A MAN OF STONE

With best wishes

Jack Wood.

A MAN OF STONE

His Life and Loves

Jack Wood

The Book Guild Ltd
Sussex, England

First published in Great Britain in 2003 by
The Book Guild Ltd
25 High Street
Lewes, Sussex
BN7 2LU

Typesetting in Baskerville by
Keyboard Services, Luton, Bedfordshire

Printed in Great Britain by
Bath Press Ltd, Bath

A catalogue record for this book is
available from the British Library

ISBN 1 85776 707 1

ACKNOWLEDGEMENTS

My thanks to Barbara Sheriff for her invaluable assistance.

– also, to my old friend Arthur Hartley, who has lived in Haworth all his life and became Chairman of the Brontë Society in the years 1986–89.

– and my family whom I love and enjoy.

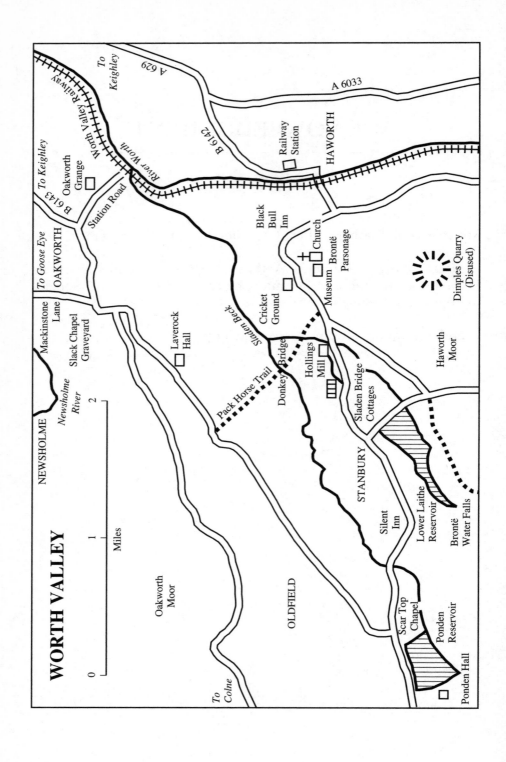

FOREWORD

When I first came to know Jack Wood he was a successful builder. We were staying in one of the Yorkshire stone holiday cottages he built at Buckden, high up Wharfedale, which are now run by his daughter Susan and son-in-law David. Jack's story of how he obtained planning permission for such a sensitive Dales site was, and still is, well worth hearing ... as are all his stories.

Not too many years elapsed before I was sharing his whisky in a farmhouse even higher up Wharfedale listening to his tales of how he had become a sheep farmer and was winning prizes in competition with lifelong Dales farmers. He took me out into his farmyard to see the pens where he was rearing young lambs and even my inexperienced eyes could see how thoroughly he was doing it – the place was immaculate, a world away from the messy farmyards you sometimes walk through on a long hike.

Jack has had other interests, too, one of which brought him a 'Best in Britain' award, though he would cut me off without any more whisky if I divulged that particular secret. His latest enthusiasm is for writing. Off to writing classes he went, after all these careers and a serious illness, at a time in life when the rest of us would be looking to sit back and reminisce. Not Jack; as with everything he has done in life, he has practised what he learned to the utmost of his ability and *Man of Stone* is the wonderful first fruit.

Story-telling, of the best kind, has obviously been a feature of Jack's 80 years and now he has drawn on all his experience, from when he was the village joiner and undertaker in Haworth and lived in the deep, half-hidden, tough and mystical valleys the Brontës knew so well, to his knowledge of the characteristic Yorkshire stone buildings and native farming, to write a historical saga – a story you will not stop reading until you finish it, which I did the day our last Dales holiday ended. I realised that instead of walking I had paid Jack's family for the privilege of sitting to read his book! That's Jack for you; nothing pleased me more, however, than being able to help him find a publisher. Now he needs you, dear reader, to read this, his first book, to the end (which once started you will be unable to avoid) and to recommend it to a friend!

Peter Harland*

---

*Peter Harland, born in Shipley, was editor of Bradford's *Telegraph & Argus* in the late 1960s and early 1970s before becoming managing editor of *The Sunday Times* 1973–1981. With his wife Jennifer, also a native of Bradford, they then ran their own company, *Bookwatch Ltd*, for 20 years. They retired recently.

PROLOGUE

The house was silent. I had a feeling of tension. The coals in the fireplace had burnt away and the room was feeling chilly. It was time to put the cat out and lock the door before retiring to bed.

I had lived alone since my husband Tom's death ten months earlier. We had been happily married for 25 years, and as Tom's job at a Bristol engineering works was steady and well paid we felt secure and content. We loved each other very much and fully expected to be sharing the same companionship in old age but all was drastically altered by a terrible accident at the foundry. The furnace exploded and molten metal spewed forth, killing three workmen, including Tom. I was devastated, and as Bristol held no charm for me without Tom I sold the house to return to our native Yorkshire. We both originated in the Worth Valley, near Keighley in the West Riding, and it was there that I looked for a suitable new home.

As soon as I saw the head gardener's cottage in the village of Oakworth I knew it was ideal. It had been part of a rich gentleman's estate and was set back from a long driveway which wound up to his large manor house. The cottage was built of Yorkshire stone, but the appearance was softened by Virginia creeper climbing across the south-facing wall.

Next to the cottage were stables and coach house and a much-overgrown kitchen garden, all of which were to be sold with the cottage. The buildings, though in need of internal repair, were sound, and I had no hesitation in making an offer to purchase them. I was lucky; the sale went through without a hitch, and after workmen had installed a new kitchen and bathroom I left Bristol without regret and soon felt quite at home in my new surroundings.

Not long after returning to Yorkshire I acquired a cat. He arrived one day while I was working in the kitchen garden. He

1

was sitting on a stone, regarding me with large, copper-coloured, understanding eyes, a big, healthy-looking cat, well-fed with a jet-black, shiny coat. We whiled away the afternoon together. He stretched out under the lavender bush, pretending to sleep, and I continued weeding. From time to time I would tell him what I was doing or comment on the state of the garden, and although he feigned complete indifference I knew he missed nothing. When I went in for tea he followed, and a saucer of milk secured our friendship. He stayed. I called him Tom, after my husband, and we soon became fond of each other.

Each evening, after the television news, Tom would have a long stretch before sitting upright to look me full in the face, asking to be let out. So it was on this evening, Tom went ahead along the hallway towards the back door. Halfway along the passage, he stopped, suddenly alert and tense and arched his back. His fur bristled and his tail stood rigidly erect. He paused for only a few seconds, then, with a note of alarm, did a complete U-turn, shooting back into the sitting room, where he cowered under a chair. No amount of coaxing could induce him to come out so I decided to leave him. Back in the hall, it felt cold and I shivered slightly, quickened my own steps and rubbed my arms for warmth. I stopped, as had Tom, before I reached the door. There was a peculiar, musty smell, and though I felt sure it must be imagination, walking sticks in the hall-stand seemed to rattle. As I reached out to turn the key in the lock, my heart jolted, for through the patterned glass panel of the door I saw the shadowy figure of a man, some 30 feet away on the forecourt of the coach house. Although I could discern no details in the poor light, I had the impression of a man powerfully built and I was sure he was looking at me. The figure was surrounded by a light grey aura, giving him an unreal quality, then he turned away and walked towards the harness room next to the stables. His feet made no sound on the gravel but just as this thought registered, he disappeared.

I did not feel like following to find out who he was or what he was doing, so still shaking, I checked the locks and bolts on the door and went into the kitchen to make a strong cup of tea. Never before had I experienced anything like this, and it shook me. I heaped three spoonfuls of sugar into my cup to help settle my nerves and went back to my easy chair. Tom came out of hiding and climbed on to my lap with a quizzical look. 'I don't know, Tom,' I said, 'I just don't know.' I slowly sipped my tea and went over the last ten minutes, trying to make sense of what had happened

Later, lying in bed, I recalled a snatch of conversation I had had with the solicitor when I visited his office to sign the conveyancing documents for the house. 'The large manor house was built around 1843,' he had said, 'by a gentleman called John Pickles, well thought-of in the district. A self-made man, he made a fortune, by all accounts, out of building materials and the local stone quarries.' I suddenly had a vivid impression of the man I had seen in the coach house yard, and I heard the name 'Johnny Big Block.' It wasn't a thought, as such, it was more as if I heard someone's voice inside my head. I heard it again; 'Johnny Big Block.' I had no idea where this name had come from, and I was certain I had never heard of him.

I tried to remember more details of what the solicitor had told me, but the name Johnny Big Block kept recurring in my mind until I knew with some certainty that, along with the property, I had bought a ghost.

Next morning, curiosity aroused, I telephoned the solicitor's office and asked for an appointment with Mr Edgar Middleton, hoping he would be able to give me more details of the history of the big house and its estate. The secretary arranged for us to meet that afternoon.

I arrived at his office on the steep hill of Main Street, Haworth, at the appointed time and was shown into a modern room which always surprised me after seeing the simple cottage exterior in its original form, in keeping with other old buildings on the cobbled street. Haworth is now a popular tourist attraction, famed as the home of the Brontë family, and as you pass the cluster of quaint buildings around the church on the hill top and descend the cobbles it is almost like taking a step back in time.

Mr Middleton was able to provide only the briefest historical details. 'The house was built about one hundred and forty three years ago,' he said, 'by a wealthy man named John Pickles. He made his money in stone and owned a quarry here in Haworth. When he died, the house passed to his daughter and was eventually pulled down in the 1930s, after the family sold it. I have

3

the transaction dates and the name of the last owner here somewhere.' He began to rummage through the thick pile of papers on his desk. 'John Pickles was a prominent figure hereabouts; the locals nicknamed him Johnny Big Block, and that's how he was known in the trade throughout Yorkshire and Lancashire.'

Searching through the old documents Mr Middleton did not observe my startled reaction to mention of Johnny Big Block. I had no intention of telling the solicitor of my 'ghost' experience and somehow I managed to keep my voice calm. 'Oh, don't bother looking for those later details. I'm really interested in the early days of the estate and this, er, John Pickles.'

'I'm afraid there's little more I can tell you.' Mr Middleton must have seen my disappointment. He smiled, 'You'd better talk to Arthur Hartley and John Wood, who both live in the village. Their families have been in business in the Main Street for generations, long before the Brontës came and long before your Mr Pickles's time. If anyone can tell you about Johnny Big Block, they can.'

After taking down their addresses I thanked the solicitor and left, feeling pleased that despite having learned little new I had not come to a total dead end; John Pickles and Johnny Big Block were one and the same. I resolved to visit Messrs Hartley and Wood as soon as possible.

That night, Tom again refused to go out, and as I went to lock the front door I was not surprised to see the same figure standing between the cottage and the coach house. He was nearer this time, only about 20 feet away, and as it was a moonlit night I could see him much more clearly. He was tall and well-built, and I had the impression he was a man of great strength. Wearing a heavy brown cloak, riding boots and a top hat, he was clean shaven with a dark complexion and the hair framing his face was jet black, though greying at the temples. Again he looked directly at me, and this time his unwavering gaze held mine for much longer before he turned, walked away and, as before, simply disappeared towards the coach house. I locked the door, intrigued by what I had seen but not unnerved, as I had been the previous evening, for I had the distinct feeling he bore me no ill.

On the third night the cat went out willingly and the coach

4

yard was empty, with no sign of the figure, and I retired to bed. My thoughts were untroubled and I slept soundly until about 4.30 a.m., when something woke me. The same musty smell that had filled the hallway two nights earlier pervaded the room. Standing at the foot of the bed was the man I had seen twice before. He was about 55 years old, well over six feet tall, and the same heavy cape hung from his powerful frame. His strong dark features gave him a gypsy look, but his face was softened by a gentle smile. There was such entreaty in his dark brown eyes that I felt certain he was trying to tell me something, but I had no way of knowing what. I wasn't really afraid; he just kept looking at me with an earnestness that was intense. He stayed beside the bed, motionless, for what seemed a very long time but in reality was probably only about a minute, before he turned towards the bedroom door and vanished.

The name Johnny Big Block again sounded clearly in my mind and I was even more certain that my night visitor was the ghost of the same gentleman, but as I lay in bed I thought about the meaning of it all. What message was he trying to convey? What did he want of me? It only strengthened my resolve to contact Mr Hartley and Mr Wood, although I could not visit Haworth that day as I intended to go Keighley to purchase material to make a summer dress.

Later, in the Market Hall in Keighley, I was browsing on a material stall, trying to choose between fabrics when I felt a hand on my arm and heard a surprised voice beside me, 'Hello, it's Valerie, isn't it?'

I turned and saw a middle-aged woman beaming at me.

'It is Valerie? Valerie Binns! How are you?'

For a moment I was nonplussed.

'Oh, I'm sorry. Do I know you?'

The woman laughed, and as she did so it was as if someone had turned back the clock. 'Barbara Lord!' I exclaimed. 'Gosh, it must be nearly thirty years since we last met. It's lovely to see you.'

Barbara and I had been at school together, and for a couple of years we were the best of pals, on the netball team, in the church choir, and patrol leaders together in the local Guides. We had drifted apart after leaving school.

'What are you doing back in this neck of the woods?' Barbara enquired. 'I thought you lived in Gloucester or Bath or some such place.'

'Bristol,' I said. 'Tom and I moved there when we married, but Tom died last year and I decided to come home.' My eyes filled with tears at this unexpected reminder of Tom's death. Most of the time I coped very well, remembering the happy times and preparing myself for anniversaries and the like, but at times like these or when someone unwittingly enquired after Tom the sadness was almost unbearable.

'I'm so sorry.' Barbara rested her hand on my arm and squeezed gently. 'How about we go and have a cup of coffee; have you time? It would be so good to catch up on all your news.'

'Yes, I'd love to,' I said, wiping my eyes and smiling at my friend. 'Sorry about that, let's get our cuppa.' We were soon sitting in the café with a steaming cappuccino each, reminiscing over our teenage antics.

'Do you remember the frothy sausages at Kildwick School?' I asked. 'We'd canoed with the Guides up the Leeds–Liverpool canal from Keighley and had permission to cook our meal in the school. You'd brought sausages but had forgotten the fat for frying them. There was a single burner for cooking and no grill...'

Barbara butted in, '...I searched round and found a cup full of what I thought was oil. It wasn't until I'd poured it over the sausages that I realized it was liquid soap!' We both burst out laughing at the memory.

'It bubbled and frothed out of the pan and all over the stove,' I spluttered. 'What idiots!'

Our conversation jumped from Guiding to school, changes in the town, college, old friends and marriage.

'I'm a widow too,' Barbara told me. 'It's six years since Richard died. I still miss him, of course, but I go to the Spiritualist Church and that has really helped me through the bad times.'

I was intrigued. I'd heard of Spiritualism but had grown up in a Methodist family where even mention of that kind of thing was frowned upon. 'How has it helped you?' I asked.

'Richard comes through to me from the spirit world sometimes and sends me messages of love and reassurance. I know he's watching over me and that we'll meet again some day in a better place than this world.' Barbara was relaxed and happy as she told me this. 'The Spiritualist Church here in Keighley has really good visiting mediums,' she continued. 'Why don't you come along with me one day? Perhaps your husband will contact you. There's nothing to be frightened of, and everyone is very friendly.' Barbara had sensed my apprehension and smiled, waiting for my answer.

I made up my mind. 'OK, I'll come.'

After arranging to meet on the Thursday evening of the same week we paid for our coffees and then, as Barbara headed for the shopping centre, I went back to the market stall for my dress material.

Thursday came round soon enough. I didn't know what to expect and was still apprehensive as Barbara and I went into the church. The lady at the door had a warm, welcoming smile which somewhat allayed any fears. She gave us each a hymn book and said we could sit wherever we wished.

I had not said anything to Barbara but felt sceptical about the visit. I had decided to go along as arranged, keep an open mind during the proceedings and later, at home, retrace what had been said to try to find a logical explanation. It proved to be a much more forceful experience than I had expected.

The leader welcomed everyone and the service began with a well-known hymn, followed by a prayer. Next the medium was introduced. She was a lady from the town of Skipton nearby and from the leader's welcoming words it was clear she had been to this church several times before and was well regarded. 'So with no more ado, I'll hand over now to Joyce Calloway.'

Mrs Calloway rose, closed her eyes and stood motionless for about 45 seconds, preparing herself for the session. As she opened her eyes she pointed to our side of the church, saying, 'I'm coming to the lady there, in the brown jacket. Are you with me, love?'

No one spoke.

'You, dear, the lady wearing an orange scarf.'

I started, as I realized the medium was speaking to me, and feeling self-conscious, I just managed to nod.

Mrs Calloway smiled, 'That's all right, then. I have here a gentleman called Tom, quite recently passed over, within the last twelve months. Are you taking him?'

7

'Yes, thank you,' I muttered.

'He wants you to know that he's with you in the new house. Is that all right, dear?'

'Yes.' I had difficulty acknowledging her as I was so amazed.

'He's also saying something about a cat.' Mrs Calloway paused. 'What's that?' She appeared to be addressing the air and was obviously concentrating hard. 'Oh, he says he's glad you have the cat for company.'

The medium moved on. 'Now, can I come to the gentleman over there? Yes, you, sir...'

I didn't hear anything more for quite a few minutes. Tears were streaming down my face. How had the medium known Tom's name? I thought. How could she possibly know about the new house and the cat? All my disbelief evaporated. I was convinced. Tom must have contacted her!

Barbara reached across and gently squeezed my hand.

Other members of the congregation were contacted through the medium, and we were nearing the end of the session when Mrs Calloway came back to me.

'I have another gentleman here for you,' she said. 'There are so many people in the spirit world trying to get through that I don't usually come to the same person twice, but he is very insistent. I don't have a name, but he's standing beside me and I can see him clearly. He's a big fellow and he's wearing a top hat. He's holding something, but I can't quite make out what it is.'

'What do you want, sir?' she asked, apparently addressing thin air as she had done earlier. 'Oh, that's better. I can see now, he's holding it up to the light from the window. It appears to be some leather straps or riding tack of some kind.' Mrs Calloway turned to me. 'He's gone now. I'm sorry I could not get more. Did it make any sense to you?'

I smiled. 'I know who it is,' I said. 'Thank you.'

My journey home was full of thoughts of Tom. I no longer felt shocked, rather I felt warm and comforted as I remembered happy times we had spent in Bristol, walking together in the Forest of Avon, attending wonderful concerts at St George's, river trips on the blue and yellow ferry boats. I thought of the little ways he let me know he loved me, the unexpected bottle of wine, the evening trip, twenty five miles, just to see a roadside banking thickly carpeted with harebells, my favourite flower, the hot bath ready waiting when I was caught out in a thunderstorm and soaked to the skin. I was still thinking of Tom when I went to bed, and I fully expected to fall asleep and dream of him.

It was as I put out the light that I remembered my other contact earlier that evening, Johnny Big Block. I wonder what he wants, I thought. Mrs Calloway had said he had a bridle or reins in his hands, but that meant nothing to me as I know little of horses and riding. I closed my eyes and tried to sleep but could not get the Spiritualist Church out of my mind. I kept going over that last part of the evening and felt sure I was missing some vital point. 'He's holding something,' Mrs Calloway had said, 'can't quite make out...' I tried hard to remember. 'I can see now, it ... appears ... to be a harness.' It still made no sense and, feeling frustrated, I buried my head under the duvet, determined to sleep.

'Oh, that's better, I can see now...' Once more the voice of the medium came clearly to my mind. 'He's holding it to the light from the window. It appears to be...' I sat bolt upright in bed. That's it! I thought. '...holding it to the window.' The window! There had been no window on the side of the church that the medium was facing, and yet she had seen the gentleman holding the harness up to the light. I remembered that on the first two occasions I had seen Johnny Big Block he was in the coach yard and had turned from me and walked towards the stables. I gasped. Had he wanted me to follow him? I wondered. Was it possible that Mrs Calloway had seen him near a window in the coach house harness room? The more I thought about it the more likely it seemed, and I felt really keyed up as I speculated what I might find across the yard. It was some time before I was able to fall asleep.

The following morning I could scarcely contain my excitement. I had difficulty forcing down my breakfast before I went out and across the cobbled yard.

I had never really explored the old out-buildings. I had been too busy over the past months, decorating the house and bringing some kind of order to the garden. It was a huge building with a flagged floor and a high beamed ceiling. The only windows were in the upper part of the rear wall, no more needed

9

as the double doors opening into the courtyard were immense. There would be no point searching there, and my main interest lay in the harness room and the cupboards I knew to be in there. As I turned the knob and pushed open the heavy oak door I paused, apprehensive, wondering what I might see behind it.

I needn't have worried, the room was light and airy, having long windows down half the length of the opposite wall. On my left was a row of tarnished brass hooks, with a slatted bench running right along the wall beneath them and a narrow shelf above. To my right the whole wall was taken up with six large built-in cupboards with a single, deep drawer beneath each. The woodwork, beautifully crafted, would once have been highly polished but was now faded and dusty, and the ornate brass handles were tarnished with age like the hooks on the opposite wall.

I opened the first cupboard eagerly but was disappointed to find the shelves bare. Without pausing I moved to the second door, but like the first that cupboard was empty too. I moved down the room, opening the cupboards in turn, but my disappointment increased with each one. All were completely empty – no riding tack, no clothes, no paper and no old tools. I moved on to the drawers underneath. The first stuck and it took a great deal of effort to prise it open. To no avail. Apart from an old chewed newspaper and some mouse droppings there was nothing. I worked back along the row, pulling out the drawers, but there was nothing in the other five either. I was completely deflated. I had felt so sure I would find something here, but now had to admit that it had been a false hope. The harness room was just so empty!

I crossed the room and perched on the window sill, wondering what to do next and trying to will the ghost of Johnny Big Block to tell me what he wanted. Of course this was a futile activity and, sighing, I rose to leave. As I turned I noticed that I had left the last cupboard door ajar and I reached out to shut it. Without knowing why, I opened the door instead and peered at the interior. This cupboard had no shelves, but it had three grooves down the back as though it had once been divided. I wondered idly what might have been stored there and was about to close the door when I noticed that a

10

small piece of timber, near the bottom of the right-hand corner, had been cut out and then replaced. It no longer fitted flush with the rest of the panel. I reached down to push it back into place, but as I touched it the whole piece pivoted and revealed a small niche behind. Kneeling down to get a better view, I saw the recess held a brass door key. I was stunned and voiced my thoughts aloud, 'Well, Johnny Big Block, it seems I've found what I've been looking for, but what on earth is this key for?'

I tried the locks of the cupboards and drawers and then, although I already had keys to the out-buildings, I tried all the doors on the ground floor, the harness room, the stables and the coach house, even when I knew that the key to that building was much bigger than the one I had found. There was a great hayloft covering the area of both the stable block and the harness room, and I climbed the ladder at the far end of the stables to explore, thinking there might possibly be something up there the key would fit. My hopes were soon dashed. The loft was bare, without even a trace of the hay once stored there. It was just one large room with a couple of lights set into the roof, no other windows and no doors. Disappointed, I went back down the ladder and into the yard. As I walked back past the stables I realized something was not quite right. It was a very long block of stables, but the hayloft I had just been in was not big enough to cover the whole length of the building, yet there was no other access to any rooms above. Puzzled, I turned back and remounted the ladder. This time I walked across the floor of the loft towards the far wall, which was, I now realized, a timbered partition. The v-jointed, vertical panels spanned the length of the room and went from floor to ceiling, but there was no indication of a door or any other form of access to the area beyond. I moved along the partition, exerting pressure on each board with my hand to see if I could detect any movement, and I was about halfway along when I felt some give in the timbers. I looked closely and saw a neatly cut-out plug which, when removed, revealed a keyhole. Further examination showed the outline of a door, cleverly concealed by expert carpentry. My heart began to beat faster and I felt frightened about what I might find on the other side. The key fitted the lock perfectly, as I had known it would, and the door opened very slightly. It was pitch black behind, and I hastily closed and locked the door, pocketed the key and, with pulse racing, left the building as quickly as I could.

Once outside I felt a little calmer but realized I would need a torch to go any further. I headed for the kitchen and a stiff drink. As I sat in my rocking chair, slowly sipping a brandy, I wondered whether I should proceed now or wait until someone could accompany me. I was feeling on edge. I have never cared much for the dark, but when I remembered how kindly my night visitor had seemed and how earnestly he had looked at me I thought he really wanted me to open that door, and I still felt there was no evil in the man. I would come to no harm.

By the time I finished my drink my mind was made up. I rooted out a large torch and went back to the hayloft. Unlocking the partition door, I pushed it gently and it swung open quite easily. I realized that the room was not after all in total darkness; there was a glass roof light, but it was covered with green moss and very little daylight filtered through. I shone the torch around. The rafters were festooned with cobwebs and everything was covered in a layer of dust. Stacked across the room were piles of identical wooden boxes. They were about four feet long, two feet wide and 18 inches deep. All were painted black with a number on the front in white – numbers 1 to 12.

The boxes were not padlocked or fastened in any way, and I went to the one on the top of the first stack, number 3, and lifted the lid. It was full of papers, neatly filed and tied in bundles. Balancing the torch on the lid of the adjacent box, I took out a batch of papers from the front and untied the string. They were in perfect condition. Unfolding the first document I saw that it was a bill of sale for stone, supplied by Mr John Pickles of Dimples Quarry, Haworth, to a Mr Jos. Fairbank at Leventhorpe Mill, Thornton, Bradford. The second was another bill, made out to a Manchester firm which had purchased extra-large blocks of stone. Details were given of the size of each block, and charges were made for 'carting of same and transportation by canal'. A note at the foot showed that this was a special order for stones to form the bed for a steam engine to power the Manchester cotton mill. I went through the rest of the papers in that bundle and saw that there was a variety of similar bills of sale to mills, factories, private houses, and one to Keighley Improvements Committee for paving stones for Brunswick Street.

I took the lid from the adjacent box, number 6, and saw that this was similarly filled with papers, estimates, orders and more bills of sale, but of a later date. I realized that these boxes, besides being fascinating, held the history of John Pickles and his company, trading as stone merchants in Haworth and, later, in Halifax. He seemed to have served all kinds of industry in Yorkshire and Lancashire, and was much involved in supplying stone and building materials for the expansion of the railways. It had obviously been a very busy firm.

Deciding it would be sensible to start at the beginning with box number 1, I put all the papers back and replaced the two box lids. It was difficult getting the top box from the stack, but, by swivelling it round and lowering it on to its end I managed it. By comparison, the second box was easily moved out of the way. I knelt on the dusty floor and opened box number 1. I was in for a shock. Instead of neat rows of documents there was a large brown paper parcel, tied with string. It contained a uniform of some sort, naval, I thought, as it was dark blue with yellow braiding and a double row of brass buttons. There was a dark hat, braided as well. It was all in excellent condition, but the short-cut style suggested it was very old indeed. Underneath the uniform was a wooden peg-leg, with leather housing and straps for attaching to the stump of a thigh, and also a leather-bound book.At the very bottom of the box was what appeared to be a scrap of old, stiff leather. I nearly overlooked it, but when I lifted it out found that it was in fact two pieces of leather and, pulling them apart, found pressed between them a single flower, a faded red rose.

Could these things have belonged to Johnny Big Block? Was he in the navy? Did the quarry owner have a wooden leg? There was certainly no trace of a limp in the ghostly gentleman in the coach yard. I had no answers and replaced the parcel in the wooden box, keeping back the book, which I now opened. It was a diary and the first entry read:

'Armley Jail, Leeds. My First Day.' Immediately below this, printed in large letters was the 23rd Psalm:

'THE LORD IS MY SHEPHERD
I SHALL NOT WANT…'

Although amazed at what I had discovered so far, nothing could have prepared me for the contents of the second chest. I lifted the lid and found inside a highly polished walnut casket, inlaid with ivory and brass marquetry. It was beautifully made, but the next sight completely took my breath away, for inside was the most exquisite jewellery I had ever seen. A necklace and tiara, both encrusted with diamonds, and a pair of earrings, obviously made by the same jeweller, completed the set. Two plain gold wedding bands gleamed from the magenta velvet lining, and next to them nestled a gold locket, delicately engraved, and a large diamond, threaded on to an intricate chain.

I could not believe what I saw. Eventually, I opened up the locket and found the two halves were sealed with small discs of glass. Behind one was a folded piece of paper and behind the other a single curl of black hair. Holding the locket, I wondered about the woman who had worn it. Was she pretty? Beautiful, perhaps? Caught up in a wonderful world of ballrooms, parties, romance and love? The hair might have been from her child, or maybe there had been intrigue and it was a memento from a secret admirer. Had he also sent the folded note, a love letter to be worn always near her heart? My imagination ran amok and only with difficulty did I return the locket to the velvet pad.

That night I could not sleep. I was worried about the valuable jewellery and uncertain as to what should be done with it. I considered telling Edgar Middleton or the police, but in the end thought I should wait until all the boxes had been searched thoroughly and I had read the diaries. After all, the hoard had been concealed in the hayloft for a considerable time; a few more days would not make a difference. As I turned these thoughts over I became aware of the now familiar musty smell which presaged the appearance of my ghost. I was not surprised, therefore, a moment or two later, to see him standing near the bedroom door, but if I had hoped for instructions or an explanation I was disappointed, for he was gone almost immediately. However, I did see his face transfigured by a great

14

smile and eventually I fell asleep, knowing that, although I did not yet understand his plan, he was happy that I had found his boxes.

It was now a priority to follow the lead from my solicitor and visit Arthur Hartley and John Wood, who, Mr Middleton had assured me, would be able to help in the quest for information about John Pickles. Hartley was a plumber and glazier who lived near Haworth church, so I went first in search of him. I found Hartley in his workshop repairing a leaded-light window. A sprightly old man in his eighties, he stopped working as I approached, adjusted his spectacles which had slipped down his nose and beamed:

'Hello!'

I introduced myself. 'Hello, I'm Valerie Feather. I married Tom Feather of Oxenhope, from Moorend Farm.'

Mr Hartley's smile widened. 'Knew the family well. Went to school with his Uncle David. Always in at the deep end was David, any pranks played and you could be sure he'd be at the centre. Good lad, though; he'd help anybody.' He paused, looking a little uncomfortable. 'I was sorry to hear of Tom's death.' Mr Hartley readjusted his glasses. 'Now then, how can I help?'

'Thank you,' I said. It was comforting to find that this old gentleman had known Tom and his family. 'Mr Middleton told me to see you. I'm trying to find out about a certain John Pickles who had a quarry here in Haworth last century. He was a...'

Arthur Hartley interrupted me with a chuckle. 'You mean Johnny Big Block,' he said, perching his bottom on the edge of his workbench and folding his arms across his chest. 'Well, what do you want to know?'

I was unsure where to begin. I did not want to tell anyone about the ghost or the jewellery and all the other things I had found, so I just said, 'I know he lived at Oakworth Grange and that he was a stone merchant with a quarry here and, later, another in Hebden Bridge, but that's about it, so anything at all that you can tell me will be helpful.'

'Thriving business he had, up on the moor,' Arthur began. 'Employed nigh on a hundred men to work that quarry, I'm told, and welcome work it was too. Lots of families in the Worth Valley relied on the full order books of John Pickles.'

15

'A hundred men!' I exclaimed. 'I had no idea it was such a big concern.'

'Oh, yes. There were quarrymen, you see, delvers, hewers, fettlers, banker hands and dressers, and then there'd be blacksmiths keeping all the tools and equipment in good order, and the wagon and horse men and the office staff, of course. My great uncle, Harold Ratcliffe, worked for John Pickles. He was an architectural draughtsman and was one of Big Block's key men. He read the plans and drawings submitted by the construction companies and provided estimates from them. Of course, he did his own working drawings from which the masons worked, and even undertook building designs when required. He was a very clever fellow.

'Why do you want to know about Johnny Big Block?' he asked suddenly, as if the thought had just occurred to him.

'I'm living in the old gardener's cottage at Oakworth,' I replied. 'I bought it along with the stables last year after Tom died, and I would just like to know about who built it.'

He nodded, 'That'll be right. I heard it was sold and that someone had moved in, but I didn't realize it was a returning local. So many properties now are bought by off-cumduns commuting to Bradford and Leeds for work. It's not like it used to be in the valley, when everyone knew everybody, is it?'

He was not expecting a reply and I waited for him to continue.

'Aye, John Pickles was a well-respected employer. He was a hard task-master by all accounts, but fair to his workmen. I've heard tell that during hard winters, when the men had to be laid off due to frost and snow, he would give each man a chit to take to the local food store for tea, sugar, flour, potatoes and beef and bags of coal. Of course, when the warmer weather came the men had to work doubly hard and work off the loan with extra long hours of labour. Still, they were glad of it at the time, I dare say.'

Mr Hartley stood up and sliding the offending spectacles back up his nose, said he would have to leave as it was time for him to wind up the church clock. Apparently, he had performed this task for many years and had been happy to do so, but since he had turned 80 the stone steps in the clock tower seemed to be getting steeper and the flight longer. He felt that it was time for a younger man to take over.

'It's been nice talking to you, Mrs Feather.' We were out in the street now, and I shivered slightly as there was a cold wind. 'Come again, any time, I'd be only too pleased to tell you what I can remember being told about Johnny Big Block. Hope it's been of some help.'

He was already starting off towards the church as I called after him, 'Yes, I'd like that, thank you very much.'

I took directions to John Wood's house from the owner of the Brontë Café, opposite the church in Main Street, where I had gone for a cup of tea and a buttered scone after Mr Hartley went off to attend to the winding of the church clock. The house I intended to visit was quite a way beyond the village, on the edge of the moor, so it was almost an hour later that I rang the doorbell of the big white house set back from the road that I had just struggled along. A bitterly cold wind had sprung up and I had been glad of my thick winter coat, wrapped tightly round me, as I battled against it.

'Mr John Wood?' I asked, as a gentleman opened the door.

He nodded, taking three short draws on his pipe, releasing the smoke with a 'phut ... phut ... phut...' sound. I politely requested his help, explaining the purpose of my visit. Still without speaking, he moved aside and gestured, pipe in hand, for me to step inside. I followed Mr Wood, thankful to be out of the biting wind, and was even more pleased when he led me into his study, where a warm coal fire was burning. The whole room had a welcoming feel to it, not just because of the open fire but also because it was comfortable, cluttered and well used. There were two tall bookcases in the alcove on either side of the chimney breast which had a high oak mantelshelf across it holding a large clock, a brass candlestick with a double twisted stem, a pair of figurines and a Royal Doulton jug with Falstaff depicted on it, sword half drawn. The jug held Mr Wood's selection of pipes. A desk under the window was piled high with books, magazines and writing materials, and on a coffee table, beside one of a pair of deep, cushion-filled armchairs, there was a newspaper, the *Yorkshire Post*, a tobacco pouch, matches, a taper and an empty coffee mug.

'Excuse t'mess,' Mr Wood spoke for the first time. 'I've lived on my own these twenty years since my wife died, and there never seems to be much point in spit'n'polishing t'place.'

17

At Mr Wood's invitation I took off my coat and sat in one chair at the far side of the fire while he sank into the other, obviously his favourite. 'Now then, where do I begin?' John Wood drew thoughtfully on his pipe before continuing. 'Johnny Big Block came here, to work in the mills, as an orphan with nothing, no family, no money, no education. But on his own merit he became one of the wealthiest men in the Worth Valley.'

Mr Wood was a born raconteur, and I spent a delightful couple of hours listening to his tales of bygone Haworth. He diverged quite a lot from my point of interest, John Pickles, following different tracks as the ideas flowed, but I learned a great deal as he wove a picture of the past which fascinated me. He told me that his great-great-grandfather, on his mother's side, William Turner, had owned Hollins Mill in the Sladen Valley, manufacturing woollen goods and building up the trade in the early days of powered looms until he had a very profitable concern, with huge consignments of fine worsted cloth being shipped out to America. It was to this mill that John Pickles, then aged about 12, had been brought from a Liverpool orphanage, where he had spent all that he could remember of his early life.

'It was common practice for the mill owners to bring orphan children to work as wool-combers. It was dirty, hot, unhealthy work, combing out the raw wool, and in many mills the children worked under intolerable conditions and were little cared for. My great-great-grandfather treated the boys fairly, by the standards of the time, you understand. He always made sure they were decently clothed and had reasonably good food. I expect he realized that on an empty stomach they would not have the strength to work the long hours required. There was no maximum working day at that time, you know, apart from a Saturday, which by Act of Parliament in 1825 had been made a part-holiday, with only nine hours' work. Imagine it, children as young as eight working twelve and thirteen hours a day.'

Mr Wood gazed at the fire and shook his head as if he could scarcely believe the information he had just given me. After a while he continued: 'The boys at Hollins Mill not only worked in the room above the boiler house but slept there too, on rough bunks with straw palliasses. No doubt during the winter

18

they would welcome the warmth from the huge boiler generating steam power to drive the textile machinery, but during the summer months it must have been unbearably hot.'

Warm and comfortable in front of the blazing fire, I realized how seldom we think about the hardships people suffered just over a hundred years ago. What a contrast to the expected norm of today. I wondered how I would have fared in those circumstances. 'The folks back then must have been a tough breed,' I commented.

'Oh, yes,' said Mr Wood, nodding. 'The harsh conditions toughened up the stronger ones, but a lot didn't make it, you know. Many succumbed to cholera, TB, pneumonia and the like. Take the Brontës, for example. Emily, Anne and their brother Branwell all died of tuberculosis, consumption as it was called then, within nine months of each other, and Charlotte only lasted another five years or so, dying at the age of thirty-eight. Patrick Brontë outlived his whole brood; his first two daughters died of the same disease in childhood. Very, very sad, but not uncommon. Many families suffered a similar tragedy.'

We were both silent for a while. Then, although I would have liked to ask Mr Wood to carry on and I was loath to leave the warm fireside, I made a move to rise. 'I really must be going, Mr Wood,' I said. 'I've had a very enjoyable afternoon, but I'm on foot and I want to be home before dark. Thank you very much for taking the time to talk to me and for all the information about John Pickles. I really appreciate it.'

John Wood stood up, stretching a little as he was stiff through sitting so long. 'You're more than welcome. I've enjoyed it too. If you're interested, I've a couple of books you might like to borrow. They were written by my great-grandfather.' He searched the bookcases and then handed the two books to me; both red and both entitled *Hollings Mill*. 'I would like them back, mind you, when you've finished reading them.' He did not quite let go of the books until he had finished speaking and I realized how important they were to him.

'Of course, I'll take good care of them.'

The wind was just as strong and cold as earlier in the day, but I hardly noticed it as I hurried home, for my head was full of mills, orphan boys and the Brontë family. I was really looking forward to reading the two red books.

19

I spent the whole of the following day perusing documents from the hayloft. It had become an obsession with me, and I spent hours pouring over the copperplate handwriting, some of it a little faded and some difficult to read because, in the florid style of the day, the letters often overlapped. With all these papers, the leather-bound diaries and the information I had gleaned from Arthur Hartley, I was gradually piecing together a picture of the quarries and the lives of those involved with them. It was fascinating stuff, but I was still no nearer to finding out about the naval officer's uniform, and I had no idea what to do about the jewellery. I knew that I could spend more time with Mr Hartley and John Wood, and I was sorry now that I had not thought to ask about the uniform on either of my visits. The jewellery was another matter. It was obviously very valuable and I just did not know who to turn to. I decided, eventually, to go back to the Spiritualist Church in the hope of guidance there.

On Sunday evening I went alone to the Heber Street Church. I had no need to feel nervous. Everyone was very friendly, and the service was similar to those of my chapel upbringing, with familiar hymns and prayers. The clairvoyant this time had travelled all the way from Doncaster and gave messages to many others present before he singled me out.

'I have a contact here from a gentleman called John. He's saying, "Get it down." Do you understand?' the medium asked me.

'I'm not sure, no,' I said.

'He's wearing a top hat and he's holding an inkwell and pen. And he keeps repeating the same thing. "Get it down, you must get it down." ' The medium paused. 'There's something else, "Leave the box where it is, just get it all down." Now does that make sense to you?'

I nodded. It did make sense. I knew now what John Pickles wanted me to do. I was sure he wanted me to write his life story; but I was also certain that John Pickles didn't know that I had never been much good at English at school and that this would be an enormous task for me.

After the service, the congregation was invited to have tea and biscuits in the back room, and I found myself sitting next to one of the senior members of the Church. He knew that I was new to these services, so he kindly told me the history of

20

Heber Street, which was the first British Spiritualist Church. It had started in the year 1853 when a certain David Richmond, who had joined the Shakers in America, had taken an interest in Spiritualism after becoming acquainted with the Fox sisters in Hydesville, New York State. He had returned to his home town of Darlington, fired by his new religion, but had found that the people of the north-east were staunch Quakers and were not prepared to hear anything about the Spiritualist Church.

David Richmond walked from Darlington to Keighley, where, with a man named David Weatherhead, he organized a public meeting, which was received with great enthusiasm and interest. As a result, Keighley derived fame as the first town in England to house a Spiritualist Circle. After everything that I had learned recently of that period, the rapid growth of the town during the Industrial Revolution, the poor living conditions and the short life expectancy, it struck me that the people of Keighley had been, in all probability, ripe for a new religious belief to cling to.

It was snowing when I left the church, and it kept on snowing for the next few days until everywhere was blanketed white. Winter had arrived and, as I was unable to venture outdoors, I decided to put my time to good use and, taking a note pad and pencil, made a start:

'The Life Story of John Pickles, Man of Stone'

1

Boston

Tied up on the dockside waterfront in the bustling seaport of
Boston, New England, was a brand-new sailing ship. She was a
beauty of some 11,500 tons, and many people stopped to
admire her. The seagoing sailors were greatly interested, marvelling at her lines and construction. The proud owner was a
Captain Blanchard, who had lived for this day and the com-
pletion of his own ship, built to his own specifications. He had
ordered the ship from McKays at Newbury Port, a renowned
shipyard which specialized in building quality ships that were
trim, speedy vessels, handcrafted with the utmost care. It was a
beautiful ship, and today she would finally be ready. Only the
blank space on the bows needed attention and the ship's painter
stood by with brush and paint. Today she would be baptized
Mary Ann, in honour of the captain's beloved daughter. William
Blanchard had broken with tradition and had not named the
ship at the launching, as he wanted his daughter's name to be
added only when the ship was at its most perfect: gleaming
paint, polished woodwork and shining brasses. As she was this
day.

Captain William Blanchard, a French Canadian, was a stocky,
thick-set man of some 56 years. His now balding head still
showed traces of the coal-black hair, which echoed in the neat
goatee beard, and the man's weather-beaten skin evidenced a
life at sea.

As a young boy he was brought up in the town of Salem, and
on leaving school he joined the whaling fleets sailing out of
New Bedford, working hard and taking few breaks. During the
early years of his daughter's life he had spent much of his time
at sea, and Mary Ann and her mother Helen had treasured the

22

few precious days he would spend with them between each trip. Looking back now, his only regret was that he had missed so much of his daughter's childhood. Like other parents, he wondered how the years had flown by so quickly, but he knew that the sacrifices had been necessary if he was to achieve his dream. The dream which was now as much for his loved ones as for himself. Captain Blanchard had been thrifty with his earnings and eventually had his own whaler, old but seaworthy. He had made good money from the whaling and had invested in a cargo ship making regular runs between Liverpool and Boston. The hard work of the past six years, building up the trade connections, taking risks and sailing in all weathers to meet demands and promises, had paid off, and having sold his old ship he had now arrived at this day. The proudest moment of his life. He leaned on the rail of his very own ship, satisfied that through his own efforts he had achieved his lifetime's ambition. Captain Blanchard smiled and turned to survey the scene on the deck.

Since early morning the forward part of the ship had been a hub of activity as her cargo was being loaded in readiness for tomorrow's sailing. There was much shouting and jovial banter amongst the crew as barrels, skips and casks were stowed in the hold. Pulley ropes strained and creaked against the wheels which winched the cargo up from the dock, and when it swung over the polished rails strong arms reached up to steady the load as it was lowered. Men, out of sight in the belly of the ship, unhooked the chains and whistled to let the winchman know the ropes were free. They were nearly done. Only a few crates and some sacks of maize remained. The barrels of fresh water would, of course, be loaded on the morrow. Captain Blanchard never tired of the loading, though he had seen it all before a thousand times. He shifted his weight and wondered whether to call a halt now. Already gathered around the main mast was a distinguished-looking group of people who had been invited to attend the naming ceremony. Mr McKay, the shipbuilder, and his wife were receiving due praise from other notable people of Boston, all, in one way or another, connected with shipping. Mrs Blanchard was talking to the priest who had been engaged to bless the ship after she was named. Mary Ann, the captain's 21-year-old daughter, standing closest to the mast,

23

was in animated conversation with Seth Snowden, the first mate of the new ship. Captain Blanchard thought he had never seen Mary Ann looking lovelier. Her eyes were sparkling and her smile was radiant. He smiled again. The young couple were so much in love and tonight, at the reception to be held later, they would announce their engagement. The captain had readily given his blessing when Seth had nervously approached him and asked for his daughter's hand.

'I could not have a better son-in-law,' he thought now as he watched them laughing together. They appeared to be unaware of all the other people around them, caught up in their own world of new plans and hopes and dreams. 'He's a good man.'

Captain Blanchard had grown very fond of the young Englishman who had joined him more than two years earlier, then aged 23. He'd proved capable, reliable and unafraid on their many Atlantic crossings. The two men worked well together, having a good understanding and a high regard each for the other, both at sea and on shore. Seth had a good physique. He was tall and slim and had a fresh complexion with a stock of sandy hair and beard to match. Before coming to New England Seth had served in the British Royal Navy as a navigation officer, and now, as Captain Blanchard watched him, he could see the qualities that had fitted him for this position.

Seth's father was a Yorkshire man, originally from Hull, Seth had told the captain, and had lost his life whilst serving as an officer in the Royal Navy when Seth was a boy only five years old. His mother had died not long afterwards, some said of a broken heart, and Seth had been boarded with an aunt whose husband also served in the Royal Navy. When Seth was 14 years old his uncle had pulled strings to enable him to be accepted as a Boy Cadet Officer. Out of a debt of gratitude Seth applied himself diligently to the training, rising to Navigation Officer in four years, a post in which he remained for a further five. He would have stayed with the British Navy, if only from a sense of duty, but on the death of his uncle, Seth felt free to make a change and had journeyed to New England to try his luck in the Merchant Navy. Lucky for me, thought Captain Blanchard.

The older man would have been content to muse further for a short while, but a sudden noise on the dock brought him out of his reverie and he turned to see that quite a crowd had now gathered below. The noise was coming from a small group of belligerent-looking men towards the back of the throng. They were pushing their way through the spectators, shouting and jeering and roughly jostling anyone who happened to be in their path, including a young woman who held a baby wrapped in a woollen shawl. She would have fallen, but the man beside her steadied her and guided her to a safer place.

'What on earth...?' Captain Blanchard was at a loss to know what had caused their anger, but he could see that the men were heading for the gangway, and he was determined that they would not board the ship. His portly figure belied his fitness, and with surprising alacrity he sprinted along the deck to the head of the gangway. Seth was already ahead of him. 'What's the trouble?' Seth looked worried. Like Blanchard he wanted nothing to mar this day.

'I'll be hanged if I know,' replied the captain, but as he spoke both men recognized the ringleader, who had now reached the bottom of the wooden planks.

'It's Vernon Seward,' said Seth, 'I might have known.'

Seward had a grudge against the world and against William Blanchard in particular. He too owned a ship working out of Boston, and over the years he had made a vast fortune doing the triangle run, taking molasses from the Caribbean to New England, rum from Boston to West Africa and then bringing back slaves on the return run. He was a gambling man and, instead of investing wisely and keeping his ship in good order, he had frittered away his wealth. Now, with the growing agitation in the north for the abolition of slavery, the slave trade had greatly decreased and the Triangle Trade had collapsed. Seward had had no other contracts and was finding it difficult to get into the North Atlantic trade. He was an ugly customer, and no one wanted to have dealings with him. The short runs he had been doing along the coast of New England brought in very little money, and with gambling debts high he'd had to lay off most of his crew. Many of them had already signed up for other ships, including the *Mary Ann*. Herein lay the trouble. Seward was envious of this beautiful new ship. He had been drinking, and in his befuddled mind Blanchard was to blame for his demise. He stood now at the bottom of the gangway,

25

red-faced and gasping for breath. He had a hand on each rail to steady himself. 'I'm coming up, Blanchard,' he bellowed. 'You're finished. Everyone knows you've taken my crew, my shipping.' He looked round, addressing the startled onlookers. 'This ship should be mine, I'm a Bostonian, lived here all my life, the ship should be mine.' His face had turned a nasty purple colour, and he swayed unsteadily.

A woman near the front of the crowd spoke out, 'Nonsense, this is Captain Blanchard's ship, and rightly so.'

Voices of agreement were heard. 'Yes!'

'Just so!'

'That's right.'

Seward took a few stumbling steps up the slope and began shouting angrily again. 'He's a blackguard,' he raged, 'stole my crew, and now he's...' Suddenly the people in the crowd began to jeer. The noise rose in a crescendo, drowning out the drunken man's tirade. As Vernon Seward looked up towards the deck, Seth took a couple of steps down the gangway. Suddenly all Seward's bravado left him. He realized that the friends who had set out with him were nowhere to be seen, the crowd was against him and now a giant was coming down to beat him. From the steep angle of the planks Seth's figure looming above did indeed appear gigantic, and it was enough to make Vernon Seward turn about and look for a way out. Seth came slowly down the gangplank, still anticipating trouble, but the worst moment had passed and the crowd began laughing as Seward, face like thunder, slunk away, muttering under his breath.

Seth ran a hand through his hair and then shrugged, before retracing his steps back to Blanchard. 'Could have been nasty,' he said, 'but it looks as if the fellow's seen sense after all, eh?'

Captain Blanchard shook his head. 'I doubt we've heard the last of him; he's a really nasty piece of work and hates me for being what he's not. However, it's not going to spoil this day. Nothing will spoil this day, and as the crew's stopped loading to watch the fun we'll have our ceremony now before they continue.'

Everyone went back to the centre of the ship. The captain welcomed them all aboard, and without further delay Mrs Helen Blanchard, beautifully dressed for the occasion in a dark blue glazed taffeta gown and coat with matching bonnet, took a bottle of Madeira wine and with all her strength took a good

26

hard swipe at the main mast. The bottle shattered and Mrs Blanchard declared loudly,

'I name this ship for our daughter, Mary Ann.'

Everyone clapped and then the whole party laughed when Mary Ann had to skip hastily out of the way of the splashed wine. The events of the last half-hour were forgotten. Each person was offered a glass of Madeira wine, and when one member of the party congratulated Captain Blanchard on his lovely wife and beautiful daughter and wonderful ship he glowed with pride. He could not agree more. It was a great day for the Blanchard family and William, wanting to share his joy, kissed Helen tenderly, simply saying, 'Thank you, dear, for everything.'

She smiled back at him, happy with the way things had turned out and immensely proud of her husband.

Captain Blanchard addressed the assembled company. 'Thank you all for coming,' he beamed. 'This has been an exciting day for me and my family, and I want to thank you all for sharing it with us. As you know, the fun has only just begun. Your rooms are ready at the Tremont, and we look forward to you joining us at our table tonight for the celebration meal. It is a wonderful hotel, as you will see.'

Indeed, the Tremont Hotel was the first word in luxury. Newly built in the broad street from which it took its name, it was an extremely elegant hotel and was attracting great interest and much curiosity from Boston's high society. A four-storey building, it boasted 170 bedrooms, many of them large and airy, and all beautifully furnished. The vast dining room, which could take 200 people at one sitting, had a magnificent marble floor. However, the main innovation at Boston's newest hotel was the installation of imported indoor water closets, which were to set new high standards for public accommodation. They were the talk of the town. A Grand Opening Ball was planned at the Tremont for this very day.

The captain had arranged for carriages to take his guests to the hotel, but Seth was unsure about leaving with the others. 'Perhaps I'd better stay here a while longer and see to the rest of the loading,' he suggested. He was usually in charge of overseeing the stowing of the cargo, and he liked to see that the job was done properly.

'No need for that,' Blanchard replied, clapping Seth on the

back. 'It's almost all aboard. Josh can manage the rest. Come with us. You've earned this day off, and I want you to enjoy it too.'

He called to Josh Mitchell, a long-time member of his crew. 'Finish off there, Josh. Secure the hold when you're done.'

'Aye, aye, Captain,' Josh raised a hand in acknowledgement. He was an easy-going character, well liked by the other sailors, and he was happy to get on with the job without Seth's intervention. He knew that Seth could be particular about the stacking and securing of the cargo, over-particular Josh sometimes thought, and they were making good time without him. The ship would be fully loaded in an hour or so, and then he and his pals would be free to wander along to the tavern at the end of the dock for their own celebration. He could already see the frothing tankard in his mind's eye.

'Aye, aye, Captain,' he said again.

Seth didn't need any more persuading. He was happy to spend as much time as possible with Mary Ann before the ship sailed.

Two barouches and a gig were drawn up on the dock, and Mr and Mrs McKay joined the captain and his wife in the first carriage. They were followed by Mr and Mrs Jackson and Mr and Mrs Collins. Tom Jackson had been a shipmate of William Blanchard in their younger days, but had since turned to banking and was also in cotton manufacturing, having numerous mills in Massachusetts. He had been nicknamed 'Mr Manchester of America' because of the prodigious amounts of cloth he produced. He and Henry Collins were great friends and had been able to help each other in their very successful business ventures. Collins owned a fleet of ships sailing between New York and England. The Collins Line was the pride of the American marine. Eliza Collins and Adeline Jackson had been friends for many years, but hadn't seen each other for some time and had much to talk about. As they drove off they were speculating about the young couple bringing up the rear in the gig.

The crowd of people on the dockside watched the little procession depart and then, knowing that the pageant was over for the day, they began to drift away.

The air of excitement in the dining room at the Tremont Hotel was almost tangible. Anyone who was anyone in Boston had tickets for this gala evening. William Blanchard had secured a top table for his party, and the evening was progressing just as he had hoped. The food had been wonderful. From the scalloped oysters, followed by glazed ham and cider sauce, to the blueberry and maple soufflé, everything was cooked to perfection and beautifully served. There had been some amusement around the table when the guests found that four-pronged forks, newly introduced from Europe, had been set at the left-hand side of their plates. 'I think I prefer normal, two-pronged forks,' muttered Mary Ann, colouring slightly as she tried to scoop up some vegetables.

Seth grinned. 'Try it the other way up and use your knife to help, like this.'

Brought up in England, Seth was quite used to this cutlery and gave a little demonstration. Everyone laughed and then, as they ate, earlier conversations were resumed. The atmosphere was relaxed and friendly. The men, of course, were talking mostly of the new vessel and shipping, whilst the ladies were hearing all about the latest fashions in New York from Eliza Collins.

'Oh, you should see the hats!' said Eliza. 'There is so much lace and so many ribbons and then, to top it all, flowers. Yes, flowers of all descriptions. Seems they think bigger is better, but I think our little bonnets are far nicer. Mind you, perhaps the hats are meant to detract from the lack of anything around the neck.' She leaned forward and lowered her voice. 'The necklines of the new Paris gowns get wider and wider, quite indecent, I say. I don't think they will be worn here in Boston.'

'Oh, I wish they would be,' cried Mary Ann. 'I'd just love to see all the latest fashions. I know that dresses now have the fullest skirts and enormous sleeves like legs of mutton. I read all about them in the new *Ladies' Magazine*. Are they really lovely? Do tell me.'

Mrs Collins smiled at her. 'They are lovely, my dear, and they have the most exquisite embroidered trimmings. But a pretty girl like you has no need for such extravagances.'

Mary Ann would have liked to have heard more about New York and the French and English fashions, but the meal was coming to an end and a five-piece orchestra was getting ready to play for the dancing which was to follow.

29

Captain Blanchard stood up and waited until he had the attention of his guests.

'I think you will all agree that it has been a splendid meal,' he began. 'Before we join the dancers, there are one or two things I would like to say. Firstly, I would like to thank Mr McKay for all the hard work he and his men have put into my ship. The deadlines have been met without any hasty work, and I know you all share my admiration for a wonderful vessel.' He reached across the table and, handing Mr McKay a cheque, he shook his hand heartily. 'That's the final payment for a job well done. Thank you.'

Mr Mckay nodded briefly and smiled as everyone clapped.

William continued, 'I'd like you all to join me in a toast. Please raise your glasses to the *Mary Ann*.'

The tinkling of glasses accompanied the chorused, 'The *Mary Ann*.'

'Now I have some news for you,' William said, beaming broadly at everyone. 'Today is doubly special, as our daughter, Mary Ann, and Mr Seth Snowden wish to announce their betrothal. My wife, Helen, and I are very happy, and we wish the young couple all the joy in the world.'

Adeline Jackson and Eliza Collins gave one another knowing glances and then smiled and added their congratulations to those of the rest of the party.

'Another toast, if you please,' Captain Blanchard was still standing and he now raised his glass high. 'To Seth and Mary Ann. May you have a long and happy life together.'

Mary Ann, flushed with excitement and not a little embarrassed, kept her head down so that her ringlets hid her burning cheeks. Seth reached across and, taking her hand in his, he kissed it tenderly. She looked up then, and seeing the friendly, smiling faces around her she laughed, her embarrassment forgotten. 'Thank you, Papa,' she said warmly, 'and you too, Mama!' She ran round the table and embraced her mother and father and then showed the ladies the sparkling diamond ring that Seth had bought for her.

'Now, everyone to the dance floor.' William held out his arm to lead Helen to where they could watch the young ones dancing. Mary Ann was radiant as Seth led her into a quadrille which was just beginning. Her new gown of white tulle, embroidered with maple leaves in gold thread, showed to advantage her tiny waist and made a stunning contrast with her dark auburn hair. Anyone watching the pair as they swirled and glided through the figures in time to the music would have been able to see that they were very much in love.

Seth and Mary Ann were laughing and out of breath as the second dance finished. They decided to sit out the next one and were crossing to join the rest of the party when they realized there was some sort of commotion at the side of the room where Captain Blanchard was sitting. Angry voices were raised, and as the orchestra had stopped playing one voice could now be heard quite plainly. Gradually everyone else stopped talking and turned to see what the trouble was about.

Captain Blanchard had seen Vernon Seward earlier in the evening. He had been at one of the other tables in the dining hall, but William had chosen to ignore the malevolent stares that Seward had given him then. He could ignore him no longer, for he was now standing only yards away from William, and with the Dutch courage from the liquor he had consumed was now giving vent to all his envy and frustration.

Captain Blanchard sighed, 'Go home, Seward, I've no quarrel with you.'

'But I've a quarrel with you,' Seward roared. 'Who do you think you are, King of the Seas? Eh? You've taken my trade, you've poached my men. You're NOTHING! You're scum!'

Blanchard sighed. 'Go home, Seward,' he said again. Vernon Seward was having none of it.

'Come outside, Blanchard, and we'll square this man to man. You've no right to that ship. You're a skunk, a low-down pig, and I'll have my men back, or else.'

'Or else what?'

Seward reeled round to see Seth standing behind him. There was no sound in the room as the two men faced each other, the one short and stout with too much to drink inside him, and the other standing tall, straight and resolute.

'What's it to you?' snarled Seward. 'Keep out of it.' He made to turn back to Captain Blanchard, but Seth took hold of his arm.

'I think you've said enough,' said Seth quietly. 'It's time you left.'

31

'Take your hands off me, fella,' screamed Seward. 'I know your game, getting in with the captain any way you can.' He leered at Seth, showing rotting teeth. 'And in with his pretty daughter too, I would not wonder.'

'That's it! That's enough!' The colour drained from Seth's face and his chest muscles tightened as he strove to control the anger welling up in him. Seward took a rolling swipe at Seth but was way off mark and only succeeded in unbalancing himself and sprawling onto the floor. A gasp went up from the onlookers, who had never expected to witness such uncivilized behaviour at an event such as this.

As Seth unceremoniously hoisted Vernon Seward from the floor, Captain Blanchard and Henry Jackson came to his aid, and between them they frog-marched the struggling, blustering man from the room.

The orchestra immediately struck up again and couples were taking to the floor as William and Henry went back to join the ladies.

Vernon Seward, still seething, staggered into the gentlemen's washroom. Seth followed him. 'Don't come back, Seward,' he said. 'You've had far too much to drink, and we've had enough of your trouble-making.'

Seward's rage boiled over again and he made to punch the younger man in the stomach, but Seth side-stepped neatly and only caught a glancing blow on the hip. Realizing that there was only one thing that this drunkard would understand, and determined that he would not let him ruin the rest of the evening, Seth gave one good solid blow to the man's ribs and Vernon Seward dropped like a stone. He lay groaning and this time made no attempt to get up. Working quickly, Seth took off both Seward's shoes and stockings and threw them out of the window, and then removed his collar and tie. Before the chap could react he had flushed them down one of the new toilets. Seth then took out a pocket knife and cut the braces supporting Seward's trousers.

'You could have saved yourself all this by going home earlier,' said Seth. 'You have only yourself to blame for all your misfortunes.'

He left Seward sitting on the tiled floor with his back against the wall. Seth was quite sure that he would not be any more trouble that night.

Back in the dance hall most people had already forgotten the unpleasant incident, and everyone was in high glee. Balloons and paper streamers had been released, and a lively polka was under way. The floor was crowded with dancers. The ladies, dressed in silks and satins and tulles of every colour, smiled happily at their elegantly attired partners. As the dancers twirled and reeled, the colours of their gowns blended in the eyes of the admiring onlookers until they were inseparable from the whole bouquet of colour filling the room. Over the heads of the dancers, Captain Blanchard caught Seth's eye as he came to join them. The young man simply gave a slight nod to acknowledge that all had been taken care of.

The celebrations continued without further interruption until 2 a.m. Music, excited chatter, lively dances, the swish of satin and taffeta and the balloons and streamers, all added to the atmosphere and everyone had a wonderful time. At last, tired but happy, the party made its way up the grand staircase to retire to their rooms on the first floor. Captain Blanchard had reserved the best rooms at the front of the hotel.

Mr and Mrs Collins and Mr and Mrs Jackson bade their hosts goodnight and went to their own rooms. As William and Helen turned to open the door to their bedroom, Seth and Mary Ann hesitated in the corridor, eager to have some time alone. Mrs Blanchard paused and then came across to Seth and spoke warmly.

'Thank you, Seth, for dealing with that objectionable man tonight. Without your intervention things could have turned really nasty. We are very grateful to you.' She paused and added deliberately, 'We'll see you at breakfast. Goodnight, Seth. Goodnight, Mary Ann.'

No one moved, Mrs Blanchard pointedly waiting for her daughter to go to her room. Mary Ann looked uncomfortable. 'Goodnight, Seth,' she said quietly.

'Goodnight, Mary Ann,' replied Seth and, turning, went into his room and closed the door immediately.

Mary Ann sighed and then, as her mother again said, 'Goodnight, Mary Ann,' she too closed her bedroom door.

It had been a wonderful evening, a wonderful day, the ring was wonderful, Seth was wonderful. Mary Ann did not want it all to end. She stood leaning against the door and closed her eyes to try to recapture the magic. She pictured her father proudly announcing their engagement, and she trembled slightly as she remembered how Seth had gently kissed her hand. She thought of the dances and how she had felt hot and excited as Seth had swirled her around the floor. Her heart swelled as she saw Seth, her brave hero, saving Papa from that awful man. 'How I love him,' thought Mary Ann. 'I'm the luckiest girl in the world.'

She still didn't move, afraid that she would break the spell. It was, at the same time, exhilarating and agonizing to know that Seth was so near, so very near. Mary Ann held her breath and imagined Seth there in the room with her, holding her close. Suddenly, a lump rose in her throat and tears welled behind the closed eyelids.

'Tomorrow he will be going,' she thought. 'The ship will sail and take him away from me. How can I bear weeks and weeks without him? This time together has been so precious, and now it is almost over.'

The euphoria of the past few hours gave way to sadness and Mary Ann raised a hand to brush away the tears. She crossed the bedroom and, with a heavy heart, took off her ball gown and threw it over the mahogany foot-board of the huge bed. Unpinning her hair, she brushed it vigorously as if this could help to brush away her melancholy thoughts.

'If you are to be a sailor's wife, Mary Ann, you'll just have to get used to it,' she told herself firmly. She continued undressing then and slipped into her kimono. It was of the palest pink silk, and as she tied the sash she caught sight of herself in the mirror. Her hair was catching the light of the lamp and hung dark and lustrous against the kimono. In the half light her eyes melted into deep pools above the still flushed cheeks. She sighed.

'Oh, Seth, if you could only see me now.'

A light tap on the bedroom door made Mary Ann start and catch her breath. Her voice trembled slightly as she asked, 'Who is it?'

There was no reply, but ever so quietly the tapping came again. She realized then who it must be.

'Seth,' gasped Mary Ann, hurrying to open the door. It was Seth, in his stockinged feet and with a finger pressed against

34

his lips, warning her not to speak. As Mary Ann closed the door behind him, Seth reached out and drew her into his arms. Their kiss was long and lingering. The kiss of young lovers alone together for the first time. The kiss awaited with such longing, as only those who have truly loved can ever know. They held each other so tightly, hardly daring to believe that this moment could be real and afraid that if they let go of each other it would melt into a dream. At last they drew apart.

'Mary Ann,' whispered Seth, 'how I love you.' He lifted her up into his strong arms as if she weighed no more than a feather and, carrying her across the room, he laid her gently on top of the coverlets of the bed.

She didn't speak, afraid that someone might hear her, but she watched as Seth undressed. He had his back to her, and the well-defined muscles of his powerful shoulders rippled as he moved. His arms, she knew, were strong, and as he lowered his trousers she saw that his legs were well proportioned and covered in fine, sandy coloured hair. Her heart beat faster as he turned towards her and she saw that the hair on his chest was the same colour, but here it was thick and curly. Now, with Seth looking at her, Mary Ann was abashed that she had been staring at him so boldly. No longer could she let her gaze wander over his body as it had been doing. She looked into his eyes instead and smiled shyly.

'You will have to tell me how to please you,' she whispered.

Seth kissed first her forehead, then her cheeks and then the tip of her nose before their lips met in a burning kiss. This was not like the kiss at the door. The feelings aroused by their passionate embrace were new and surprising to Mary Ann. Her heart raced and she was aware of a stirring deep within her, strange but exquisitely intense. A burning in some part of her, until this moment quite unknown. She clung to Seth and was aware of the hot hardness of his manhood pressing against her through her nightdress. She felt no apprehension, her only thought, 'Please let me please him.' Seth gently ran his hand down the silk kimono and, finding the sash, released it to let the garment fall apart. He drew in a long slow breath, for in the soft glow of the lamplight Mary Ann's body looked as smooth as the silk that had been covering it.

'I can't believe how lovely you are,' murmured Seth, easing

the kimono from her shoulders to reveal firm, round breasts. Gently he cupped one breast in his hand, softly kissing the nipple, circling it with his tongue. Her flesh tingled at his touch and both their hearts beat even faster. He moved closer, enjoying the feeling of their naked bodies touching, flesh on flesh. Seth's hand moved down from her breast to the soft mound of her fluttering belly and she moaned slightly, beginning to ache for him. His hands traced the contours of the little hill. Trim smooth flesh gave way to a thicket of dark hair. Seth paused. Her velvety skin and the sight of her dark brown nipples, now hard and pointed, increased his desire. He wanted to be gentle, he wanted Mary Ann to delight in him and in their love-making, he wanted her to reach the heights with him, but she was so soft, so beguiling, lying there so utterly beautiful, and the urgent throbbing in his groin would not let him wait. He thrust his hand deep between her thighs and, parting her legs, he came to her. Mary Ann moved with him. They were as one, he giving all and she, with a slow moan of ecstasy, wanting more and yet more until they united in the sweet, dark wonder of abandonment.

They lay together, blissfully relaxed, drifting in and out of sleep, until Seth got the desire again and Mary Ann wanted more of him. After they had made love a second time they dropped fast asleep in each other's arms.

2

Dockside

There was the usual hurly-burly of the busy dockside: the loading and unloading of cargoes, the mending of sails, the wag-
goners quietening their fretful horses, the retarring of life-rafts
and barrels, the checking of ropes and sheets, the shouts of the
peddlers hoping to make a small profit from those embarking,
'A trinket for the lady for the long voyage, sir?' 'A St Christopher
for luck?' Besides all this, on the harbour front a large crowd
of eager spectators had gathered to see the *Mary Ann* set sail
for Liverpool on her maiden voyage.

It was a beautiful clear day with a bright blue sky painted
with the occasional snowy cloud. The sea was calm here in the
harbour, but there was a light fresh breeze to take the sails
when they were unfurled. Captain Blanchard was looking forward with anticipation to the voyage to come. He wanted to see
how his ship handled, and he felt confident that she would ride
the waves well, on an even keel, and make good headway.

Barrels of fresh water had been taken aboard, and Seth was
already making fast the hold. He had been annoyed that morning, on arriving at the ship, to find that the wooden covers and
tarpaulins were not secure. He had sought out Josh Mitchell
and upbraided him.

'You were left in charge, Josh, and could not even be bothered to batten down the hatches. Had your mind on the ale,
no doubt!'

Josh looked aggrieved. It was all fast after we left.'

'Oh. come on, Josh. The tarpaulins were loose. I know what
I found. It's not what we've come to expect from you.'

Seth was angry with Josh but also angry with himself for not
staying aboard the previous day to see the job done.

37

Josh tried again. 'I'm telling you, we fastened everything before...'

'Don't let it happen again, Josh. We've no place for heedless seamen on this ship.' Seth hadn't given Josh a chance to reply before standing angrily away. A more experienced mate might have seen the truth behind the perplexed expression on the other man's face.

'The battens were fast when we left,' Josh muttered, shaking his head as he looked after Seth's receding figure.

Seth secured the last bolt and signalled to let the captain know that all was now ready. They could sail as planned with the ebb tide in an hour or so. The throng on the wharf included Mrs Blanchard and her daughter. Helen knew how frantic the final preparations for sailing could be, so made it a rule never to go on board. Both women were hoping that their menfolk would have a chance to come and see them, but Seth had said his goodbyes after breakfast and didn't want to repeat the experience. Mary Ann smiled bravely and wished him 'Bon voyage', but her eyes had remained sad and had briefly filled with tears. When he had embraced her she clung to him as though she would never let him go. He was surprised at his own reluctance to leave her. In the past, the excitement preceding each new voyage had filled his whole being. He had always been impatient to cast away and eager to face the adventures of the sea. Today a part of him wished to remain in Boston and felt strongly aware of Mary Ann's unhappiness at their parting. He shared the feeling and forced back the threatening tears as he busied himself.

He occupied himself with last-minute checks, giving Mary Ann a salutary wave whenever he was at the starboard side, but being careful not to pause too long in his tasks in case the sight of his loved one weakened his resolve to stay aboard.

At just turned 2 p.m. the ship cast off. The people on the quay waved and cheered as the *Mary Ann* slid gracefully from her moorings. Helen Blanchard had a lump in her throat as she watched her husband giving the orders, but her emotion was pride at all he had achieved and not sadness at his leaving. She had long become accustomed to William's departures and was resigned to their long separations. Mary Ann, on the other hand, was quite forlorn. She felt sad and disappointed that Seth

38

hadn't found time to come and see her one more time.

'If it had been the other way round,' she thought miserably, 'I would have made time to see Seth. He would have been first in my thoughts. Why didn't he come?' Tears filled her eyes and trickled slowly down her cheeks, but as the vessel pulled away she forced a bright smile and blew Seth a kiss before waving until the ship was clear of the harbour. She watched as the enormous white sails were unfurled into the sun, and she didn't turn away until the *Mary Ann* was no more than a speck on the distant horizon.

They had been at sea for ten days. The weather remained clear, with a fair wind to fill the four-masted, fully rigged vessel. The *Mary Ann* ploughed through the waves as though she had had a lifetime of practice and as if each new dip and rise filled her with immense joy. She made good speed.

'I hope the weather holds,' thought Captain Blanchard, scanning the azure skies for sight of any change. 'At this rate we'll cut our usual crossing time by four days and be in Liverpool by the seventeenth.' He was elated and full of optimism. Not for the first time on this voyage he allowed himself the luxury of admiring his ship. He ran an approving eye over the billowing canvas stretched above him, noting with satisfaction the neat twists of pleated halyards. He found pleasure in the scrubbed decks and the polished wood and brasses of rails, binnacle and helm. All was shipshape, as he liked it. The crew were working well together, without the usual spats and tension that normally occur when men are together 24 hours of each day. They worked as a team under himself and Seth, and William was pleased that there had been no resentment harboured over Seth's harsh words on the day of departure.

William Blanchard would not have felt so confident if he could have foreseen the events that were to occur over the next few days. There was no warning of the bad weather to come. As the evening drew in, the skies were still clear and a moderately fresh breeze was blowing them on their chosen course at a steady rate of knots. Before sunrise, however, a northeasterly wind had seized the ship and her progress was considerably slower as she battled against an ever-increasing swell on the ocean. The wind howled through the rigging, tearing at the sails, and in no time at all it had risen to gale force.

'All hands on deck,' roared Captain Blanchard. 'Lower the mainsail!' 'Hold that halyard, man!' 'Belay!' 'Look out there!' 'Trim fore and aft!' The orders came thick and fast as the crew struggled to keep the ship under control and set her back on course.

The weather worsened. The wind raised a higher sea, the waves curved higher and higher above the ship's deck, the gale increased in ferocity. As the hours wore on the sky became dark, bleak and desolate, the grey, scudding clouds low over the racing billows. The voice of the wind, the constant repeated surge of the sea lashing the crew, bombarded their ears and senses. After a struggle the crew managed to get the sails down hard and fast. Their oilskin clothes had been ripped, and some of the men's seaboots had been sucked off their feet. The ship climbed and dived, climbed and dived, as she met the formidable waves, but it was when one crosscurrent roller hit her broadsides and she reeled from the force that Seth heard, above the noise of the wind, a thump, a crash and the cry that followed as the ship began to yaw.

'Cargo's shifting!'

Seth raced towards the forward hold, shouting as he went, 'Josh! Andy! David! Wilf!' He collected six of the strongest hands to go down into the hold with him.

'I know I should have stowed the cargo myself,' muttered Seth, glowering at Josh as he swung himself onto the ladder. But this was no time for reproach; there would be plenty of time for that later. Another crash from below hastened their descent. Seth hoped that it was only a minor mishap, perhaps one crate that had broken loose, but he knew that if the barrels of turpentine and tallow were to topple it would be a difficult and dangerous task. The barrels were stacked seven high, and if the ropes and leather strapping had given way they would need to fix heavy timbers into position to make everything safe. The bales of cotton on the port side were less likely to move, but they too were heavy and could pose a real threat if they were shifting.

It was worse than Seth had thought. Many barrels of turpentine and tallow had crashed against the bulkhead, splattering

40

their contents over the wooden floor, making it slippery and almost impossible to get a firm footing. Seth and Josh Mitchell were the first crew members to step off the ladder into the hold, and as they did so the *Mary Ann* reeled violently and the man at the bottom of the ladder shrieked with alarm and leaped back up three rungs. As Seth turned he saw a whole row of barrels falling towards them.

The barrels seemed to leap from their places and float through the air towards Josh and himself. He heard Andy yell and added his own voice, but it was as if someone else shouted.

'Josh, watch out!'

He saw Josh's horrified expression and saw him, turning, slip on the greasy boards. He saw him stumble just as the barrel hit him with fearsome force. It didn't break but bounced off Josh, stunning him and leaving him lying on the deck to take the full weight of the other barrels following the first. There was nothing Seth could do. As he watched he had instinctively moved backwards, away from the collapse, and only when a barrel of turpentine smashed against his leg was he fully aware that the scene was real. Flung sideways, Seth grabbed at a vertical beam to steady himself, but before he could get a firm grip he was knocked to the floor by a rolling barrel which came to rest against a cotton bale, pinning Seth beneath it.

3

Josh Mitchell was dead. The men who found him were afraid that Seth had suffered the same fate, but when they moved the barrel off him they were relieved to see that he was alive, and on Blanchard's orders they took him to his cabin.

Captain Blanchard looked down at Seth. The young man was ashen and was having difficulty breathing as he'd sustained damage to his chest when he was trapped beneath the barrel. Seth's leg was shattered just above the knee a jagged piece of bone protruded through the flesh and the wound was smeared with tallow and turpentine from the floor of the hold. There was a real risk of infection setting in, and the Captain had not much hope that he would be able to repair the leg with splints.

'It is too badly broken,' he thought, 'still I must try.'

He had set broken limbs on numerous occasions aboard the whalers and knew the importance of immediate action. He gave Seth a dose of laudanum and then made every effort to remove all traces of the tallow and turpentine before calling on three strong men to hold Seth whilst he straightened the damaged leg. Seth was determined to be brave, but as the captain wrenched his leg back into position his scream was heard all over the deck and he was sick immediately the deed was done. Splints were applied and held fast by strapping them at intervals all the way up the leg.

William laid a hand on Seth's shoulder. 'Well done, young man. Now you must rest as much as possible and give your leg and ribs chance to heal.'

The storm blew itself out as quickly as it had come, and the captain ordered full sail in order to make a run for Liverpool where Seth could be seen by a doctor and nursed in hospital.

He knew that if they altered course to catch the Gulf Stream over the top of Ireland they would gain another five knots – valuable time for Seth.

Over the next few days they again made good speed and were cautiously hopeful that the outcome would be good; although Seth was in great pain, he was a better colour, was breathing more easily and eating well. He even managed to joke with one of the crew who brought him some rather stodgy porridge.

'Thanks, this should help. If it makes its way straight to my leg it will set solid, and I'll be up and about tomorrow!'

Later on the third day after the accident there was a sudden and dramatic change in Seth's condition. When summoned to his cabin, Captain Blanchard found him to be flushed, with glazed, staring eyes. His temperature had soared and he was breathing with slow rasping breaths. Obviously in tremendous pain he moaned whilst gritting his teeth in his effort not to shout out. Blanchard whipped back the bed sheet and knew by the smell, before he even looked at the wound, that the leg was necrotic; gangrene had set in! His heart sank. He knew what this meant, what he had to do, and a great weight seemed to bear down on him as he realized the enormity of the task ahead. The leg would have to come off. There was no alternative. They still had three days' sail before reaching Liverpool, and if he didn't amputate the gangrene would spread and Seth would die.

William Blanchard stood stock still, looking down at the young man whom he had come to regard almost as a son. This tall, strong, young man who was in love with his daughter would lose a leg ... or die. He could not do it!

He had witnessed a few amputations during his years at sea and had helped with some, but he had never performed the operation on his own ... and never had the amputee been anyone to whom he was so close. How could he face Mary Ann if anything went wrong?

He could not do it!

Seth groaned and began to ramble – something about angels in white brandishing wine bottles and battening down the hatches with oranges – he was delirious, and the sound of his rambling snapped Captain Blanchard out of his inertia. His moment's indecision was gone, he was the only chance Seth had. He sent for the ship's carpenter.

'Get your best saw and some knives. Sharpen them, clean them with alcohol and sterilize them in a flame. Do it now.'

Other members of the crew were set to scrubbing a table with boiling water, fetching clean linen, thread, needles, soap and whiskey. Blanchard knew that the latter was essential. They had given Seth about as much of the laudanum as they dared, and it didn't seem to be deadening the pain as it had at first. They would have to get him drunk to help him through.

Captain Blanchard went to his own cabin to scrub for the operation. He needed a short while alone, and although he wasn't a religious man he found himself asking God for courage and strength for both himself and Seth in the hour to follow. He thought of Mary Ann and wondered what news he would have for her. How happy the young couple had been at the celebration dinner on the night of their engagement.

'Dear God, give all of us the strength we will need to face today and the uncertain future. Amen.'

Much calmer now, he went back to Seth.

The captain had appointed three men to assist him with the operation. Between them they lifted Seth onto the well-scrubbed table. The fever was running high and with the combination of delirium, drugs and inebriation from the whiskey, Seth drifted in and out of the terrible pain. One moment he was ranting, arms waving frantically, the next there was silence as he lost consciousness, only to surface a few moments later with a scream that reverberated around the ship. Then ranting again; another scream; unconsciousness!

Captain Blanchard knew that he must work quickly, allowing as little blood loss as possible. Sweat was pouring from him, and throughout the operation one of the helpers was required to mop his brow to prevent the sweat from running into his eyes. Never for a second did William Blanchard let his mind wander from the job he had to do. He concentrated solely on the leg, as though it were a thing apart, blotting out Seth's agony and all thoughts of Mary Ann.

The arteries were the difficult part. The blood supply. He mustn't lose too much blood. He must work quickly. Quickly. Done! It took him less than ten minutes then to saw through

44

the bone and sinews. Then stitches, bandages, and all was finished. The ship's carpenter took the amputated leg and threw it overboard.

William Blanchard felt weak and very, very tired. Up on deck, breathing refreshing gulps of clean air he said, to no one in particular, 'Pray to God that I never, ever have to face anything like that again!'

Seth had by now fallen into merciful unconsciousness and was kept in this state with the help of drugs for the rest of the voyage. He was in a critical condition, and no one knew whether he would make it or whether the shock of the amputation would be too much even for a healthy body such as his.

The day after the operation Captain Blanchard went down into the hold to check that the cargo had now been made secure. He didn't want a repeat performance if they hit another gale. Very much saddened by the death of Josh Mitchell, he was still puzzled by the whole event. William had known Josh for many years and had always found him to be a trusty seaman. He had liked him and had come to have complete confidence in him. Never had his seamanship been in question – until now.

Everything was ship-shape again in the hold. The barrels were neatly re-stacked and fastened in position with wooden planks. The floor had been scrubbed, and there was no evidence of the disaster that had happened a few days earlier. Blanchard searched for the leather straps that had been holding the barrels when they left Boston and which had always proved sufficient to stabilize the cargo on his previous trips. The straps on the bottom two tiers were all still in place, and at first he could not see those from higher up, but when he did find one he stared at it in amazement. The leather had been sliced right through, a clean edge. The strap had been deliberately cut! The captain sat down heavily on one of the crates. Who would do such a thing? A member of his crew? Did someone have a grudge? It came back to him then. The open hatches. Josh swearing he had made them fast. The disruption on the quay on the day before departure and the scene at the Gala Evening at the Tremont when Seth had ousted Vernon Seward...

Vernon Seward? Could he have boarded the ship and cut

45

these straps? Vernon Seward had a grudge. Would he have sabotaged the *Mary Ann*? Captain Blanchard thought this much more likely than anyone on board being involved. After all, if it had been done at sea there would have been a real danger of being caught, or worse, of the perpetrator being in the hold when the barrels came down. Who would take that double risk? And why? He decided to say nothing. He would keep a keener watch from now on and leave the matter until he returned to Boston.

4

Under normal circumstances there would have been great rejoicing on reaching Liverpool. The successful crossing of a ship on her maiden voyage was a good excuse for merry-making, but Seth's condition was still critical and the whole crew were in a subdued mood. When the ship docked Captain Blanchard made immediate arrangements for Seth to be taken to the Royal Liverpool Infirmary on Brownlow Hill, and then he wrote a difficult letter to Mary Ann, telling her of the accident, and despatched this with the captain of the ship just casting off for Boston.

Whilst the *Mary Ann* was in dock Captain Blanchard went to the hospital daily to visit Seth. At first the prognosis wasn't good; the doctor had praised the captain for the good job he had made of the amputation but said Seth was still in shock and was very weak from blood loss, fever and lack of nourishment, and might yet die.

In the first few days William sat beside Seth's bed and related to him the daily activity aboard the *Mary Ann*; the progress of the off-loading, details of another contract for shipping out woollen and cotton cloths, and anecdotes about crew members getting drunk in one of Liverpool's shabbier alehouses. He also told him about the cut leather straps and his suspicions that Vernon Seward may have been involved in that. He had no idea whether or not the invalid heard him, for he never acknowledged his presence, nor even opened his eyes during his visits. However, with constant care from the nurses Seth, very slowly, began to make progress. Day by day he was a little stronger. Each day the nurses managed to persuade him to take a little more food and drink, and gradually, very gradually, the pain diminished.

Within ten days the ship was turned around and was sailing down the Mersey, heading back to Boston.

On his last visit William had been overjoyed to see Seth propped up against the pillows, still very pale but obviously on the road to recovery.

'Seth, good to see you! How are you feeling? You certainly had us worried there for awhile, but now you're on the mend it won't be long before you are your old self again.'

Seth managed a weak smile to hide the thoughts that were screaming round his head. Old self! I'll never be my 'Old self' again. You should have let me die!

'We'll be leaving tonight,' Blanchard had continued, 'I've made arrangements for you to stay here as long as necessary, so don't worry about anything except getting well. You're in good hands here.'

Seth hadn't trusted himself to speak but had managed another faint smile and a slight nod, so the captain had left, thinking that he was still very weak and tired, and had never guessed at the turmoil in the young man's mind.

For five weeks Seth lay in the hospital bed waiting for the stump to heal. He had no visitors after Captain Blanchard's return to Boston and, although the nursing staff were kind, he was very lonely, left alone for long periods with too much time to dwell on what had happened, resulting in him having in- ordinate mood swings.

At first he had been in so much pain that he wished they would let him die. Finish him off even, anything to stop the pain. When the pain eased a little and the drugs were reduced, he realized with horror his leg was gone. They had told him, he knew that. He remembered, through the haze of pain, that they had explained what they had to do. It hadn't mattered. Do anything to stop the pain! Only now did the full meaning of the words sink in. His despair was total. Now he wanted to die for different reasons. What sort of useless being was he with only one leg? What good would he be now on board ship – with only one leg? What good was making his body strong again – with only one leg? Only one leg! ... He didn't want to eat, he didn't want the nurses' help. He was full of self-pity. He wanted to die!

Then when he was stronger, the anger came. He raged and

fumed, trapped in his hospital bed, frustrated that he had no means of giving vent to his fury except by shouting. He raged against the captain for cutting off his leg. He hated Vernon Seward – yes, he had heard what the captain had said – he hated Vernon Seward with a passion he never knew he was capable of.

He loathed himself for blaming Josh, and was incensed at the needless waste of Josh's life. He was angry at the nurses who were kind, but firm, 'No nonsense, Mr Snowden, come now, eat your dinner.' Couldn't they see he did not want to eat? Would Mary Ann want a useless, one-legged man?

He was consumed with an anger that absorbed his whole world.

Then when it was spent he lay quietly with the dawning realisation that he felt much stronger and that, unlike poor Josh, he was alive and still had one *good* leg. He had been given a chance. His self-pity evaporated, and in its place was a determination to make something of his life, despite his injury.

I will get a false leg and learn to walk, he thought, and who knows what I'll be able to do then. He knew that the life he had planned with Mary Ann was now a past dream and with great will power he locked away deep inside him any thoughts of her and turned to the challenge of taking his first steps.

Upon receiving the letter from her father, Mary Ann had straight away booked a berth on one of the fast ships of the Collins Line. She had had to wait 24 hours before it sailed, and had hardly known how to contain her impatience and anxiety.

Now, on board ship and with another two days' sail before they reached Liverpool, she took her father's letter from her pocket and read it for the umpteenth time.

Liverpool
October 1829

My Dear Mary Ann,

It is with sadness that I write to tell you the news. You must be brave, dear daughter, and trust that all will be well in the end. We have had a terrible accident on board ship.

49

Josh Mitchell was killed by falling barrels in the hold, and Seth has been badly injured. He is now in the Royal Infirmary here in Liverpool, and in the very best hands, so try not to worry too much.

I am sending this letter on a ship leaving here today so that you may have it with all speed.

Your loving Father,

William Blanchard

Mary Ann remembered now her panic on first reading the opening lines. She had been sure that Seth was dead and had hardly dared to read the rest of the letter. She had been relieved, therefore, to find that he was alive, and she felt guilty later that she had felt no emotion when reading of Josh's death. Since then she had worried constantly about Seth and wished that her father had given her more details of the accident. What exactly had happened? What did 'badly injured' mean? Would Seth still be in hospital now?

She refolded the letter and returned it to her pocket and then oblivious of the cold and rain she went on deck and paced backwards and forwards scanning the horizon for some sign of the coast.

When they finally reached Liverpool Mary Ann, having arranged with the captain that she would collect her luggage later, immediately hailed a cab, asking the driver to make all haste and take her to the hospital.

Seth's whole existence over the past three weeks had been focused with determination on his plan to walk again. He had been fitted with a wooden leg, a stump padded at the cup with kapok and soft leather, but at first he could not take his weight on it even with the aid of crutches. Despite thick bandaging his tender stump was chafed and raw. Seth had felt that he was taking one step forward and three back; almost literally, except that he hadn't managed even one step at that point. The nurses were infinitely patient. Time and again they had run to help him or to lift him from the floor, only to be pushed away.

'I need to do this on my own!' Seth had gasped, sweat streaming down his face.

Slowly and painfully he had progressed. One step. Two! Another fall and then the nurses had insisted that he rest.

Two steps! I took two steps, Seth had thought, lying on his bed. If I can do two today, I can do four tomorrow, then 40, then 400!

He was up now, eager to try again. Still euphoric from yesterday's success he refused the crutches and with new confidence he hauled himself from the chair. The nurses knew better than to interfere and stood back, each silently willing him to succeed.

Taking time to get his balance right, Seth grinned at his audience and then, gritting his teeth, he swung his peg leg forward – one step! Seth paused, sweat beginning to glisten on his brow. Swing, step, pause – swing, step, pause – Seth took four steps before crashing to the floor with a shout of triumph and a huge grin on his face.

5

Arriving at the half-glass door of the ward just as Seth was struggling out of his seat, Mary Ann was amazed at the sight which met her eyes. She was rooted to the spot, with one hand resting on the door handle. Her eyes filled with tears when she saw the wooden leg, but her heart filled with pride as she watched Seth, her Seth, take his first awkward steps. She had thought to find Seth pale and sickly in a hospital bed; instead, here he was full of life and strong, eyes sparkling...

Even as Seth fell Mary Ann flung open the door and was running, running to him down the long ward.

'Seth.'

Her voice was choked with tears and Seth, still laughing thought she was a dream. He could not believe his eyes. Was this Mary Ann? She knelt beside him on the floor, throwing her arms around him.

'Seth, my darling.'

When he heard her voice again and felt her hot tears fall onto his cheeks, he knew he was not dreaming.

With the help of two nurses Seth was soon back in his chair, but his laughter had gone and he looked sadly at Mary Ann.

'I didn't think you would come,' he said, 'I'm not the man I was, and I'll understand if you no longer want me. I am...'

'Seth! Don't talk like that. Of course I want you.'

She took his hands in hers and looked straight into his eyes. 'I was so proud of you just now, and I will always be here for you. From now on we face this together.'

Seth could not speak, but his wonderful smile was all she needed to see, all doubts behind them, they felt secure in each other's love.

Mary Ann looked up from her knitting for a moment to watch Seth. After his unaided first steps he had been persuaded to go back to the crutches to 'learn to walk before you run,' as Dr Moorcroft had put it. He was determined to succeed, still allowing no one to help him. Two days ago he had managed half the length of the ward, and the doctor had promised that when he could walk from one end of the ward to the other he would be allowed to leave the hospital. The limb was still sore, chafing on the leather padding of his wooden leg, and yesterday he had to forgo all practice to give the skin chance to heal.

Mary Ann had been into the city to purchase knitting needles and the very softest wool that she could find. She was now busily knitting a cover for Seth's stump, hoping that this would ease, if not solve, the problem, and feeling glad that she had something useful to do. Mary Ann had been coming daily to the hospital, bringing tasty food and bottles of stout and was happy to see Seth regaining his appetite and putting back some of the weight he had lost, but she had wished that she could do more to help him, not realizing how beneficial her presence, chatter and laughter were to his recovery. She smiled now as she watched him struggle past the halfway mark and reach the bed beyond before giving in and dropping onto it for a rest.

The next time she glanced up Mary Ann saw Seth shaking the hands of two well-dressed gentlemen. She put down her knitting and stood up as they all came forward to her. They walked at Seth's pace and, a little breathless from the exertion, he spoke as they drew near.

'Mary Ann I'd like you to meet Mr Murgatroyd and Mr Turner. Gentlemen, this is my fiancée, Miss Mary Ann Blanchard.'

'Pleased to meet you Miss Blanchard.' Mr Turner's smile was warm as he shook her hand. Aged about 45 he was fair-skinned with very blue eyes. He had a well-built frame with large practical hands and a quiet voice and a polite manner. Mr Murgatroyd, by far the taller of the two gentlemen, was thin with dark hair and a moustache. He also smiled and asked Mary Ann if she had seen any of the fine buildings in Liverpool.

Mary Ann replied, 'The weather has been so cold and wet

just now, and I spend most of my time here at the hospital, so I haven't seen much of the city at all.'

Mr Turner's eyes twinkled, 'Not the best time of year to choose to come for a visit!' Then he added more seriously, 'I hope that some day you will see our country at its best.'

'I hope so too.'

In truth, Mary Ann had given very little thought to the fact that she was in England; her only concern had been helping Seth back to good health. Now it crossed her mind, for the first time, that it was a shame to travel so far and not see something of a different country.

Seth had met Mr Murgatroyd on previous crossings, and he knew that Mr Turner was one of the Yorkshire mill owners whose woollen cloth they transported.

'What brings you here?' Seth hoped he didn't sound rude but he could not imagine why the two men had come to the hospital.

'I'm in Liverpool to arrange further shipments of our cloth,' Mr Turner explained, 'and when Mr Murgatroyd told me of your plight I thought the least that we could do was to come and visit you and find out how you were getting along. I see that you are a good way to walking again. Well done. It can't have been easy.'

Seth could see that Mr Turner was impressed, and felt a surge of pride.

'I'll get there, no worry about that.'

'I'm sure you will, but you'll not be back on board ship for quite some time, eh?' Mr Turner didn't wait for a reply, but went on, 'What are your plans for when you leave the hospital?'

Seth and Mary Ann looked at each other a little perplexed. They hadn't really discussed what would happen when Seth was discharged. Mary Ann had been secretly hoping that Seth would go home to New England with her, and all Seth could think about was getting back to sea! He looked a bit embarrassed as he admitted, 'We don't really have any plans...'

Mary Ann remarked that Seth needed more rest and required a quiet place to get his strength back. Mr Turner had been weighing up the young couple and liked what he had seen of them, and replied,

'I think I have just the place for you both. It's a little cottage in Yorkshire, near to where I live and close to the village of Haworth. It is very comfortable, situated in a lovely setting among green fields, and a nice little garden with a stream flowing in front of the cottage. My aged parents used to live in it.'

Mary Ann looked at Seth and smiled, and with a nod Seth thanked Mr Turner for his kind offer which they would accept. Mr Turner stated it was his intention to return back to Haworth the next day, and would be only too pleased to accompany them both.

Mary Ann had warmed to Mr Turner and remarked, 'We do not want to impose on you.'

The two gentlemen both smiled and Mr Murgatroyd said, 'Don't worry, I think you will be happy with this idea. Yorkshire has some wonderful countryside.'

Mary Ann protested, 'Seth won't be able to leave the hospital for quite some time. Not until he's reached the targets set by Dr Moorcroft.'

Seth didn't speak but grabbed his crutches, and with a look of grim determination he set about walking the full length of the ward. All those present held their breath until he reached the far door, then everyone clapped and cheered.

'Well done, Seth.' 'Good on you, lad.' 'Bravo.'

A broad grin split Seth's face.

'Thank you again, Mr Turner. We accept, and we WILL come to Yorkshire with you tomorrow.'

'Good then it's decided. We shall have an early start,' said Mr Turner.

Next day as they travelled through the countryside, Seth filled his lungs with the fresh air, a treat after being confined in the hospital for so long. Both he and Mary Ann felt more relaxed, and all three enjoyed each other's company. After two and a half days' travel from Liverpool they approached Haworth up the steep cobbled hill of Main Street past the church gates, taking the left-forked road to the moors and then began to descend down a steep hill into Sladen Valley below. Mr Turner stopped the horses and with his whip pointed to a row of seven cottages lying in the bottom of the valley, and indicated the end cottage, saying it was the one where his mother had lived and that he would instruct his housekeeper and the maids to have the house warm. At the garden gate Mary Ann noticed the gardens all neat and tidy and that the windows and curtains were clean.

Mr Turner remarked, 'The other cottages are occupied by my mill workers, all nice families. It's very sheltered here, being tucked under the hill. You'll love it, I know you will. This was the family house where I was brought up as a boy. We caught trout in the stream and swam in the mill dam, caught rabbits and went bird-nesting along the river banks.'

Mary Ann's heart skipped a beat as they reached the garden gate and saw the neat gardens. When they went inside she was hardly able to contain her excitement, the little cottage was all she could have dreamed of. So cosy, with the well-polished furniture shining; there were comfortable rocking chairs, one each side of the fireplace. The kitchen at the back of the house was bright and clean and well-equipped with everything they might need. Upstairs there were two good-sized bedrooms with large feather beds, each with clean bed linen and beautiful hand-embroidered counterpanes. Seth and Mary Ann were each thinking that only one of the beds would be needed, but they kept their thoughts to themselves. It was perfect, just perfect.

'Mr Turner, I can't thank you enough for all your help,' Seth began. 'The cottage is wonderful, we don't know how to thank you.'

'Just get fit and well, lad, that's all the thanks I need.'

Mr Turner insisted that they should go down to his home and have a meal whilst he instructed the housekeeper and the maids to light a fire, get the cottage warm and ready, and provide more blankets and linen. His own house and mill was another quarter mile down the lane from Sladen Bridge, which was through three field lengths, the lane running parallel with a chattering stream. Round a sudden bend in the lane was a large, well-built stone farmhouse with mullioned windows. The entrance had an imposing arched doorway with a solid oak door. As the door opened they were greeted by Mrs Turner and their daughter Ruth, and with a smile on all their faces were introduced by Mr Turner, who explained how Seth and Mary Ann had travelled with him from Liverpool.

Mrs Turner held out her hand and said, 'I'm very pleased to

meet you both, I hope you've had a good journey. At least the weather has been kind to you, not a drop of rain over these last three days, which is most unusual for this time of the year. You must be tired, I know how uncomfortable it can be over some of these rough roads,' and with a simple gesture she said, 'will you please come through into the drawing room.'

Mrs Turner and her daughter were quietly well-spoken, and their clothes, without being showy, were obviously of the best quality. Mrs Turner was a tall, good-looking woman with a fair complexion and a clear skin, very much like her husband. Her hair was swept back high into a bun, giving her a rather regal appearance. The tone of her voice was gentle and welcoming.

Ruth was also fair like her parents with the same kind of expressions. She was a little younger than Mary Ann and was relaxed, and chatted merrily as they all sat around the table having a meal, telling her father all that had happened at the mill and in Haworth during his absence in Liverpool.

'Oh, some more news for you, Papa! Mrs Hartley gave birth to twin girls whilst you were away. Seven children, just imagine! I hope their ironmongers shop is doing well with all those mouths to feed.

'There was also gossip up in Stanbury last week, about the funeral of an old lady called Mrs Sunderland, who lived down by Lumb Foot Mill. The road, from the house where she died to the churchyard, was impassable owing to storm damage, and the undertaker, Mr George Shackleton, wanted to take the funeral cortège across some fields, but the farmer would not allow it, saying that if the coffin passed over his land it would make it a public right of way, and he would not give consent.'

Seth and Mary Ann liked Ruth and were happy to listen.

'...and the fox has been in Greenswood's chicken pen again ... and killed six chickens. Do you have trouble with foxes in America, Mary Ann?'

'No, it's the coyote that we have to watch out for, and in winter wolves and bears.'

'Wolves, gracious me. I'm glad we have nothing like that here. Foxes are bad enough.'

Ruth turned to her father and said, 'I think I have told you all the news locally, but there is trouble in the Bradford woollen mills. There have been militant strikes, with woolcombers and workers damaging machinery and power looms. They had to get the troops out.'

Mr Turner's face looked grim as he remarked, 'I hope the workers' unrest doesn't spread to the mills in the Keighley district and the Worth Valley.'

After the meal Mrs Turner suggested that Mary Ann and Seth would be tired after the long journey from Liverpool and a good night's sleep would be the best thing for both of them. It was suggested that Mr Turner should take them back to the cottage. On returning to the cottage, there was a welcoming coal fire blazing away and a copper bed pan warming up the beds.

Mr Turner moved towards the door to leave them and bade them to 'Sleep well, and tomorrow Mrs Turner will be calling with more food and milk for you ... that is er ... for Mr and Mrs Snowden,' he winked at Seth then, but the young couple didn't see the broad smile on his face as he went back to his carriage.

Immediately Mr Turner had left and the door was closed to the outside world, Seth and Mary Ann fell into each other's arms and wept for joy, smothering each other in tears. It had felt a lifetime since their last time alone together in the Boston hotel. Seth would have liked to have carried Mary Ann up the narrow, twisting staircase to lay her on the bed as he had done in Boston, but he was still learning how to negotiate stairs with a wooden leg, and by the time he made it to the bedroom Mary Ann was already snuggled into the soft feather mattress.

This was the second time that Mary Ann had watched Seth undress. The same powerful shoulders and broad back, the same strong arms, the same soft hair. Mary Ann felt the same deep longing, but there was an added tenderness as she sensed a self-consciousness in Seth that he hadn't had in Boston.

Seth spoke as he took off his shirt and trousers.

'Remember the Tremont? It was a wonderful night. The dancing ... you were the belle of the ball ... and later, together...' he paused, and then, 'I had two legs then, I'm sorry I'm not...'

Mary Ann stopped him quietly.

'It doesn't matter. You are still my Seth. You will always be my Seth. You have lost a leg but you've gained my heart, and that is yours forever.'

They were together then. All that had happened over the last few weeks was forgotten. The accident, the fear, the pain, the dread, the struggles and the longing were behind them as they melted into each other's embrace. Seth need not have worried, Mary Ann delighted in him, if possible, even more than before. She was hungry for his lips, his hands, his arms, his strength. She soared to heaven in a series of leaps as he kissed first her face and neck, then her breasts, her tummy. Gladly she let him take control, surrendering to his superior strength. No one-legged weakling this, but a giant, a warrior, a conqueror, her hero. He was on top of her now, kneading into her, on and on until it seemed his power was so great that it would engulf them both and then he burst into her, long and deep and she cried out as she held him to her, nails biting into the flesh of his back. He shuddered, and they were spent. Finished, exhausted, helpless. Neither spoke, it had been all they remembered and more, secure in the knowledge of their love.

The next morning it was late when they awoke. Mary Ann got the fire going and the kettle singing, and prepared breakfast on a tray. She had found a brightly coloured apron and wore it to protect her dress as she busied herself making Seth's breakfast.

On entering the bedroom with the tray in her hands she found Seth sitting up in bed. His face broke into a broad grin. She looked so radiant and cute in the apron. Mary Ann smiled back and remarked,

'This little cottage is heaven-sent bliss.'

She knew that Seth would soon recover and gain strength and regain confidence.

Mary Ann had decided to inspect the plants and shrubs in the garden when Mrs Turner appeared at the garden gate, carrying a large wicker basket and, giving a warm smile, enquired if they had had a good night's sleep. She placed the basket containing bread, butter, milk, eggs, tea, sugar and a joint of lamb on the table.

'There's a vegetable garden across the lane near the stream,' she said, 'just help yourself to potatoes, herbs, carrots and such.'

Mrs Turner stayed for upwards of two hours, and as the three of them sat beside the blazing fire Mary Ann found her to be warm-hearted and easy to talk to.

'How do you like the cottage Mary Ann?' she asked. 'Are you comfortable here?'

'Oh yes, thank you, it is really lovely. This cottage reminds me of my grandparents' house in Vermont.'

'Did you stay often with your grandparents?' asked Mrs Turner, noticing how the girl's face had lit up when she mentioned them.

'I was brought up on their farm,' replied Mary Ann. 'Papa was so much away at sea it was better for everyone. Mother and Grandmother were company for each other, and Papa didn't have to worry about us whilst he was gone. The dairy farm was quite large, and Grandpa was glad of the extra hands to help with the butter-churning.' She laughed, remembering. 'I think I was probably more of a hindrance than a help, but I felt so important patting the butter into blocks and Mother always said "Well done, Mary Ann," but I'm sure she re-shaped the butter when I was gone. I was very happy there.'

'Whereabouts is the farm?' Mrs Turner had only a scant knowledge of the United States, but she resolved to look at the map book when she returned home.

'It is near to the town of Dorset in Vermont. My grandparents are no longer there. After we moved to Boston in 1825, so that I could attend the new English High School there, Grandpa and Grandmother found the farm too big, and last year they sold it and moved to a house in the town.'

Mrs Turner said, 'We started married life with the farm, and a flock of sheep also, keeping pigs and poultry with just a couple of cows for our own milk and butter. In the beginning Mr Turner ran the farm and I wove cloth, from the sheep's wool, on a hand loom in the spare bedroom. What a long time ago it all seems now.' She smiled at the memory of the dusty room and the long hours she had spent at the loom whenever daylight permitted.

Seth was interested to hear how the Turners had built up their textile trade as Mrs Turner continued.

'Mr Turner saw the potential in the new power looms and knew that was what we needed. We managed to invest in a small steam engine which powered just ten looms, and we set them up in one of the barns. At first that was enough, but we found new buyers and the market has steadily grown. I think it was because our sheep produced such good wool that things went so well. Of course, now we have to buy in wool to meet the demand.

'We now produce some of the best-quality worsted cloth in Yorkshire, which is in great demand in London, Paris and America. We have installed a larger steam engine and more machinery and looms, and employ some seventy workers. My husband has worked many long hours to get the mill on to a sound footing.

'Our son David would have inherited the mill, of course.' Mrs Turner seemed to be talking to herself. She was gazing into the fire and looked quite sad.

'I didn't know you had a son,' exclaimed Mary Ann.

Mrs Turner turned to her.

'He died eleven years ago, when he was just ten... David was fishing in the mill pond ... no one was with him ... must have slipped ... he drowned.'

'Oh, I'm so sorry,' Mary Ann didn't quite know what to say, but Mrs Turner smiled then and spoke more brightly.

'It's all a long time ago, and we are blessed with our daughter, Ruth. She's a good girl and a great help to her father in the office, keeping all the books in order.'

Just as Mrs Turner rose from the chair to depart she produced a small box containing a gold wedding ring and said it belonged to her great-aunt. 'Folks in Haworth ... very narrow-minded ... stop the gossiping if you wear it ... we'll keep it between ourselves ... you'll be known as Mr and Mrs Seth Snowden.' She smiled then put her fingers to her lips. Mary Ann knew she meant well but she didn't know what she should do. She sighed again.

'Why the sighing, Mary Ann?' Seth had been watching her and knew that she was troubled. 'Wear the ring. We were to be married at Easter if all had gone according to plan, but circumstances change things, and now that we're here there's no point upsetting people. We love each other. That's all that matters.'

He hobbled across to her and, taking the ring from its box he slid it onto her finger. Mary Ann smiled.

'Are you sure it will be all right, Seth?'

His eyes twinkled mischievously as he replied, 'Well, we're as good as man and wife now, after all.'

Seth kept admiring Mary Ann's ability and confidence in preparing the meal in the kitchen. The smell of the lamb roasting in the oven and the fresh vegetables boiling in the pans. Before they settled into their rocking chairs for the evening, Seth drew her into his arms.

'That was a delicious meal. Even better than the celebration meal in Boston, thank you.' He kissed her lightly on the cheek and then drew back a little so that he could look at her. 'And you look so cute in your pretty apron. I really am a very lucky man, MRS Snowden.'

'And I'm lucky too, MR Snowden.'

Mary Ann smiled. All her reservations about wearing the wedding band were gone. They were very much in love, and she was happy that they could be together.

6

Each day Seth grew stronger, and the weather being particularly mild for autumn, he was able to get out for plenty of exercise. He began to venture up the steep hill towards Haworth and onto the edge of the moors overlooking the Sladen Bridge cottages. Both he and Mary Ann enjoyed this time together. They absorbed the panoramic views across the valley and, from higher up the moor, could see for miles around. Still green, the pocket-sized fields divided by stone walls gave way to the wild expanses of moorland beyond. Farming families were taking advantage of the good weather and were busily tending their lands: clearing field drains or rebuilding walls where young lads had clambered over displacing the topstones and causing the upper layer to fall into the grass. Sheep and cattle contentedly grazed in the fields, and overhead lapwings soared and dived and skylarks sang as they flew ever higher. Behind them, hidden amongst the heather of the moors they heard the occasional grouse call, 'go bak, go bak, bak, bak, bak'. This countryside was new to Seth and Mary Ann, but they both soon grew to love its many moods. The bleak moors were in stark contrast to the quiet intimacy which they felt between man, bird and beast all living together in harmony in the valley. Mary Ann had loved the beautiful, fertile land of Vermont, but here she felt an excitement and a oneness with nature that she never knew were possible.

Seth's whole life had been spent in seaports or on the wide expanses of the ocean, and this tiny village in the Yorkshire Pennine hills was a totally new experience and one that he adjusted to so easily that he surprised himself.

Village people on their way back and forth to Haworth would

always stop to talk with the young couple, and Seth and Mary Ann were delighted but, in truth, found it difficult at first to understand the strong Yorkshire dialect. They soon realized that these people were a breed on their own: very independent and outspoken, but hard-working and friendly, once they had got to know you. They disliked authority, were straight-thinking, very stubborn types, and they were fiercely Protestant. The mill-workers going to their work each day at Hollings Mill had to take the little track in front of the row of cottages and, without fail, they each bid 'Good-day' to Mary Ann and Seth as they passed, the men touching the neb of their caps as they spoke. These people never moved far out of the valley, and work, family life and attending church or chapel was their whole existence. Everyone knew everybody else, and Mary Ann and Seth, like other strangers moving into the valley, were made welcome but were always known as 'off-cumduns'.

At first these walks into the countryside, chopping wood ready for the winter and getting under Mary Ann's feet whilst she busied herself cleaning the cottage and preparing meals were enough for Seth, and they were blissfully happy. As the weeks passed Seth grew fitter and stronger, and with the fitness came a restlessness and frustration and a feeling of uselessness. He began to feel guilty about staying in the cottage on Mr Turner's kindness.

Consequently one morning found Seth up earlier than usual and heading down the track to Hollings Mill. He sought out Mr Turner, who welcomed him with a strong hand-shake.

'Seth, good to see you. Particularly good to see you looking so well. What can I do for you?'

'I'd like to offer my services, Mr Turner. I'll try anything you can give me. I'm keen to start work to repay you for your kindness to us. Any job that you need doing I'll give it a go in return for the cottage and our food.'

Mr Turner looked into the eager face in front of him.

'I told you, I don't ask for repayment and I'm sorry, but I don't have a full-time job available at the moment, Seth.' He paused, seeing the disappointment, and thought for a moment before continuing, 'I could do with someone to check the weight and quality of the raw wool coming into the mill, and there are various other ways in which you could be of assistance; ordering corn fodder for the farm and recommending payments of accounts at the end of each month ... yes, I think we can work something out.'

Seth was delighted and shook Mr Turner's hand again.

'Thank you very much, sir. I'll not let you down. When can I start?'

'There's no time like the present,' said Mr Turner, pleased and a little amused at Seth's eagerness. 'You can start straight away, but first I'll show you round the mill so you know what's what. Come on.'

They began in the woolcombing room. The glow from the charcoal burners used to heat the metal combs was quite welcoming to Seth and Mr Turner coming in from the December cold, but the young men pulling the heavy combs through the tangled wool had their shirt sleeves rolled up and the boys were sweating as they worked in the smokey atmosphere, where only small windows gave poor ventilation.

'Most mills still send the wool out to cottages to be washed and combed,' Mr Turner explained as they went, 'but I wanted to bring the whole process under the one roof, so we begin with the washing of the raw wool and take it right through to the woven cloth.'

They continued by way of the smelly drying room, where steaming skeins of wool were draped over wooden beams above hot pipes, and on into the lower level of the spinning room. The gleaming machines were simultaneously spinning, twisting and winding reel after reel of spun yarn, whilst the workers kept a keen eye out for any broken threads or entanglements. Seth was very impressed with the efficiency, and surprised by the speed of output from the machines.

'We've another floor above,' said Mr Turner, 'more or less identical to this one, so we'll not go up just now.'

He was aware that steps were still not easy for Seth, and there would be no advantage in taking him up there.

Seth was watching the machines and their operators with interest. His life at sea had kept him fairly ignorant of any other kind of life, and he said, 'You must have created quite a number of jobs in this valley.'

'Folk don't see it that way,' replied Mr Turner. 'They don't like these powered looms, and I'm getting worried about the unrest in many mills of Yorkshire and Lancashire. The workers are becoming militant and are breaking up machines. In Bradford mobs broke into the mills under cover of darkness and smashed the power looms with sledge-hammers. A mill owner in Colne, not ten miles away on the Lancashire border, has been killed trying to protect his property from a violent crowd. The red-coated military men are now patrolling the area, but they are having difficulty catching the rebels, as there is such a large area of countryside to cover and no way of knowing when they will strike next.'

Seth had heard nothing of this unrest, and seeing how worried Mr Turner was, he felt quite alarmed by it all.

'What precautions are you taking here?' he asked.

Mr Turner struggled and moved on again as he spoke.

'Oh, we're quite isolated here, and so far there's been no trouble. I like to think my workers are happy and that any such uprisings will be confined to the larger mills in the towns.'

They were now entering the weaving shed, and the noise of the looms, with warp and weft threads shifting and shuttles flying to and fro, prevented any further conversation until they had walked the full length of the long, low building and out through the far doors.

'That's the main part of the mill, Seth. Over there is the finishing and packing shed and the warehouse. We'll not go round those today. Come on, lad, let's sort out a fair wage and then get you started.'

Christmas was almost upon them, and there was great excitement at Sladen Bridge as the coach drew up. Mary Ann, running to meet it, hugged first her father and then her mother, who held her tightly before taking her shoulders and gently pushing her back.

'Let me look at you, Mary Ann.'

Mrs Blanchard had been worried about her daughter so far away from home, and although Mary Ann's letters had been bright and cheerful she could not help wondering if she had done the right thing in allowing her daughter to come alone to England when the news of Seth's accident had reached them. She hadn't been able to forget the sight of Mary Ann leaning

66

on the ship's sail as she sailed out from Boston. When the letter came, telling them of the protracted stay in Haworth, she had thought at first that Seth and Mary Ann were staying with the Turners and was dismayed later to understand that they were living together as man and wife at Sladen Bridge. William Blanchard, on the other hand, had remained unperturbed.

'It's best that they are together,' he had said. 'Fate plays strange games, and everyone has to find his or her own way through life. If you're worrying what people will think, Helen, don't! No one need know.'

She had felt a little better then, but not until she looked into Mary Ann's face, and saw joy and fulfilment and eyes that sparkled with happiness, were all her fears allayed.

'Welcome to England, Mother,' said Mary Ann, laughing. 'Papa, I'm thrilled that you could plan for the *Mary Ann* to be in Liverpool over Christmas. What a wonderful idea. Wait until you see our cottage. You will love it, just as we do.'

Suddenly, noticing the amount of luggage piled onto the carriage, she gasped, 'Goodness, where will we find space for all of that!'

Besides Mr and Mrs Blanchard's portmanteaus there were three travelling trunks of Mary Ann's clothes, books and other personal effects, a large barrel of New England red apples, a cask of maple syrup and a crate containing good American food for the Christmas celebrations.

There was much to catch up on. Mary Ann delighted in showing her mother the cottage, and as they unpacked the trunks they talked non-stop; of Haworth, the Turners, Boston and all their friends, Seth's accident and recovery and much more.

Seth and William Blanchard also had much to talk about and settled down by the fire. Seth was 'all ears' as the captain brought him up to date.

'We're making record sailings, cutting as much as five days off the old ship's time. We've still the same cargoes; wheat, turps, tallow etc from New England, then mostly cotton piece goods from Manchester and the worsteds from here in Yorkshire on the return run. I've also managed to secure a contract for fine pottery from the towns in Staffordshire – our reputation for efficiency and reliability went before us, Seth, and I was

67

approached through Mr Murgatroyd for this trade. The ship's running well. Many of the crew send their regards and wish you a happy Christmas and a speedy return,' he paused, glancing up. 'I miss you, Seth. We're a good team,' he paused again but when Seth made no reply he changed the subject, turning to tales from Liverpool docks and, finally, to Boston.

'I didn't write this news to you Seth, because I wanted to tell you face to face. That rascal Seward was brought to trial for sabotaging the ship and consequently causing your accident and the death of Josh Mitchell. We tried our best, brought witnesses to the fight at the Tremont, to his threats and to the fracas on the waterfront. We made much of the open hatches and cut strappings but the judge ruled that all the evidence was circumstantial and the case was overturned.'

William leaned forward with a sigh. 'I'm sorry, I would have liked to have seen him convicted.'

Seth shrugged, 'It doesn't matter, Mr Blanchard, you did your best. Nothing can alter what happened, but I don't like to think of Seward free to cause more mischief.'

'He'll not do that,' Blanchard replied. 'The night after the trial he got rolling drunk in the Blue Whale Tavern and was bragging to anyone who'd listen that he'd "Fixed the Captain" and "Got away with it". He left the inn after midnight and was last seen staggering along the quayside, bottle in hand – they fished him out of the harbour the following morning.'

'I can't feel any pity for him,' said Seth. 'Josh Mitchell was a good man, and if Vernon Seward was responsible for his death he paid a just price.'

The captain nodded. 'God moves in mysterious ways. Isn't that so, Seth?'

Christmas Day was spent at the cottage. A wonderful meal, blazing fire and the warm closeness of people who love one another savouring every moment of precious time spent together. William Blanchard, seeing how fit and strong Seth was, talking often of the ships and the sea and watching for Seth's reaction. Helen Blanchard delighting in her daughter's company. Realizing how much she had matured in these few short months. Mary Ann bubbling with excitement, chattering ten to the dozen and happily playing hostess for the very first time. Seth, feeling lucky to have been accepted into this family, proudly watching Mary Ann and wondering how he could ever tell the captain of the decision he had made.

The four at Sladen Bridge were invited to a party at the home of Mr and Mrs Turner. It was to be only a small gathering, and Mrs Turner thought that it would be an ideal opportunity for Seth and Mary Ann to meet some of their friends. As they were welcomed into the entrance hall, Mary Ann caught sight of three young girls peeping round the drawing room door. Their faces were a picture of wonderment, mouths open and eyes wide they watched as the ladies removed their wraps. It is no wonder that they were amazed by the sight of these people from overseas, for Mary Ann and her mother had decided to wear the gowns that they had had made for the night of the Boston party, and the menfolk were resplendent in their naval uniforms, dark blue with gold tassels and buttons. The people of Haworth were unaccustomed to such finery. By the time the group was ushered towards the drawing room the girls had disappeared and were next seen along with a red-headed boy of about 12 years, standing quietly in a row beside a middle-aged gentleman, whom Mary Ann took to be their father, and other guests waiting to be introduced.

Mr Turner did the honours.

'Reverend, may I present Mr and Mrs Blanchard and Mr and Mrs Snowden. This is the Reverend Partick Brontë, vicar of Haworth parish, and his children Branwell, Charlotte, Emily and Ann.'

The girls, aged between nine and thirteen years, each gave a slight curtsey when introduced, and the boy nodded but never took his eyes off Mr Blanchard, already imagining himself a pirate on the high seas, single-handedly taking over the captain's ship.

Mrs Blanchard was sad later to learn that the children's mother, Maria, had died some years earlier and that two other daughters had died of tuberculosis in 1825. She knew none of this now and she told Mr Brontë that she was 'Delighted to meet your lovely family.'

69

Next to be introduced were the local bank manager and his wife, Mr and Mrs Jonas Fisher. Grey-haired and refined in appearance, they were very smartly dressed, but in comparison with the Blanchards' fine clothes their attire appeared rather sombre. The dark brown frock-coat which Mr Fisher wore was only slightly relieved by the grey cravat knotted at his throat, and Mrs Fisher wore a dark green gown of heavy satin, full-skirted and with wide shoulders, but it had very little orna-mentation save for some paler green ribbon at the collar and cuffs and on the waist sash. Mr and Mrs Blanchard noticed only the kind expression on the faces of the elder couple and the sincerity of their pleasure in this meeting.

Ruth, in yellow silk which highly complemented her fair hair, and a young man, Mr Robert Butterworth, son of a wealthy Keighley mill owner, completed the line up and, introductions completed, the party were invited to make their way through to the dining room to take their seats for dinner. The meal was good, plain cooking of roast leg of pork with sage and onion stuffing served with boiled vegetables and followed by apple pie and cream. Conversation flowed around the table.

Mr Brontë was interested to hear about life in Vermont and in particular the life of the Quakers and the spread of their religion. The children said very little, but they listened intently and absorbed every word. They wanted to know about the wild animals of America, especially the big brown bears, and about the Red Indian tribes and their wigwams. Captain Blanchard and Seth soon realized that they had a captive audience and regaled them with sea-going yarns of other countries they had visited. They told of whaling off Iceland and of the crystal-clear air of that land of contrasts with its icy-cold cascading rivers and its hot geysers spouting from the rocky landscape. They painted pictures of the Breton fishermen with their woollen caps and leather-sailed boats who, though French, spoke a special Celtic language all of their own, and they told how the Portuguese, though poor and barely scraping a living fishing for sardines, were always merry and bright. The children hung on every word and, more than once, Ann, the youngest, had to be reminded to eat her food.

Before they left the dining room a treat awaited the Americans when a Yorkshire custom was followed. Cups of tea were poured

70

and slices of rich fruit cake were served with portions of cheese. Mary Ann and her mother thought this very strange but Mrs Blanchard enjoyed it so much that she took the custom back to New England and served the same combination at many gatherings in the future.

The meal was over, but the evening had scarcely begun. Mr Turner led them all into the music room where they gathered around the piano to sing carols to Mrs Turner's accompaniment. Ruth then sang for them a ballad called 'As Morning Dawned'. She had a clear, sweet voice, and as she finished everyone clapped and shouted 'Encore!'

Ruth blushed, 'No, I've done my turn, perhaps Mary Ann will sing for us now.'

Mary Ann's singing would best be described as mediocre, and she didn't want to follow the lovely performance just given. She felt awkward refusing, but managed to side-step the moment by saying quickly, 'Seth has brought his flute. He'll play for you.'

The children clapped happily as Seth played sea-shanties and reels, but they were highly delighted when he began to play a horn-pipe and Captain Blanchard, caught up in the mood, took to the floor and leaped and kicked and mimed all the sailor's work in the steps he'd learnt as a young lad on the whaling fleet. Faster and faster Seth played; faster tapped the captain until with a final step and bow he collapsed into his chair, red-faced and out of breath, mopping his brow with his handkerchief. Everyone laughed.

'It's a long, long time since I last did that,' he puffed to another round of applause; the children, fascinated by their new acquaintances, clapped loudest of all.

It was a wonderful party with games of Blind Man's Buff and Crambo especially for the children, another song from Ruth, and Mr Fisher surprised them all by producing a pack of playing cards and amazed everyone with his sleight of hand. His tricks kept them all guessing, and the children's faces were a picture of puzzlement.

Time passed all too quickly, and gone 10 p.m. Mr Turner ordered the waggonette to be made ready to take everyone home to save the tired children the long walk back to Haworth village.

71

Everyone thanked Mr and Mrs Turner for a truly wonderful evening, and the children waved until the house was out of sight.

It was a clean night with a sprinkling of stars and a bright moon to help them on their way. The coachman stopped at the Sladen Bridge Cottages to allow Mr and Mrs Blanchard, Seth and Mary Ann to dismount. Mary Ann went to the front of the waggonette.

'Wait here a few moments, please,' she instructed the driver.

She and Seth hurried to the cottage and reappeared a minute or two later with a basket of red American apples for the children and two jars of maple syrup, one each for Mrs Fisher and Mr Brontë; they were all delighted and agreed again that they had had a very happy evening. Amid calls of 'Thank you' and 'Good night' the horseman flicked his whip to bid the horses forward up the steep hill to Haworth.

Later, snuggled into their feather bed, Seth and Mary Ann finally discussed the subject that had been uppermost in both their minds, but which neither of them had really wanted to mention. Their return to America. Mary Ann had been so very happy here in the cottage, and as long as Seth never mentioned the ship or the sea she felt that they didn't exist and that the past was another life; one to which they would never have to return. She knew that being a sailor's wife could be hard. Her mother had had a lonely married life, waiting months for her father's return and then, after only a few short days, watching him sail back out to sea.

'I would rather you were here, Seth, in bed with me every night,' she said as she leant over to kiss his cheek.

'I've been thinking,' said Seth, 'that life on board ship can be hard for anyone, and with my wooden leg I'd probably be more of a hindrance than a help when the seas were rough. I'd be useless now.'

Mary Ann hid her own feelings and responded with wifely pride.

'You'd be just fine. Papa really wants you back, just as you are, wooden leg or not. He knows you well and he misses you. You must do what you think is best, Seth.'

Seth answered carefully, 'I don't know whether Mr Turner will have full-time work for me at the mill or whether we'll be able to stay here at the cottage, but if you're willing to chance it I'm sure we can work something out. I'd really like to stay here in England.'

Mary Ann flung her arms round Seth and almost whooped for joy.

'That is exactly what I want,' she said. 'I know it will work out, Seth, so long as we're together.'

He kissed her then, saying, 'This is heaven for me, darling,' and folded in each other's arms they dropped off to sleep.

Time had passed all too quickly; the ship would soon be ready to sail, and next day Mary Ann's mother and father had to begin the journey back to Liverpool to join her. Over breakfast Seth had told Mr Blanchard of his decision to stay in Yorkshire, and although the captain had anticipated this news he could not conceal his deep disappointment.

'I'll miss you, Seth,' he said. 'I'll not deny I've been hoping you'd be coming back. You've been good to work with and a valuable member of the ship's crew. Still, I wish you all the very best for the future.'

Mrs Blanchard made no remark, but was silently pleased that Mary Ann would not know the aching loneliness that she herself had known. She could see how happy her daughter was with Seth, and although she would have preferred her to be in New England near to them, she knew that she would be able to make regular visits to England on board the *Mary Ann*.

They didn't linger long after breakfast, making their goodbyes brief. The days were short and the weather had turned cold and wintery, so Mr Blanchard was eager to make an early start.

'Be sure to write, Mary Ann,' said her mother as she hugged her, 'and be sure to eat well and keep wrapped up in this cold weather, and make sure...'

'Oh Mother! I will,' laughed Mary Ann. 'Have a good journey.'

Captain Blanchard took Seth's hand. 'All the very best, Seth. Remember, if you change your mind there's always a place for you on board my ship.'

'Thank you,' said Seth. 'I'll remember, but I won't change my mind.'

'Goodbye! Goodbye!'

7

The militant trouble-makers were becoming more active in the Worth Valley, smashing up machinery in the weaving sheds, destroying finished cloth and even setting light to one mill. In that instance the fire had been spotted and put out before any real damage was done but nevertheless it was very worrying for all the mill-owners. Just after Christmas Mr Turner had voiced his fears to Seth and had asked him if he had any ideas for extra protection of the mill. Seth had promised to give the matter some serious thought. Although there had been no trouble so far at Hollings Mill it had become a constant cause for concern, and Mr Turner was glad now to have something to take his mind off it all.

The three boys standing below him in the mill yard shuffled uncomfortably as Mr Turner looked them over, weighing up their potential. They had been quite talkative on the journey from Liverpool, asking Seth endless questions about the mill and Haworth and the work they would have to do.

'There'll be plenty of time for you to find all that out when we get there,' Seth had said, laughing at their excitement.

Now they had actually arrived they were a little in awe of the gentleman who had sent for them, and they stood quietly waiting for the mill-owner to speak.

Two of the boys were of a very healthy appearance, well-developed with good limbs and stocky frames. The taller of these two had a darkish face framed by thick, black, curly hair and studded with the deepest brown eyes Mr Turner had ever seen.

'Latin blood in him,' thought Mr Turner, summing him up. 'Coming from Liverpool it's possible his father was a foreign seaman, Mediterranean probably.'

'What's your name, lad?' he asked kindly, 'and how old are you?'

The boy answered quickly and clearly with a bright grin that lit up his dark features.

'John Pickles, sir, and I'm ten years old.'

Mr Turner asked the same questions of the second boy, who was almost the same height but who was as fair as John Pickles was dark.

'Paul Ryan, aged ten, sir.'

Paul, freckled-faced with light blue eyes and a fresh complexion, pushed his mop of blond hair from his face as he spoke. He didn't smile, but Mr Turner saw an air of quiet confidence in him.

'And you, lad, who might you be?' said Mr Turner, addressing the last of the three boys.

'I'm Albert Holmes. I'm eleven, sir,' replied the boy.

Although the eldest boy of the three Albert was small for his age and not so robust as the other two; his blue eyes stared from a pallid, pinched face, and his hair was lank and straggly and needed cutting. The mill-master noticed immediately the effects of under-nourishment, for the lad suffered from rickets and had badly bowed legs, but he also noticed the rather shy, winning smile the boy gave him as he answered.

Mr Turner wondered why Seth had chosen this boy to work in the mill. He was obviously not strong and mill work could be very hard and tiring.

It had been a week earlier, shortly after Christmas, that Seth had left Haworth for Liverpool to visit the Blue Coats Orphanage with a view to selecting six boys and bringing them back to work in the woolcombing department of the mill. They would have to be taught the craft, but young boys are quick to learn, and Mr Turner had been confident that Seth would choose well. In fact, as Mr Turner found out later, when Seth arrived at the orphanage he was told that there were just three boys available, as only days before ten boys had been taken to a cotton mill in Rochdale. Seth had no choice of selection but had to take the last three boys, John, Paul and Albert. It was plain to see that Albert was not a strong lad, but he had begged to be allowed to go with his friends, and Seth hadn't the heart to leave him behind. In any case he felt sure that good food would build up the boy's strength.

75

Mr Turner nodded at the boys.

'Welcome to Haworth. I hope you'll like it here. We've fair hours and good food. Work hard and you'll be well looked after. Mind you, we'll have no trouble and we don't put up with shirkers, so see that you do as you are bidden and behave yourselves.'

Mr Turner broke off then for he had noticed a large pile of rope netting in the corner of the yard.

'Where's this come from, Seth? What's it for?'

Seth grinned.

'It's a ship's boarding net. I got it from the docks in Liverpool. I'm going to fasten it under the wooden canopy over the doors to the loading bay. If any militant machine-wreckers try to get into this mill in the dead of night we'll be ready for them. They'll be very surprised to find themselves neatly captured. Hopefully no one will get hurt, but we'll have the culprits red-handed. Not a bad idea, eh?'

'Splendid idea, Seth.'

Mr Turner was impressed. He already had night watchmen, and he knew they would feel easier knowing they had a means of dealing with any intruders.

'Now take these boys and show them where they'll be sleeping, and it looks as if a bar of soap would not go amiss. There's plenty of hot water in the boiler house, and there's the wooden vat for bathing. Tomorrow morning take them up to Haworth and get them all fixed up with working clothes and footwear at Brown's outfitters in the main street. Mind you, lads, I want you back at the mill by ten o'clock sharp, ready to work. Now off you go.'

Across the yard, through a door next to the boiler house, a flight of stone steps led to a warm room above. Two long rows of single beds lined the walls, and at a large, wooden table in the centre of the room four older boys were busy making fishing rods. Three other boys lounged on their beds. John, Paul and Albert were introduced by Seth, who then allocated them each a bed at the far end of the room before organizing the prescribed baths in the boiler room below.

'When you're done there'll be soup and bread for you upstairs,' he said. 'Have a good night's sleep, and I'll see you in the morning.'

The boys were quite sure that they would be awake all night, so excited were they by all the new sights of the day and all the new people they had met. They had so much to talk about and had found that being together meant that they felt unafraid of the unknown future. In the event they fell asleep almost as soon as their heads touched the pillows, and they slept soundly until they were woken for breakfast.

The trip to Brown's outfitters shop was the most exciting thing ever to have happened in the boys' young lives. They were kitted out with not one, but two pairs of trousers, two shirts, two pairs of socks, a tailored, worsted tunic and a pair of wooden clogs to work in. Lastly, and by far the best, they were each fitted with a pair of shiny 'Sunday' boots. Mr Turner expected the boys to look clean and respectable to attend the church services on Sundays. As the boys headed for the mill, each with a brown paper package under his arm, they felt like lords and whistled all the way back.

Their first job in the mill was to learn how to hand-comb the raw wool. It was a dirty, smelly job, and in the summertime it could be unbearably hot.

The men had small metal pots, containing charcoals from the main brazier, on which they heated the metal combs used to untangle the matted wool draped over high wooden frames. It was not easy work. The wool had to be combed repeatedly until the knots were loose and the strands were all lying the same way. It was expected that each man would produce a stipulated weight of combed wool each day, and often John and Paul would help Albert make up the required amount when the smaller boy was not feeling too good. They didn't mind; they thought of themselves as a team and each looked out for the others. The hours were long, beginning at 7 a.m. and working through on five days of the week, until 6 p.m. with only a 50-minute break for the mid-day meal. On Saturdays they had a half-day holiday, working only until 1 p.m.

By the standards of the day Mr Turner was a fair employer and the workers' wages were slightly better than those paid by other mill-owners, but as the boys had free bed and board their pay amounted to very little. William Turner was a practical and wise man and saw to it that the boys had plenty of good, wholesome food, for he realized that if they were not well fed they would be unable to work the long hours needed at the mill. They were provided with porridge oats, sheep's head broth, turnips and carrots, mutton stew, pigs' trotters and, on Sundays, roast pig's head and apple pie. Most of the food came from the farm, and there was always plenty of skimmed milk and duck eggs. There was a large vegetable garden and fruit trees, and on top of all this there was an abundance of wild rabbits in the fields and fish to be caught in the mill pond.

Despite the long working hours John and Paul grew fit and robust on this healthy diet. Albert lost his thin, gaunt appearance, but he was never as strong as the other two.

On Saturday afternoons the boys all bathed in the vats in the boiler house and, when necessary, they cut each other's hair. Seth insisted that they should look clean and tidy for the weekends, and he lined them all up for inspection before their weekly visit to the church on Sunday evenings.

It was springtime, and by early May the countryside around Haworth had awoken from its winter sleep. Hollings Mill and the farm had been built at the confluence of the Sladen Valley Beck and the River Worth, and the little pocket of land was lush with new vegetation. The trees had burst into leaf and the first pale green of the hawthorn bushes had disappeared under a cloud of snowy-white blossom. Primroses peeped shyly from hollows on the river banks, and in shady corners bluebells spread a misty carpet. Stretching up from the grass pretty pink milkmaids swayed gently in the light breeze. The lane leading down to the mill from Sladen Bridge was flanked with hedgerows bright with stitchwort, red campions, cowslips and forget-me-nots, and everywhere birds sang their hearts out as they busily built their nests and fed their young. Wrens flitted through the bushes, blackbirds grew fat on juicy worms, the wistful song of the willow warbler descended from the branches overhead, and the slightest disturbance sent a pair of goldfinches flashing up the track and out of sight. In the fresh green fields black-faced lambs gambolled, enjoying the sunny day and almost forgetting to heed their mothers' warning bleats when people passed.

It was a magical place to be in spring, and with lengthening days and warmer weather it was a happy time for all.

John, Paul and Albert, although new to the countryside, soon learnt how to tickle trout from under the rocks in the river and how to snare a rabbit. They climbed trees 'bird-nesting' and had a wonderful time swimming in the mill pond. Albert often found it hard to keep up with the other two and was usually at the foot of the trees whilst Paul and John raided nests, but he was best of the three at catching trout, as he had endless patience. The boys were inseparable, and Mary Ann called them the 'Three Merry Men'. Despite their long hours in the mill they were very happy in their surroundings.

Seth and Mary Ann were busy during the evenings tending their gardens, and the boys willingly helped them with the rough digging work. Mary Ann did the hoeing and planting of seeds, but when it came to setting potatoes it was a team effort to get the job done. Seth walked up and down the prepared trenches making holes with his peg leg, and the boys followed, Albert dropping a seed potato into each hollow and Paul following to level the earth. John was no use at all as he collapsed in a fit of giggles as soon as he saw Seth – up, down, up down, up down across the vegetable patch. It took much longer than intended to complete the task, for there was much laughter and they all had great fun. It was almost dark when Mary Ann brought nettle beer and raisin pasties for their supper.

Mary Ann and Seth were well settled in the cottage now. It had been decided shortly after Christmas that the young couple would stay on at Sladen Bridge and that Seth would have full-time employment in the mill. When Seth had broached the subject with Mr Turner, the mill owner, he had been delighted. He liked Seth, and watching him over the previous few weeks, had found him to be diligent and capable. He had seen that the young man was amiable with the other workers and had a natural ability to get the best out of people. William Turner knew that Seth would make a tactful and discerning overseer at the mill.

The spring and summer of 1830 was an idyllic time for Seth and Mary Ann. Their first year together was a learning process as for any young couple. They were full of hopes and dreams and each day, each step drew them closer, for after that first trauma of Seth's accident they knew that together they could face anything that life might send their way. They were so very much in love that nothing seemed impossible. They wanted to start a family straightaway, and Mary Ann often imagined what it would be like with their children's laughter filling the cottage. Meanwhile it was often filled by the three exuberant boys, who thought the world of Mary Ann and idolized Seth, their 'Hero Sailor', who compared with anyone they ever knew had led a very exciting life.

It was during that summer that the boys were introduced to the sport of knur and spell. Hollings Mill had a team whose reputation was known for miles around the Worth Valley. The game, popular throughout Yorkshire and Lancashire, with every mill or village having a team, attracted an enormous following. Crowds of 2000 people would attend a big contest, and there was heavy betting with men playing for high stakes of £10 or £50. In Haworth knur and spell was played in a large open field on the edge of the moor, and as the game progressed the excitement of the crowd grew. John, Paul and Albert, caught up in the atmosphere, loved every minute of it cheering on as the big, strong men from the mills and stone quarries swung the heavy spell, a specially designed stick to thwack the knur. It required balance and strength to drive the hard ceramic ball, little bigger than a large marble, some 200 yards. The lads shouted themselves hoarse when one of their own Hollings Mill men hit a particularly long shot, and were quite downhearted when, on rare occasions, their team lost.

Of course after seeing their very first match the boys were straight off into the woods to find suitable sticks for their own spells and using whatever they could find as a knur, they lobbed, swiped, pitched and lammed it. It was a little while before they could actually hit the knur, but once they had the knack they soon became quite good and hour after hour they practised, flicking their arms and swinging the spell hard, hitting the knur true, and longing for the day when they would be big and strong enough to join the Hollings Mill team.

Seth had taken a keen interest in the boys' progress at the mill. Paul and John were quick to learn. They both showed initiative and a willingness to get on with their tasks and produce good work. Seth had no worries there, but he had seen how hard the work was for Albert, who suffered from a bad chest which was aggravated by the hot, smoky atmosphere of the woolcombing room. Seth had hoped that Albert's health would improve once he was well fed and able to get out into the countryside more often, but instead it seemed, if anything, to be worse than when he had first come to Haworth. He asked Mr Turner if there was another part of the mill in which Albert could work which would be better for him.

'I'll think about it,' Mr Turner had said. 'Bring the boy to see me this afternoon.'

Albert and Seth now stood in Mr Turner's office. The boy looked very worried. Seth had said nothing on the way across the mill yard about why Mr Turner had asked to see him, but Albert knew full well that he didn't pull his weight at the woolcombing, and he was terrified that he would be sent back to the orphanage. Please God, not that! He liked it here in Yorkshire and he just wanted to be able to stay with the two best friends he'd ever had, John and Paul. He would promise to work harder. He would stay later to get the work done. He would ... a fit of coughing stopped his thoughts, and when the spasm finished Mr Turner spoke.

'You're finding it hard in the mill, eh, lad?'

'Not too bad, sir,' Albert tried to sound confident.

'Isn't it true that you don't always produce the required amount of combed wool?'

Albert's heart sank.

'Yes, sir,' he mumbled, not daring to look up.

'Speak up, lad,' said Mr Turner.

'Yes, sir.'

'Well, I think we'd better have you out of there...'

Albert interrupted him and Mr Turner saw the boy's frightened expression.

'No, sir. Please, sir. I'll try really hard. Please don't send me back. Let me stay...' he pleaded, looking first at Mr Turner, then at Seth and then at the mill-owner again.

'Hold on there, lad,' Mr Turner interrupted the outburst. 'No one said anything about sending you back. I thought you might like to work on the farm instead of in the mill. Mrs Turner could do with some extra help in the garden and help on the farm, and the fresh air will be better for you. Now what do you say?'

Albert's face was transformed, wreathed in smiles, the relief was very apparent.

81

'Oh yes, sir, Mr Turner. Thank you very much.'

Mr Turner smiled too.

'That's settled, then. You can start in the morning.'

Seth winked at Albert and watched a very happy boy race across the yard to tell his friends the news.

8

The demand for good-quality worsted cloth in London, Paris and Boston had continued to increase, and Hollings Mill was on full production. Mr Turner had installed extra power looms, bringing the total up to 100 but he had no ambition for further expansion on the scale of some of the large mills in the towns. He was still very worried about all the industrial unrest in other parts of West Yorkshire and in Lancashire, and he hoped that smaller mills like his would not be targeted. Realistically he knew that he had just been lucky and that he might be affected at any time. There were strikes and lock-outs, and factory hands were becoming increasingly restless. There was a more sinister, political protest against ruthless, powerful mill owners, many of whom were self-made men who had begun with nothing but burning ambition and had succeeded at the expense and degradation of their workers. They had prospered beyond their wildest dreams but had no consideration for the people they employed, who worked long hours for inadequate wages and who were housed in poor conditions. It was no wonder that there was unrest for leaking roofs, children piled five to a bed in a room shared by three generations of the family, no money for winter fuel, and totally insanitary conditions were to be found in every town.

As he had promised, Seth had rigged up the rope boarding net he had brought from Liverpool. It was made fast above the loading bay doors and fixed in such a way that one tug on a restraining rope would release it and send the whole lot down. He also filled six buckets with lime wash, and these too were concealed in the rafters of the wooden canopy and could be tipped over unsuspecting intruders.

Perhaps the best idea Seth had come up with was to erect a small wooden hut in the lane leading down to the mill and fill it with geese. The birds were let out during the day and, being rather aggressive, they were not popular with mill workers coming to and fro, but Seth knew that locked in the shed at night they would be an ideal early warning arrangement, for if disturbed they always made a great din, cackling noisily.

One day, shortly after the installation of the geese, a young man arrived on a pony asking to see Mr Turner 'with all haste'. Both the man and the pony were hot and sweaty, for it was a warm day and they had travelled some miles.

'I've come to warn ye,' he said as soon as he was ushered into the office, 'they're coming tonight, six of 'em. We overheard 'em at the inn. "Tonight," they said, "Hollings Mill"!'

Mr Turner jumped from his chair.

'Slow down, young man, let's be hearing what you know, all of it.'

'Sorry, sir. I'm Wilf, Ned Barnes' lad from t'Herders Inn on t'moor on the border between Lancashire and Yorkshire.'

'Aye, I know Ned,' Mr Turner nodded. 'Go on, lad.'

'Six men came in for refreshment this morning, dirty they were. Looked as if they'd been out all night. My dad overheard them talking about Hollings Mill and a raid here tonight. I came as fast as I could to warn you.'

'You did well, Wilf. Six you say, are you sure there are no more? How are they travelling?'

'They're on foot, sir, and far as I know there's just the six of 'em, never saw no more, anyways. We don't like all this trouble, and my dad thought as how you ought to be warned.'

Mr Turner shook Wilf's hand.

'Forewarned is forearmed, and we'll be ready for them, thanks to you and your father.'

A meal was arranged for Wilf Barnes, and one of the older lads was set to rubbing down the pony and giving it a bucket of oats. They would both need a rest before starting the six-mile journey back over the moorland road to the Lancashire border. Mr Turner would have liked to have shown his appreciation somehow but that would have to wait. Right now there were plans to be made.

Seth, Mr Turner and ten other men laid in wait that night.

John, Paul and Albert, seeing this as a chance to prove they really could be like Robin Hood's Merry Men, had begged to be allowed to help, but Mr Turner had said things might turn nasty and it was no place for such young boys, and they were sent off to bed.

Just after midnight the expected cackling of the geese began. In the darkness the noise of whispering voices coming down the lane approaching the mill yard was quite enough to warn the hidden men. They tensed, listening for the first sounds of intruders. Quite a while passed. The cackling had ceased and all was silent again before they heard the low muttering of men's voices as they approached. Seth, from his vantage point on top of the wooden canopy, saw shadowy figures entering the mill yard ... three, four, five, six. Just as Wilf had said. He held his breath and wound the rope he was holding once more round his hand in reassurance. They were a motley crew, each carrying a hammer or crowbar. None of the watchers moved, but they all saw when, from a signal from the front man, the raiders made straight for the big doors and began to smash them down.

One strong pull on the rope was all Seth needed to release the netting, and pulling out a wooden stay he sent the buckets of lime crashing down after it. The men below cursed and shrieked as they struggled to get out of the net, but with lime wash in their faces and on their hands and making the floor slippery, they hadn't a chance. Mr Turner and his men moved swiftly from their hiding places and encircled their uninvited guests with another rope, pulling it tight around them. They were caught like fish in a net and were suddenly quiet.

'What shall we do with them?' Seth asked as he climbed down from the canopy. 'Shall I send the boys up to Haworth for the police and the Redcoats?' Then, winking at Mr Turner he continued more loudly, 'You'll go, won't you, boys?'

John, Paul and Albert came out sheepishly from behind a jutting wall where they had been hiding so as not to miss the excitement. They thought they would be in trouble, but Mr Turner had more important things to deal with and just shook his head in disbelief.

The mill-owners had recognized one of the gang as a man who used to work for him as a weaver. Changed from the militant hammer-wielder of a short while before, this man was now pleading to be released, saying that he had a wife and nine children at home to feed.

'You should have thought of that before you came here with mischief in mind,' said Mr Turner shortly, but he was disconcerted to think of the wives and families of these men left without a breadwinner to support them. He knew full well that if the police were brought in the men would be taken to York and imprisoned in the castle and be hanged, or if spared, they would be deported to Australia.

'I'll not have these men on my conscience,' he said to Seth and to the men he said, 'You must swear on the Holy Bible that you'll take no more part in destroying mill property and that you'll never again set foot in Hollings Mill yard.'

'Are you mad?' Seth cried angrily. 'These men would have smashed up your looms, burnt the mill, anything! Now you're just going to let them go. Fetch the police, I say.'

Mr Turner was adamant.

'I think they've learnt their lesson. They'll not be back. Fetch the Bible from my office, Paul, please.'

The men, still trapped in the net, knew as well as Mr Turner what fate awaited them if they were turned over to the military or police, and they all remained silent, each praying that they would be allowed to return to their families. Somehow, smashing up machinery didn't seem quite so important now, nor such a clever thing to do.

The Bible was brought; the men, prompted by Mr Turner, each swore never to return, and then Seth, much against his will, cut the rope that bound them and set them free. The cackling of the geese signalled their departure as it had announced their coming.

9

1839

It was 9 p.m. on a cold, frosty, moonlit night as the three boys
made their way back to the mill after the church choir practice.
They had grown into fine young men. John and Paul had done
well at the mill, for Mr Turner had seen their potential. John
had been put into the office in charge of production of cloth
going from the weaving sheds to the dye works and then for-
warding the finished cloth on to the customers. Paul was training to be an overlooker in the weaving shed, and was well
respected despite being so young. Albert was quite happy still
on the farm, as he enjoyed working with the animals and in the
large kitchen garden. He had benefited from all the fresh air,
and his health was very much improved.

They were talking about cricket, for although the season had
ended some weeks earlier it was still their favourite topic of
conversation. They had developed good use with bat and ball,
and their cricketing skill was recognized by the Haworth Church
Cricket Club. The boys' main typical conversation was about
tactics and the other village teams they had played against.

'I still say Hebden Bridge's umpire was biased,' said John.
'He called "wide" when the ball was clearly on line and "not
out" when anyone could see the chap was well outside his
crease.'

'And he didn't like the speed of Paul's bowling,' Albert put
in. 'I think he's against round-arm bowling altogether.'

Paul struggled, 'A lot of people think it's dangerous – remember Alfred Mynn who played for Lancashire; laid up in bed,
bruised so bad the docs thought they might have to take his leg
off! I think they'll have to try leg-pads again – that's the
answer.'

They continued along the pack-horse road on the edge of the moor near to Oldfield Gate Farm, and it was Paul, slightly ahead, who spotted what he took to be a bundle of rags in the gutter at the roadside. As they neared they could see that it was actually a man. He appeared to be unconscious, and rolling him over to take a closer look, they saw that it was Branwell Brontë. They knew Branwell quite well for he had been one of the organizers of the Haworth Boxing Club. The boys had taken boxing lessons from John Brown in the stables behind the Black Bull Hotel.

Branwell was in a dreadful condition, his clothing was wet and his face and his red hair were plastered with mud. It was common knowledge that the vicar's son drank gin, and he had been seen to take laudanum in the Black Bull. The boys had thought that he was in Bradford, where he had set up a studio for portrait painting.

'I didn't know he was back,' said Paul. 'Poor Branwell, he's in a right state.'

'Serves him right.' John hadn't much tolerance for anyone who drank to excess.

'That might be,' Albert reasoned, 'but we can't leave him here or he'll freeze to death. Do you think we could carry him?'

Paul was unsure. 'I doubt it. He'll be a dead weight, and it's a long way back to the parsonage.'

John hit on the idea of borrowing a wheelbarrow from the farm and raced off to get one.

The farmer didn't mind lending his barrow, but he laughed when he heard what they wanted to carry.

'I've been mucking out t'byre,' he hooted, 't'barrow's full o' cow shit!'

John took the emptied wheelbarrow, and Albert and Paul helped him lift the still unconscious Branwell into it. They took turns to push their load back along West Lane and up the cobbled street past the graveyard to the parsonage.

Tabitha Ackroyd, 'Tabby', who had been cook to the Brontës for many years, answered the insistent ringing of the door bell.

'Oh my! What have we here?' she said, dismayed at the sight that met her eyes. 'What are we going to do with him? Mr Brontë's not in, and I can't lift him. You young chaps must help me get him up the stairs to bed.'

It wasn't too hard for the three of them to carry Branwell to his room. With John at his head and Paul and Albert taking a leg apiece, they made light work of it and soon had him on his bed. They removed his shoes and then his jacket and trousers, which were covered in cow dung and smelled none too good. Throughout, Branwell was completely unaware of what was going on. They washed his face and hands and covered him with a blanket over his prostrate form before leaving him to sleep off his stupor.

Tabby was waiting for them at the foot of the stairs, and thanking them profusely she ushered them into the kitchen for a cup of tea and a slice of her home-made fruit cake.

10

Mary Ann had been very content in the cottage at Sladen Bridge. Her only sadness was that she had never had the children which she and Seth had longed for. She had accepted now, that after ten years together, this probably would never happen, and with all other aspects of her life she was truly happy. She still took pride in the cottage and in looking after Seth. She enjoyed tending her flower and vegetable gardens, and she specialized in growing herbs for medicinal purposes. Gone was the bubbly young girl who had come from Boston full of eager excitement, and in her place was a deep-thinking woman who was very aware of the beauty of nature and the power of God's presence in everything around her.

Over the years she had befriended the young Emily Brontë, the quietest of the vicar's children who had few friends and generally preferred her own company but who enjoyed walking with Mary Ann and taking tea with the Heaton family at Ponden Hall. Although ten years apart in age Emily and Mary Ann had much in common, being of a more spiritual nature, and both appreciating the serenity and solitude of the moors. They would walk together for hours, often not talking yet each instinctively knowing that the other was at one with nature just as she herself was. They shared a love of poetry, and Mary Ann lent Emily a book of poems she had compiled as a young girl on her grandparents' farm in Vermont. Their favourite from the book was one given to Mary Ann by an old Iroquois Indian called White Eagle, who lived in a wooden hut at the edge of her grandparents' land. They often read it together.

With beauty before me may I walk,
With beauty behind me may I walk,
With beauty above me may I walk,
With beauty below me may I walk,
With beauty all around me may I walk.
Wandering on a trail of beauty lively I walk.
A joy shared is a joy doubled.

White Eagle had taught Mary Ann all she knew of nature and
had instilled in her an awareness of the tremendous splendour
of the earth. From him she had learned how to treat sick and
injured animals and birds, and had grown to know that we
should all live in harmony together, understanding the value of
all living things which together display the wonder of God's
world.

Emily Brontë eschewed the Church of England, the religion
in which she had been brought up, and turned rather to God
the Creator, whose truth and beauty were manifest everywhere
around her.

On one of their walks, taking them this time past Lower and
Higher Heights and across the wide sweep of moorland to Top
Withens, they were deep in conversation about the possibility
of reincarnation.

Keeper, Emily's dog, ran beside them sniffing at rabbit holes
and chasing any birds which stayed too long hidden in the
heather stumps. They were on their way back down towards the
waterfall when Keeper suddenly darted off across the moor
chasing a rabbit. The little animal soon outran him and disappeared into a burrow. Keeper, still in pursuit, jumped onto a
loose stone, dislodging it and sending himself spinning into a
little niche below. He yelped loudly two or three times, and
when Emily and Mary Ann reached him they found a very
frightened dog who was obviously in great pain and unable to
get up. He was panting fast and he stared at them with eyes
wide as if to say 'Help me'.

Mary Ann thought of White Eagle and all that he had taught
her. Kneeling in the heather, she held her hands over the trembling dog, and closing her eyes she quietly asked God to send
his healing power. She remained perfectly still for almost ten
minutes, and her quietness seemed to transmit to the wounded

91

animal, for gradually his breathing slowed to a gentle rhythmic rising of the chest and his eyes slowly closed. Mary Ann then moved her hands over Keeper, gently stroking his head, his back, his legs. Over and over she stroked, all the while aware that healing energies were being gathered from the divine source and were flowing through her to the injury. She pictured white light surrounding Keeper and making him whole.

Emily stood beside them watching. She loved Keeper and prayed fervently that he wasn't too badly hurt, for she could not bear to be without him. She trusted Mary Ann and knew that her friend would do all that she could for Keeper.

After 20 minutes or so, Keeper suddenly sat up. He looked up at Emily and cocked his head on one side quizzically. It looked for all the world as if he was saying, 'What are you standing around here for, let's get going!' and with no more ado he set off on the path home.

Emily and Mary Ann laughed with relief and, quite out of character, Emily embraced her friend because no words could thank her enough.

John and Paul were practising cricket in the mill yard. The mill now shut down between 12.30 and 1.30 for the mid-day meal, and summer and winter, weather permitting, these two could be found with bat and ball cultivating the skills which had already earned them a place on the Church Cricket first team and reputations as formidable opponents. They were alone in the yard since no one wished to get in the way of a ball hit by one of these two, and in any case the day was cold and most people preferred to spend the whole lunch resting in the works' canteen.

Paul was bowling to John, who was using the boiler house door as a wicket, and the batsman had just deflected a low bouncer when they heard a series of bangs and what sounded like small explosions coming from inside the boiler house. Running to investigate they soon saw that something was seriously wrong. The boiler house was full of steam which was escaping from the front of the boiler with a menacing hiss. The walls were running with condensation and the door of the boiler appeared to be bulging under pressure. It was obvious that the boiler was about to explode, and John and Paul knew that the millworkers were in terrible danger.

'Get out of here!'

As John shouted he saw the corpulent figure of the stoker man propped against the wall. He was dead drunk, and had an empty bottle beside him. Taking the man roughly by the feet, John dragged him out into the yard before leaving him to run for all he was worth, shouting as he went, to warn the mill workers.

'Get out, everyone! The boiler's going up! Get out! Get out!'

Paul had realized that the boiler was short of water and was running dry. He didn't think of the consequences, but knew that he had to open the water valve, and that he had very little time to do it. He sprang across the room and grabbed the stop-cock, but he shrieked and let go immediately, for the metal was too hot to hold. Looking round he grabbed an old cloth, and with this over the valve he tried to turn it. The valve would not move; harder and harder he pushed until his arms ached. Paul was sweating profusely, conscious that at any minute the whole building could be blown apart but also aware that he was the only person with any chance of averting a terrible tragedy. He tried again, mustering all his strength and was just about to give up when he felt the screw move. He threw his weight onto it and the valve opened sending water hissing through the pipes. Immediately Paul was enveloped in a seething hot steam. It scalded his arms, his face and his chest. Stumbling towards the door, Paul had to hang on to his senses to find his way out of there and into the welcoming cool of the October day. He collapsed just as Seth came into the yard.

A loud cheer went up when everyone realized that the mill was safe but the hero didn't hear it as, mercifully, he was out to the world, flat on the cobblestones beside the drunken sloth who had caused this mishap.

The waggonette was quickly brought, and lifting Paul onto it Seth took him with all speed to his cottage. Mary Ann took charge of the situation and knew just what to do. She bathed Paul's wounds with clear cold water to help take out the sting and to reduce the swelling, before covering the burns with clean linen. She asked Seth and John to carry the patient upstairs to the spare bedroom and put him to bed.

Fully aware that in cases such as this the worst thing could be the after-shock, Mary Ann never left Paul's bedside for the next 48 hours. When tiredness overcame her she dozed in a chair under the window. He slept fretfully at first, and when he awoke he was in a lot of pain. Seth made a wooden cage to keep the weight of the bedclothes off his body, and Mary Ann mixed some herbs to give him some ease. She cleaned and redressed the wounds daily, hating to inflict more pain but knowing that without this attention the risk of infection was too high. She also used the healing technique taught to her by White Eagle, laying her hands gently over the scalded areas just as she had done with Keeper. She felt the warm glow of radiant energy transmitted through her fingers, and the feeling of peace and tranquillity which it brought to Paul was very beneficial to the healing process.

Very gradually the pain diminished and Paul began to eat a little, but he was very weak and had continuing dreams of explosions and boiling water and wheels that would not turn. The doctor had visited and had said that on no account was Paul to get up from the bed. In truth he had no strength and no desire to be anywhere else.

Suddenly, after ten or twelve days the dreams stopped and Paul was able to talk about the accident without panicking and breaking into a cold sweat. The worst was over, and with another week of tender nursing and Mary Ann's good food he was up from his sickbed.

As soon as he was allowed visitors a whole string of people wanted to pay their respects, and Mary Ann had to limit the callers. John and Albert had been allowed short visits throughout, as Mary Ann thought they would cheer Paul, but the first real visitor was Mr Turner.

'I am ever indebted to you, young man. You saved the mill but more, much more importantly, many lives were saved through your courage. You were very brave. Thank you.'

The Brontë family had been concerned for Paul and had sent every few days for news of his progress. Now the Reverend Patrick, Charlotte and Branwell walked down to Sladen Bridge to see for themselves how the young man was faring. Branwell brought Paul one of his oil paintings, of a famous champion London boxer, in appreciation for 'help earlier in the year when you brought me home'. Branwell looked a little shame-faced, so Paul made no more reference to the episode with the wheelbarrow. Charlotte had brought a book of her poems for Mary Ann, and in return a jar of maple syrup was produced for the family. Mr Brontë had acquired a taste for this New England delicacy. He particularly liked it on the porridge he had for breakfast every morning. He had taken to walking down to Sladen Bridge to visit Seth and Mary Ann whenever his supply ran low in the hope that he would be offered replenishment, for he knew that Captain Blanchard never failed to bring a cask of syrup when he visited from Vermont.

Paul stayed with Seth and Mary Ann for another month, and although he went for short walks, under no circumstances was he allowed anywhere near the mill.

'We want you fit and well first,' Seth had said. 'You've had a nasty shock, and you're not coming back until the doctor has given his consent.'

Six months had passed since the accident at the mill, and life had long since returned to its normal routine. Paul was fit and strong again, and the burns had left no physical scars to mar his good looks, thanks to Mary Ann's careful ministrations. Seth had promised Mary Ann that as soon as the weather turned fair they would all have a day out and go by horse and trap to Wycoller Dean. The hall there had stood empty these past 20 years and was beginning to fall into disrepair but the village, nestling deep in the valley below the moor road was a lovely place for a picnic. The sparkling stream, tumbling from a wooded dell, widened near the cluster of houses so that carts could ford it, but it was also crossed by two picturesque bridges: a narrow pack horse bridge with well-worn stones and mossy sides, and a clapper bridge reputedly dating from Roman times. It was a magical place to spend an afternoon. A hidden village, untouched by the revolution of the grimy industrial towns, with its quiet beauty inviting all who came to linger by the bright water and enjoy its peace.

Paul, John and Albert were enthusiastic about the outing and arrived just as Mary Ann finished packing the hamper. They loaded this onto the back of Mr Turner's trap together with rugs and a flagon of ale and set off in high spirits.

The day was warm and still with no clouds in the sky, and birds were singing heartily as though to cheer the little party on its way. Seth was content for John and Paul to take turns driving the horse, and Mary Ann reflected on the three young men who were sharing this day and who had become almost like family to her. She was especially close to Paul now since his enforced stay at the cottage last winter. They had walked for hours and he had told her of his life before he came to Sladen Bridge; the orphanage in Liverpool and vague memories of a time before that – of a woman who had smelled of gin and who sang lullabies to him. Mary Ann had always liked John, as everyone did. He was a natural leader, gregarious and charming, and had a way of making people listen to him and of making them laugh. Albert would always be much smaller than the other two and his legs were permanently bowed from the rickets he had suffered as a child, but he was a happy chap with a ready smile and he was always game for a prank. Sometimes the joke would turn on him, but he would only shrug his shoulders and laugh with the rest.

As Mary Ann mused they were making good progress. Stanbury was behind them. They had passed Ponden and the Wesleyan Chapel at Scar Top and were climbing the hill from the Oldfield Road junction to Two Laws, just past the halfway point, when they came upon a man, his wife and their three small children. They were ragged and barefooted and, unsmiling, they moved to let the trap pass. The oldest child, a girl of about five years of age, was wearing a thin, tattered shift which could not disguise her emaciated frame. Her hair was thin and straggly, and there were bald patches on her head where clumps of hair had fallen out. Holding tight to the mother's skirt was a little boy of three. He was crying with pain, for his feet were swollen and red raw. Wrapped in a shawl in the mother's arms was an unweaned baby, just a few months old. Its feeble cry brought an expression of hopelessness to the mother's face.

At Seth's request John reined in the horse and Seth greeted the unfortunate family.

'Good-day to you. Where are you heading?'

The man spoke quietly, almost as if he no longer believed in what he was saying.

'We're going to Bradford. I hear they're wanting weavers in the big new mills there and I'm needing work. We've walked thirty-five miles from Rochdale. There's trouble o'er there; riots and demonstrations and the like. We didn't want to be part of that.'

'Surely the police will sort it out,' said Seth.

'The military are standing by at the barracks in Rochdale, but t'mood's angry and t'workers are on the point of rebellion. There'll be trouble there, mark my words.'

Mary Ann spoke for the first time.

'Have you eaten?' she asked.

The man shook his head. 'Not today. It's taken us longer than we thought to get this far, and the food we brought is long gone.'

'Then you must share ours,' Mary Ann declared, and without further ado she climbed down from the trap, and taking the rugs from the back she quickly organized everyone.

'Come with me, Mr – er – I'm sorry I don't know your name.'

'Hollindrake, ma'am. Arthur Hollindrake, and this 'ere's my missus, Glenda.'

'And I'm Mrs Snowden and this is my husband, Seth. Now if you will all please follow me. Albert and Paul bring the picnic hamper and the drink, please, and John, if you would get the trap off the road and see to the horse.'

Very soon they were settled in a nearby field. Seth, Mary Ann and the boys ate only a very little, leaving most of the food for the hungry Hollindrake family. It quite distressed Mary Ann to see just how ravenous they actually were. Meat, sandwiches, cakes and scones disappeared at a great rate until, at last, all were satisfied. Sensing that the Hollindrakes could do with a long rest, Seth made no immediate move and engaged them in conversation, telling them a little of Hollings Mill. Arthur Hollindrake looked up eagerly and asked Seth if he had any work for him.

'I'm a weaver by trade. I was a pattern weaver in a cotton shed, but I'd be willing to do anything, anything at all. I'm quite handy and I'm not afraid of hard work. I'm desperate, Mr Snowden, I've my family to feed.'

Seth could see that he really was desperate, and he felt sorry for them all being in such adversity. Besides, he had taken quite a liking to the chap, who seemed a decent sort despite his ragged appearance.

'We'll have to see,' he said. 'I might have something.'

The trip to Wycoller was abandoned and the horse's head was turned to home. John, Paul and Albert were quite happy to walk, leaving room in the trap for Mr and Mrs Hollindrake and the children. It was quite an adventure for the little girl and boy, who had recovered their spirits remarkably quickly once there was food in their tummies. Of course the tiny boy didn't remember much of the journey, for he was soon sound asleep with his head resting on his mother's arm.

They soon covered the miles back to Stanbury and were dropping down the hill towards Sladen Bridge when Seth turned the horse down a track on the left, leading to Milking Hill Farm. George Greenwood, the farmer, was in the farm yard and called out as they approached.

'G'day, Seth. What brings you here?'

Seth left the trap so that he could speak with George out of earshot of the others. He told him about the family they had met and of their dreadful plight.

'I was wondering if you have a barn that they could sleep in for a week or two until I manage to find them somewhere to live?'

Seth wasn't sure what reaction to expect from George, for some farmers could be notoriously narrow-minded and stuck with their own ideas, but he needn't have worried.

'The barn o'er yonder 'd do. There's a well wi' fresh water nearby,' George replied. 'T'winter hay's all but finished, and I'll not be needing it till we bring t'next lot in summer. Aye, they'd be right enough there for time bein'.'

'Good, that's settled then. Thank you, George. You'll not be out of pocket, and if you could let the family have milk, eggs and butter I'll pay you later.'

Mr and Mrs Hollindrake could not believe their luck. After days on the road it was wonderful to have a roof over their heads and to know that they would be warm and dry at night. Mary Ann was quite embarrassed when Mrs Hollindrake fell to her knees, kissing Mary Ann's hand and crying as she tried to thank her.

'There's no need. Please, get up,' said Mary Ann. 'We just hope that everything will turn out well for you now.'

Seth turned to go saying, 'Someone will be back with blankets and more food. Come to the mill at six-thirty in the morning, Arthur, and I'll find some work for you. Good-day.'

When Arthur reported for work he was put into the weaving shed and given four looms to mind. Mr Turner and Seth kept a close eye on him, as they did with all new employees, and were surprised to see that he soon produced exceptionally good-quality cloth with few faults. When a loom broke down Arthur was able to mend the machine with a minimum loss of working time. After only two weeks Seth had seen enough to know that it would be well worth giving Arthur a permanent job, and a cottage was found in Stanbury for him and his family to live in for a very reasonable rent.

Arthur continued to work well, and Mr Turner and Seth were impressed by his output and by his knowledge of weaving. He suggested ways of making the worsted cloth more attractive by introducing cotton threads into the pin stripes and of making lighter weight material for ladies' dresses, suitable for the American market. The first of these ideas was taken up and proved successful, but Mr Turner wasn't sure at first about the lighter fabric and held back from experimenting with it. However, Arthur hadn't been at the mill long when Mr Turner made a snap decision. He sent for the weaver and told him that he could have a free hand with the pattern loom and see what he could come up with. Within three weeks Arthur had produced a sample swatch of fine dress material which caused great excitement when shown to Seth and Mr Turner, and which proved exceptionally popular with the customers, who placed large orders for this cloth.

Mr Turner knew a good man when he found one, and wanting to keep up Hollings Mill's reputation for the finest cloths, it wasn't long before he promoted Arthur Hollindrake to weaving shed manager in charge of all production, giving him a big enough raise in his wages to ensure that his wife and family had a good standard of living and a quality of life they'd hardly dared to dream of only a few short months before.

* * *

One Friday, soon after the aborted trip to Wycoller, Seth and Mary Ann were following their normal weekend routine. The fire was blazing and the tin bath in front of the hearth had been filled with water. Mary Ann bathed first, savouring those first moments as she slid into the hot depth, her pale skin turning pink and rosy. As she took the soap and lathered her still firm body, Seth thought as always how beautiful she looked, her wet skin shining in the glow from the fire.

'I love you, Mary Ann,' he said gently. He had noticed a quietness about her of late and wondered what was troubling her. She had said nothing, but he knew her too well and could sense her unease. There had been a time, a couple of years back, when her longing for a child had been almost unbearable. She had been quiet then, but Seth thought she was over that and had accepted that they would probably never have a baby. He could think of no other reason for her melancholy mood.

Mary Ann took the towel he handed her.

'I know you love me, Seth, and I love you too.'

It was Seth's turn in the tub now and, as always when she had finished drying, Mary Ann took the loofah and scrubbed his back.

Curled up soon after in the large feather bed they called 'The Love Nest', Seth ran his fingers through her hair and over her naked body preliminary to their love-making. Mary Ann's response was warm yet somehow distant, as if her body only was there in bed and her thoughts were elsewhere. Much later, whilst still folded in his embrace, when normally they would have discussed their plans for the weekend, Seth asked Mary Ann what was worrying her.

'Let me share it, Mary Ann, we're a team and there's nothing I would not do for you,' he said.

'Oh, Seth, I've been so happy here with you,' sighed Mary Ann. 'I don't want you to think I haven't been happy, but always at the back of my mind is the disgrace of not being properly married.'

Seth sat up. 'Disgrace? What's been said? Who has been upsetting you?'

'No one has said anything Seth. It's me. *I* know that I'm not legally your wife, and I have always wished I was. In the eyes of God we are living in sin. It came home to me again recently when we met Arthur Hollindrake, the day we set out for Wycoller. I introduced you as my husband, and even after all these years felt myself blushing. I know it's silly, but there it is. You have it now. I want to be married.'

Seth had never really thought about marriage since the day long ago when he had slipped Mrs Turner's ring onto Mary Ann's finger. To him she *was* his wife. He had no idea that Mary Ann felt this way, but he was relieved that this was all that was wrong and before they fell asleep he had promised that he would speak with Patrick Brontë as soon as possible.

That Sunday an ideal opportunity presented itself to Seth and Mary Ann when no other members of the congregation lingered after the evening service. They told the Vicar everything. About Seth's accident, how they came to be at Sladen Bridge, and about the ring and the deceit. If Mr Brontë was surprised at their disclosures he didn't show it, and there was no form of censure in his voice as he replied.

'I was vicar of the Thornton Parish Church, near Bradford, before I came to Haworth,' he said, 'and I'm on good terms with my successor.' Perhaps you could be married in that church instead of here in Haworth. It is not usual for people to wed outside their own parish, but the circumstances are rare. I'll see what I can arrange.'

'Thank you,' said Seth, quite relieved. 'We'd prefer to keep this a very quiet wedding to forestall any village gossip.'

Within the week Mr Brontë had visited the couple at Sladen Bridge to tell them that the wedding was arranged for the week after Whitsuntide and, if it was their wish, he would be only too pleased to officiate.

So it came about that after ten years together Seth and Mary Ann were finally married and became, in the eyes of the law and of God, man and wife. Mary Ann would have liked her parents to be with her on this day, but it was impossible to arrange for them to visit England at such short notice. Instead, she wrote and told them the news, giving the date and time of the service, so that in their heads they could share the moments.

Mr and Mrs Turner stood as witnesses for the happy couple, and when the marriage vows had been taken the party of five

101

had a celebratory meal of roast beef and Yorkshire pudding at the Flappit Hotel, halfway between Thornton and Haworth. The Reverend Patrick Brontë proposed a toast of continued happiness for Seth and Mary Ann and all of them this day, shared with good firm friends who were truly special. For Mary Ann there was the added bonus that their secret was now safe.

11

'Roll up! Roll up!'
  'Best pies only twopence!'
  'Have your fortune told, sir – just cross my palm with silver!'
  'Bright ribbons, fine lace!'
  'Two goes for a penny on the coconut shy, laddie!'
It was the first week in August and Haworth Feast Week –
the greatest event of the year for the village folk, who saved
what little money they could to buy from the travelling sales-
men who came with pack-horses laden with all manner of good
things. There were travelling showmen, too, and musicians, jug-
glers, fortune-tellers and performing bears. There was always an
air of excitement around the boxing tent, and it was here on
the first morning that Seth found himself listening to the promoter as the boxers were exhibited on a rostrum outside the
tent. The boxers' manager was a rough-looking customer with a
heavy frame, more fat than muscle, and an ugly scar across his
left cheek, but his patter was glib and well-rehearsed.
  'Now who can box? Who'd care to have a go against one of
my boxers here? Come on chaps, don't be shy. Show the ladies
what you're worth! Three guineas for anyone who can knock
my man down. Come on. Who's to be first? ... Haworth men
all cowards, eh? Three guineas says no one can do it!'
  Rather hesitantly a young chap stepped forward, egged on by
his mates. Another followed and a third. The tent was opened
and the spectators started filing in to see the show. Seth joined
the queue. He was wearing his naval uniform, and being tall
too, he stood out amongst the crowd. The promoter's eye fell
on Seth and he beckoned to him as he neared the pay desk.
  'How much for the uniform?'

'I'm afraid it's not for sale,' Seth replied. He was particularly proud of his jacket and would not have let it go for all the tea in China. The promoter tried again.

'Oh, come on. I can pay, just name your price. Everyone has a price.'

Seth didn't like the tone of the man's voice and repeated, 'It's not for sale.'

There was a nasty glint in the man's eyes, and Seth could feel those eyes boring into him as he made his way into the boxing arena.

The three bouts of boxing were over rather quickly, with only the second of the three lads putting up any sort of a fight. It was obvious that none of them knew anything about the sport, and the professionals played with them like cats with mice before delivering an uppercut or hook to send them reeling to the floor and ending the contest. The fun over for the time being, the crowd began to make an exit.

At first Seth thought that folks were just being over-boisterous as he was jostled and bumped about, but he sensed trouble when he realized he was hemmed in by three burly men who were edging him towards the rear flaps of the tent. He tried to resist and struggled to get past them and join the main throng, but it was to no avail and almost before he knew it he was outside, behind the tent and out of view of all the hundreds of people who were milling around the fairground. Seth was pushed to the floor and kicked hard. He hadn't a chance against the three thugs, but he continued to resist as they stripped him of his jacket and took his hat. This only enraged the men, who kicked him even harder, and then the biggest of the three sat on Seth's chest, completely winding him and pinning him to the ground, whilst one of his accomplices fetched a saw and callously sawed through Seth's peg leg. They laughed then, setting into him again, and they left him lying behind the tent only semi-conscious, with blood pouring from his nose and beginning to trickle from a nasty gash above his right eye. By the time someone found him huge bruises were beginning to appear all over his body.

Back at Sladen Bridge Mary Ann bathed his wounds but she was so angry and upset that she could hardly speak and when John and Paul heard what had happened they were furious and

104

decided there and then that they would take revenge. Seth was worried when he heard what they intended.

'Let it be,' he said. 'They're bad beggars, bad through and through, and we don't want anyone else hurt.'

John and Paul were quite determined not to let it rest. They recruited Albert and Arthur Hollindrake and a couple more volunteers from the mill and asked Mr Turner if they could borrow his horse and flat wagon for the following day. The six of them set off down the main street to the showground at Coldshaw Fields and left the horse and wagon to the rear of the boxing booth. They joined the crowd which had already gathered, and watched the same spectacle that Seth had witnessed the previous day. Boxers paraded before them on the rostrum and the promoter rattled out his inducements to all the young men of Haworth.

'Three guineas says no one can do it!'

The only difference from the day before was that now the boxing promoter was sporting a smart naval uniform jacket and hat. John stepped forward.

'Make it five guineas and you're on.'

'It's three guineas,' the man snarled.

'Five guineas says I can knock him out in five rounds,' John persisted.

The crowd cheered John's offer, and the promoter accepted the challenge.

'Five guineas it is,' he sneered, confident that this smart young man would hit the deck in the first couple of rounds. He wasn't a boxer. He was like the lads yesterday, and the boxers would make mincemeat of him.

'Same for me,' shouted Paul, 'five guineas for five rounds.'

The promoter laughed, rubbing his hands. Another sucker, he thought, nodding to accept the bet.

The tent was filled to capacity, and the air of anticipation could almost be cut with a knife. When John entered the ring, stripped to the waist, an enormous cheer went up. Acting as John's second, Paul took his place at the edge of the ring and looked across to the opposite corner where John's opponent sat. His heart sank; the boxer was a thick-set, heavily built man with muscles that stood out in glistening bands. Much older than John and far heavier, he was grinning in a contemptuous

105

way at the young man who had dared to challenge him.

When the bell rang for the first round John was up from his stool in a flash and running smartly across the ring he delivered a blow to his opponent's head before the chap had even decided what he was going to do. Taken completely by surprise, he looked quite stunned to find that John had drawn blood. The crowd roared with delight, but the man's surprise turned to anger then and he came across the ring toward John and threw a punch aimed at the side of his head. John ducked under his arm and round to the man's left, getting in another jab before the boxer could defend himself. The crowd was really excited and cheered John on. He was quick on his feet and went in again and again, delivering heavy blows to the body whilst his opponent appeared to be in a daze and could not keep up with the speed of John's movements. By the second round the boxer was flat on his back on the canvas. The crowd went wild, shouting, whistling and cheering for all they were worth.

John went to the manager and insisted that he should be paid his five guineas immediately, and when he received his money he held it high in the air for everyone to see. The crowd cheered again and stamped their feet.

Paul whipped off his shirt and ducked under the ropes into the ring to take up his challenge with the second boxer. At the bell he tried the same trick as John, but this man had been watching the first fight and was ready for him, catching Paul a glancing blow on his cheek. The fight became a hard slogging match with the boxer on a par with Paul, blow by blow. They were evenly paired and each gave as good as he took. In the second's corner John was anxious by the fourth round, and he had no more tips for Paul. They had tried all the tactics that they had learnt at John Brown's boxing club, and he was clean out of ideas. Paul was beyond thought by the start of the fifth round, but he was still determined not to be beaten and went in with renewed vigour. In contrast his opponent's stamina began to wane and just before the final bell, in the nick of time, Paul delivered a right to his jaw which sent the other man crashing to the floor, to the cheers of the spectators.

Carried shoulder-high round the perimeter of the ring Paul went to collect his winnings but the promoter turned on him in an ugly mood and refused to pay up. Paul leapt down and let fly with his fist, hitting the manager full on the jaw, and he also dropped like a stone.

John's first thought was to retrieve the naval uniform for Seth, but as soon as this was done he called to Arthur Hollindrake and the other mill men and together they took hold of the two boxers and their promoter. The men would have resisted arrest, but there were plenty of willing helpers in the crowd, men who had seen an injustice done and were glad to be of assistance. The three men were thrown into the wagon like sacks of corn, and the lads sat on them.

Albert took his pocket-knife, and going round the boxing booth he cut the guy ropes, one by one, until the whole tent collapsed. No one stopped him as he took a match and set fire to the canvas.

An excited crowd of people followed the wagon as it conveyed its protesting load up the steep Main Street. John brought the horse to a halt by the church steps, and the three miscreants were stripped of their trousers before being fastened in the stocks. Everyone else was in high glee and laughed to see the near-naked men sitting on the cold flag stones. The two village constables, quite aware of what was happening, turned a blind eye and went off to investigate a 'disturbance somewhere over the moor!'

A kind of euphoria seized the onlookers and many of them, including John, Paul, Albert and Arthur, ended up in the Black Bull drinking much more of the home-brewed ale than usual and enjoying the sort of fun which this kind of heady excitement brings, when spirits run high.

It was six hours before the men were set free from the stocks, and they were jeered and pelted with rotten vegetables as they made their escape running down Main Street, still only half-dressed. (They were gone from the showfield by nightfall and were never again seen in Haworth.)

Seth heard the revellers long before they arrived at Sladen Bridge. They were all very merry from the ale they had consumed and were singing at the tops of their voices. He smiled to himself. Lads will always be lads, he thought. Any excuse for jollification. Little did he realize the excuse included his beloved officer's uniform, and he could not believe his eyes when John laid it on the table.

12

Ruth Turner was silent. Sitting bolt upright beside the bed, her hands clasped tightly in her lap, she never moved as the doctor spoke. She kept her head down in the hope of hiding the tears which had begun coursing down her ashen cheeks.

'I'm afraid she won't last the night, miss. There's nothing more that I can do for her now.'

When Ruth didn't reply, Dr Bolton walked across the room and placed his hand gently on her shoulder.

'I'll be back in the morning,' the doctor sighed. He wished, as always, that there was something more he could say. As he left he closed the door quietly behind him.

Ruth stayed beside her mother for four more hours, gently bathing the sweat from her clammy brow and offering sips of water when her mother momentarily regained consciousness, moaned weakly and turned unseeing eyes towards her daughter. At some point during that long evening, probably shortly after the doctor departed, Mr Turner returned to his wife's bedside. Neither he nor Ruth spoke. There was nothing to say. At the end it was Ruth who held her mother's cold hand, telling her how much she loved her but unsure whether she was heard or not.

Lying on her own bed later, Ruth felt numb with shock. Three days ago her mother had been well! Five days ago there had been no hint of what was to come. Dear Lord, please let it not be true. Let this be a dream. If only she could turn the clock back, just five days. Back to when everything was normal and as it should be! There had been deaths, Ruth realized. In Haworth, not here. Not people she knew. Someone down Mill Hey and another on Belle Isle, and a little girl who lived in

Changegate. But they were strangers. Just names. People who had passed on suddenly to the other side.

Five days ago Albert had been taken ill. Dear, kind, funny little Albert who never had a bad word for anyone. Ruth had heard what happened from Mary Ann. The sickness had begun with violent vomiting and diarrhoea and a weakness which drove Albert to his bed. John and Paul, anxious about their friend, had reported his condition to Seth, who in turn had sent for the doctor. Dr Bolton, by all accounts, was run off his feet, for many people in the area were ill. As soon as she had heard of Albert's sickness Mrs Turner had hurried to the mill, taking extra bedding and hot-water bottles. By the time she arrived at Albert's side the skin on his face had shrivelled, his eyes were sunken and his body temperature was dangerously low. There was little she could do for him except wash his face, keep him warm and as comfortable as possible. When the doctor finally arrived, his diagnosis came as no surprise to anyone. Albert had cholera. It meant isolation, for the disease was spreading rapidly and must be contained at all cost. The lads who slept in the same room were immediately moved to other quarters, John and Paul moving into the cottage next door to Seth and Mary Ann, which by chance had become vacant only a few days earlier. Albert lived for only eight hours more. Never a strong lad, he'd succumbed to the disease more rapidly than some and died in an agony of cramp spasms, whilst Mrs Turner looked on helplessly. Everyone was in shock. Albert was popular, and his death touched them all.

Not two days had passed before Mrs Turner also took ill. The sickness and diarrhoea were not at first as bad as with Albert, and it was thought that, being of a strong constitution, she might pull through. It was not to be. Little by little her condition worsened. Unable to keep down any liquid, she became dehydrated, and within three days the epidemic had claimed another victim.

Haworth Church was full that Saturday afternoon in early September. People had travelled far and wide to pay their last respects to Mrs Turner. Mill-owners, farmers, shopkeepers, nobility and weavers all came, united in their sorrow. Churchgoers and chapelgoers alike all held Mrs Turner in high esteem, for she had been a good-living Christian and was well-liked. She would be greatly missed, not only by Mr Turner and Ruth but by everyone in the village and at Hollins Mill.

The funeral cortège moved slowly up the church steps, Mrs Turner's coffin first, carried by four men from the mill. All wearing black, the pallbearers were solemn and dignified in their duty. Albert's coffin followed, with John and Paul in front and two other friends behind, who held it shoulder-high. Through the graveyard and on into the church. They proceeded slowly up the aisle between the silent mourners to the chancel.

'I am the resurrection and the life...' Though spoken quietly, Patrick Brontë's words filled the huge church as the two identical oak coffins were placed side by side before the altar.

'...he who believes in me shall have everlasting life...'

Mr Turner and Ruth, who had walked behind the coffins, now took their places in the front pew and bowed their heads.

'...let not your hearts be troubled...'

Ruth did not hear most of the words, only the tone of the vicar's voice floating over the coffins and down the church, wrapping itself around each member of the congregation like a velvet mantle, comforting each to their needs.

'...I go to prepare a place for you ... if it were not so I would have told you...'

She still found it hard to believe her mother was gone. Even here at her funeral, she half-expected her to turn up with a comforting word for those who mourned. It all still seemed like a bad dream, one from which she would awaken to the bright, sun-filled skies of August. Her father, sitting beside her, seemed to have shrunk over these last few days. He had eaten almost nothing, spoken only when necessary and had, Ruth suspected, slept hardly at all. Mr Turner had taken his wife's death very badly, as if a light had gone out inside him, and she wondered if it would ever shine again.

With a start Ruth realized that Mr Brontë was talking about her mother now, praising her warmth, love and charity.

'...she was a woman of truly Christian spirit who will be sorely missed by all. May she now rest in everlasting peace.' Patrick Brontë paused before he continued, 'We are also here to remember Albert Holmes and to say farewell to a young man taken from us in the prime of his life at the young age of twenty years. Albert came here from an orphanage in Liverpool to work in the mill at Sladen Bridge. He didn't have the best start in life, but he had grown into a fine young man. He had not had the chance to experience much of the rich tapestry of life that this world has to offer, and he died without accumulating any wealth, but worldly possessions are only on loan to us and when we leave this world it is as we came into it – with nothing. Dust to dust! Albert was a good man, and we recommend him to the Father as someone who appreciated the little things, the true things in life. He would do anything for anyone and was a truly good friend to those who knew him.'

The Reverend Patrick Brontë was a deep-thinking man with a genuine concern for his flock. He had been known to use his pulpit as a means of putting across his views with regard to social and moral reform, and he had decided to put the timeliness of this tragedy to good use. He had a packed church. Among others, wealthy manufacturers filled the pews, many of whom made vast profits from their mills with no concern for the welfare of their workers. Mr Brontë was determined that they would not leave without a piece of his mind. Members of the Haworth Council Board were also present, and they certainly needed waking up to the dreadful living conditions of most of the villagers. August had been a particularly hot month, and drinking water in Haworth had become so putrid that even the cows would not drink it. There was severe overcrowding, and the lack of drainage meant that human excrement fouled the streets. It was time for change.

Mr Brontë climbed the steps to the lectern and read the Bible passage on which his address would be based.

'Matthew chapter 6, verses 19 to 21. "Lay not up for yourselves treasures upon earth, where moth and rust doth corrupt ... but lay up for yourselves treasures in heaven ..."'

He spoke eloquently about the suffering of the poor and the disease of deprivation.

'Everywhere we turn there are people who are undernourished, sick and living in appalling conditions, with no hope of a better life. How many more from our village will die of cholera? How many more have to waste away from consumption? The Lord gave us life, and we selfishly indulge it whilst squandering our neighbours' lives through our neglect. The rich of this world suffer from the disease of excess. True harmony will reign only when the "Haves" begin to look at the "Have-nots" as brothers and sisters in the Lord. "Lay up for yourselves treasures in heaven ... for where your treasure is there will your heart be also." Amen.'

Every one of the wealthy members of the congregation – landowner, mill-owner or gentry – was left in no doubt that the sermon was addressed to them.

To the strains of the well-known hymn 'The Lord's my Shepherd,' the coffins were carried out of the church and into the graveyard. A newly dug grave waited to take Albert into its eternal safe keeping, and on the other side of the path the large Turner vault had been opened to receive one more family member. Despairing in their grief, Ruth and Mr Turner held onto each other for support, and John and Paul cried unashamedly as Albert's coffin was lowered into the ground.

13

During the long weeks and months following the death of his wife Mr Turner could find no interest in the mill which had been his life's dream. At first, out of habit, he went along to the office each day, but he would sit for hours, submerged in grief and vacantly staring at the walls, thinking of happier days. He remembered the beginnings of his married life; the small farm and the two hand looms. How he and his wife always pulled together working as a team and building up to this mill with its 100 power looms. Now she was gone. Without her there was no point to anything. His dreams were shattered. There was Ruth, of course. She was a good daughter, but she had her own life to live and would soon be married. More and more the running of the mill was taken over by Seth, who was unhappy to see Mr Turner in such a sorry state and tried to involve him in whatever way he could, asking his advice over any matter that came up.

Mr Turner's reply was always the same.

'Do whatever you think fit, Seth. I trust your judgement.'

Ruth didn't come into the office now. She had taken over her mother's role at the farm, trying to keep things running as they always had. She was to be married in the spring, having at last become engaged to Robert Butterworth, but she never mentioned the wedding now, unsure how her father would be if she left. When Mr Turner returned each evening she welcomed him warmly and made light-hearted conversation, but no matter how she tried it was impossible to cheer him.

It was events of March 1841 that were to save Mr Turner from his slow decline. It was particularly cold weather, with traces of snow still lingering on the moors and under the wall sides. The sheep lambed early when cruel north-easterly winds were drawing icy-cold rain across the fields. The farm hand had been taken ill with bronchitis, and with Albert gone, there was no one left to tend the flock.

Ruth was concerned when her father said that he would check the sheep himself.

'It's too cold, Father. You're accustomed to the office and a warm fire.'

She needn't have worried. Her father threw himself into the task with new-found energy. He was out at all times of the day and night checking the sheep, delivering lambs and feeding two whose mother had died at their birth and who had been rejected when he'd tried to mother them on to another ewe.

The farm was Mr Turner's salvation. He gave up his daily visits to the office, leaving everything in Seth's capable hands. He had found a new purpose in life, realizing how much he had missed the outdoor life and working with the animals. For the first time since his wife's death he was sleeping well, and when the lambing season was over he took a quiet pride in having lost only five lambs. One old sheep from his flock of 60 had died, but he had 109 quickly-growing lambs gambolling in the fields when the April weather suddenly turned milder.

It was on one of these days when the clean air and soft spring breezes bring fresh hope to the most dejected of hearts, that Mr Turner decided what he would do. After walking through the fields, checking the sheep, he was dropping back down to the farm when he paused at the stile to watch a kestrel hovering above, keen-eyed, searching for its dinner. The bird swooped and was lost to sight, but as Mr Turner followed its dive his eyes fell on the roofs of the mill buildings in the valley below him. It all looked alien to him somehow, as if he were a stranger seeing the lines of the different sheds and the tall main mill for the first time. It seemed, then, inconceivable that he had created that hive of industry and that a good part of his life had been spent making a dream into reality, building up a tiny empire which no longer felt a part of him – no longer mattered. It had been *their* dream, his and his dear departed wife's, and without her there was no longer any point to it.

He breathed deeply, filling his lungs with clean April air.

Feeling the wind in his face he knew, in that moment, that he would leave the mill, leave the Worth Valley, find a new place and make a fresh start. He would farm, he thought, but on a bigger scale than was possible here in this wild, narrow valley.

'Somewhere up the Dales,' he said aloud, recommencing his walk with a new spring in his step, 'as soon as Ruth is wed.'

His thoughts turned then to his daughter, and he felt ashamed that he had given her wedding no attention. He had taken no part in any plans and had not even thought to enquire if all was going well. Dear, sweet Ruth! She had always been there for him, patient, kind and cheering, but he had been so wrapped up in his own grief that he'd spared no moment to wonder how his daughter was coping with the loss of her mother. It must be especially hard for Ruth at this important time. He would make amends. He resolved to speak with her as soon as he arrived home.

The wedding of Mr Robert James Butterworth and Miss Ruth Elizabeth Turner took place at Keighley Parish Church on the Monday after Whit Sunday. It was a grand occasion. Highly connected people from the county and from London and even Paris had descended on the town. Polished coaches, pulled by gleaming horses, stopped in front of the church, where the alighting passengers immediately became the objects of speculation and admiration for the huge crowd that had gathered on Church Green.

'Who do you suppose that is, then?'

'A Duke, I'll be bound. He looks that important!'

'Cor look at them feathers!'

'Oh, Mam, see that lady, isn't she beautiful?'

A young girl turned shining eyes to the older, care-worn face beside her and then, not wanting to miss a thing, she turned her attention back to the wedding guests.

'I want a dress like that one day, same colour as t'sea and so much stuff it looks like waves an' all!' she said her face taking on a dreamy expression.

At the back of the crowd another child was crying until her father hoisted her onto his shoulders.

'There, Ellen, can yer see now?'

Two young boys, not interested in all the silks and satins of high fashion, were enthralled by the many coaches rattling to a halt one after another, and more especially by the splendid horses which drew them. Greys, chestnuts, bays – whatever their colour, all were immaculately groomed, and when they stopped at the church some snorted and pawed the ground or tossed their manes in a gesture of impatience, eager to be on their way. As the boys edged closer for a better view a liveried coachman, smart in black and red, warned them back, fearful that they would startle the horses and be trampled under their hooves.

Rarely had the townspeople of Keighley witnessed such a spectacle as this. The workers from Butterworth's and Turner's Mills, who had been delighted to receive a day's holiday with pay, had turned out in droves to watch the fashionable parade, hoping to catch a glimpse of the bride as she arrived at church. They were not disappointed, and the sight of the carriage coming into view from the Halifax road produced a cheer from the crowd. It was drawn by two fine strawberry roans, each of which had a white rose behind the ear. Matching flowers were worn by the coachman and his companion, both attired in blue coats trimmed with gold braid. The bride, as brides always do on their wedding day, looked radiantly beautiful. Her gown had three very full layers of white satin, each layer edged with lace, and the neckline, trimmed with yet more lace, was fastened with a single white rose. Ruth's fair hair was adorned with a circlet of orange blossom from which a veil of finest Honiton lace hung almost to the ground.

Mr Turner, alighting from the coach, proudly offered his arm to his daughter and led her into the church.

14

The ballroom extension at Cliffe Towers, newly built with a
hardwood floor for dancing and a stage to accommodate the
orchestra, was full to capacity. The 200 guests who had attended
the wedding ceremony and had enjoyed the lavish reception in
the mansion's dining hall, were now in high spirits. Whether
dancing, conversing or spectating, all were enjoying the celebratory atmosphere. A request had been sent out with the wedding invitations that any lady intending to dance bring with her
a white ball gown. The request had been unusual, but everyone
agreed that the effect was stunning – a striking success. There
was a colourful border to the room. Ladies whose dancing days
were behind them wore gowns of different hues, ones more flat-
tering to their paling complexions, but on the dance floor there
was only white. Dresses were of taffeta, figured silk, muslin,
moiré, organza or satin, they had full skirts, tiered skirts, split
skirts with petticoats – long sleeves, puffed sleeves, trimmed
sleeves – wide necklines or ruched necklines – the styles and
materials were many and varied, but all the dresses were white.
The dancers glided, turned and curtsied so that the spectators
saw a swirling, billowing, ever-changing, froth of white. Like
clouds on a breezy summer's day.

John Pickles and Paul Ryan were watching the quadrille. They
had already partnered two pretty girls, beside whom they had
been seated in the dining room and with whom they had felt
obliged to take the first dance, but they were content, for the
moment, to join the spectators and watch the dancers as they
progressed through the complicated set patterns. They drew
admiring glances from all sides, for they had grown into attractive young men. At twenty-one both were tall and well-made,

and the contrast in their colouring, Paul as fair as John was dark, made them outstanding in the throng.

It had been a busy and exciting day for the two friends. They were proud to have been asked to undertake the important part of ushers at the marriage ceremony. Arriving early at the church, they had cut a dash in matching grey dress-coats, patterned silk waistcoats and knotted white cravats. They were agreeable young men, unflappable and enthusiastic in whatever they were doing, and they had carried out their commission with charm and efficiency, expertly directing the invited guests to their allotted pews in the church so that no one was left standing for long, and despite the excitement of the occasion everyone remained calm. After the ceremony it had been their task to organize the coaches, giving the cab drivers directions to Cliffe Towers, the Butterworths' home on the outskirts of the town and ensuring that all the guests were conveyed there with as little delay as possible in readiness for the reception dinner and dance.

Now, with their duties for the day completed, John and Paul were enjoying the experience of their first ball. Although this was a new environment for them, they were completely at ease. No one present would have guessed that ten years earlier these two confident young men had arrived in Haworth from the Liverpool orphanage with little more than the clothes that they were wearing. Many young girls were sneaking sly glances at the pair, hoping to be introduced and be the next to be asked to dance. As John or Paul caught their gazes young women blushed and looked away, a half-smile at their lips.

Paul was flattered by all the attention and laughingly pretended to be perplexed.

'Who shall I dance with next, John?' he joked. 'That girl wearing white or the one there in – er – white?'

John had no such dilemma. He had already fixed his eyes on an exceptionally beautiful girl at the other side of the ballroom. She had not danced and was engaged in conversation with an older couple whom John took to be her parents, for all three had the same olive-coloured skin. From this and the unusual style of their dress, John guessed that they were from some foreign country. He was intrigued and could not take his eyes off the girl. She was about his own age, tall and with a lovely figure. Her dress sparkled with sequins which caught the light as she moved, but it was her hair which he had noticed first. It was thick and lustrous, rolled in a chignon high on her head, with thick ringlets at the neck and was as black as the night, darker even than his own. Against the white of the dress it was breathtakingly beautiful. John felt a surge of excitement as he watched her.

'That's the girl *I* shall dance with,' he told Paul.

When he looked across the room again she was looking at him, and as their eyes met she smiled before turning to answer some question from the older woman. It was enough, that smile, to send the blood rushing to John's head. Her eyes, though very dark, had sparkled as the smile lit up her face, and John had never before been so enraptured. He left Paul to make up his mind which 'swan' he would dance with next, and began to make his way around the edge of the ballroom. He wondered how he should approach the girl; he wanted to go straight to her and whisk her onto the dance floor, but knew that this would be frowned upon. He must introduce himself and speak with the other members of the party. However, one way or another, he was determined to dance with her! On drawing close he saw that Mr Turner had joined the group and had already seen John threading through the spectators. It was made easy for him.

'John, come and meet my friends.' Mr Turner's outstretched arm drew John into the circle and introductions were made.

'This is John Pickles – Mr and Mrs Ferrari – and their daughter, Leonora.'

'I'm very pleased to meet you.' John took Mrs Ferrari's hand and bowed slightly.

'This is a wonderful occasion, yes?' Mrs Ferrari smiled. 'I like always the wedding.'

John murmured some reply, but his attention was on Leonora. She was even more beautiful than he had thought, and his pulse was racing. He was aware that the quadrille had ended and that the orchestra were now playing one of the new Strauss waltzes and he didn't want to be drawn into conversation with Mrs Ferrari. He didn't hesitate, but asked, 'Leonora, will you do me the honour of dancing with me?'

It was as if they had always been partners. The music flowed

through them and into their feet, taking them around the ballroom in perfect unison. Their steps were light and their movements graceful, and the excitement that the pair felt radiated
from their faces. Many of those assembled turned to watch the
dark young couple with shiny, jet-black hair, and were for a
moment caught up in their happiness as they swirled around
the floor. They sat out the next two dances, eager to talk and
learn as much as they could of each other.

'I live quite near to you,' said Leonora in answer to John's
questions. 'My home is Laverock Hall at Oldfield, only a mile
away from Sladen Bridge. I can look down at the mill in the
bottom of the valley.'

John was astonished.

'I can't understand how I've never seen you before when you
live so close!'

Leonora laughed, 'We only came to the Hall about six months
ago, so I know very few people here.'

'Where do you come from?'

John knew that though she had perfect English she was a for-
eigner, and he wasn't at all surprised by her answer.

'We're Italian. My father is a wool merchant and came here
to export Yorkshire wool to Italy. He thinks your Pennine wool
is the best of all. We came first to Bradford and then, as I told
you, about six months ago we moved to Oldfield. We are very
happy here. The house is beautiful and the countryside is so
different; peaceful little fields and the wide, bleak moors
beyond. I hope we can stay forever.'

I hope so too! thought John, but he kept his thoughts to himself and told her instead of his life at Stanbury and his work in
the mill. Leonora was interested in all he had to tell her and
listened attentively, only interrupting once when he mentioned
Paul.

'Is he the young man you were with earlier, before we
danced?'

'Yes,' said John. 'He's the best friend anyone could wish for.
He, Seth and Mary Ann are all like family to me.'

'I've seen you both fishing near the little bridge below our
home – the Donkey Bridge, I think you call it.'

'That's right, we often go there for trout. Perhaps one day
you would like to join us?'

Leonora smiled, 'I'd like that very much.'

They were so wrapped up in their conversation that they almost missed another dance, but Leonora realized just in time that a gallop was about to begin

'Oh, this is my favourite. Let's dance!'

It was the simplest of dances, couples zigzagging down the floor with long, gliding, chassé steps, but it was danced at a furious pace and Leonora and John sparkled with such happiness that everyone near them felt lifted by their energy and merriment. They were laughing and out of breath when the dance finally ended, and all were glad of the respite when it was announced that the bride and bridegroom were about to depart for their honeymoon to the South of France. Everyone was invited to go out onto the terraces to wave good-bye and give the happy couple a fitting send-off.

Outside John and Leonora found themselves next to Seth and Mary Ann.

'I'm very pleased to meet you,' smiled Leonora when John had introduced them all. 'I've heard so much about you both.'

'What, already?' laughed Seth. 'Nothing too bad, I hope!'

John grinned, 'I told her how you beat us daily and Mary Ann fed us only bread and water, but otherwise it was all good, I promise you!'

They all laughed, but Ruth and Robert had come out of the house and were ready to depart and, for the moment, all else was forgotten as everyone cheered and waved, sending good wishes to the newlyweds as their carriage slowly pulled away and disappeared down the curving drive.

When they had gone most people filtered back inside, but Seth, Mary Ann, John and Leonora remained on the terrace, enjoying the coolness of the clean night after the heat of the ballroom.

'How's the new leg, Seth?' asked John.

'Fine, thank you. I've managed a couple of dances, but I passed on the gallop. I doubt I could have kept up with you two!'

Seth and Mary Ann smiled at each other. Tonight had been special for them too. It was the first time they had danced together since the ball in the Tremont Hotel, Boston, all those years ago on the evening of their engagement, and it had

121

evoked sentimental memories. Also, they could see that a new romance had begun with the young couple beside them, and they both thought that it was special. They had liked Leonora immediately and secretly they wished them all the joy they themselves had known.

Soon after the wedding Mr Turner put into action his plans for leaving the Worth Valley. He bought a large estate of 250,000 acres in the village of Buckden in the Yorkshire Dales. Beside the big house it had three farms and a number of workers' cottages, and the land could carry some 2000 sheep and 250 head of cattle. He had no regrets on giving up his home. The farm was let to a tenant, and Mr Turner knew that he was leaving the mill in capable hands. There had been yet more re-organization in its management, and a firm of accountants had been brought in to do the main book-keeping. Arthur Hollindrake was now in full charge of the production of cloth and Paul and John had been promoted, Paul being in control of the combing and spinning mill, and John in the offices dealing with orders, workers' wages etc. Mr Turner was confident that all would run as smoothly as ever. Local people were sorry to see him go. The Turners had been good and fair employers, but those who knew him well realized how unhappy he had been since the death of his wife and felt that new surroundings would be good for him. The biggest surprise to everyone was the news that Seth and Mary Ann would also be leaving the valley. Mr Turner had asked them to accompany him to Buckden.

'The house is huge, plenty room for all of us, and I'm sure that you and Mary Ann would like it there. Wharfedale is a beautiful place. What do you say, Seth?'

Mr Turner had been sure that Seth and Mary Ann would jump at the chance to live in a fine house as his companions, and was unprepared for their hesitation. They loved their little cottage at Sladen and had been very happy there, and therefore spent long evenings sitting in their rocking chairs or on the low wall around the garden trying to make up their minds.

'I'll miss this place if we go, Seth,' said Mary Ann quietly. 'Our first home. It has been wonderful here, every year, every month, every minute.'

122

'Life moves on,' Seth had said. 'We should move with it and seize opportunities.'

Things at Sladen were changing anyway. The orphan boys were grown and had lives of their own to lead so they seldom came to the cottage any more, Ruth was married now, and Emily Brontë was away at school in Brussels so Mary Ann had no companion for her moorland walks. Finally it was decided they would join Mr Turner, and in late July the pair left Sladen Bridge for Buckden. John and Paul were saddened by their leaving, but promised to come and visit them all just as soon as the cricket season was over.

As the horse plodded up the hill pulling the laden carriage, Mary Ann thought of that day, a long time ago, when after long weeks in Liverpool they had come down the hill and seen the enchanting little cottage for the very first time. A tear trickled down her cheek, but she turned away quickly so that Seth would not see, and as they left Haworth behind she was already looking forward to her first glimpse of their new home in Buckden.

15

Leonora could see John already waiting. He was sitting on the stone parapet of the bridge with his legs dangling over the river, and he was looking up the fields to the little pack-horse lane so Leonora knew that he would have seen her too, and her heart beat a little faster in anticipation of their meeting. She wasn't late, so John must have arrived well before the chosen time, and it made Leonora smile to think that he was as eager to see her as she him. It was a warm sunny day, two weeks after the wedding, and they had arranged to meet at the Donkey Bridge, just half a mile from Laverock Hall, at 2 p.m. John had promised to teach her how to fish with a rod and line and Leonora could see that he had with him the fishing rods and a small wicker basket.

As she made her way down the narrow track Leonora had a sense of heightened awareness, as if the countryside had taken on a brighter cloak especially for her. The grass was greener, the lambs whiter, the birds sang more sweetly and the sun shone in a bluer sky than ever before.

As she reached the bottom of the lane John swung his legs back onto the bridge and came to meet her. They ran the last few yards and then stopped, facing each other, smiling. Neither spoke. John thought Leonora was even more beautiful than he had remembered, and Leonora's heart was beating so loudly she feared that he would hear. Simultaneously each reached out to take the other's hand and, still without speaking, they went down to the bridge. At last John found his voice.

'I've brought all the tackle if you still want to learn how to fish. Of course, if you've changed your mind it will...'

'I do want to learn, really,' Leonora laughed. 'Do we fish here from the bridge?'

'No, we'll have to walk upstream. There's a really good pool not far off, and I think we'll try our luck there.'

'It *will* be luck if I catch something. I've never fished before.'

'Don't worry, I'll teach you all you need to know.'

John was as good as his word. He knew every inch of this river and besides knowing the deepest pools to fish and where to find the juiciest worms, he knew the names of all the flowers and recognized the calls of the birds darting among the bushes on the river bank. He pointed out a pair of yellow wagtails, and Leonora was thrilled to see a kingfisher skimming low over the water.

They soon reached the pool. Half the river was darkly shaded by the branches of low-growing alder and hazel trees, but the nearer trees half glistened in the sunlight, and the grass banking was warm and green, catching the heat of the sun but sheltered from the breeze. It was a lovely place to spend the afternoon. Leonora was keen to start, but when John found red worms beneath a tuft of grass and cut them up with his penknife she shuddered and declined the invitation to fix her own bait, letting John do it for her.

He showed her how to cast the line towards the running water on the far side of the pool, explaining that the trout often rested in the deep, shaded areas, and he told her to keep a sharp eye on the yellow float. John demonstrated the cast with his own line and Leonora took the other rod and drew it behind her, as John had done, and then swung it forward with a sweeping motion. She hadn't got the movement right, and the line fell short and trailed back towards the bank.

'Here, let me help you.'

John reeled the line and then, standing behind Leonora he put his arms around her and, holding her wrists, drew back her arms to the correct position. They were so close. Her hair was in his face, she smelled sweet and the skin of her neck looked soft and inviting. For a moment they stood motionless, rod held aloft, each very much aware of the other.

John drew in a deep breath and concentrated hard on the fishing line. With a quick flick he sent it flying over the river to fall into the middle of the fastest water. Reluctantly he released Leonora's wrists and said, a little gruffly,

'Keep your eye on the float and be ready for a bite.'

John cast his own line and they waited, side by side on the bank, content to let the minutes pass by in silence whilst they enjoyed the sun, the sound of the river and the nearness of each other. A water vole appeared on the opposite bank, and scuttling down to the water it pulled up some new green shoots and began eating them, unconcerned by, or unaware of, the couple's presence. A dragonfly droned by, hovering over some pondweed before continuing its flight up-stream. Its wings were a beautiful iridescent blue, and Leonora was watching it when she felt a sharp tug on the line. She shrieked with surprise and John instructed her on how to strike, hold the rod firm and play the fish. Leonora was excited by the catch, and carefully following what John told her, she managed to land a fine trout. John was as thrilled as she was and was full of praise.

'Well done, Leonora!'

Before long Leonora had caught a second and third fish, but John only managed to land one trout all afternoon. In the wicker basket were ham sandwiches and wine, and as they picnicked on the grassy bank John said again, 'Well done. You've really taken to fishing – a natural angler.'

'I had a first-rate teacher,' replied Leonora, blushing.

The afternoon had slipped by, and Leonora knew she should be going home.

'Would you like to come back to Laverock Hall to show my parents our superb catch? If we hurry, we may be in time for the fish to be cooked for the evening meal, and you could stay and eat with us. Do please say yes.'

Leonora was kneeling in the grass. She was so alive in her eagerness, cheeks flushed and dark eyes sparkling as she pleaded with him. John moved towards her.

'Of course I'll come,' he murmured, kissing her gently on her cheek.

Leonora lifted her face to him and they leaned closer.

As their lips met he drew her into his arms for their first real kiss.

Mr and Mrs Ferrari were sitting on the veranda when John and Leonora arrived at Laverock Hall. Mr Ferrari did not look pleased and Mrs Ferrari appeared a little flustered, sitting bolt

126

upright and glancing from her husband to Leonora and back to her husband, for all the world as if she expected trouble.

Mr Ferrari spoke sternly as the couple approached.

'Where have you been, Leonora, and who is this young man?'

'Oh, Papa. This is John Pickles,' exclaimed Leonora, 'you met at the wedding ball, remember? We've been fishing.'

Mrs Ferrari gasped, 'Fishing! Oh my goodness!'

Mr Ferrari opened his mouth to speak, but before her father could say anything more Leonora continued excitedly.

'Look what we have caught. Trout! Enough for dinner and, if you'll allow it, John has promised to show me how to cook it. A special recipe; his favourite! What do you think, Mamma, would you like trout tonight? Look, Papa, isn't it wonderful?'

Leonora had opened the basket to show her parents the brown fish. She was flushed with excitement and, seeing her so happy, her father's quick Italian temper dissolved and his face broke into a smile. He adored his daughter and could not stay cross with her for long.

'The fish look tempting,' he said, 'and yes, if you wish to be the cooks we will sample your meal. Mr Pickles, I do remember you now, yes.'

Mr Ferrari rose and took John's hand, and then looking into his eyes, he said purposefully.

'Our daughter is very precious to us, please remember that!'

Mrs Ferrari smiled and relaxed, glad that the angry scene she had anticipated had not come about. John, however, was embarrassed and angry with himself. How could he not have realized that he was putting Leonora in an awkward situation by asking her to meet him alone? He had distressed her parents and shown himself in a bad light. Others should have been invited to the picnic. He resolved to be more thoughtful in future, to be sure that Mr and Mrs Ferrari would look upon him favourably.

The meal was a great success. Leonora had smoothed the cook's disgruntled feathers when they invaded her kitchen, and with her help they had assembled everything John required. Fresh parsley, bay leaves, onions and lettuce were brought from the kitchen garden, and the cook produced a glass of white wine, butter and a poaching pan. Leonora had never done anything like this before, and they had great fun putting the meal together.

'This is a day of firsts,' exclaimed Leonora. 'First time fishing, first time cooking!'

'And our first kiss,' whispered John.

'Sh!' Leonora glanced anxiously towards Mary, the cook, but she was busy washing the lettuce and hadn't heard a thing. Leonora was so bubbly and happy that John soon forgot his disquiet at having upset her parents, and they laughed together when the onions brought tears to Leonora's eyes.

All was finally ready and carried through to the dining room. A large platter held the four trout garnished with lettuce and onion rings. They were served with crusty bread with parsley butter and washed down with wine, making a splendid meal which drew hearty approval from Mr and Mrs Ferrari. As the meal progressed John and Mr Ferrari found they had much to talk about, the state of the woollen trade in Bradford and current prices being of great interest to both of them.

'There is great demand in Italy,' said Mr Ferrari. 'I export to Milan, and garments made from your Yorkshire wool are much sought after by the fashionable society there. It seems you only have to name your price and the deal is done.'

'Oh yes, we Italian ladies love to follow the fashions, just as you do in England and France,' Mrs Ferrari joined in for the first time. 'We are lucky now, for we have the best of both countries. We have the Italian designs – wonderful colour and flair – and your fine wool!'

The conversation was pleasantly relaxed, and John felt relieved that both Mr and Mrs Ferrari appeared to have forgiven him for the afternoon's *faux pas*. Certainly Leonora wasn't troubled. She was bright and merry throughout the meal. Excited and sparkling – so obviously happy in his company.

After such a poor start the evening had turned out splendidly, and John left with warm invitations to call again very soon. He whistled all the way home. Leonora! Her thick, black hair, bright eyes, lovely smile and merry laughter filled his thoughts, and as his feet skipped along the rutted track his heart also skipped a beat.

The summer of 1841 was idyllic for John and Leonora. John called at Laverock Hall whenever time allowed, and they spent hours deep in conversation sitting on the veranda looking out across the little fields. Leonora liked to sketch and paint, and she tried to persuade John to try his hand with the water-colours.

John had laughed. 'You paint, I'm content to sit and watch you. I could never capture your beauty, and I don't want to paint anything else!'

Mr and Mrs Ferrari soon grew to like John and welcomed him at the Hall. They thought he was a 'very nice young man', rather more agreeable than the usual local lads, and they were glad of his company for Leonora, who was restless if she had to spend a lot of time alone at Laverock Hall. The Ferraris were happy to see their daughter happy, and because Mr Ferrari still thought of Leonora as 'his little girl' and Mrs Ferrari could not bear to think of a time when her daughter would not be with them, and because John was careful to show no impropriety, they were completely blind to the romance blossoming between the two young people. In any case, if they ever did think of Leonora marrying, it was to some high-ranking Italian gentleman or, at least, an Englishman of some wealth and standing, and they just never considered John as a prospective husband for their daughter.

Whenever opportunity arose, John and Leonora sought each other's company. They spent many balmy summer evenings along the riverbank following the river source high on the moorland above Ponden Kirk, but there were not only moorland rambles; they were invited to musical evenings with the Heaton family at Ponden Hall, and Leonora became an avid cricket supporter. She attended every game of the Haworth Church Cricket Team and, although new to the sport, she soon learnt all the rules and flushed with admiration when John excelled and drew the cheers of the spectators. The young couple were content together, and their love for each other grew deeper with every meeting. They would have liked to have spent even more time together – for Leonora at least every minute spent apart felt like time wasted, but John could not neglect his work, for he had been entrusted with responsible jobs, and above all he wanted to prove to Seth and Mr Turner that their faith in him hadn't been misguided.

16

Under the new management, production at Hollings Mill had actually increased. Arthur Hollindrake, John and Paul were all respected by the workers, and John, in charge of the wages, had offered incentives for quality and production. The employees, on the whole, were happy and loyal, working hard for the fair wages they were given. Profits were high, and soon the management were able to invest in a larger, more powerful steam engine that gave combined power to the spinning mill and the weaving sheds. Sixty Jacquard power looms were installed to produce an endless variety of new patterns.

Since Mr Turner's departure the finances of the mill had been overseen on his behalf by Messrs Hayward and Sutcliffe, accountants of Keighley, but John was in charge of the day-to-day cashflow and in particular the wages. Each Friday morning he strapped a leather bag to the saddle and rode his horse up into Haworth to visit the Yorkshire Bank. Cheques and receipts from the week's transactions were paid into the mill account, and monies were withdrawn for the wages. John looked forward to this part of the week, as he always enjoyed a long chat with Jonas Fisher, the bank manager. Mr Fisher was a gentle, considerate man who had been the bank manager in Haworth for as long as most people could remember. He was quiet and tactful and could extract from his customers any information he needed without ever stirring up ill-feeling, and he was well-liked by all the mill-owners, businessmen and farmers who were customers of the bank. He and John would discuss mill business, and then their conversation would drift to cricket and other events in the valley. It was Jonas Fisher who told John just how influential the Ferrari family were back home in Italy.

'Their wool trade is a very lucrative business, John, but they are merchants by choice, not necessity. Mr Ferrari built up and expanded his company, but his grandfather made a vast fortune trading in silk from the Lombardy Plains, and Leonora's grandfather has a country estate on the shores of Lake Como, north of Milan. As her father is the only son of an only son, he will inherit all the wealth too!'

John was interested to discover this, but it made no difference as far as he was concerned, for he could not love Leonora more if her father were the King of Italy!

One Friday morning in August John had tied up his horse outside the Black Bull Hotel as usual and was about to unbuckle his saddlebag when he noticed two men approaching the bank. They were strangers to Haworth and were shabbily dressed and none too clean. One was about 5 feet 10 inches tall, with straggly red hair, and the dirty leather jerkin he wore over a rough collarless shirt had seen better days. His expression was sour, and as he spoke his lip curled back revealing yellowed, and broken teeth. Under his arm he carried what appeared to be a rolled sack. His companion was shorter and looked as if he had been sleeping rough, for although the day was warm, he had on a heavy mud-stained coat and his trousers were badly creased. His face was obscured by a brown felt hat pulled well down over his ears. He had his arms across his chest, keeping the coat wrapped tightly around him, for all the world as if it were the middle of winter instead of a sunny August day. John knew that they were up to no good, but held back from entering the bank, wondering what he should do.

An empty wooden barrel had been left outside the public house, and John rolled it across the street, clambering onto it beneath a small window high in the bank wall. Standing on tiptoe he could just manage to look through the glass and had a good view of the manager's private office. He was aghast at the scene he saw below. Jonas Fisher was slumped over his desk. The smaller of the two men was bending over him with a pickaxe handle held high in the air, ready to strike again should the bank manager stir. His filthy coat was now hanging open, and John cursed himself for being such a fool not to realize the shaft must have been concealed beneath it. If only he had acted sooner, his friend would not now be lying injured. The second

131

man was on his hands and knees in front of a large safe, attempting to lever open the door.

John knew he had no time to lose. He doubted that he would have the strength to overcome two men, but on the other hand he was determined that they would not get away after hurting Mr Fisher. Racing across to the public house, he grabbed two empty bottles from a wine case near the door and then quietly made his way into the bank and took stock of the situation.

The cashier, white-faced and trembling, was leaning heavily on the counter. He had a nasty gash on his forehead and was trying to staunch the flow of blood with his pocket handkerchief. The clerk looked terrified but otherwise unhurt. He was in the corner, rooted to the spot with his mouth open in a silent scream. John put a finger to his lips before he realized that the man was so shocked that he probably could not move. It was clear to John that neither of the employees would be of any help to him and that he must tackle the intruders alone. His heart beat a little faster as the muscles of his stomach knotted, and unconsciously he tightened his grip on the bottles. The door to the office was slightly ajar, and John could see that the safe was now open and the two men were hastily stuffing bank notes into their sack. He could not see Mr Fisher, whose desk was obscured, but as both men were at the safe John presumed that he was still unconscious.

He didn't wait. In a single motion he burst through the door and sent one of the bottles zooming though the air. It hit the nearer man on the side of his head and his knees crumpled beneath him as he dropped to the floor, his hair now a little redder where a trickle of blood began. In a flash the second man was up and across the room trying to reach the pick-axe handle. John took aim with the remaining bottle, but it went wide and as the thief reached the desk where he had left his weapon John took a flying leap and grappled the man to the floor.

They rolled and fought for some time, crashing into a filing cabinet and upsetting the coat stand, sending Mr Fisher's hat skimming across the room. John was the stronger of the two, but the little chap was cunning and just as John thought he had him he wriggled out of his coat, and turning he kicked John in the ribs, winding him so that as John fought for breath the intruder had time to retrieve the sack and make for the door. John started after him, but the red-haired man had regained consciousness, and managing to get to his knees he lunged at John, tripping him and helping his friend in his escape.

John rolled over and leaped back to his feet, pausing long enough to kick the man hard between the legs and send him crashing back to the floor before pursuing the first man, who had now reached the outer door of the bank. John was just in time to see him apprehended by the village constable and a shopkeeper, alerted by the bank clerk who had snapped out of his paralysis at the sound of the first bottle smashing.

It was all over in a matter of minutes. When they saw that they were outnumbered the two robbers put up little further resistance, and they were taken into custody.

Jonas Fisher was alive, but he had taken some nasty blows to the head and the fingers of his right hand had been shattered as he'd tried to protect himself. He was still unconscious when John went back into the office.

'Send for the doctor,' he told the clerk, 'and we'll need a carriage to take Mr Fisher home.'

It was many months before Jonas Fisher recovered from the savage attack. It had left him with impaired vision and prone to violent headaches, but the ordeal had taken its toll in other ways. For the first time ever he really felt his age. A temporary replacement had been drafted into the bank, but as the months dragged by it became clear that Mr Fisher's working days were over, and reluctantly he decided to retire.

The Deputy Manager was appointed to be the new Branch Manager. He moved from the lodgings he had taken for a month at a time and bought a house on West Lane, which he considered to be the 'best' part of the village, and he expected that everyone would now look upon him as an important person, which he certainly considered himself to be. His name was Oscar Beale. He was 25 years old, but having spent years carefully cultivating his outward persona he had none of the spontaneity of youth and often seemed more like a man of middle years. He was small and dapper. His clothes, of the latest style, were considered rather flashy for Haworth, and his light ginger hair, smoothed across his pale brow, was held in place by some aromatic preparation which made it sleek and shiny. He was a smooth talker with impeccable manners and a false charm which opened doors, enabling him to move in the circles of more wealthy people. He appeared to be dedicated to his work in the bank, but it was only his obsessive ambition to improve his status in life which drove him on. He resented having to earn a living at all and secretly hated those more wealthy than he, just as he despised the poor who had nothing and had been born without his single-mindedness – and luck – to raise them from their poverty.

No one in Haworth knew anything of his origins. He never had visitors and he never spoke of any family. It was as though he had no past. Folks in the village had their own ideas – background of poverty, skeletons in the cupboard, a maid in distress somewhere – but it was all bare supposition and, without fuel for the fire, the curiosity soon wore off as people became accustomed to his presence in the bank. Oscar Beale was polite and punctilious in his dealings with the customers. No one could fault his efficiency and the service he provided, but he had none of Jonas Fisher's warmth and easy manner. No one was encouraged to stay and chat after their business was concluded, and nor did anyone seem particularly keen to do so. He had previously worked at the bank's headquarters in Bradford, beginning as a junior clerk but ingratiating himself with the manager and making a quick rise to First Cashier before putting himself forward for the position of Deputy Manager at Haworth during Mr Fisher's illness.

The Haworth branch was an important bank with some very good customers. Wool merchants and mill owners banked there, and transactions were made involving large sums of money. The branch had prospered over the years, largely because of the goodwill and trust developed between old Jonas Fisher and his customers. Oscar Beale, riding on Mr Fisher's reputation, took over the management of a very successful establishment and felt that this was enough to earn him the elevated position in society that he craved. For a time it seemed that this was to be the case. No one had any complaints, and he managed to procure invitations to many of the fine houses in the area, thereby mingling with the 'best' of local society.

When it came to religion the folk of Haworth were roughly split down the middle; half belonged to the Methodist faith and

134

were known as 'Methody', whilst half attended the Church of England and were called 'Churchers'. Oscar Beale was a lay preacher in the Methodist Church and preached at West Lane approximately once each month. If the truth were known, he had no strong religious convictions, but he felt it enhanced his status to be seen in the pulpit and known as a God-fearing person. He was quite sure that being a preacher in the Methodist Church elevated him from the level of the ordinary 'Methody' and put him on an equal footing with what he saw as the lofty ranks of the Church of England, thus securing his position in all parts of the community.

There was some prejudice and intolerance between the two groups; the 'Churchers' looked down on the 'Methody' who, in turn, thought the 'Churchers' were snobs. Nowhere was the rivalry greater than between the cricket teams of the two churches. From the time of his arrival in Haworth Oscar Beale had played cricket for the West Lane Methodist Church side. He had let it be known that he was available, but he had made it quite clear that as Bank Manager he felt he could only play as opening batsman. The captain of the team, Vic Wilson, had thought this a balmy idea – 'a chap opens 'cause he's good wi't bat not wi' figures' – but he had let him lead the field anyway and was surprised to find that Mr Beale was a first-class batsman.

Oscar didn't particularly like sport of any kind but had decided years before that it was useful to be seen to be taking an active part in the community, and in any case he took great pleasure in outshining others in any way he could, and when Oscar Beale put his mind to something he usually made things turn out the way he wanted them to. He wasn't an especially good bowler, but hours of practice had refined his batting skills and he was making a name for himself in the valley. The two church teams met quite often, and each time it was a needle match, with villagers turning out in great numbers to watch the sport. They were vociferous in their support, shouting and cheering on the players. Oscar Beale was the star of the Methodist eleven, and at all other matches he would have the highest score of the day, often making a half-century and once scoring 137 not out by the close of play.

It was a different story the first time he played against St

135

Michael's. John Pickles' batting was quite equal to that of the bank manager. Along with Paul he had practised for years in the mill yard and, of late, Arthur Hollindrake had helped them with the finer points of the game, coaching them until they were a formidable pair. Known locally as the Black and White Twins, they struck terror into the opposing sides. John was the hardest-hitting batsman in the district and could place the ball at will. He too frequently made high scores and, on the occasion that they first played against Oscar Beale, the church team batted first and John scored 57 runs. Everyone was expecting a close contest, but they had reckoned without Paul Ryan's bowling. Paul was an exceptionally good fast-bowler, he could send a ball whipping down the pitch like a thunderbolt and had some trick – a flick of the wrist – which made the ball bounce back six inches, surprising everyone. It was an extremely destructive, hostile action, and Oscar Beale had no answer to the speed and accuracy of the balls Paul delivered. He had only scored eight runs when his wicket fell. The 'Churchers' in the crowd roared with delight, quite making up for the stunned silence of the 'Methody' supporters.

Oscar Beale could not disguise the anger and frustration he felt and to make matters worse, as he turned to leave the pitch the first person he saw was John Pickles, who had been fielding near the wicket. John's delighted grin was enough to send Oscar into a quiet fury, and from that day forward he harboured resentment against the two friends, who had, in his eyes, totally humiliated him in front of the very people he had been trying so hard to impress.

17

That summer Julius Ferrari Snr, Leonora's grandfather, died in Italy. He was 79 years old and left business interests and estates which amounted to considerable wealth. Leonora's parents immediately made plans for a lengthy stay in Milan to oversee the distribution of the family assets. Grandfather had owned land, property and a huge art collection and many decisions would have to be made. Mr Ferrari estimated that they would be away for at least six months, and expected his daughter to accompany them. Leonora was dismayed. She was so very much in love, and the thought of even a brief parting was enough to bring tears to her eyes, but six months! No, she could not bear it. She would die! She must be allowed to stay! The floods of tears which flowed as soon as her father read the letter and put forward his plans were at first misinterpreted.

'There, there, Leonora. Grandfather was an old man. He had had a good life. Don't be too sad.'

Leonora felt guilty that her tears were for herself and not for her grandfather, who had been a remote figure in her life, always busy, often away, but it did nothing to stop the tears. When she came down to breakfast the following morning, red-eyed and drawn-looking from a sleepless night, her parents were concerned.

'Leonora, you mustn't upset yourself so, Grandfather would not have wanted it.'

'Oh, Mamma, don't you see? It's not that. I can't go to Italy. I will die if I have to go. I just can't leave John for six whole months! Please don't make me go.'

Mr and Mrs Ferrari were quite taken aback.

'That's enough, Leonora. You'll have a wonderful time in

Milan and meet many new young people. You'll soon get over this foolishness. I don't want to hear another word about it.'

As far as he was concerned the subject was closed, and he would not discuss it further. Leonora was distraught. Between bouts of hysterical tears she begged and pleaded with her mother to talk to Papa and make him see that she just could not go to Italy.

'It's no good, dear, Papa has made up his mind.'

Mrs Ferrari was in a quandary. Like her husband she was at first upset by Leonora's disclosure, for though she liked John she considered him an unsuitable match for her daughter, but she was a romantic at heart and could now see that Leonora was very much in love.

'I can't go, Mamma. I won't be able to breathe. How will I ever be able to sleep? What reason will there be for me to get out of bed each day? Please, please speak to Papa, make him see. Please, Mamma.'

In the end, against her better judgement, Mrs Ferrari agreed to speak with her husband.

'Leonora is making herself ill with this foolishness, Vincente. I fear for her health if we take her to Milan. She'll pine constantly, be sure of it, and all the time she'll be waiting for the return. What young person hasn't had these times when they fancy they are in love? If we let her stay this infatuation will wear itself out, like countless ones before it, and when we come back to England everything will be fine, you'll see.'

Mr Ferrari was finally persuaded, and when the older couple left for Italy Leonora remained at Laverock Hall with Mary, the housekeeper, promising to 'look after Miss Leonora real well'.

Whilst Mr and Mrs Ferrari were away, Leonora spent many happy hours with John. The summer evenings were warm and long, and the young pair often walked along the riverbank or through Ponden Woods to the moors beyond. Sometimes John waded into the river and tickled the brown trout hiding beneath rocks in the shadowy pools. He showed Leonora how to trap and skin rabbits, which they took back to the Hall for Mary to cook. Whatever they were doing they were happy to be in each other's company. The more time they spent together, the harder they found it to be apart. On occasions Leonora would chatter excitedly, but at other times they would stroll in silence, hand in hand, with no need for words, each totally absorbed in the other's presence. It was a heavenly time for both of them.

Mary, the cook, had suggested that they gather bilberries from the bushes on Stanbury Moor so that she could bake a pie for supper, so on one particularly warm evening they set out carrying a basin to hold the fruit. The bilberries were big and juicy, and in no time at all the bowl was full. Setting it down, Leonora looked across the huge expanse of open hillside above them. As far as the eye could see there was nothing but heather, bracken and ling spread in a luxurious carpet of pinks and greens under the brightest blue sky. Nothing stirred except the occasional sheep and a curlew flying overhead, calling clearly, 'coorli – coorli'. Leonora laughed. She was filled with excitement at the beauty of the day and the freedom of the moors.

'I'll race you to the big rock, John.'

She was away as she spoke, leaping over the tufts of heather and plunging through the bracken, but John was past her and already on top of the rock when she reached it. Jubilantly he pulled her up to join him, and standing behind her, he put his arms around her waist drawing her to him and rested his chin on her shoulder so that cheek by cheek they surveyed the landscape falling away below them to the village and beyond. This place, which could be so wild and unforgiving in the winter, was now beautiful and tranquil, and John felt a wholeness of body and spirit.

'This must be one of the very best places on earth,' he murmured. 'God has given it a special magic. I could stay here for ever.'

'Well, you can't, Mary's waiting for the bilberries!' Leonora laughed quietly but made no attempt to move. She too wanted to hold the moment.

Suddenly John stood back.

'Hide and seek!' he said. 'I'll count to fifty – you hide, one, two, three, four...'

Leonora leapt lightly from the rock and running across the moor, quickly found a place to hide in a small grassy hollow just below the moorland track. She was out of breath and was sure that her gasps would reveal her hiding place, but soon it was clear the John was searching in the opposite direction.

139

Leonora lay back and watched the small white patches of cloud drifting across the blue sky. The ground beneath her was warm and soft. There was no breeze, and although the evening shadows were lengthening there was still heat in the sun's rays. Leonora could smell the fragrance of the heather and somewhere a lapwing was calling, 'p-wit, p-wit, pee-wit, pee-wit...'

John was laughing. 'There you are, sleepy head!'

Leonora opened her eyes to see him silhouetted against the sky.

'I must have drifted off...'

She raised her arms above her head in a sleepy stretch but made no attempt to get up. Gazing down at her, John thought he had never seen her looking so lovely. Her face was flushed with warmth and her sleepy brown eyes were deep, fathomless pools. Strands of her tousled, black hair fell across her cheek, and as she stretched her whole body seemed to ripple before melting back onto the soft blanket of earth. Quietly John lay down beside her in the hollow, and propping himself on one elbow he leant across, kissing her lightly on the forehead.

'Did I ever tell you, Miss Ferrari, that you are a very beautiful woman?'

He didn't wait for a reply but moved closer and kissed her lips, very gently at first and then more urgently as she kissed him back. Leonora's arms came round his neck and John felt her tremble slightly as their bodies touched. Their lips parted and their kisses were hot and sweet, ever more insistent. Breathless in their anticipation they moved together, and swooping Leonora from the ground John pulled her on top of him and then, as quickly, rolled her over until he lay on top of her kissing her again. He kissed her cheeks, her eyes, her nose, her mouth. She didn't stop him when his hand moved down over her body, lingering a moment as he felt the soft curve of her breast beneath his fingers and then sweeping on past her tiny waist. He felt her tremble again at the pressure of his hand on her hips – it was at that moment that they heard the approaching footsteps and the heavy, laboured breath.

Horrified, they lay perfectly still, hardly daring to breathe. They had seen no one on the moors but knew that they were about to be discovered, and in dread they both turned their eyes to the spot where the track passed the hollow where they

140

were concealed. The footsteps halted momentarily and then resumed, and the young couple had no time for escape. Leonora's cheeks were already burning when an old sheep peered over the heather and gazed down at them, nonchalantly chewing grass. John and Leonora fell into fits of hysterical laughter. What happy, sweet relief! And what a joke – to have been fooled by an old ram! Their laughter hid the disappointment for what might have been, but their mood had changed, and the moment had passed, so retrieving the bowl of bilberries they wended their way off the moor and back to Laverock Hall.

Later, having safely delivered the bilberries to Mary, John and Leonora were enjoying a glass of Italian wine in the drawing room and were laughing again at the memory of that moorland visitor.

'I really thought we were to be found out,'

Leonora got another fit of the giggles as she remembered the horned face appearing above them.

'Silly old ram, frightening us like that!'

Bright-eyed with laughter, she refilled their glasses.

'I really am the luckiest man alive,' thought John. 'To be here, in this lovely old house, with the girl of my dreams is more than I could have dared to wish for.' He wasn't accustomed to such sumptuous surroundings. Compared with the cottage, the furnishings at Laverock were very splendid. He liked the Italian furniture and style of decoration, and felt privileged to be there. Today his, already strong love for Leonora had deepened, and he was now more sure than ever that this was the woman with whom he wanted to spend the rest of his life.

Leonora was still chattering.

'I wonder how Mamma and Papa are getting on in Italy. I expect they are catching up with all their old friends and will have lots to tell us when they come home. I wonder if they will see an opera whilst they are away. Oh I'm sure they will, they will not miss visiting La Scala – it was always a favourite with them. They'll probably bring home new furnishings when they come back and...'

'Leonora,' John interrupted her suddenly, 'I don't want to talk about your parents. I'm sure they're having a wonderful time, but I need to talk about us – about our future.' He spoke

141

quietly, but Leonora was silenced by the intensity in his voice. John looked long at her before he continued.

'I love you, Leonora, and I want us to be married. Darling, will you be my wife?'

Leonora needed no time to think. She ran to John and threw her arms around him.

'Oh, John, there is nothing I would like more. Yes! Yes, I'll marry you – of course I'll marry you!'

Lifting Leonora's feet from the floor and whirling her around ecstatically, the serious expression left John's face and he grinned broadly.

'You've made me the happiest man alive.'

He set her down again and kissed her long and passionately. At last they parted and John led a radiant Leonora to the sofa and seated himself, facing her. His face had once again taken on a slightly worried expression, and she wondered whatever could be wrong.

'It won't be easy, Leonora. As yet I have little to offer you. A horse and gig and fifty pounds in the bank is not enough to persuade your father to give me your hand. I have no property of my own, the cottage belongs to Mr Turner, but in a year's time I hope to be able to buy a house and then I can approach your parents...'

'John, I don't care about the money, and I'll be happy to live in the little cottage at Sladen.'

Leonora didn't want anything to mar the joy she was feeling, and she refused to even consider that John might be right.

'Papa will give his consent. Oh, he's sure to agree – he always says he only wants me to be happy!'

'I think this time he will not agree.'

John was equally sure that Mr and Mrs Ferrari would never allow their daughter to marry him unless he could make something of himself and offer her a lifestyle more like that to which she was accustomed.

'We must be patient, Leonora. I love you so very, very much, and I will do whatever is necessary to win your father over.'

Leonora waved aside all John's objections. What point was there to thinking up reasons why her father would object to the marriage? There must be as many reasons why he would agree. In any case, he was in Milan now. It would all have to wait until he came back. She didn't want anything to spoil her happiness.

Leonora rose. 'Don't let's talk about it anymore now, John, come with me.'

She was smiling and holding out her hand. John followed her from the drawing room and up the broad stairway. Neither of them spoke, but as she stepped lightly ahead of him John's heart skipped a beat and his pulse began to race. He was very conscious of the scent of her hair and the soft radiance of her skin so near to his. They reached the upper landing and Leonora paused before one of the doors, half-turning to John.

'This is my bedroom,' she said, with a smile and added as she quietly closed the door behind them, 'we won't be disturbed, there are no sheep in here!'

18

The wages had been counted and checked, and as the cashier handed him the bags John breathed a sigh of relief that the morning's business was concluded and he could return to the mill. The cashier, who had seen the expression on Mr Beale's face when he left the premises a few minutes earlier, was well aware that trouble had been brewing in the office, and gave a sympathetic half-smile.

'See you next week, sir.'

'Yes, see you next week. Good-day.'

John had come to Haworth as usual on this Friday morning in August to pay into the bank all the cheques and receipts from the week's transactions at the mill and to draw the workers' wages. The cashier had been busy when he arrived, so John had decided to go through to the manager's office and speak with Oscar Beale, as he had been used to doing when Jonas Fisher was in charge. He had one or two small banking matters to discuss, but besides this he knew that he and Mr Beale had got off to a rather bad start, and he hoped that he might be able to remedy the situation and put an end to the animosity which had sprung up between them. He saw no reason to quarrel, and besides, he mused, it was always useful to have a bank manager that one could count on as a friend. On seconds thoughts John decided that friendship was probably not possible, or even desirable, with someone like Oscar Beale. He didn't like the man, but that didn't mean that they had to be uncivil, and someone had to wave the olive branch.

The bank manager had received him courteously enough, and the banking matters had been discussed and dealt with swiftly and efficiently. When Oscar Beale rose, intimating that the meeting was over, John had pretended not to notice, and settling himself in his chair he had tried talking generally of things that were happening in the village and down the Worth Valley. The conversation was strained. Oscar was not making it easy for John; it was clear that he had no intention of being on friendly terms with the 'Mill Messenger', as he had once scathingly called him, and it seemed that John would be unable to draw him into discussion. At a final attempt, John turned the conversation to cricket.

'It looks as though it will be our two teams in the final for the cup. We're through, and your match against Oakworth tomorrow is almost a sure win for you. There's not much opposition apart from Albert Hardacre, and perhaps a bit of a run from Ernest Peacock.'

'We're quite capable of dealing with the Peacock boy,' said Oscar Beale frostily. 'I'm sure it will be a good match, but we'll have no difficulty putting them out of the cup.'

Oscar leaned forward and his lip curled slightly as he sneered.

'At least Oakworth play *clean*.'

John bristled, but managed to hide his annoyance.

'What do you mean, Mr Beale?' he asked lightly. 'Have you had some trouble in your other matches?'

'You know full well what I'm talking about!'

Oscar gripped the edge of his desk in an effort to control the anger rising in him. He flushed slightly, and glaring at John he spoke through gritted teeth.

'Paul Ryan's bowling. That's what I mean. He should be banned.'

John was amused to see how aggrieved the bank manager had been over a lost cricket match. He smiled as if he hadn't noticed the other's ill humour.

'Why is that, because he's too fast for you?'

'He's dangerous, that's why,' Oscar snapped. 'Dangerous and careless. Someone will be injured if he's not stopped. I'm going to see to it that he's banned!'

Oscar Beale was now red in the face and struggling to keep his composure. John thought it was all rather ridiculous and could not resist needling him some more.

'Paul's a good bowler and a highly regarded cricketer. Perhaps you should go down in the batting order and let someone open who has a keener eye – someone who can play the ball and is not afraid to face a fast bowler,' he suggested.

This had the desired effect. Oscar was suffused with rage and banged his fist down hard as he hissed, 'I'm not afraid. I would not want another of my team to face that maniac's first over. He should be banned, I tell you. Everyone should stick to the normal underarm bowling and keep the sport safe.'

'Maybe you'd like to play with a soft children's ball as well!'

John's sarcasm was too much for Oscar, who looked as if he would explode. Leaping up, he banged his fist down on the desk with such force that John's bag fell over and the contents, cheques, papers and receipts, spilled out over the floor. The sight of all the strewn papers brought Oscar Beale up short, his temper left him, but in its place a cold anger settled. Anger at himself for having shown a weakness; anger still at the memory of his defeat by Paul Ryan's bowling, but most of all anger at John Pickles who had revelled in that defeat and had come here, to his bank, and made fun of him! He would get even. He didn't know how, but one day, he would get even with this 'Mill Messenger'. Without another word and without even glancing in John's direction, he walked out of the office.

Left to retrieve his papers, John knew that he had wasted his time coming to see Oscar Beale. He had only made matters worse. There was no hope now of a congenial relationship such as he had enjoyed with Mr Fisher. He could do nothing more. With a shrug he gathered up the last of the cheques, and stuffing them into his bag he went through to the public counter and handed it to the cashier.

Affairs in Milan had been put in order far more swiftly than Vincente Ferrari had anticipated. The will had been simple and clear – Vincente himself inheriting the greatest bulk of his father's estate – with only one or two minor legacies to cousins and friends to be dealt with. He had decided to keep the house on Lake Como, with only a skeleton staff to run it for most of the year. The intention being that he, Mrs Ferrari and Leonora would go there for their summer retreat, and the option of returning there in the future was always a possibility. When these matters were settled and Mr and Mrs Ferrari had renewed

146

acquaintance with old friends, visited Milan and enjoyed a couple of performances of the opera at La Scala, Vincente saw no reason to remain longer in Italy, and their visit was cut short.

So it was that on the day of the Cricket Cup Match, the final between the Parish Church Team and West Lane Methodists, Mr and Mrs Ferrari were with their daughter, Leonora, among the throng of spectators who, in anticipation of an excellent match, had come from far and wide to watch the game. It was mid-September and a warm, Indian summer kind of day. Chairs and benches, carried out from the chapel, were already full, and other spectators had spread blankets and rugs on the grass and were settling down to watch the afternoon's sport. A marquee had been erected at the edge of the field, and the ladies were busy setting out cups and saucers on the trestle tables in readiness for serving of tea and cakes at the halfway point between the two teams' innings. There was an exciting air of expectation; the friendly rivalry which had always existed between the two teams could be felt amongst the crowd. Everyone felt sure that it would be a sensational match, but no one could have foreseen just how sensational the afternoon would turn out to be.

The Methodist team, winning the toss, decided to bat first and, as usual, Oscar Beale was their opening batsman. John had told Paul nothing of the unsettling incident at the bank, so the steely-cold determination which John saw in the bank manager's face went completely unnoticed by Paul, who walked slowly back from the crease to take his first run-up. Paul had already worked out his tactics, and the first ball he sent was fast but wide, way off target, causing Oscar Beale to smirk before retaking his position for the next ball. For the second one Paul took a fast run-up but checked his speed at the last moment and sent a perfectly straight medium ball, which Oscar had no difficulty placing deep between the fielders, giving him time to score two runs. On his third delivery Paul took a long run-up but the ball was slower still and Oscar, seeing his chance, swung hard and scored a boundary four, drawing loud cheers from the 'Methody' supporters in the crowd. Paul sent a couple more medium-paced balls which Oscar blocked competently, but from which he was unable to score. For his sixth delivery, having lulled Oscar into a false sense of confidence, Paul sent down a thunderbolt, whipping off the pitch like lightning and turning, taking out the middle stump to send the bails flying through the air.

It was with the excited cheers of the St Michael's supporters ringing in his ears that Oscar Beale walked from the pitch. What little colour he had normally had drained from his face. He was pale with anger, and once again it was a smiling John he had to pass as he crossed the field. The hatred he expressed was all too evident and, as their eyes met, John felt a shiver run down his spine. If looks could kill, thought John, I'd be a dead man. What kind of sportsmanship is this? It was Paul who conned him and for whose bowling skills he has no answer, but all his wrath seems directed at me.

Fred Hobson, number three, was already coming out to bat so John hurried back to face the wicket, trying to forget the malignancy on Oscar Beale's face. Paul switched into top gear after dismissing Oscar, and with Harold Bottomley and Sydney Ratcliffe, who were both good bowlers, they had the Methodist team all out for a total of 124 runs.

The teas were served a little earlier than expected, and Paul received much praise from the team's followers for his part in the innings. One of the mill workers came up and slapped him heartily on the back.

'Y'er a champion bowler, lad. I've nivver seen aught like that 'n 'at copped t'bank manager.'

'Yes, yes, excellent bowling, well done!' A tall gentleman in a smart suit and bowler hat, whom Paul recognised as one of the wealthier wool merchants, added his rather more restrained, but nonetheless sincere, praise.

Everyone was eager to compliment the team, Paul in particular. Even the 'Methody' team supporters were full of admiration for him, but they were careful to add a warning for the second innings.

'Good bowling, lad, but we've some good lads of our own so you'll have your work cut out after t'break.'

Joining Leonora and her parents in the refreshment tent, John was pleased to see that Paul was the centre of attention and receiving due praise, but he wondered how Oscar Beale would be taking it, and found himself searching the sea of

148

heads for sight of that pale gingery hair. Surprisingly Oscar wasn't in the marquee and, wanting to satisfy his curiosity, John excused himself and went outside and scanned the spectators in the field. There was no sign of Oscar Beale; he was nowhere to be seen. Surely he can't have gone home and walked out on his team? He knew how humiliated and angry Oscar had been the last time Paul bowled him out – John would not forget the absurd scene in the bank's office in a hurry – but surely he wasn't such a poor loser that he would slink off without completing the match? Puzzled, John went back into the tea tent to join Leonora for the rest of the interval.

When the spectators returned to their seats and the teams reassembled on the pitch for the second innings there was still no sign of Oscar Beale, and the reserve man had taken his place on the outfield. John was batting first. He was on great form, and as he notched up the runs the spectators cheered ever louder. He played to the crowds, placing the ball wherever he wanted it to go. His hard-hitting stroke sent many balls to the boundary, scoring four runs each time. When the 'Methody' tried a change of bowler he found that he could swing out at this chap's deliveries, and three times in succession, he hit the ball clean over the boundary line. Three sixes! The crowd went wild, cheering and shouting their support. Leonora, proud of his popularity with the crowd, flushed with admiration of him.

'Isn't he wonderful, Papa? Isn't he just the best cricketer you've ever seen?'

Mr Ferrari laughed at his daughter's excitement, but he too was impressed by John's batting. It certainly was a fine display. Mrs Ferrari didn't take too much interest in cricket, and had agreed to come to the match only because it was such a lovely afternoon and she could enjoy sitting in the sun with the two people who, in all the world, were most precious to her, but even she was caught up in the excitement when, after one and a half hours, John scored his century. A great roar broke from the crowd, and some local lads ran onto the pitch and hoisted John shoulder-high. They carried him between the wickets shouting, 'Three cheers for John Pickles, hip-hip-hooray! St Michael's for the Cup!'

It was some minutes before the umpire could clear the pitch

and restore order to continue the match. Only a couple more balls had been played when there was a new commotion near the gate. Two burly policemen, a sergeant and a constable, walked onto the pitch. Ignoring the shouts from the spectators that this was 'The Cup Match', and also ignoring the ball which came perilously close to the constable's ear, they marched straight up to the umpire, who had no alternative but to stop play.

Leonora, watching from the sidelines was, like everyone else, interested to know what the trouble was. The sergeant appeared to be asking the umpire something, and the poor fellow kept shaking his head and making a broad sweep with his arms as if to tell the policeman that an important match was in progress. The sergeant, putting his thumbs under his lapels, drew himself up to his full height, and under his intimidating stare the umpire pointed down the wicket to John Pickles. As the policemen approached John the crowd fell silent, waiting to see what would happen. John greeted the officers with a smile, but Leonora was alarmed to see that the smile soon disappeared as he listened to whatever it was that the sergeant had to say. The men were deep in conversation for a few minutes and then, to everyone's astonishment and to Leonora's horror, the constable took out a pair of handcuffs, and snapping them over John's wrists led the young man across the cricket pitch towards West Lane.

No one could believe what they were seeing, least of all Leonora and Paul, who were deeply concerned about John's plight.

'Don't worry,' he told them as he was marched away. 'It's all a big misunderstanding. I'm sure it will be sorted out in no time.'

John smiled brightly in an attempt to hide his anxiety from Leonora, but he was badly shaken, for although he was certain that the matter would soon be cleared up it was not at all a pleasant experience to be handcuffed and taken into custody in front of 2000 amazed onlookers.

As they neared the field gate John caught sight of Oscar Beale on the edge of the crowd. He was no longer dressed for cricket, but was wearing a suit and had on a bowler hat, which he mockingly raised ever so slightly as their eyes met. The

150

expression on his face would stay in John's mind for a long time to come. He looked smug and self-satisfied, and a cold shiver went through John when the absurd thought struck him that Oscar Beale was actually enjoying his downfall.

When the police had departed with their charge it took the umpire quite some time to restore order and get the cricket match under way again, and even then no one's heart was in it any more, for everyone was agog with the mystery of the arrest. The final score of 217, securing the cup for the Church team, seemed a hollow victory without their star player to share the triumph, and there was no jubilation and not much celebration. There was, however, a buzz of excitement amongst the home-ward-bound spectators, but it was conjecture as to the downfall of John Pickles that filled their thoughts and not the defeat or victory of their favoured team.

Speculation was rife, and many theories were put forward regarding John, who now became 't'Liverpool orphanage lad', or 'that upstart' and even 't' off-cumdun', for although after ten years John and Paul were usually regarded as local lads, their 'foreign' roots were now quickly pointed out in the light of a possible misdemeanour. When gathered in crowds, people are fickle and easily swayed and always seem to want to believe the very worst thing that they hear. By the time the last stragglers had left the field John had become in turn a smuggler of con-traband, an arsonist, a cat-burglar and even a murderer – though no one could produce a body or other evidence of wrongdoing to support any one of the many theories.

Vincente Ferrari was, of course, unable to provide answers to his daughter's frantic questions. He, like everyone else, was com-pletely in the dark regarding the arrest. He was already think-ing that he had been wrong to encourage Leonora's friendship with John, and wished to distance the family from him.

'We shall know soon enough, Leonora. Whatever it is, it has nothing to do with us. It is not our problem. Don't worry your-self about it.'

Very soon everyone knew what it was all about, for two days later the local paper ran bold headlines:

'WELL KNOWN LOCAL SPORTSMAN ARRESTED ON SUSPICION OF MISAPPROPRIATION OF MILL FINANCES'

151

The local people were quick to quote the old adage 'There's no smoke without fire'. In most folks' minds John Pickles was already guilty.

19

'The Lord is my Shepherd, I shall not want.'

It is at the suggestion of my good friend, Harold, that I begin this diary. I have been here now for almost three months, and it has been the very worst time of my life. Indeed I have known the depths of despair, frustration and anger and have at times wondered if I would keep my sanity, cooped up here knowing that I am free of any blame and having no way to prove my innocence. Harold has shown me the way to survive. He has proved to be a true friend and my only real help. I cannot hope to tell in detail the events leading up to my incarceration and all that has happened since, and I do not wish to dwell on it too much, but I will set down a brief record of what has passed.

I was arrested on the afternoon of September 18th 1841 in front of a huge crowd of spectators during the cricket cup tie. I was shocked and embarrassed, but because I knew that I had done no wrong a part of me also found it quite amusing. I was so sure that I would be back to finish the match just as soon as I'd had time to sort everything out. This was not to be.

A discrepancy of £2000 in the mill accounts had been brought to the notice of the police, and after a short appearance at Keighley Magistrates' Court, where I was charged with theft, the case was referred to the Bradford Assize Court. Of course I pleaded 'not guilty'. Mr Fisher spoke at length on my behalf and Mr Turner travelled down from Buckden to give a character reference for me, but it was all to no avail. The prosecution had a tight case against me, for I alone had dealt with transactions at the mill and there was clear evidence of a payment by a Leeds tailor in the sum of £2000, but no proof of this having been paid into the bank. I was completely baffled, for I had always been careful to keep all charges and cash in the office safe until paying them into the bank each Friday, and had no idea how this money could have gone missing.

Oscar Beale brought the bank's ledgers for examination by the court (and I would swear that he enjoyed the situation). On taking the witness stand he said that he could understand why I might have taken the money, as I was an orphan who aspired to a way of life above his station! I was incensed, and even though the judge ruled this 'inadmissible conjecture' the damage was done and I knew my fate was sealed. I felt helpless and frustrated. My cry of 'Not guilty! I'm not guilty!' fell on deaf ears and the judge's words sent a chill down my spine.

'John Pickles, you were placed in a position of trust by your employer and you abused that trust. I find you guilty of deception and theft, and hereby sentence you to be detained in Her Majesty's Prison at Leeds for five years.'

It felt like a life sentence, and during my first weeks here I was so low and so angry that I made no friends and fellow prisoners gave me a wide berth to avoid my bitter tongue. My first sight of the bare cell which was to be my home for the next five years filled me with despair. A wooden board and a sack filled with straw serves as my bed. A blanket, chair and slopping-out bucket complete the furnishings, and the only window, set high in the wall, is filled with strong metal bars. That first night was the hardest. A dreadful feeling of isolation engulfed me as the heavy metal door clanged shut. I could not sleep and I spent long hours standing on the chair with my face pressed against the barred window hoping for a view of familiar stars, but the night was black and overcast and offered me no hope.

The next morning, my own clothes having been confiscated, I donned the prison uniform and joined rows of similarly clad prisoners from all four blocks of the prison, A–D. I was marched off, with six rough-looking customers, to the boot repair shop where we were each issued with a leather apron, shoemaker's needle and thread and a sharp knife, all of which had to be returned at the end of the shift. The warden, a burly, unsavoury character, gave us brief instructions on boot repair

154

and told us to be economical with the leather, sneering as he added 'any waste and you'll have me to answer to.' We were left in no doubt that if we didn't comply, the consequences would not be pleasant.

It is the most loathsome place. The stench from the pile of dirty, sweaty boots turned my stomach, and I made no secret of the fact that as an innocent victim of the judicial system I considered myself above the low-life and scum incarcerated here and was determined to keep my distance. The prisoner sitting next to me at the bench, a small, bald-headed man with bowed legs and broken teeth, between which an empty clay pipe was permanently wedged (and whom I later came to know as Harold), tried to warn me of my folly.

'Keep your counsel, lad,' he muttered. 'Remember t'old sayin' "Hear all, see all, say nowt." Just do a good job and you'll get by.'

But I would not listen. I didn't do my share of the work for I could not see the point of slaving over other men's boots and trying to keep up to the expected output of ten pairs per day. I scoffed at the other prisoners' labours, and before the week was out I was nicknamed Snooty and had had my eyes blackened when the warden's back was turned. Come Saturday, when everyone else was enjoying the only recreation time of the week and receiving visitors, I was back in the sweaty repair shop making up my quota. It did nothing to endear me to the warden, who also lost precious leisure time. I learnt the hard way!

Over the next couple of months, although I now worked as hard as any man, my anger and frustration grew deeper, and my intolerance of the others was plain to see. Had it not been for my neighbour in the repair shop there would have been some ugly incidents. He had a knack of calming the waves when my arrogance riled another prisoner, and I am now ashamed to remember how, on more than one occasion when he had intervened, I snarled at him, 'I can do without your help.'

It was after one such incident, when I had been particularly disdainful refusing to share a good piece of leather and Harold had defused the situation, that he had cornered me later and quite uncharacteristically, for he is always such a mild-tempered man, gave me a piece of his mind.

'Who do you think you are, John Pickles? You're no better than t'rest of us. We are what we are, and whether you like it or not we're all in this together. T'sooner you get off yer 'igh 'orse and walk wi' t' rest of us the better. You're full o' self-pity and self-righteousness, and we're all about fed up o' your airs and graces!'

I was furious, and if Harold hadn't walked away smartly I would have hit him.

Back in my cell I was seething with frustration. As always during the long nights, memories of my life came flooding back to me. I thought of the young boy in the orphanage in Liverpool and wondered, as I had done then, about the parents I had never known and what circumstances led to their abandonment of me. I thought of Paul and Albert; the three of us playing in the river, birds-nesting and catching rabbits and later looking at the club behind the Black Bull Inn. Happy days! I remembered, as if it were yesterday, the day we had arrived at the mill... 'John Pickles, sir, ten years old.' My thoughts turned to Seth and Mary Ann, who had been like father and mother to the three of us. Always helpful and encouraging, and I thought of Albert now in Haworth churchyard, six feet under and hidden from the sun for ever. It brought my five years into new perspective, and I suddenly found hot tears coursing down my cheeks but I was unsure then and I don't know now whether the tears were for Albert or myself.

My anger subsided, but I was filled with remorse and self-pity. I hated what I had become, but I was full of despair at the long years stretching ahead of me. I closed my eyes and immediately saw a pair of bewitching black eyes dancing in front of me ... so close, so close. Leonora! What of Leonora? Seldom from my thoughts, she pulls at my heart strings and I long to see her, touch her, kiss her. I remember every detail of our time together last summer. Wonderful, heady days when the world was at our feet. Yet I have no word from her, and I am torn apart with the agony of not knowing. Will she wait for me? Five years is such a long time, and sometimes I tell myself it is unfair to expect it, and I want her to be happy and live her life now but the next moment I am certain she will wait and I know that I cannot live without her. Why does she not come? Does she believe in me? Surely she can't think I stole the money? Does she still love me? Oh Leonora!

With a deep sigh I opened my eyes to dispel the image and, as had become my habit, I took the chair to the window, and climbing onto it I prayed for sight of something new – anything to bring a ray of hope to my despondent soul. As usual all I saw was mud below and a heavy grey sky above. It was then that Harold's words came back to me.

'We're in this together ... walk wi' t' rest of us.'

I realized then how badly I had behaved, and I knew that I must do something about it, but I also knew how hard that would be with all the anger turning inside me. I thought of Harold, always so calm and pleasant. He was amiable with everyone, even me, who had rejected all attempts at friendship. I saw that Harold could somehow rise above any situation. The prison life didn't appear to get him down, for he worked cheerfully and could always turn a problem into a laugh and joke. I decided then to eat humble pie, apologize to Harold for my bad behaviour and ask him for the secret of his contentment. This is what I later found out about Harold.

At the age of 45 he is the father of six children and worries that his wife and eldest boy will not be able to support the others whilst he is in prison. He is sad that he doesn't see his wife, who cannot afford to travel to Armley to visit him. By trade Harold is a blacksmith, but business has been slack for some time and, desperate to feed his family, he had resorted to sheep stealing. It was on one such night mission that he was caught and sent down for two years, fourteen months of which he still has to serve. Despite everything he is always ready for a laugh and a joke, and never gets downhearted. He is respected by the prison wardens and the other convicts alike, and from what he told me, the secret of his fortitude seems to be faith! I was amazed at the strength of Harold's belief and at the way this uneducated man described it to me. I will write it in Harold's own words, for I cannot do better.

'I repeat the Lord's Prayer every night before I go to sleep, and each time I think anew on the clause about pardon: "forgive us our debts as we forgive our debtors". You must let go of the hate, John, for if you hold a grudge it will fester in you and block God out. Pray from the heart for your own forgiveness and for help to overcome the bitterness you feel toward others. St Michael of All Angels will protect you. He is the

157

greatest angel and understands all wrongs. If you pray to him he will help you, for he is the leader of the struggle against the powers of evil and darkness. God can carry us through any trials if we really want him to – and ask him. I have some paper in my cell and I cross off the days each week until Sunday, and then I write down something good that has happened and follow this by a verse of the 23rd Psalm. You know the one: "The Lord is My Shepherd". I find it really helps. You could give it a go.'

I thought Harold had finished but, with a twinkle in his eye, he added, 'I knew you'd come to your senses before long – I've been praying for just that!'

So here I am writing a diary of my own. I don't quite know what to make of Harold's conception of St Michael of All Angels, but I decided that it won't hurt to try this praying thing. I'm not sure that I am rid of all the anger yet, but I am certainly feeling more positive and more able to face each day. Last night the sky above my window was bright with stars – all shining out new hope for the future.

20

Ponden Hall, February, 1842

The music had been delightful. The small orchestra of local musicians, conducted by the host Mr Heaton, had excelled themselves, and their rendition of the Mozart sonata had been especially well accepted by the assembled company. The monthly soirées at Ponden Hall had become very popular with the invited guests, and on this particular evening, February 3rd 1842, about 20 people had braved the winter weather to attend. These included Vincente and Mrs Ferrari and Leonora, Mr and Mrs Jonas Fisher, Stanley Greenwood, who owned a small mill in Oxenhope, accompanied by his wife and his daughter, Molly, Oscar Beale, Ruth and Robert Butterworth, and Charlotte Brontë with her father Patrick Brontë (now in his mid-sixties the old incumbent was becoming rather reclusive, but his daughter had been eager to hear the music and Ann having returned to the governess post in York, and Emily, as always, shunning society gatherings of any kind, Charlotte had finally persuaded her father that the evening would be to his liking). Also in the party were Paul Ryan, William Weightman, curate of Haworth, and of course several members of the Heaton family.

Paul had arrived quite late with just enough time to take a seat next to the two young Heaton boys at the back of the room, before the music began. From this vantage point he had plenty of time, as he listened to the music, to digest the scene of all the familiar people gathered there. Robert and Ruth Butterworth were the picture of happiness; he proud, she radiant. Their first child was expected in about eight weeks time, and they were obviously overjoyed at the prospect. Married life seemed to be good for them. Jonas Fisher looked frail and

159

much older than Paul remembered him. His wife sat straight-backed and had a protective air. She laid her hand on Jonas' arm where it remained all evening as if to reassure him that no more harm would befall him whilst she was present.

Mr and Mrs Greenwood listened attentively and looked just a little uncomfortable. Paul suspected that this was a new experience for them. He had not seen them on previous visits to Ponden, and he doubted very much that they would host parties such as this at Old Oxenhope House. Seated next to her mother, Molly Greenwood sat perfectly still, wrapped up in the strains of the music. Paul had seen Molly on several occasions but had never been introduced. Despite looking only at the back of her head, he could picture her open, friendly face with its rosy cheeks and smiling eyes. Paul felt a quickening of his pulse and a slight nervousness as he resolved to speak with her during the evening.

On the front row were Leonora and her parents. Seeing them brought thoughts of John, and a sadness swept over Paul. He missed John more than he could ever have imagined, and it was always the unexpected things which reminded him of his friend. He wished with all his heart that John could have been there that evening. They had been like brothers, had fought, laughed and cried together, and it was one of the blackest days of Paul's life when he listened to the judge's sentence. Paul was suddenly jerked out of his reverie when he saw who was sitting next to Leonora. It was Oscar Beale! A sick feeling began in the pit of Paul's stomach and gradually grew as he continued to stare at the bank manager. What is that smarmy fellow doing with the Ferraris, he thought. He's worming his way into every niche in society. Paul's dislike for Oscar Beale deepened every time they met. Although Oscar was clever enough never to do or say anything that openly gave grounds for offence, Paul was sure that his politeness and ingratiating charm masked an underlying devious character. He didn't trust Oscar Beale an inch.

As the music finished and appreciative applause reverberated round the panelled room, Oscar turned to Leonora with some remark. Paul could not quite put his finger on what it was that alarmed him, but a sudden chill went up his spine and filled him with foreboding. Whilst refreshments were being served there was much praise for the musicians and discussion about the

160

pieces they had played, but gradually conversation turned to other topics and quite a large group of people gathered round.

Paul didn't join the group, as he was hoping to speak with Molly just as soon as an opportunity presented itself. He was joined by Mr Fisher.

'I'm glad to see you, Paul. I only wish young John were here too. Sorry business that. He's a good lad and I'm still sure he had nothing to do with that missing money, but I can't figure out what did happen to it. I'm off to Leeds this week to see him and wondered if you'd like to come too? I know he'd be pleased for you to visit him.'

They arranged to meet for the 11 a.m. train from Keighley to Leeds, which would give them plenty of time to make it to Armley for 2.00 p.m.

'What do you make of that Beale chap, Paul? Have you had much dealings with him?' Mr Fisher kept his voice low and Paul answered likewise.

'Only at cricket. I'm not often at the bank so I see little of him in the winter time but, between you and me, I don't like him. He's a poor loser at cricket, and besides, there's something underhand about him.'

Mr Fisher nodded, 'Much my own thoughts. He's too big for his own boots. Some of my old customers at the bank are complaining; he's really put their backs up with his superior attitude, and if he's not careful they'll be looking to taking their business elsewhere.'

They were interrupted by Leonora, who had only just caught sight of him.

'Paul! Oh Paul, I didn't know you were here. How good to see you.'

She came swiftly across the room, glancing over her shoulder to make certain that she wasn't followed, and as soon as she was near enough she asked quietly, 'Have you news of John? How is he? Have you seen him?'

Paul was shocked by Leonora's appearance. She smiled a greeting, but gone was the vibrant girl who had cheered them on through last season's cricket matches. Her features were tense and strained and her eyes, once so bright and sparkling, were dull and lifeless. He wished fervently that he had some news for her, some words of comfort.

'He's allowed visitors now, and Mr Fisher and I are planning to go to Armley this Saturday. Come with us, Leonora, see him for yourself.'

The smile faded and a frown furrowed Leonora's brow. Mr Fisher felt sorry for her and reinforced Paul's invitation.

'You're more than welcome to make the journey with us, Leonora, Paul will tell you the arrangements.'

He could see her discomfort and tactfully excused himself and left the young people together.

Leonora took Paul's arm and led him into a window recess where they were less likely to be overheard.

'I cannot come, Paul. Father says John is a no-good, swindling thief, and has forbidden any mention of his name at Laverock Hall.'

Her lips trembled slightly and tears filled her eyes.

'Papa would never allow me to visit John in prison.'

Leonora turned towards the window, hoping that Paul would not see her tears, and as she did so a thin branch of rose bush blew against the window-pane, scraping the glass. Without really thinking what she did, Leonora opened the window, letting in a cold blast of air. She was astonished to see a single red rose clinging to the stem. Despite the cold this late flower had blossomed, and its deep red petals filled Leonora with a moment of hope. Quickly she plucked the rose and closed the window. Sobbing slightly, she handed the rose to Paul and whispered.

'Take it to John. Tell him I love him with all my heart and he is in my thoughts every day. I hope the rose will remind him of me.'

Paul watched as Leonora rejoined her parents and Oscar Beale. His earlier fears dissolved, and he would tell John how much Leonora loved him. With a lighter heart he crossed the room and, responding to the extra beating of his own heart, made himself known to Molly Greenwood.

21

Armley Jail

February 7th 1842

Paul and Mr Fisher came today. How good to see them, but how it makes me wish that I were free. The assault at the bank has made an old man of Jonas, but he assures me he is in good health. They brought me news of all my friends, many seen quite recently at the Heatons, and reassurance that my horse, Casson, is well cared for. Most of all I have been longing for news of Leonora. She is well. She loves me! Paul said he was to tell me that she loves me dearly and I am ever in her thoughts. Oh Leonora. So too are you in mine! I have a rose. One deep, red rose which Leonora sent. I am holding it now as I write, and when I am done I'll put it in some water. Leonora, thank you. The rose is beautiful, but why did you not come?

February 10th 1842

Another day with stinking, rotten boots. How will I endure five years of this place? Even thoughts of Leonora cannot lift my spirits. I pressed the rose she sent between scraps of stiff leather which I took from the repair shop when Beefy wasn't looking. I didn't want to watch it wilt! It is under the mattress, and knowing it is there brings Leonora closer. Harold says I must stay cheerful and remember the Lord's Prayer, and all he told me. I have lost my faith. It is not easy to believe, in a god-less place like this!

February 16th 1842

I've been taken out of the boot shop! For two days I've been marking out the foundations of a new prison chapel. I can't believe my luck. The fresh air smells very sweet after all that old leather! Yesterday morning the Governor came with a Mr Calvert and, although I don't know why, I was the one singled out to help him. The construction plans are in a site hut in the exercise yard and are quite impressive. Mr Calvert seems to be a good man to work for, and he gave me clean instructions for holding the tape and accurately measuring and pegging the lines of the proposed building. It's been cold work, but it's surprising what a few hours of bright sunshine can do for a man's spirit.

February 20th 1842

I am to remain on the building site a little while longer and help with the digging for the foundations. Thank God! It was bitterly cold today and there was no sun, but the hard work kept me warm and my heart is lighter than at any time since my arrival here.

February 21st 1842

The foundations are completed and I fully expected to be returned to the boot shop today, but somehow Mr Calvert has managed to arrange for me to continue to work with him on the building of the church. He's been pleased with my efforts, and despite my being a prisoner we have developed a good relationship.

We are having problems working the stone. It is very difficult to square the stones to fit together, as the chisel tips are too soft for the hard Yorkshire grit. I've been thinking that, with all his years as a blacksmith, Harold will have the experience to temper and harden the metal to get the results we need. I'll suggest to Mr Calvert that he is the man for the job and get Harold out of the workshop too!

Still no word from Leonora. During the day the hard work keeps my thoughts in check, but at night there is no rein. My head is full of Leonora. Her smile, her sparkling eyes, her laughter, the scent of her hair, the sway of her hips, her touch. Why does she not come?

February 28th 1842

Harold has been with us this past seven days now, and work is progressing much more quickly with the sharper tools. The building is beginning to take shape, and in the process I am learning a great deal. It is good to be alongside my friend again, and the days are passing quite agreeably.

Today the Governor and his wife came to see what progress has been made with the building work. They are very excited about the chapel project and took a keen interest in the construction and materials used. The Governor's wife has a good eye and has made one or two constructive suggestions, regarding the outside appearance of the church, which are to be incorporated in the building.

I never expected to enjoy my time in prison, but now I get up with renewed energy and an eagerness for the work waiting to be done. Harold says 'God moves in mysterious ways.'

March 1st 1842

It is snowing quite heavily. I hope it doesn't stick as Mr Calvert expects we should be ready for the roof to go on the chapel in about ten weeks time, and a heavy fall of snow will set us back. The last snows lay on the ground for almost a week, and everything ground to a halt. (The worst part was spending four days back in the boot shop. UGH!) Still, I've heard that there has been much worse weather further north, so perhaps we've been lucky in Leeds.

* * *

The evening at Laverock Hall had been quite a success after all. The Bradford wool merchant, Samuel Ickringill, and his wife, Dorothy, had turned out to be much livelier company than anyone expected. Samuel related many stories from the early days of his business, when he built it up from small beginnings to the successful enterprise he now enjoyed. He loved the cut and thrust of the trade, bartering for the best price for his cloth, and managing to undercut his competitors just when it mattered and coin in huge profits whilst others struggled to find a niche in the market. Since he dealt mainly in stuffs and worsteds rather than the fine wool which Vincente Ferrari exported, they had never been rivals for trade and had formed a good friendship as they prospered alongside each other. Dorothy Ickringill liked nothing better than to listen to her husband's reminiscences, and she glowed with pride as everyone laughed over yet another of his anecdotes of yesteryear. Chuckling, their host reached for the decanter.

'Another glass of wine, Samuel?' Vincente had heard most of the stories before, but always enjoyed his friend's company and never tired of listening to him. He himself had grown up with the security of family wealth and had never experienced the struggles which Samuel had had to firmly establish his business. Vincente had wondered if his wife and daughter might be a trifle bored by all the wool-trade tales, but he needn't have worried for they had laughed as much as he had. It was good to see Leonora in a merry mood again. He was glad he had invited young Mr Beale; it was nice for Leonora to have the company of someone of her own age for a change, and perhaps she would now forget all about that scoundrel John Pickles.

'And you, Oscar, more wine?'

Oscar Beale nodded.

'Thank you, sir. It's very good wine. Italian, I presume?'

As always, Oscar was polite and deferential to Mr Ferrari, who saw no reason to suppose that he was any other than what he seemed, a charming, upright young man who was, moreover, a bank manager of some standing who had recently purchased a fine new house in Haworth and was obviously making his mark in local society.

Oscar Beale was in fact totally uninterested in the silly stories of wool merchants losing whole cartloads of their precious homespun, horses going lame and some well known bigwig getting the wrong cloth for his suit, but he had laughed along with everyone else and pretended to find the tales highly amusing. It was all so trivial and banal, and besides, how could he impress Mr and Mrs Ferrari and interest Leonora whilst this upstart was droning on? He hadn't had a chance to get a word in edgeways. The three ladies and Vincente appeared to be thoroughly entertained, but it wasn't quite what Oscar had hoped for when he had been invited to make up the numbers for this small dinner party.

He knew, even before the invitation arrived, that he was making good progress with Mr Ferrari. Oscar had made himself known to Leonora's father soon after the exhilarating day of the last cricket match. He had managed to worm his way into the Italian gentleman's company on several occasions since and had recently offered him good terms at the bank (better than he should have done for, if the truth were known, he would be in trouble with head office, but Oscar was confident that he could cover his tracks and keep the books looking good); in this way he hoped to make Mr Ferrari think highly of him and at the same time open up many more opportunities to get closer to his daughter.

He was having a rather more difficult time working his way into Leonora's affections. She was still sighing over that Pickles fellow and, despite all his efforts, Oscar felt she still barely noticed him. He had the beginnings of an idea about how to deal with this and make Leonora forget about John Pickles, but he needed time with her; time alone so they could talk without the ever-present parents. Then there would be no obstacle to his attentions, and Oscar was conceited enough to believe that with John out of the picture Leonora would readily accept his advances.

Samuel Ickringill had run out of wind and seemed to notice for the first time that Oscar Beale had been rather quiet. Thinking that he was probably shy Samuel felt guilty that he had monopolized the conversation.

'You see the other side of the trading, don't you, Mr Beale? The good and the bad; those who flourish and those who flounder. Of course you could say that to some extent you have a hand in their destiny, don't you think?'

Mr Ickringill intended only to draw Oscar into the conversa-

167

tion and meant no offence, but Oscar bristled and found it hard to conceal his annoyance.

'There is success and failure too, and I see some businesses bankrupt, yes. It is inevitable, but I don't agree that I must shoulder any responsibility. I try always to be fair and as helpful as I can be – of course taking into account the best interests of the bank, where my first priorities lie.'

Samuel Ickringill looked rather uncomfortable but had no time to reply as Vincente said quickly, 'Of course. Just so, Oscar. In fact it is because of your integrity that I have decided to follow the advice you gave me when we last met and transfer my business from the Bradford bank to your branch in Haworth. It makes sense. As you said, it would be much more convenient for me near at hand. There are just a couple of points I would like to discuss further with you.'

Leonora sighed. It looked as though this was going to turn into another dull evening after all, just when she had begun to enjoy herself. Mrs Ferrari, however, having seen her daughter smile for the first time in months, was determined this was not going to happen.

'Now, now, Vincente. No business talk, please. You promised to forget all about it for once. Why don't we all go through to the drawing room and I'll ask Mary to bring some coffee. I'd like to show Dorothy the paintings we brought back from Italy.' Mrs Ferrari turned to her guest.

'They're by a little-known artist, Alberto Guillo. He paints mainly views of the Italian lakes, but also scenes from the operas. I have a feeling he will become very popular. Come and tell me what you think, Dorothy.'

The move to the drawing room gave Oscar time to regain his composure and present his usual façade of interest.

'What is the artist's name again, Mrs Ferrari? – ah yes, I see the signature – A. Guillo – well, I must say this landscape is very pleasing. Brighter colours than those the English artists favour and very effective. Do you like it, Leonora?'

'It is my favourite lake, Lake Orto. It's smaller than many, but oh so pretty, and we spent many happy times there when I was little, and I think Guillo has captured it perfectly. The colours are vibrant and yet the overall effect is very peaceful.'

Leonora had been delighted by all six paintings her parents

had brought back from Milan, but her favourite was the scene from Purcell's opera, *Dido and Aeneas*, picturing the Queen of Carthage receiving Aeneas at her court. She showed it now to Oscar. The painting had a dreamy, ethereal quality which appealed to Leonora's romantic nature.

Oscar Beale nodded his agreement, but secretly he detested the picture, thinking it far too fanciful for his refined taste.

'I didn't know you were interested in art, Leonora. I have an invitation to a reception at Cliffe Towers on Saturday. Mr and Mrs Butterworth are showing their newly acquired artworks, and it promises to be a splendid afternoon. I wonder if you would care to accompany me? I'm sure you would enjoy seeing the paintings.'

Mrs Ferrari didn't give Leonora chance to reply.

'Oh, Mr Beale, how very kind. Of course Leonora must go. It is just what she needs. Say you'll go, Leonora; I'm sure you'll have a jolly time.'

Leonora didn't really want to accept but found it hard to disappoint her mother, whom she could see was thrilled at the prospect of something new to interest her daughter.

'It seems I have no choice, Mr Beale. Thank you very much for asking me.'

'That's decided then,' said Mrs Ferrari, looking as pleased as if she had thought up the whole idea herself.

Later, when their guests were taking their leave, both Mr and Mrs Ferrari thanked Oscar again.

'You are so kind, Mr Beale. It will be good for Leonora, a change of company and something new to think about. So kind, thank you.'

Before the carriage had rattled out of sight they had both decided that Oscar Beale was a very agreeable young man.

22

'I can see you are not impressed, Leonora. Surely there must be one painting which takes your eye?'

Oscar was feeling a little exasperated. The afternoon was going from bad to worse. Firstly, they had been delayed on the journey by a problem with the carriage wheel which had taken some time fixing. Secondly, when they finally arrived at Cliffe Towers, Ruth Butterworth had claimed Leonora for the best part of an hour, and now Leonora could not say she liked even one out of the many pictures hung here!

'They are all so heavy,' sighed Leonora. 'Those landscapes by Edward Carter are summer scenes, but they are sombre and dull and have none of the freshness and light that I admire in our Italian paintings. As for the others, all those portraits of dukes, squires and ladies – not one of them with a face worth painting – no, I don't really like any of them!'

Seeing her companion's disappointment, she added hastily, 'It's not your fault, Mr Beale. I'm grateful to you for bringing me and I've had a very pleasant afternoon. I just don't much care for the paintings here.'

'Tea is being served in the ballroom. Perhaps you'll enjoy that more – and please, not "Mr Beale", do call me Oscar.'

Leonora took the arm he offered her, and they joined the other guests as the tea and cakes were being served. Oscar led Leonora to a seat a little apart from the rest. He had something to say to her which he definitely didn't want others to overhear. He was unsure how to broach the subject of John Pickles, but was determined to find a way. In fact Leonora did it for him. The tea had been served, but she wasn't drinking it but was staring into space lost in her thoughts, and then said,

170

as if to herself, 'The last time I was here was Ruth's wedding day. I met John and we danced together all night.'

Oscar could not believe his luck, and he didn't miss the chance.

'You are better off without him, Leonora.'

When Leonora's eyes filled with tears he added in a sympathetic tone, 'I didn't mean to upset you, but there are things you don't know about John Pickles, and you would be wise to forget him.'

Leonora looked puzzled.

'What do you mean, Oscar?'

'No, I mustn't say more. It would only distress you. Just believe me, he's where he belongs.'

'Oscar, if you know something you must tell me, I want to know. I'm sure there isn't anything too bad. Not of John. Please, do tell me.'

'Well, I'm not sure. I haven't said anything before. John was well-liked and I didn't want to be the one to blacken his seemingly good character in the public eye. I'm not one to spread scandal.'

'Scandal! Whatever do you mean?'

Oscar looked around carefully to make sure no one was within earshot. He was pretty sure that Leonora would not breathe a word of what he was to tell her, after all it would seem she was the one duped and made to look a fool, but he didn't want anyone else questioning it. He was really rather proud of the story he had concocted.

'Very well, but you must know that I tell you this only because I care for you, and I don't want you to distress yourself any longer over that fellow. It is for your own good; to make you see the true nature of the man you admired. It is of rather a delicate nature, but I'm sure you'll take my meaning. There was a certain woman – no, I'll not give her name – who left the area very suddenly, and word has it that she was paid a considerable sum of money and given a ticket for the Liverpool boat to New York so that she could settle in America before anyone knew – er, hum – before anyone knew about the child. Yes, I can see you understand, Leonora. After all no one has even found any trace of the missing £2000. The police won't have been looking in America! I'll spare you more details

171

for I can see how upset you are. I shouldn't have told you. I wish now I hadn't, but you did press me so, and I really believe it will help you to come to terms with what has happened.'

Leonora could not breathe. The room was spinning and hot tears pricked her eyes. She fought very hard to stop them flooding down her cheeks as she tried to make sense of what Oscar had just told her. Surely it could not be true. Had she been wrong about John all along? Who was this other woman? No! She would not believe it! But it was strange about the money; it had been proved that it had passed through John's hands and it had not been seen since. Could he really have paid off this other woman?

The cake and the tea remained untouched on the side table, and Oscar began to wonder if he had gone too far as Leonora looked as though she might faint. Gradually the colour returned to her cheeks, and finding it hard to speak, Leonora just managed a choking whisper.

'Thank you, Oscar. You did right to tell me.'

After a few moments she spoke in a more normal voice.

'I would like to leave now. Would you be so kind as to fetch me my coat and bonnet?'

Leonora was silent on the journey back to Oldfield. Oscar knew that he had given her much to think about, and was careful not to be too cheerful. He appeared to be concerned and understanding and didn't press her into conversation. When he left her at Laverock Hall she took his proffered hand and quietly but calmly thanked him again for telling her the truth. As he drove away Oscar had to admit that he'd done very well that afternoon, very well indeed!

*　　*　　*

March 3rd 1842

'Seth is dead! I can't take it in. Paul and Mr Fisher brought the news today, and a part of me wishes I still did not know. He was buried last week – and I wasn't there! Oh Seth, you were like a father to me, the only father I've ever known, and I should have been at your funeral to say good-bye.

172

This is what Paul told me: in February the weather in the Yorkshire Dales turned pretty nasty. Snow began falling, and the heavily laden skies promised much more to follow. The shepherds were worried that they would not have enough time to fetch the sheep down to the low pastures from the slopes of Buckden Pike which rises some 2300 feet above sea level and gets the very worst of the weather. Despite anxious pleas from Mary Ann and Mr Turner, Seth set out to help. Within an hour of his departure the snowstorm worsened. A blinding blizzard raged over the fells blotting out all trails and familiar landmarks, eventually leaving the craggy hillside as smooth as an iced cake. Later many sheep were found to have perished.

It is thought that Seth fell through deep drifting snow into a rock crevice and, hampered by his wooden leg, was unable to haul himself out. He froze to death and despite many frantic searches when the storm abated his body lay concealed for six weeks until the snow melted. Poor Mary Ann and Mr Turner. Paul says they have taken it very badly and can't forgive themselves. Neither they nor Seth deserved this. But they mustn't blame themselves. I knew Seth and when he had set his mind to something he would do it, no matter what others said. No amount of pleading would have stopped him going out when he felt his help was needed.

Paul dug his grave. It should have been the two of us. My frustration at being held here is burning up in me again. Why did this have to happen now? Seth is buried in Hubberholme Churchyard. Paul says it's a beautiful place beside the river and only a mile from where Seth died. One day I will visit him, but tonight I will pray to St Michael to give me strength and help me at this sad time, for I am very low and miserable. The night will be very long.

Hearing that Seth had died drove all other thoughts from my mind yesterday. When Paul and Mr Fisher first arrived I was bursting with impatience for news of Leonora, but it was only much later during the night that I realized they had brought me no word of her. No letter, no message. Paul told me his news; that he has been courting Molly Greenwood from Oxenhope for some weeks now, and I am pleased for him. I know Molly, and they'll make a good pair. Perhaps he forgot Leonora's message. After all, I forgot to ask him! That must be it.

May 1st

Winter has now gone. The building proceeded at a pace, and the timbered roof is now completed. Large Westmoreland slates have been delivered, and we're all eager to get them up. It should look well. Mr Calvert has pneumonia, and we're more or less left to get on with things. Surprisingly every man pulls his weight. The prisoners working on the chapel all seem to have pride in their work, and a lot of that is down to Mr Calvert being so enthusiastic, treating everyone fairly and, most importantly, praising good work. If I ever have men working under me when I get out of here I will remember all this. I've been nominated as overseer in Mr Calvert's absence and, strangely, the others seem to have accepted this without resentment. The Governor and his wife come daily to make sure all is going to plan.

May 15th

The Governor's wife wants a marble altar, and I've agreed to try my hand at carving it! I hope I haven't bitten off more than I can chew, but I'm determined to do my best. She has asked for a station of the cross showing Jesus being nailed to the wooden cross by Roman soldiers whilst Mary, his mother, and a remorseful Mary Magdalene look on. I've asked for sketches and a scaled drawing to work from and she's promised to have these ready in about a week's time. I feel excited.

May 20th

The Governor's wife brought the drawing for the altar and the marble will be delivered; the anticipation of making a start is giving me something to take my mind off the events outside the prison! Harold is to do the metal ornamental work for the altar – the candlesticks and communion rail and he'll make the tools I need for the sculpting. Meanwhile work has begun on the inside of the chapel and the first pews have been fitted.

May 26th

I am agreeably surprised to find that I am making a reasonably good job of the altar. After one or two blunders at first I've got into the way of working with marble, and I'm pleased with my results. The Governor's wife is really enthused with her idea, and is often here to see how the altar is coming along. She talks at length with Harold and me and we have begun to look forward to her visits. It is rather a strange situation – Governor's wife and prisoners. She is kind and friendly (and even brings us cakes sometimes), but we are careful not to take advantage of her kindness for we know how lucky we are to be working on this project.

May 27th

Saturday, and again no visitor. I have been standing on my chair for almost an hour looking at the stars. I have heard nothing for so long from Leonora and I've been looking for a sign – anything – something to tell me that all is well, but everything is the same as ever. It is quite a clear night. To my right Orion, the mighty hunter, strides the sky, and if I press my face to the glass I can just make out the Plough to my left. These stars have shone through the night for countless millennia, unchanging, inspiring us to dream. Whilst filling me with awe at the sheer magnitude of the universe they make me feel insignificantly small in the vastness of space, and yet their constancy reassures me. It was foolish to look for more – for shooting stars, for meteor trails, for magic – tonight these bright specks fill me with the power to rise above the wrong I've been done and assure me that all will be well.

June 2nd

The altar is finished, and we're all overjoyed that it has turned out so well. It's been a joint effort, and the Governor's wife is particularly delighted and says we are to be congratulated and should feel justifiably proud of the result. Now she has more plans! She feels that the rear of the church with its bare stone wall needs some decoration, and it was Harold who suggested that a large piece of oak roofing timber could be carved in the figure of St Michael of All Angels slaying a dragon. The Governor's wife thinks it is a splendid idea and has gone away to draw yet more plans and get hold of some wood carving tools.

June 10th

Paul came alone today. I knew something was wrong the moment I saw him, for he was uneasy and would not look me in the eye. The fact is Leonora is to be married! I could not take it in when Paul told me. My mind was whirling through all the times we'd had together and the promises we'd made. Since coming to Armley I have often told myself that I could not expect Leonora to wait five long years – it was too much to ask. I knew now that I had expected it; I'd felt sure of her love! And now I am told she is to be married. However, that wasn't the worst of it. I almost screamed when I found out whom she is to marry. It's Oscar Beale. How can this be, Leonora and Oscar? No! Apparently he was in the Ferraris' company at every available opportunity; over-solicitous to Mrs Ferrari, laughing too loud at Mr Ferrari's jokes and making the most of every chance to woo Leonora. Paul says he's bought a large house in Cooke Gate, Town End, Haworth for £1200 and furnished it quite lavishly, no doubt to impress the Ferraris and further his chances. Well, it worked! They fell for it. They are blinded by Beale's flattery and false charm. I can understand Mr and Mrs Ferrari, who are only looking for the best prospects for their daughter, but I'll never understand Leonora. How could she? Surely she cannot be in love with Oscar Beale? I had come to think of late that I could endure my five years here, but without hope of Leonora my sentence seems interminable, unbearable. No wonder she did not visit me. I thought she loved me as I love her, but how easily she is betrothed to that loathsome man, how quickly her affections have changed. I am angry, hurt, afraid for her, and I feel as though I have been torn apart.

176

June 20th

The design for the carving came today. Thank God for something to take my mind off Leonora. I lay awake all through the night, and every time I closed my eyes I saw her face, so close, smiling, laughing – mocking me. I will NOT think of her!

The drawing shows a large figure of a fine-featured young man with eyes that glow like the hottest embers of the fire. A white cloak hangs in heavy folds from his strong shoulders and is fastened at the waist by a broad golden belt. I am struck most of all by the feeling of compassion radiating from the saint's face. I dearly want to capture that expression in the carving but fear that it will be beyond me.

June 27th

I've no incentive to write. I am continuing with the woodcarving, but my heart's not in it and it is taking a long time to complete. The weather is warm now and I am able to do the work outside, but I find no joy in the sunshine, for every day that the sun rises brings us nearer to Leonora's wedding.

July 3rd

Harold is to be released! He has been granted eight months remission of the sentence for good conduct – and well he deserves it. It is truly good news, but for all my joy for Harold I am sad and even a little frightened that he is going. He has been such a good friend to me. I never would have made it in here without Harold, and tomorrow he'll be gone. I shall miss him.

July 8th

Leonora's wedding day, and I must somehow get through it alone without the support and wise words of my friend, Harold.

I have had many sleepless nights these past weeks, and long

177

hours to wonder where it all went wrong. I thought our love was strong enough to survive anything, but I was wrong. Leonora was my sunrise and my sunset, she gave me endless joy and made me whole. I wanted to fill her as she filled me, and I thought we were joined forever. I was wrong. I realize now that I was blinded by my own love for her and saw only what I wanted to see. Leonora cannot have loved me. She is married, and I have lost her to Oscar Beale.

July 22nd

At long last the carving is done. The Governor's wife is pleased and has had it hung on the bare stone wall at the back of the church as planned. It looks well enough, but I never did manage to capture the saint's expression of gentleness and love.

I am not to be returned to the boot repair shop. What a relief. Instead I've been given the task of maintenance and cleaning of the church. It suits me fine. I prefer my own company, for these days I'm in no mood for banter or ribaldry. The chapel is quiet and calming, and I am hoping for a new contentment.

23

December 1842, Haworth

Six months had passed since Leonora's and Oscar's wedding, and in that time things had deteriorated at the bank. If Oscar's supercilious manner had deterred a few customers in the early days, his attitude after his marriage was far worse. He had little understanding of the woollen industry and didn't try to learn, and he treated the tradespeople of Haworth with such disdain that, one after another, they transferred their funds to the Keighley branch, choosing to make the four-mile journey each way rather than put up with the young upstart who was trying to tell them how to run their businesses.

Though Oscar never discussed his affairs with her, nonetheless Leonora knew that things were not as they should be at the bank. Whenever she went to Haworth she sensed that the shopkeepers were uneasy with her now, and on one or two occasions she had been sure people were talking about her and had caught sympathetic glances from her acquaintances. The atmosphere in their new home at Cooke Gate was not what Leonora had hoped for, either. Oscar had been so caring and considerate before their marriage that Leonora had fooled herself into believing that she was especially fond of Oscar. Being so badly hurt by John had left her susceptible to his charms, and her parents had been so keen for the union that she had gone along with their wishes. Now Oscar was domineering and patronizing. When Leonora laughed he told her not to be frivolous, and when she ventured to comment on any serious subject he ridiculed her ideas, contriving to make her feel rather foolish.

In company Oscar was proud to have a beautiful wife on his arm. He showed off Leonora like a prize, but he was obsessively jealous and would become angry in an instant if he considered the smile she bestowed on another too bright, or if she laughed too merrily at someone else's wit. All pretence of charm and courteousness had disappeared once the wedding vows were safely taken. At first Oscar had been careful still to appear the same in public, but as his reputation at the bank crumpled he stopped pretending altogether, and all his resentment towards a world which he felt had always treated him badly was directed at Leonora. The only people who failed to see the truth of the situation were Mr and Mrs Ferrari. They loved to visit the house at Cooke Gate but their daughter, pleased to have their company and not wanting to waste that precious time together, was careful not to let them see how unhappy she had become.

Leonora would never forget the day Oscar came home with news of his demotion. He stood with his back towards the fire, pale and silent, looking at her with such hatred that for a moment she felt almost afraid. Some minutes later the fear turned to disbelief, and Leonora fought back a sudden urge to laugh out loud as Oscar accused her of undermining his authority.

'What have you been saying? How have you managed to turn so many people against me? I should never have allowed you to walk alone around Haworth; how do I know what you get up to whilst I was striving to improve the bank and uphold our position in society. You are not fit to be my wife! This is all your fault!'

'Oscar, what has happened? I have done nothing ... this is ridiculous...'

'Ridiculous, is it? Am I ridiculous? Is that what you think? Well if I am, then you have made me so. You think yourself better than me, always hoity-toity and full of airs and graces!'

Oscar was purple in the face and shouting at the top of his voice. Taken aback, Leonora tried to calm him down enough for her to find out what had happened but to no avail, he only screamed louder.

'You want to know what is wrong. I'll tell you. I'm to leave the bank. LEAVE THE BANK! I'm to go back to Bradford. Me,

180

Oscar Beale, back as an under-manager. I'm disgraced, and you're to blame. I don't know how you've done it, but I'll find out and then you'll be sorry!'

Oscar stormed out of the room, slamming the door behind him, leaving an open-mouthed Leonora alone beside the fire.

It was so ridiculous it was almost funny. How could he possibly think that she had brought this about? Once again Leonora had the urge to laugh. Oscar brought down to size! Well no doubt he deserved it, and she could not feel sorry for him. It served him right if he had to go and live in dirty Bradford! It wasn't long before all amusement left her when she realized that if Oscar had to go back to Bradford so must she. It would mean leaving her parents and this village, and she would be miles away from the open moors that she loved. All that she held dear would be far away, just when she would need support and reassurance, for she was almost certain now that she was carrying Oscar's child. Leonora sank to her knees and wept.

The local carter, George Binns, moved the Beales' furniture. The two wagons were almost full, and despite the January cold George and his man were sweating by the time they came to move Oscar's heavy oak desk. It was quite a task negotiating the front steps, and George was relieved when they got down to level ground, but halfway along the garden path his assistant slipped on a patch of ice and let the desk drop. No real damage was done to the piece, but a drawer fell out, scattering its contents. Some papers blew across the garden and George scurried after them, stuffing each one into his pocket as he retrieved it, and then he hurried back to make sure his helper wasn't hurt. As they loaded the desk onto the wagon it began to rain heavily, and in their haste to cover the furniture with a tarpaulin George forgot all about returning the papers to the desk drawer as he had intended.

How suddenly our destiny is changed! Oscar Beale's fate was sealed the second the wagon-man fell and the drawer flew out of the desk, but it was some weeks later that George called on Mr Fisher for advice.

181

'No, I'm afraid I can't help you there. I don't know where Mr Beale is living now, except that it is somewhere in Bradford.'

Mr Fisher thought for a moment. 'We can't post the papers on to him directly, but don't worry, I'm sure we can find some way of returning them.'

George Carter looked a bit sheepish.

'I'm only bothered that they might be important, like. It's a few weeks since we moved 'im, see, and I've only just come across 'em. There might be summat 'ere that 'e's been wantin',' he paused before adding, ''e can be a reight nasty piece sometimes.'

Mr Fisher could see that the carter was troubled, and he had a point. Oscar Beale would probably think the chap took the papers on purpose to inconvenience him.

'If you'd like to leave them with me, George, I'll see that they are returned. It was a genuine mistake, and there's no need for you to worry.'

Later Mr Fisher sat down to write to Oscar Beale. He hadn't read the papers, for they were no concern of his, but they were on the table in front of him and only slowly did it dawn on him what he was seeing before his very eyes. This was not some private correspondence of Oscar Beale's, it was a Yorkshire Bank official receipt slip, and moreover it was made out to Hollings Mill for the sum of £2000. Jonas hurriedly took up the rest of the papers and began to look through them. Some were insignificant and he discarded those, but there was a paying-in slip from Hollings in the same amount, and at the bottom of the pile was Oscar Beale's bank book. A cold sweat broke out on Mr Fisher's brow. He knew before he opened it what he would find. The entry was clear, September 22nd 1841, Deposit £2000.

Without delay Jonas Fisher donned coat and hat and set out to see the chief executive at the Yorkshire Bank's head office in Bradford, with the evidence of John Pickles' innocence carefully locked in his briefcase.

How quickly the wheels of justice turned to right the wrong. The police arrested Oscar Beale the following day, and not long afterwards he was found guilty of embezzlement and of conspiring to incriminate another.

Judge Avery was stern in his summing up.

'We have here a man with no thought for anyone but himself, who sought to further his own interests and establish himself in society by whatever means he chose and without regard for those he damaged along his path. Due to his wickedness an innocent man has spent over a year of his young life locked away in jail, and a well-known bank has been brought into disrepute. Oscar Beale, I have no alternative but to punish you severely, and I hereby sentence you to ten years' imprisonment in Her Majesty's jail at Armley.'

It was exactly double the sentence that had been handed to John Pickles!

* * *

Armley Jail

Thursday, January 25th 1843

It is over. I can't believe it. I am a free man! The governor and his wife came together to give me the good news, and I think they are almost as pleased as I am! Despite the bars I have counted them as my friends this past year, and I can see today that they are really happy for me.

It was Oscar Beale who framed me. I think I should have known. Everything has fallen into place now; the argument at the bank when my satchel went flying and all the papers fell out ... Oscar's disappearing act at the cricket match ... and the look he gave me as the police led me away, which I could not quite fathom. Well, now I understand it – triumph! He may have scored miserably in his first innings, but he knew he'd won the game! Well, Oscar Beale, I've finally got the Cup, and when you get out of here you'll be too old for any more cricket.

Oscar is to have my cell. I've brought a tin of black paint from the stores and painted a huge number 10 on the ceiling so that every time Oscar Beale awakes he will be reminded of just how long he must remain in jail.

Paul and Mr Fisher have arrived to take me home, but I'm

183

not going yet. I'm going to wait until that scoundrel is brought in. I want to see his expression when he sees this cell and comes face to face with the reality of the next ten years. I want to turn the key and lock up Oscar Beale. Only then will I walk away, happy to be free.

Armley Jail – farewell

24

A new John came back to Haworth. Working on the chapel in Armley had given him confidence in his own abilities, and talks with Harold, followed by long hours of thought when he could not sleep, had allowed a dream to spring up in him. John wasn't going back to the mill. He wanted to work for himself – and he wanted to work with stone. He had 70 gold sovereigns saved and owned a fine horse, and he felt the world was at his feet.

John and Paul decided that they would go together and visit Mary Ann and Mr Turner at Buckden, in the Yorkshire Dales, some 30 miles away.

As they travelled up the dale in John's trap, they were captivated by the beautiful River Wharfe and the lush green fields, with their cattle and sheep peacefully grazing amongst the limestone rocks. Passing through farmsteads and pretty villages, they eventually reached the big house where Mr Turner and Mary Ann lived. All four were overjoyed on their arrival, and there was great excitement all round. While John fed and watered his horse Mary Ann went into the garden, where she gathered a bouquet of flowers. Then the four of them walked along the riverside to the ancient church at Hubberholme, where they placed the flowers on Seth's grave.

After a good meal, they spent the evening sitting by the fire, reminiscing and bringing Mr Turner up to date with the news from Sladen Bridge. The following morning they said their goodbyes and retraced their steps to Haworth.

It was Jonas Fisher who pointed John in the direction of

Dimples Hill Quarry. He knew his old friend Jos Barrit was feeling his age and ready to retire, and Jonas felt sure he would jump at the chance of selling his business if he were offered a fair price.

'But I've no idea what would be a fair price,' said John. 'I only have the money I told you of, and I doubt if that will be enough.'

'Offer him one hundred and forty guineas. Seventy pounds to be paid now and the balance in six months time.'

It was just as Mr Fisher had said it would be, and without further to-do Jos Barrit and John Pickles shook hands on the deal and John became the proud owner of Dimples Hill Quarry. It was hard work. The weather was cold and often wet, but John worked all the daylight hours, whatever the weather, revelling in his freedom. Freedom to be where he wanted to be. Freedom to do whatever he chose, freedom to work hard enough to drive Leonora completely from his thoughts! He had nobody else to think about now, and he enjoyed the physical work of getting the big blocks of stone out of the quarry and splitting them up to sell for wall stones. Very gradually he began to make a profit, and as the days lengthened so did his working hours until by June he was falling into bed exhausted at 11.00 p.m. and was up again by 6.00 a.m. ready for another day. His debt to Jos Barrit was due on 1st August, and he was proud of his accomplishment.

Now the quarry is really mine, thought John, and somehow I'm going to make it a success. He left the quarrying for a couple of days and went on his horse to visit all the builders he could reach. The local ones knew he'd had a rough deal, and as a gesture of goodwill put in an order, but when they saw the quality of the stone they wanted more. It wasn't long before John was employing five extra men, and they were still working flat out to meet demand.

Unbeknown to John, Jonas Fisher had taken out a writ against damages for his friend's wrongful imprisonment. The Yorkshire Bank had defended the action at first, but, afraid of yet more adverse publicity, they had finally settled out of court, and John was delighted to receive a cheque for £2000. He put the money straight into his business. Visiting John Smith & Co, crane makers of Keighley, he invested in a steam crane which enabled him to lift much bigger blocks from the bottom of the quarry and a steam driven frame stone-saw. The town was expanding rapidly, and architects were designing ever more imposing buildings and were demanding fine-sawn stone for the frontages. It soon became known that the stone from Dimples Hill was the best to be had, and it was in great demand.

The noisy bunch of children playing cheerfully with a barrel hoop and stick were suddenly silenced by the sight of the smart horseman riding into the communal yard. The gentleman stopped his mount and asked the biggest lad where he might find Harold Wainwright.

'I'll fetch 'im, sir, wait ye on,' and, his clogs clattering on the cobbles, he disappeared through an open door halfway along the row of scruffy cottages. A moment or two later he reappeared with Harold behind him. John's one-time prison mate still had his clay pipe clamped between his teeth, but now there was a thin wisp of smoke swirling from the blackened bowl.

'Can I 'elp yer Mr? – Well! If it isn't John Pickles! Good to see you, lad. I 'eard you were out. What brings you 'ere?'

John swung himself from his horse, and the two friends greeted each other with a warm handshake.

'I've a proposition for you, Harold. Have Alice make a pot of tea, and I'll tell you all about it.'

They'd finished the tea by the time John had finished telling them of his plans.

'What's it to be then, Harold? Are you going to join me at Haworth?' John laughed before Harold could reply. 'And bear in mind that I didn't ride all the way from Haworth to Wainstalls for a "no"!'

Harold puffed on his pipe and grinned.

'Well, it looks like I 'ave no choice, then.'

He looked across to where Alice was busy washing the cups. 'What do you say, Alice?'

His wife hardly dared to believe what she had heard. They were to get out of here at last. Live in a house in Haworth, that this John had found for them, high up near the moors, and 'er 'Arold would have a secure job and a real good wage – double

187

what he was earning now! It was wonderful. A bloody miracle. Alice could say nothing at all.

'We'll take that as a "yes", eh, John? We can't thank you enough. We'll never be able to repay you, but you can be sure that you'll 'ave the best maintained machines of any to be found.'

'There's nothing to repay, Harold. You did more for me in Armley than you'll ever know. You saved me from my own destruction. I owe you.'

'Quits then?' laughed Harold.

'Quits!'

John was light-hearted as he rode back home. It was good to be getting Harold on board. They worked well together, and John knew he had the right man for the job; hard-working and trustworthy. Long before he reached Haworth his new cottage on West Lane, near the quarry, was beckoning him. He was saddle-sore but happy. The look on Alice's face was enough to tell him that he'd done a good day's work and had left behind him a very happy family.

Delivery of the steam crane and saw caused quite a stir in Haworth. The horses hauling the huge parts up the steep cobbled Main Street were sweating and straining taking the load. People came out of the houses and shops to watch the slow progression of the wagons, and an unruly bunch of local lads fought for a position clinging to the tail boards until, for their own safety, they were warned to keep clear. Everyone was keen to see these huge machines, but equally they were determined not to miss any excitement. Here was a potential calamity. Anything could happen – a broken wheel or chassis, a shifting load, a lamed horse – and if anything did go wrong the folk of Haworth wanted to be in on it!

There was no catastrophe, and eventually the machines were safely delivered to the quarry. An engineer from John Smith's crane works had come to oversee the assembly of the parts, and both Harold and John joined in to help. It was an interesting task, and following the engineer's instructions piston was joined to crank, crank to flywheel, and so on. The men worked patiently, making sure that every moving part was well oiled

188

and greased. Finally the flywheel was bolted to the shaft, and after making a few minor adjustments and lavishing yet more oil and grease wherever possible, they were ready to steam. John noticed for the first time that quite a crowd had gathered on the edge of the quarry, and he winked at Harold.

'Say a prayer, Harold, we don't want to disappoint the spectators.'

Harold laughed, 'I don't think there's any fear of that. She's a beauty – raring to go!'

All three men leaned their weight on the flywheel. Sweat poured from them as they pushed the wheel round by hand several times. The crowd had fallen silent and watched expectantly as the engineer cautiously opened the valve. With a fierce hiss of steam the engine finally burst into life and the wheel made its first trembling, powered revolution, to a rousing cheer from the bystanders.

John had bought the business at just the right time. Quarrying was becoming a thriving industry supplying the heavy demand for stone in the expanding towns of West Yorkshire. The population of the Borough of Bradford had grown from 13,000 in 1800 to over 60,000 in 1840. Thousands of young people were flocking to the town in search of work in the mills and factories of this new industrial era. They all needed homes, and row upon row of back-to-back houses were being built to accommodate these immigrants. Other towns had a similar phenomenal growth, and also some stone was being shipped abroad. Dimples Hill Quarry was stretched to meet the demand, and soon more men were employed. In particular John's became known for supplying the large blocks of stone used for engine beds for the steam-powered mills. Already his dream was taking form and the hard slog of the first months was paying John good dividends.

25

The Sun Inn on Ivegate, Bradford, was a busy hostelry. Besides being one of the leading coaching inns of the town, it was used by local businessmen as a venue for meetings for their many commercial projects. The Leeds and Liverpool canal, the Halifax Piece Hall and the Worsted Committee all had life breathed into them under the Sun's roof. John had taken accommodation at the back of the inn, overlooking the yard but away from the hustle and bustle of the day-to-day activities. He had an appointment with a firm of architects in Bradford and was hoping to gain the contract to supply stone for their latest building project. He wanted a quiet room where he could peruse the detailed plans of the buildings, study the designs of doorways and window surrounds without distraction, and then he would be able to make an accurate assessment of the stone required. He expected to be in Bradford for about three days, and since he could not meet with the architect until morning he saw no reason why he shouldn't have a drink or two at the bar and catch up with the local news.

The group of men he joined were discussing the recently passed law to prohibit women and children working in the mines.

'A jolly good thing too,' said a stout gentleman sitting opposite John. 'The conditions in those mines is deplorable, "dark, damp and dangerous" so they say. I'd not want my wife and child down there.'

The men all seemed to be in agreement, with 'Hear, Hear' and 'Quite so' voiced around the table.

'Yes, yes, I agree.'

A gentleman, whom John recognized as the owner of one of Bradford's larger mills, sounded rather as if he disagreed.

'But who knows where it will stop. These so-called reformers want them out of the mills too, and where would they be, then. They'd not have enough money to live on.'

Someone at the back spoke up.

'You mean where would you be then, without your cheap labour!'

'That's not what I meant at all. My concerns have always been for my workers.'

'Oh yes? Pull the other one. For your pocket, more like.'

The debate was beginning to turn nasty but an older man, who had said very little, intervened.

'The government is only seeking to reduce the long hours worked by the women and children. They'll not go hungry, and the workforce will still be there. I'm sure we all feel this is a good move forward. Most of our mill owners are doing all they can to improve working conditions.'

Although this last bit was rather stretching the truth, it seemed to diffuse the anger and the conversation drifted onto other topics: the expansion of the railways and the great steam ships that were now being built; the new column monument to Viscount Nelson erected in Trafalgar Square with which one gentleman, newly returned from a visit to the capital, had been very impressed; and Charles Dickens' latest book, *A Christmas Carol*, which had been a sell-out in December.

It was late when John went back to his room, and he intended to go straight to bed and get a good night's sleep in readiness for the important day ahead. He drew the curtains and as he began to undress he heard a noise and paused to listen. He was just thinking that he had imagined it when he heard scuffles outside in the yard and a woman's voice saying, 'Get off me, don't do that, leave me alone.'

Followed immediately by an angry yelp and a man's voice snarling, 'Ow – you bitch. Come 'ere, I'll show yer.'

John could make out three figures below, two men and a woman. Probably she'd enticed them there, he thought. It was none of his business. He dropped the curtain, but then heard the woman scream frantically, 'Help! Help me! Please, some-body help me.'

The panic in her voice spurred John into action, and he was through the door in a trice and taking the stairs three at a time. He found the back door and flung it open with a bang, alerting the two men. The first made off across the yard and disappeared down a dark alley, but the second man wasn't so fast and John charged at him, hitting him full in the face with his fist. The man staggered and John punched him again and sent him reeling down a flight of steps. John was ready for him should he come back at him, but the man had had enough and slunk off after his accomplice swearing under his breath.

The woman had crawled across the yard and was sitting huddled against the wall with her arms wrapped tightly around herself. She was barefoot, bedraggled and mud-spattered, and her blouse had been taken in the struggle. She was trembling, there was blood on her cheek and her right eye was beginning to swell. John felt sorry for her and helped her to her feet.

'Where do you live, miss? I'll see you safe home.'

'I have no home, sir. I came to Bradford to look for work and those two said they'd help me – help themselves, more like!'

She tossed her head angrily as she said this, and John was struck by her fiery spirit which had obviously not been quenched by the attack. He didn't quite know what to do, but he could not leave the woman here in the yard with nowhere to go so he decided to take her indoors and have her wounds attended to. He only got as far as the back corridor and was met there by the innkeeper who was, to say the least, surprised to find John Pickles coming in by the back door with a dirty-looking woman.

'You can't bring her in here. This is a respectable establishment. Sorry, miss, I'm afraid you'll have to leave.'

'She's been attacked, Mr Sanderson, if we could just...'

'Rules is rules! No women, and that's that!'

John reached in his pocket and took out a folded note.

'She has nowhere to go. Your reputation will be intact if no one sees her. My room is at the back, and there'll be no trouble. Perhaps you'll arrange for a bath and hot tea to be sent up.'

Mr Sanderson's eyes narrowed when he saw the money, and snatching it he said gruffly, 'All right, then, but keep her out of sight. I'll send up the tea, but there'll be no bath. Not at this hour!'

With that he turned on his heels and John led the still trembling young woman up the stairs to the sanctuary of his room.

His first priority was to staunch the blood which was oozing down her cheek and inspect a wound at the back of her head, which he hadn't noticed at first. Neither was as bad as he had feared. They were superficial cuts, and once they were bathed and he had given her a cold pad to hold over the bruised eye John felt less anxious.

A pot of tea for two arrived, along with a large pitcher of hot water. John smiled at this.

'It seems our host is not so unkind after all.'

The woman's clothes were dirty and wet so, giving her one of his own clean shirts, John said he would go out for a while and leave her to wash and clean herself up.

At Reception John asked for another room but, as he had feared the hotel was fully booked and there was no other accommodation available. As the lounge bar was by now in darkness John went out into the town. The streets were dark and empty at that time of night, and he hoped he would not meet a policeman and have to explain himself. The time passed very slowly and he was cold when he returned and keen to get back to the warmth of his room, but he hesitated outside the door, apprehensive about entering and wondering what on earth he was going to do about the night's sleep. He knocked lightly and waited until he heard 'Come in' before opening the door.

The woman was sitting before the dressing table mirror, and John was taken aback by her appearance. Despite the bruising he could see that she was a good-looking woman, much younger than he had supposed – she could not be more than 20 years old. His shirt, though far too big for her, could not disguise her shapely figure, nor hide her long legs. Their eyes met for the first time, through the glass, and she smiled. She had regained her composure and thanked him for rescuing her from the pair of ruffians. She had a quietly self-possessed manner and a gentle way of speaking which took John by surprise. This was no rough girl from the slums, and he was intrigued to find out more about her. She answered his questions easily, without embarrassment and told him how she came to be in Bradford.

'My name is Isabella Outhwaite, and I'm from a little village the other side of Keighley. My father has a farm, but he lost all his animals – sheep, cows and pigs – when the dreaded foot

193

and mouth disease struck the farm. Not long after the fox got in and killed all our hens and ducks. It's been a terrible time. I had a job at the bobbin mill, but now that's closed down and there's no other work in the village. Dad was desperate, what with three little ones to provide for as well and said that I'd have to go and find work somewhere else. I went into Keighley first, but I'd no luck there so I walked another ten miles, all the way to Bradford. I would have given up at one point, but the two fellows you saw swore to me that I'd get work at the Sun Inn and I walked with them from Frizinghall. They seemed right enough then.' She looked down, a little self-conscious. 'They didn't even give me chance to ask for work, they were after something else entirely! I can't thank you enough for coming out when you did.'

'Don't think any more about it. I just wish that I'd caught the pair of them and given them what they deserved.'

John felt even more sorry for Isabella than he had done before.

'You shall have the bed – no, no argument please – I'll have one of the pillows, and then I'll be fine on the floor here.'

He thought she might be afraid, being alone with a stranger, but he needn't have worried, for not long after he had covered himself with his coat, blown out the candle and settled down; he could hear the rhythmic gentle breathing of a deep sleep.

It was not a comfortable night for him, and by 7 a.m. he was washed and shaved and smartly dressed in a new suit which he had had tailor-made by Mr Brown at Haworth. He had a white rose for the buttonhole, and as he fixed the flower he appraised himself in the mirror. He cut a fine figure. His dark features were set-off by the moss-green, velvet corduroy of the suit, which in turn toned well with the new russet-brown shirt and matching tie. He was pleased with the result – you'll do, John Pickles – and decided there and then that this was to be his standard dress when meeting business associates in Bradford and Manchester. In truth he did look exceedingly smart, and his new attire made him look – and feel – full of confidence.

Isabella slept on. She must have been exhausted, for she never stirred during John's preparations, and not wanting to wake her he left a note, telling her that her meals would be sent up to the room and he hoped to return around 3.30 in the afternoon.

After ordering Isabella's meals, John breakfasted alone. He ate heartily, unsure how long it would be before he had time for the next meal, and was about finished when the landlord appeared with a shabby ladies' shoe.

'I think this must belong to the lassie. I found it out t'back this morning, but where t'other is I don't know. Looks as if it's seen better days.'

It certainly does, thought John. He thanked Mr Sanderson, and when his host left him he wrapped the shoe in his serviette and put it into his pocket.

His walk to the architect's offices took John past Brown, Muff's, a select ladies' outfitters, and having time to spare before his appointment, he went in and looked at the clothes on display. He hadn't really any idea what he wanted, and when the girl behind the counter asked if she could be of assistance he made her smile with his request.

'I want a nice-quality, warm dress, please.'

'Could I ask what size, sir?'

John hadn't thought about that.

'Well, she's about five foot six or five foot seven tall, well-made, young – and she has long brown hair. She'll be needing a shawl to match, too.'

The shop assistant was too polite to show her curiosity and said only,

'I'm sure we can find something available, sir.'

John took the worn-out shoe from his pocket.

'I'll need shoes too, this is the size. Could you also provide – er, what I want is – she'll need er, undergarments.'

The assistant tried hard not to smile.

'Of course, sir, a full set? And stockings too?'

'If you would be so kind as to parcel everything up ready for me to collect about three o'clock, I'll settle the bill when I return.'

John was glad to leave and was already on his way out as the assistant replied, 'I'll do that, sir. Thank you. Just leave everything to me. Good-day, sir!'

* * *

195

It was exactly 9.30 when John arrived at the premises of Messrs Lockwood and Co and was ushered into the private offices of the senior partner. Mr Lockwood, a balding man of about 50 years of age, rose from his desk as John entered. They shook hands and exchanged pleasantries, but both men were eager to get down to business, and they were soon engrossed in the plans for the new block of shops and offices to be built in Forster Square. The older man could see immediately how keen John was to land this contract, and he understood why. Securing the order for the stone for such a huge building project would make his name in the fast-developing towns of West Yorkshire. They pored over the plans and detailed drawings for some time, discussing the stone required: ashlar for the frontages and flag rock for the roof slates and paved areas, and so on. John produced a sample from his quarry to show the quality that he would provide. Mr Lockwood found the stone pleasing to the eye. It had a light greyish, sand colour and was smoothly finished. Taking up a magnifying glass he examined the piece for what, to John, seemed like a very long time, finally saying, 'Hmm! Good stone.'

He could see from the grain and texture that it was first-rate.

'But can you guarantee this quality throughout?'

Mr Lockwood and John both knew that it is impossible to be absolutely sure of what a quarry will yield; a seam can narrow and run out at any point, but all the signs were good so far and John wasn't going to let doubt creep in and ruin his chances.

'All that we've taken out to date is consistent with what you have there. I'm confident that we can maintain this quality. Yes, I'll stand by that.'

The architect wanted assurance that transport schedules would be met and, although he thought it unnecessary, John agreed to a penalty clause in the contract should he fall down on deliveries. Finally they negotiated the price per cubic yard. John hoped for some reaction from the older man which would have told him what the architect thought of the terms he stated, but Mr Lockwood was impassive and, as to be expected, haggled a bit until they reached a price acceptable to them both. Pushing back his chair. Mr Lockwood rose.

'A good time for a break, don't you think? What do you say to refreshments at the Rawson Arms?'

They put buildings, plans, stone and quarrying right out of their minds, and over lunch of beef sandwiches and ale they talked of their mutual interest in cricket.

'I've heard all about your batting, John Pickles. Hard hitter, aren't you? I never could get the force behind the ball, although I had a reputation in my time for being able to place it pretty neatly, like you.'

'I didn't know you played. Which club were you with?'

'Lidget Green. I'm the Chairman now. My playing days are long since over,' Mr Lockwood chuckled. 'Short of wind and shaky on the legs – it comes to us all! Perhaps we can arrange a friendly match between our two clubs. I know our chaps would love the chance to take you on, and that fast bowler you've got too. What's his name – Ryan?'

'Paul Ryan. He is pretty good and, yes, I think that would be a great idea.'

Back at the office it only took about an hour to go over what they had discussed earlier. John was satisfied with the morning's work and confident in the prices to take away. Mr Lockwood asked him to submit on paper the price quoted and estimates together with a written guarantee of quality and an undertaking to meet due delivery dates.

'All things being in order, I think we have a deal. When I have the documents I've asked for, the contract is yours, Mr Pickles.'

John could not stop the grin which spread across his face as they shook hands.

'Thank you very much, sir. You'll have my guarantee in just a few days, and you won't be disappointed.'

As Mr Lockwood escorted John to the main office door the young man was very happy with his first important deal in Bradford.

During the past few hours John's mind had been so full of his new venture that he had not given a thought to the woman who occupied his hotel room. Now he began to wonder what would become of her. What would she do? Where would she find work? He quickened his pace and was soon back in the ladies' department of Brown, Muff's Emporium. The assistant, who had everything parcelled up in readiness, handed him a bill for 14 guineas and said she hoped the lady would like her choice.

Arriving back at the Sun Inn earlier than expected and eager to give Isabella the clothes he'd brought, John bounded up the stairs and along the corridor to his room. As long as he lived John would never forget the sight that met his eyes as he opened the door. Isabella, completely naked, was stepping from a tin bath. She reached for the towel draped over the foot of the bed, but in her haste dropped it into the soapy water, and having no other means of covering herself she just remained still, her cheeks flushed with embarrassment. John had never seen such a perfect creature, and for a moment they were caught as in a tableau; he transfixed, his hand riveted to the brass doorknob, and she a statue of Venus rising from the sea. Her newly washed dark hair hung over her shoulders, with long, wet tendrils clinging to her firmly rounded breasts. The whole of her body glistened in the sunlight filtering through the lace curtain at the window. She was lithe and beautiful. With a sharp intake of breath John tore his eyes away and quickly closed the door. Crossing the room, he handed her his towel and placed the brown paper parcel on the bed, muttering, 'These are for you. I'll come back in about thirty minutes.'

Without waiting for a reply and without a backward glance, he left.

Isabella towelled herself dry and then put back on the shirt which John had loaned her the previous evening. She picked up her own discarded clothes from the floor and examined them. Her skirt, though very dirty, was otherwise undamaged. It might be old and worn, but it will see me through awhile yet. It only needs a good wash, thought Isabella, and she dropped the muddied article into the bathwater. However, the blouse, which had been ripped by her assailants, was beyond repair, and Isabella wondered anxiously where she could possibly get another one. Perhaps the gentleman will let me keep this shirt, she thought, not entirely convinced. He had been very kind, but there was a limit to everyone's kindness. It was then that she remembered the parcel on the bed, and it crossed her mind that the gentleman must have seen her torn blouse and perhaps he might have replaced it. She hardly dared to hope so, but felt quite excited as she began to undo the string.

What she saw as the wrapping fell away was beyond her wildest dreams. A whole set of brand-new clothes! A beautiful brown dress, shoes, cape and some underwear. Isabella had never seen anything like it. Only rich ladies had the privilege of wearing fine silk underclothes, and she had never owned a dress of such quality as this. Jumping up, she spun around the room with the dress held against her, feeling like a princess at a ball. She stopped suddenly remembering that the gentleman would soon be back. Hurriedly she put on the clothes, glad to find that the dress buttons were at the front where she didn't need assistance. She took care with the silk stockings, the first she had ever owned, and then was amazed to find that the lovely leather shoes were an exact fit. When she had finished she stood before the mirror and stared open-mouthed. This can't be happening to me, she thought. It can't be true. Out loud she said,

'Isabella Outhwaite, is that really you?'

And when the reflection in the glass beamed back at her she knew she wasn't dreaming.

The russet-brown of the dress brought out the hints of chestnut in her long brown hair, and the fine wool hugged her figure before falling in soft folds from her tiny waist to her ankles. It fitted perfectly. The bruising on her face was receding and, with eyes sparkling with excitement, Isabella knew that she looked good.

Downstairs at the bar John ordered a double brandy and tried not to think of Isabella in the room above. He was stunned by her beauty; she was gorgeous! How had he not noticed yesterday how pretty she was? Was it just her nakedness that had fired him, enticed him, or was she truly beautiful? All he knew was that he had wanted to run to her, take her in his arms and kiss her. John sipped the brandy slowly and tried to think of other things to rid himself of the vision. He still had the architect's plans in his pocket and, relieved to have something to do, he took them out and spread them on the table. He tried to concentrate on costing for the stone for the buildings and did a rough calculation for the end wall, but it needed a clearer head than his just now and he soon found that his thoughts were once again full of Isabella. Asking for another brandy, he surprised the barman by downing it in a single mouthful.

This time John knocked before entering his room. Isabella turned from the mirror to face him and John once again stood in the open doorway, unable to move. Neither spoke as they held each other's gaze until John finally found his voice.

'Isabella, you look wonderful!'

She still didn't speak, but her smile told him that she was pleased with his gift and that his generosity was appreciated.

'The shop assistant made a good choice,' said John. 'They seem to fit, and I'm glad you like them.'

Isabella spoke at last.

'She obviously took notice of the colours you are wearing. My dress matches your shirt, and look, the cape is exactly the same green as your suit! I can't believe they're mine.'

John laughed at her obvious excitement and made a sweeping bow before her.

'Would the lady care to accompany me into town and dine with me at a restaurant I know of?'

Isabella laughed too and, joining in the fun, she gave a jaunty curtsey.

'Sir is too kind. That would be very agreeable, thank you.'

Still laughing, they left the inn. The landlord was in the lobby as they passed and nodded a greeting to the smart pair.

'Good afternoon, Mr Pickles. Good afternoon, miss.'

He then stared after them, scratching his head and trying to figure out where it was that he'd seen the young lady before.

This was a new experience for Isabella. She had never sat down to a meal anywhere other than in her own home. There were quite a few other diners in the restaurant, and she felt a little self-conscious as the waiter showed them to a table for two in a corner. They ordered roast lamb and a bottle of wine to be followed by sweet trifle and coffee, and before the food arrived Isabella had time to look around. Unaccustomed as she was to any prosperity, she was impressed by her surroundings. Full rose-coloured curtains, trimmed with gold braid, and a deep red carpet gave an air of luxury to the spacious room, with huge potted plants and gilt candelabra the only decoration against the cream walls. On a raised area near the far wall a string quartet was playing soft, romantic music, pleasantly relaxing the diners without disturbing their conversation. The people here were smart and fashionable, but Isabella thought none of them cut a dash such as she and her escort in their matching outfits, and the admiring glances which her new attire drew gave her confidence to relax a little.

'Do you realize, I don't even know your name?'

She spoke quietly, not wanting anyone else to hear this admission, and John was rightly ashamed of his oversight.

'I'm so very sorry. Forgive me. My name is John Pickles, but I have a nickname now. The folks at home call me "Johnny Big Block"!'

'Why do they call you "Big Block", do they think you're big-headed?'

He laughed. 'No, nothing like that. I'm a stone-quarry man and sell the biggest stone blocks in Yorkshire.' He went on to explain. 'They're used for the steam-engine beds for the new factories. We have a reputation for accurately sawn blocks, and as there's little opposition we get a good price from them.'

'Is that all you do, just supply huge blocks?'

'No, I'm in Bradford at the moment to fix a contract supplying building stone for some new shops and offices to be built in Forster Square.'

Isabella leaned forward, obviously interested.

'How exciting to be directly involved with the growth of the town; to be taking part in something that is to benefit so many people.'

'Yes, I hadn't seen it like that. I just saw it as expansion for my quarry and plenty of work for the local men. It's a good thing for the village. Haworth has had some tough times.'

'Haworth!' Isabella exclaimed. 'Why, we're almost neighbours. My dad's farm is at Newsholme, not five miles away!'

The good food and wine relaxed the pair, and as the evening progressed they found they had much in common and shared the same sense of humour. They talked easily with one another, and John became enchanted with the dimple which appeared in Isabella's cheeks whenever she laughed. She also had a way of tossing her head, flicking her hair back over her shoulders, which he found extremely attractive. Isabella was very happy. She felt she was on a cloud – and it showed. Her skin glowed and the pupils of her sparkling eyes grew wider and wider.

201

She told him much about her life at Newsholme. They had only recently fallen on hard times, she said, for in the past, besides farming, her father had owned a wagon and four horses. He did a daily run from the Keighley Mills to Ripley's Dyeworks at Bradford, taking a wagonful of plain grey cloth and returning with a dyed and finished load. The new L & M railway between the two towns had put him out of business, and he'd had to let the horses go. John already knew about their bad luck on the farm and asked her then about the job she'd had at the bobbin mill. He almost wished he hadn't mentioned it as her face clouded for a moment.

'I loved my job. At first I was in the mill, turning out wooden bobbins by the hundred like everyone else, but last year I was moved to the offices to help with the wages. It was long hours, and I had to work Saturday mornings and I had to make sure I turned up to play the organ in church on Sundays, but it was a good job, and when Dad sold the wagon and horses it helped to feed us all.'

Isabella fell to earth with a bump.

'Oh, Johnny, I should be out looking for work and a place to live, not sitting here with you eating all this good food whilst my family are struggling to survive!'

She looked as if she would have run from the restaurant if John hadn't stopped her by putting his hand on hers.

'No, Isabella. It is too late to do anything today. You had a nasty shock and needed a day to recuperate. Enjoy the rest of your meal. You deserve it, and no one's much use with an empty belly. Tonight you can stay with me, and tomorrow – well, we'll see what tomorrow brings.'

She was pacified and sat down again.

'You're right, and thank you for this meal. Thank you for everything.'

They were soon chattering and laughing again, enjoying each other's company, but over coffee they grew quiet and John, watching Isabella across the table, had a curious thought.

'Just think, Isabella, twenty-four hours ago we had never met. Now I feel as if I've known you all my life!'

They walked arm in arm back to the Sun Inn and, if asked, neither would have remembered what they passed, for they had eyes only for each other.

202

By the time they were back in the hotel room John was finding it hard to contain his feelings for Isabella. He wanted to
reach out and hold her, kiss her and make love to her. She had
been delightful company, both interested and interesting, and
she looked gorgeous especially when she laughed and tossed
her head in that way of hers. He had been more and more
attracted to her, and coming back into the hotel room had
brought back the afternoon's picture of Isabella as she had
dropped her towel into the bath. He could not forget the sight
of her naked, wet body – and the close proximity of the double
bed didn't help!

He asked Isabella, rather brusquely, if she would care to see
the architect's drawings and hurriedly spread them on the low
table under the window. John was surprised by her pertinent
questions about the design and the stone needed. She was
really interested, and he was impressed to find that she had a
keen mind and took in all that he told her. Using a scale ruler
John took the length and height of the main building, jotting
down the measurements, and after a quick calculation he
arrived at the cubic footage of stone required for the front ele-
vation. Isabella had been watching over his shoulder and stated
bluntly that his figures were incorrect.

'I make it nine hundred cubic feet more than you've got.'

To humour her John agreed they should go over the figures
together, but after double-checking he had to admit that Isabella
was right. He had made a mistake, and errors like that would
cost him. He put down his pencil, smiling.

'You're not just a pretty face, are you? There's quite a bit of
sense in that head of yours!'

He leaned towards her and kissed her lightly on the tip of
her nose. Her response was immediate and unexpected. She
lifted her mouth to his, and for an instant he felt her hot, sweet
breath on his lips before they met in a passionate kiss. The
floodgates were opened and all the pent-up excitement of their
evening together burst through. They were on fire and it
seemed that kiss would never end. At last John drew away and
kissed her forehead, eyelids, cheeks and nose, but their lips
were magnets and they were drawn together once again in an
even more passionate kiss than before. He ran his hands
through Isabella's luxuriant dark hair, following it down round

her neck, over her shoulders and lightly over her bust. Tentatively he began to undo the buttons of her dress, slowly, unsure of her reaction, one, two, three, four. She offered no resistance but drew back slightly to make it easier for him. His hand slipped under the soft folds of wool and through the cool silk beneath he felt her breasts, firm and round, thrusting forward eager for his caress, the nipples hardening at his touch. How quickly fire can spread. They were consumed in its flame now, and all tenderness was gone. Urgently they undressed each other, even as they kissed, struggling to free themselves until their smart new clothes lay in a crumpled heap on the floor. John swept up Isabella and half-tossed her onto the bed where she lay smiling, arms stretching up for him.

'God you're beautiful,' he breathed. His pulse was racing, and in a trice he was with her on the bed. Another fiery kiss engulfed them and their legs entwined, sending shivers of delight through Isabella. This was her first time with a man and she had had no idea what it would be like, but never could she have imagined the delicious darts of electricity surging through her body nor the overwhelming yearning deep down inside her. She ached for this wonderful man and she wanted more. Roughly John pulled her to him. A fleeting thought that he should be gentle came and went without his heeding it, for he was a slave to his needs now, desperate to make love to this enchanting creature who had bewitched him. The fire had taken hold. He couldn't wait, and only her acceptance could quench its flame. Isabella moved with him, moaning at the unbelievable power of her new-found desire. The fire raged on, hotter, hotter, burning them up in its heat until at last Isabella arched and stretched, crying out with a mingling of pain and ecstasy as John, deep inside, amazed her as the last mighty flame blazed and was spent. They lay together then in the warmth of the fire's embers. Isabella nestled into the crook of John's arm and he kissed her gently on her damp forehead. They were utterly at peace, and each was deeply thankful to have found the other.

They had breakfasted early at the hotel, but by the time they had eaten the Sun Inn was already buzzing. Merchants of all types and from all areas, even from the continent, were trading in textiles, steel, building materials, oils, and so on. The Sun was recognized far and wide by mill engineers and builders as the Stone Exchange, and if you wanted to buy or sell anything this was the place to be. John intended to keep his ear to the ground for first-hand information of future projects requiring stone, and had insisted that Isabella join him amongst the builders and stone merchants. She had found it all very exciting and had been listening intently to the haggling and bartering going on around her when she heard a cheerful voice behind them.

'John Pickles! Just the man I want. How are you?'

Isabella had turned in time to see an agreeable-looking man stretching out his hand in greeting to John.

'Good to see you, Mr Fairburn. I'm well, thank you. What can I do for you?'

'I need some whopping great blocks of stone for engine beds at the mill, and I'm thinking that you're the chap to supply them. The last lot we had from you was real good quality.'

As he spoke Mr Fairburn had taken a drawing from his pocket.

'I need to be sure of what I'm getting, mind, they'll have to take a hell of a weight, you know.'

Holding the paper for John to see more clearly, he said, 'Now see here. These are the sizes and I'll need these bolt holes here, and here, to the exact diameter for the engine to be bolted down onto the stone. What do you think? Can you get out blocks as big as this?'

John assured him that he could and Mr Fairburn continued. 'I'm putting up a new extension, a weaving shed, and I want six-inch straight-faced wall stones for that. I'll need nine hundred square yards, all the same colour. I was well satisfied with the last lot you supplied, and if you can deliver the same quality, and if the price is right, the contract's yours.'

Isabella had watched as John pulled out a pocket book and did a quick calculation before telling Mr Fairburn that he could supply the stone with only a three per cent increase on the prices of the last order. Without more to do the deal had been struck, and the mill engineer grasped John's hand.

'It's a deal then, John. I'll be requiring the stone in three weeks' time, and I'll pay on delivery.' He had made to leave then but had turned back for a moment adding, just loud enough for Isabella to hear, 'Pretty wife you have there. Take care of her!'

He didn't see the faint blush which coloured Isabella's cheek, and John had just smiled at her and had made no attempt to enlighten Mr Fairburn as the mill engineer moved away.

Sitting in the trap on Brow Moor, Isabella remembered how proud she had been of Johnny's dealing methods and how nice it had felt to be taken for his wife. John was talking about Haworth now, pointing out familiar landmarks, but for once Isabella was only half-listening. Her mind had wandered back to the scene in the Sun Inn that morning, going over every detail of this astonishing day.

When Mr Fairburn had left them Isabella had told John that she too must go.

'I have to get some work today, Johnny. You'll be going back to Haworth, and I haven't even found a room. The Sun Inn is far too expensive for me. I can't thank you enough for all that you have done for me, and I wish you great success with your quarry.'

John had taken her arm and guided her to the lobby where it was quieter, away from the throng of traders, then he had turned her to him and taken both her hands in his. Isabella trembled slightly again as she remembered his words.

'Don't go, Isabella. Why not come back to Haworth? I have a cottage near the moors, and you can stay with me.'

When she protested that he had done enough already and that she could not possibly impose on him, he had silenced her with a little laugh.

'Impose! Isabella, you won't be imposing. This is a purely self-ish request. I *want* you to come. I don't want to lose you,' he paused and then said quietly, 'I think I am falling in love with you, Isabella.'

When she hadn't responded he'd given an embarrassed laugh.

'In any case, with that clever head of yours you'll be a great help. You can do the wages at the quarry. What do you say?'

He had taken her back to Brown, Muff's then and had bought her a warm coat for the journey. The same assistant had served them and had produced a lovely moss-green coat of fine-quality Melton cloth trimmed with a strip of brown fur. When Isabella had tried it on they had all agreed that it suited her very well, and John had said she looked very classy. They had not needed the shop assistant to point out that the colour was an exact match for John's suit. Whilst the assistant went in search of a matching hat and gloves John had kissed Isabella lightly and told her again that he was falling in love with her and could not believe his luck.

He can't believe *his* luck, thought Isabella. I must be the luckiest lass in Yorkshire. Here I am dressed in fine clothes and starting a new life with the most wonderful man I have ever met. She resolved there and then to make John proud of her. She didn't know how she would do it, but she was determined to find a way.

They were heading down the hillside now, and Isabella was jolted out of her daydream by John poking her with his whip.

'You haven't heard a word I've been saying. What are you thinking about, Jezebel?'

Isabella blushed, but she knew that John was joking and laughed as she retorted,

'Wouldn't you like to know! And I'm not a Jezebel – you are the only man I've known!'

They continued with their merriment chatter and they were both overjoyed at being together.

As the trap reached the brow of the hill John reined in the horses. Haworth lay ahead of them on the opposite hillside. Thin wisps of smoke curled into the dull sky from the chimneys of the buildings clustered below the church, and on the skyline beyond plumes of steam billowed against the smoky clouds. John pointed across the valley with his whip.

'That's Dimples Quarry, there. It looks as if the steam crane is working on full power, but with the orders I've taken in Bradford we'll be needing another crane and two more larger mechanical frame saws. I expect to be setting on another twenty men or so to get all the work out. Things are really looking good.'

He turned to Isabella sitting beside him and smiled.

'You'll have plenty to keep you busy with all those wages!'

Isabella smiled too, but she didn't reply. She still felt it was all a dream and that at any moment she would wake up and find herself in some dusty lodging house in Bradford, cold and hungry.

As the trap reached the brow of the hill and they were making their way up the steep hill of Haworth's Main Street, local people waved to them and Isabella was amused when little children shouted after them.

'Hello, Johnny Big Block.'

John stopped the trap briefly outside the baker's shop and went in for a fresh loaf. Then they made their way past the church and took the left fork in the road, heading towards the village of Stanbury, until they stopped outside John's little cottage in West Lane. On reaching the door John unlocked it and then turned and handed the key to Isabella, saying, 'This is your key, and you can keep it for ever if you wish.'

She thanked him with a kiss and went through the doorway into her new home.

26

It wasn't the first time that Mr and Mrs Ferrari had asked Leonora to come back to Laverock Hall. When Oscar Beale had been sent to prison they had begged and pleaded with their daughter to come home, and when the baby had been born they had once again tried to make her see sense, thinking that she would need help with the child now and would be glad to return. However, Leonora had been adamant; she would stay in Bradford and bring up her daughter, Sarah, alone. Her parents had helped her financially, as otherwise the house would have been taken from her to pay Oscar's debts, and she had coped really well. Her mother had gone to stay in Bradford for a couple of months when the baby was born and Leonora had put on a brave face whilst she was there, but afterwards, alone in the house with her daughter, she had spent long hours wishing that things had turned out differently.

Leonora could not go back to Laverock Hall and face all the sniggers of her old acquaintances. What would they think of her now, marrying that despicable man? Worst of all, she might bump into John, and that she could not bear. He must really hate her. Although she had had no part in his misfortune, she felt as if she were to blame because she hadn't stood by him. She hadn't even spoken out in his defence, and had almost believed that Papa and Oscar must be right when they had said that John was no good. Many times she had wondered what John was doing now, but her parents had never mentioned him and she hadn't liked to ask. Leonora was lonely and depressed, and her mother was concerned to see how pale and thin she had become.

When Sarah was ten months old Mrs Ferrari finally persuaded Leonora to bring the child to Oldfield for a visit.

'I'll come for a month or so,' said Leonora at last. 'It will be good for Sarah and she will get to know you better but I'm not staying on. My home is in Bradford now.'

She had been at Laverock Hall for almost three weeks and had enjoyed the familiar surroundings and her parents' company. Her mother had made sure that she ate well and had been pleased to see some colour returning and a smile back on her face. In truth, Leonora was happy to be home and knew that she would find it hard to go back to the empty house in Bradford. Perhaps after all she might stay.

One Wednesday afternoon Mrs Ferrari had said that she would look after Sarah, and she had encouraged Leonora to go out for a walk.

'It's not a bad day for the time of year, a little grey, but it doesn't look like rain. If you wrap up warmly you'll be fine. It's good to have some time to yourself. Little ones can be so very demanding.'

Leonora hadn't needed a second bidding. She loved her daughter dearly, but sometimes found it trying to be always with her, for in Bradford she had no one to turn to for help. She set off with no clear intention of which direction she would take, but soon found herself heading down past the Donkey Bridge and then on up the hillside to Stanbury. She felt free, and as the day was chillier than she thought she was glad to keep moving and walked on over Sladen Bridge and up the last steep hill to Haworth. Once in the Main Street she dawdled, looking in the shop windows until a child's bonnet in the draper's shop caught her eye and thinking how sweet Sarah would look in it she went inside to ask the price. The clang of the doorbell brought the shopkeeper hurrying from a room at the back, obviously pleased to have a customer. She opened the wooden panels that gave access to the window and placed the bonnet on the counter.

'It's a lovely little cap. Only two shillings and sixpence, and the buttercream colour will suit any child. What age is it for?'

Leonora didn't answer. Through the open panels she had seen a smart young man in a green suit coming out of the baker's shop opposite. Her heart skipped a beat. It was John Pickles! All thoughts of not wanting to see him flew from her head. She must speak with him...

'What do you think?' the shopkeeper was saying. 'Would you like the bonnet?'

Distractedly, Leonora fumbled in her purse for money.

'Yes, I'll take it, thank you. There's no need to wrap it. Thank you. Good-day.'

Hurriedly she left the shop, only half-hearing the shopkeeper calling after her, 'Your change, madam, I haven't given you your change!'

Out into the street Leonora turned to hurry up the hill after John, but was stopped in her tracks by the sight of him climbing onto a trap beside a beautiful young woman with thick auburn hair. As John took up the reins the woman linked her arm in his, and he smiled at her the way Leonora remembered him smiling at her. Hot tears stung her eyes – she pressed herself back against the shop door, afraid of being seen. She needn't have worried, for the pair had eyes only for each other and, not giving her a second glance, they were soon out of sight past the church.

Leonora felt as if she had been hit with a sledgehammer. She could not breathe. How could she have been so stupid? She had got everything wrong; she hadn't realized until this very moment that she was still in love with John, and now it was too late! All the pleasure had gone from her afternoon's excursion, and the walk back to Laverock Hall was long and dreary.

Mrs Ferrari was expecting Leonora to be refreshed by her walk, and was worried to see her daughter so dejected on her return. She knew her too well to ask what had upset her, but by next day she also knew that whatever had happened that afternoon had ruined the hopes she had built up of persuading Leonora to stay on at Laverock Hall.

'I'm going back to Bradford tomorrow, Mamma. The sooner the better. That is my home after all.'

With a sad heart Mrs Ferrari waved goodbye to her daughter and granddaughter, promising to visit very soon. She could only speculate on Leonora's unhappiness, but she did wonder if it might have anything to do with young John Pickles.

27

John could not wait to show Isabella his quarry, and they were up on Dimples Hill quite early the following morning. First they visited the quarry face, and John explained the different layers of rock which were clearly visible where the hillside had been worked.

'First we have to remove all the clay and topstone using picks, shovels and wheelbarrows to get to the gritstone, which is poor-quality stuff and only good for crushing for sand and gravel. Of course that has its uses too; gravel is needed for roads and for infill. Below that you can see the narrow band of freestone – or flagstone as it's usually known, which is removed by following any natural cracks in the rocks.'

'Is that what is used for flags for pavements?' Isabella asked.

'Yes, it is. It splits easily but it has many other uses too, such as wall stones, kerbstones, landings, roofing slates and the likes.'

'Surely roofing slates need to be much thinner than flagstones – would not they be much too heavy for roofs?'

John was pleased at Isabella's interest and explained.

'Lifts of flagstone are left to dry for a few weeks, and then the slate strikers are able to split off the slates, but we don't do much of that here, as we concentrate on the block stone from deeper in the quarry.'

He pointed to a bed of rock well below the flagstone which looked about nine feet thick.

'That's ashlar or block stone. It can be as deep as one hundred feet into the quarry, which is why we needed that monster steamer crane. The ashlar is what we'll get out for the building work in Bradford, and in a minute I'll show you the power saw that cuts it. It's exciting lifting these blocks.'

John's eyes lit up when he was telling Isabella about it, and she could see how much he loved his work.

'In the old days men called "huggers" used to bring out the rock. They wore leather saddles on their backs and were incredibly strong, lifting slabs of up to seven hundredweight. Of course, nowadays with the steam-powered cranes we can lift much bigger blocks. We have to, the slabs for the steam beds in the mills are often over ten feet long and four feet thick – that's some weight of stone!'

John took her next to see the blocks of ashlar being cut to size on the frame saw. He explained how the abrasive action of iron shot and water, sprayed from overhead, work with the oscillating blades to saw through the stone.

'I didn't realize these machines were so huge,' said Isabella. 'Is the stone ready when it comes off these saws?'

'No. The wall stone dressers square and dress the stones for use on the fronts of buildings. They use a nicker and mallet, and get wonderful results.'

John's enthusiasm was rubbing off on Isabella, and she was keen to learn all she could, so he took her next to see the piles of dressed stone awaiting delivery.

'What are those men doing over there with the sand and water?' she asked as they made their way to the delivery yard.

'They are polishing flagstone. Some flags are self-faced, but most need to be ground level and polished for a good finish.'

Isabella laughed. 'I've never really thought about stone, but I suppose I just imagined someone digging it up and carting it away to build with just as it came out of the ground. It is all very interesting.'

'Well, you can work here full-time if you would like to. There's plenty to do besides the wages: book-keeping, letter-writing, and so on. I'll gladly pay you a weekly wage.'

Her reply took her by surprise.

'I'll be happy to do it for nothing, for you, Johnny.'

However, Isabella felt guilty when John pointed out that she would hardly help her brothers and sisters with no wages. She had given her family little thought since her new-found happiness which was so unlike her, and she was glad now to accept the offer.

The blacksmith's shop was their next stop, where Harold, pipe-in-mouth as usual, was busy sharpening tools. Chisels, nicking-tools and quarrymen's wedges were neatly lined up, ready for his expert crafting. He grinned impishly as the pair came through the door, and with a twinkle in his eye nodded towards Isabella.

'Fine filly you got there, John. She'd win first prize at Haworth show, for certain!' and before either of them could respond he continued, 'Nah then, lassie, can ye bake a good apple pie, 'cos sure as eggs is eggs t'quickest way to John's heart will be through his stomach! Likes 'is food, the lad does.'

Isabella smiled at Harold. She had been taken aback when he called her a filly, but she could see that he was only teasing.

'If that's the quickest way, just provide the apples, and within an hour I'll be Queen of Hearts.'

They all laughed, and John introduced his friend to Isabella.

'It was Harold's humour and common sense that got me through my time at Armley and helped to keep me sane. I'll never forget that. How are all the family, Harold? Are they happy living in Haworth?'

'Well, we aren't going back to Halifax, that's for sure! The missus thanks the Lord night and morning for all our good fortune,' and he added quite seriously, 'we're all 'appy. Yes, very 'appy and it's down to you, John Pickles.'

They left Harold to his sharpening and leaving the quarry walked down into Main Street, calling at the butchers and the grocers for provisions. John introduced Isabella to Mary Firth, who owned the ladies' outfitters opposite the church, and then left the pair of them to choose some everyday wear for Isabella, which Mrs Firth promised to parcel up and have delivered to West Lane.

Whilst they were busy sorting out stockings, skirts and blouses John nipped into the greengrocers and bought three pounds of shiny green cooking apples.

Later, back at the cottage, Isabella laughed when John produced them, saying, 'Now prove it if you want to be my Queen of Hearts!'

She had no trouble producing two delicious pies, and she sent the larger of them for Harold and his family with a note that read: 'Fine fillies are not only long legs and a pretty face!'

* * *

214

The large engine-bed slabs for Mr Fairburn's mill at Saltaire were ready for delivery and had been hoisted onto the heavy wheeled block-wagon. It was a terrific load for the four tough horses – probably upwards of ten tons, John estimated, and he was worried about taking it down the steep main street. He knew that if the brakes failed it would be disastrous both for the horses and the occupants of the street. The wagon-driver was a little fellow called Tom Knight who, despite his years of experience with wagons and horses, looked decidedly nervous as the wagon rolled along West Lane towards the hill. He stopped on the last flat stretch of road just before the church, to put on slipper brakes and fasten the rear wheels with chains to prevent them running too fast. Then he gently eased the horses forward and began the descent. He reined the horses back and they struggled to hold the load.

Slowly the wagon rumbled over the cobbles, the chains creaking and straining and the brake shoes screeching against the iron wheels. Slowly past the shops, slowly, slowly past the row of neat cottages. Almost halfway now and John, walking beside the wagon, began to relax slightly. All seemed to be going well. It was then that one of the chains snapped, and the wagon lurched forward dangerously before Tom Knight threw all his weight on the brakes. With the extra strain the wooden brakes shrieked and whined, and the friction caused sparks to fly and flames suddenly licked around the wheel.

'Whoa there!' shouted Tom, hauling on the reins for all he was worth. And as John darted behind the wagon, grabbed the water bucket hanging on the back rail and doused the flames, Tom pulled on the safety brake and jammed the wheels with a stout pole. Wiping his hand across his brow, John checked that the wheel was not too badly damaged, fixed the chain and shouted to everyone in the street to stand clear. Then he told Tom to proceed cautiously. Carefully the pole was removed and the brakes were released and thankfully the wagon made it to the bottom of the hill without further mishap. John congratulated the driver.

'Well done, Tom. You did a good job. You're over the worst and should be fine now as far as Saltaire. See you when you get back.'

As the wagon moved away John made a decision. He would

find another quarry for the big blocks. One from which the stone could be transported safely. He had put Tom and others in great danger today, and it must never happen again!

One morning in late April John showed Isabella a letter he had received from a Mr Fielden, inviting them to visit him at his home in Todmorden.

'I've never heard of the fellow,' said John, 'but it seems that the reputation of Dimples Quarry is spreading further afield. He wants some decorative stonework for a chapel he's building, and has heard that our masons are noted for their artistic ability. He's a cricket fan too, so we'll have plenty to talk about!'

Mr Fielden had suggested early May for the visit, and on the appointed date John and Isabella donned their smart green clothes and, as a mark of respect, John sported a red rose, the Lancashire emblem, in his lapel and Isabella wore a white rose – Todmorden town is half in Yorkshire and half in Lancashire. They set off early in the trap, and on the way John told Isabella what he had managed to find out about Mr Fielden.

'He's a very prosperous cotton manufacturer. Apparently the family started with just a few hand looms, but now have many large cotton mills in Lancashire and also own three ships sailing out of Liverpool carrying their cotton goods around the world. Mr Fielden is a very wealthy man. So wealthy in fact that he has strong influence with the Bank of England and knows all the right people in the City of London.'

'You're making me nervous about meeting him,' said Isabella. 'I'm not used to these well-off folk.'

John smiled reassuringly.

'You'll be fine,' he said, but he didn't tell her that he too was feeling a little apprehensive by the time they turned into the wide drive leading up to the house.

A maid answered their ring at the door and escorted them through the large entrance hall to a drawing room, where two men were waiting to receive them. The taller, and slightly younger looking of the pair came across to meet them, hand outstretched.

'John Pickles? Pleased to meet you. I'm Fielden, and this is

216

Mr Crowther, my architect. You must be Isabella, my dear. How do you do!'

Both men were down-to-earth Lancashire men, open and friendly, and Isabella needn't have worried that she would feel ill at ease. She wasn't excluded as the men got down to business and discussed the decorative details of the stone-work required for the chapel. They were happy to hear her views on their ideas.

'Are you a chapelgoer, Isabella?' asked Mr Fielden.

'Yes, but I'm afraid our chapel is a very plain affair compared to the one you are building. However, even though it is quite small the acoustics are good, and the organ sounds wonderful.'

'Do you play, Isabella?

Isabella nodded.

'It is such a gift. Perhaps you'd play for us when we are through with the plans? I don't have an organ, but the piano is newly tuned and I'd love to hear it.'

Isabella didn't really know what to play, and to warm up she began with a couple of hymn tunes, but after that she played a Haydn piano piece that she knew well. The three men were delighted, especially John who had never before heard her play. He was impressed and looked very proud.

They stayed for afternoon tea, and over scones and cake Mr Fielden quizzed John about the quarry. John was full of enthusiasm as he told about his new cranes and saws and the full order books, and although Mr Fielden didn't want to dampen his spirit he had a word of advice for the young man.

'Always remember, John, the bank is ever-willing to lend you an umbrella when the weather is fine, but when it rains they will want it back again! You seem to be doing fine, but my advice to you, now that you are an established quarry man, is to join the Freemasons. They can be a great help. Just one more piece of advice, keep yourself out of politics. At least, avoid any strong connections with either party and stay neutral. Who knows which way the pendulum will swing?'

'I've never been too interested in national politics,' said John, 'so it shouldn't be too hard to steer clear of that, but I'm grateful for your advice, and I'll remember what you've said about the banks as I'm looking now to expanding and opening a new quarry.'

217

Mr Crowther had been quietly listening, but now joined the conversation.

'There's a great demand for stone in Lancashire, John, especially in the Manchester area. Have you ever thought of coming this way?'

Tea was finished and, although reluctant to leave, the young couple knew they should be heading home if they were to be over the bleak Cock Hill Moor before dark. John had the detailed chapel drawings in his pocket and told Mr Fielden that he would be happy to supply the ornamental stone and would submit a price by letter within the week.

Whilst they had been talking Isabella had been admiring an oil painting in a large gilt frame, which hung over the mantelpiece. It was of a low farmhouse set in a patchwork of green fields, and despite the rural calmness of the work the painting seemed to dominate the room.

'What a beautiful painting. Did you used to live there?' asked Isabella.

'How perceptive of you,' said Mr Fielden. 'That is where I was born and where my family started to weave cloth. We began with just four hand looms, and I have the painting there to remind me of our beginnings. No matter how well you succeed in life, never forget your roots.'

On this note they made their farewells and started the long journey home. Their route took them first along the valley bottom, where the road runs parallel with the canal, and Isabella was thoughtful as she watched heavily laden barges carrying building bricks or coal for the mills. She remembered what Mr Crowther had said about the ever-increasing demand for stone in Manchester, and as the trap began the long ascent of Cock Hill she turned excitedly to John.

'If we could find a quarry at Hebden Bridge, as you've planned, we could send all the stone we wanted into Manchester on the canals. We would not use the wagons; the canal barges can take huge amounts at a time. What do you think, Johnny?'

Before he could reply she rushed on, 'We could go further – right to Liverpool, and then bring back timber from the docks on the return trips. We could be stone and timber merchants. It's a good idea, isn't it?'

John laughed. 'You've got it all worked out, haven't you? It does sound like a good idea, but it needs some looking into. First we have to find a quarry where we can produce big blocks of stone as good as those at Dimples Hill. But it's right what you say. A horse-drawn canal barge can transport six hundred times the load of one packhorse or twenty cartloads of goods. Wagon transportation is getting very expensive. And timber? Yes, there's a great demand for that too. I'll make some enquiries. It's certainly worth considering. Thanks, pretty face!'

Each Saturday, when the cricket match was over, Paul and his girlfriend Molly would spend the evening with John and Isabella at their cottage. They would have an evening meal together and talk at length on all manner of topics. The four of them got along extremely well, and when the subject of marriage was raised it was almost a forgone conclusion that they would have a double ceremony and share their special day. There was much talk in the village about the coming wedding, and when the day arrived, June 16th 1844, there were crowds of people outside Haworth church to wish the couples well. The rival cricket teams, Methody and Church, had for once joined forces and, smart in their white outfits, they lined the church pathway, cricket bats held aloft, to form an archway for the brides and grooms.

The wedding reception was to be held at the Black Bull Inn, and the invited guests made their way the short distance from the church to the hostelry. John and Paul welcomed each of them, including Mr and Mrs Jonas Fisher, the Butterworths, Ruth and Robert with their new baby daughter, Harold and Alice Wainwright and Mr Turner and Mary Ann, who had travelled down from the Dales the previous day. John and Paul had gone up to Buckden with their news and the wedding invitations, and had been shocked to see Mary Ann looking much older than when they had known her at Sladen Bridge. She no longer laughed in the light-hearted way that they remembered, and though still only in her forties her hair was streaked with grey and there were care lines on her forehead. She had found it hard losing Seth, and now her elderly parents were in need of her in Vermont and she had decided to return to the United States to care for them. Paul had suggested that if she waited until after the wedding they could escort her to Liverpool and see her safely aboard ship, and she had been only too pleased to accept.

Now at the wedding breakfast they honoured her with pride of place at their table and during the speeches both John and Paul gave thanks to Mary Ann and Seth for their devoted care of them when they arrived at Sladen Bridge as orphans from Liverpool all those years ago, and a toast was drunk to Mary Ann to wish her well in America.

Next day Mary Ann had a surprise for John. Before she left for Liverpool she gave him a parcel containing Seth's naval officer's uniform and his wooden leg.

'I thought you might like to have these. They're all I have to give you, and I know that Seth would have wanted you to have them.' As he unfolded the blue jacket John had a lump in his throat and found it difficult to speak. He knew how much the uniform had meant to Seth, and he would treasure it always.

The four young people standing on the dock waved to Mary Ann as the crew cast off and the liner moved slowly away from the quayside. They continued to wave as the ship sailed down river until they could no longer make out the figures leaning against the rails, then a little sadly they retraced their steps to the hotel, where they were to spend another night before they caught the following morning's paddle steamer to Bangor in North Wales for their two-week honeymoon.

When Isabella found that she was pregnant both she and John were a little taken aback. Although they had talked of children, it had always been 'sometime', 'when', 'in the future', and now it was to happen sooner than they had anticipated. They had been intent on building up the business, and both had worked long hours thinking of little beside stone, timber, barges, cranes and estimates, orders, bills and wages. They had acquired a quarry at Hebden Bridge bearing good-quality stone and had quickly installed cranes and frame saws and then implemented Isabella's idea, buying two barges for transportation to Manchester, where the demand for stone seemed endless. They brought back huge long lengths of timber to the timber yard they had developed in Halifax. These were sought after for the large

220

official buildings springing up throughout West Yorkshire. Business was booming on all fronts, and John and Isabella were making vast profits.

They realized now that the little cottage in West Lane was not large enough for a family, and John told Isabella she could have a house anywhere in the Worth Valley, providing it was no more than three miles from Dimples Quarry. Their order books were full and their profits and bank balance were good. John wanted to build a house befitting their station in life.

Within a couple of weeks Isabella had found the very place for her new home. It was at Dockroyd in the next village of Oakworth. The field faced south with a lovely view across the valley, and had a small, natural waterfall where spring water gurgled out from beneath a banking and bubbled its way down the gentle slope. Isabella was delighted.

'This spring will make a wonderful garden feature. I want the whole area landscaping and a kitchen garden at the back.'

'There's a lot to do before we worry about a garden,' laughed John. 'First we must negotiate a price for the site, and then I'll get Fred Day, an architect, to come and discuss designs for the house. I'm happy to leave it to you, Isabella, but don't forget to include a billiard room for me!'

The architect was duly engaged and Isabella gave him clear instructions as to what she had planned for her new home. She wanted seven bedrooms, all of which must face south, a music room, an oak-panelled dining room and, of course, John's billiards room. The servants' quarters would be at the back and must not be skimped on, but should be comfortable and light. There was to be a large kitchen garden, a stable block with coach house, and a cottage for the gardener. Lastly she told Mr Day about the conservatory she envisaged connected to the drawing room at the front of the house. Much discussion went into the design of the conservatory, as Isabella wanted this to be the main feature of the house, and the final plans were for a large, ornate, airy and, hopefully, sun-filled room. Isabella had always loved plants and had hopes of growing a vine under the glass.

The architect was not surprised by the stipulation that all the stone must come from Dimples Quarry, nor the fact that John wanted a local builder, Wilfred Bottomley, to carry out the work. It was well known that John Pickles favoured local businesses, and although Fred Day had had no prior dealings with him he had heard much that was good about the builder. It was said that he worked hard alongside his men, setting a good example to all who worked for him. He was fair and just, but would not tolerate a slacker who didn't pull his weight.

John was highly pleased with the final drawings and ordered an immediate start on the building. At first progress was slow, owing to incessant rain and frost in the early months of 1845, but as the days warmed and grew longer the external structure quickly grew and took shape. Isabella, though now heavily pregnant, spent much of her time at Oakworth making sure that all was going to plan. It was impossible to finish even the main house before the baby was born, and in early July Isabella was safely delivered of her child in the little cottage at Haworth. It was a fine lusty boy, weighing eight and a half pounds and with curly black hair just like his father's. They named him Robert, and Isabella and John were delighted as they had both secretly hoped for a son. God was good and he had granted them their wish.

Over the next few months Isabella saw the finishing touches put to the house. A large heating boiler was installed to give comfort throughout their home, even in the conservatory. Carpets were obtained from a Halifax firm renowned for the quality and design of its stock, curtains came from Brown, Muff's of Bradford, and Italian workmen laid the flooring in the front hallway and conservatory. Bob Wood, carpenter of Changegate, Haworth, recommended for his craftsmanship and artistic talent, was commissioned to make fine mahogany and walnut furniture, and another local firm landscaped the garden with trees, shrubs, rockeries, waterfalls and pools which were filled with goldfish. John left everything to his wife. He was busy at the quarries, and he knew that he could rely on Isabella's good sense over money. Besides, the order books were still full – there was more work available than they could take. Both quarries were running to full capacity, and the timber yard in Halifax was also doing good business. By the time Mr and Mrs Pickles moved into their new home, 'Oakworth Grange', Robert was ten months old. He was a sturdy little chap, already walking and trying to talk. To his parents it seemed that they had all that life could offer.

* * *

The years passed happily for John and Isabella. The businesses prospered and they became more and more wealthy. Although Isabella now stayed at home with her young son, John still consulted her on decisions at the quarry or the timber yard. He had been right when he had said she was not just a pretty face, for she proved to be an astute businesswoman. She was far-seeing and had the abilities to put their priorities in the right order. It was Isabella who foresaw the demand for the extra long lengths of heavy timber that the architects and builders would require for the support of large-span buildings and for the new factories which were being built. When the orders came in, they were ready to supply. They made special purchases at the docks in Hull and Liverpool, bringing the wood to Halifax and Bradford on their own canal barges and creating a monopoly of the larger timbers sized in the area. In Halifax John was re-named 'Johnny Big Plank', and he would smile when he heard that and say, 'We can supply. How many do you want?'

Although Isabella missed the bustle of the quarry, she was never despondent at home with Robert. She spent many hours in her garden and was never happier than when, trowel in hand, she helped the head gardener, George, with re-potting, separating, or bedding out the plants. George had a wealth of knowledge where the garden was concerned. The Latin names for all the flowers rolled off his tongue like music, and he knew the best plants for the shade and for the sun and which ones needed richer soil or a wetter area. Isabella had an eye for colour and shape so that splashes of brightness contrasted with the varied foliages of the greener plants. In the short space of five years she and George had between them created a garden of incredible beauty.

From the conservatory there was a splendid view of the garden, and when John was home, during the long spring and summer evenings, they spent their time there looking out at the bright banks of colour and the soft evening sunlight glinting on the fishpond or catching the water as it trickled over stones on its course down the garden. The trees planted at the bottom of the garden already afforded privacy, and John reflected that when they matured the garden would take on a dream-like quality, hiding them completely from the world beyond.

Visitors were always impressed by the garden, but even more so by the conservatory. Isabella's vine had grown well from its first planting and had now spread upwards and across the glass roof. It provided shade on the hottest summer days when the cool of the conservatory was unexpected and welcome, bringing a feeling of tranquillity to those seeking respite there.

On one such afternoon, Isabella and Ruth Butterworth were taking tea in the conservatory, watching their children playing with a ball on the lawn beyond.

'How do you make your plants flourish like this?' asked Ruth looking in wonderment at the vine above them, so vigorous and healthy. 'My plants are all small and pale by comparison.'

'When I'm working amongst the flowers I find myself talking to them. I'm on good terms with all the flowers, and I give them my love,' replied Isabella.

If Ruth thought this strange she didn't say so, and Isabella never admitted to anyone what was, she suspected, a big part of her success – that George, the gardener, had put a dead sheep at the vine's root to make it productive!

Every Friday afternoon Isabella took her son to visit his grandparents at Newsholme. It was a two-mile walk, and sometimes Robert would ask if they could take the trap in order to get there more quickly, for he loved every minute at the farm: collecting eggs with Grandfather or watching Grandma skim the thick, yellow cream from the milk in the wide bowl. However, Isabella always insisted that they should walk, no matter what the weather was like, no matter how hard Robert pleaded, they always walked. She had never forgotten what Mr Fielden had said when they visited him at Todmorden. 'No matter how wealthy you become, never forget your roots.'

Walking to the farm took Isabella back to her childhood days. Somehow it didn't seem quite right to draw into the old farmyard in a smart coach and, besides, the coachman would have nothing to do whilst waiting to take them home. No, far better to walk. Having once started out Robert enjoyed those outings running on ahead looking for hedgehogs, rabbits, birds' nests and a host of other things to be found among the hedgerows. They usually took the lane past the old bobbin mill, and Isabella told Robert stories of the time she worked there as a girl and of the time when foot and mouth disease killed Grandfather's cattle and he'd had to start all over again. She didn't tell her son that it had been John who had restocked her father's farm, for Grandfather was a proud man and had insisted on repaying every penny once he was back on his feet.

Mr and Mrs Outhwaite were always overjoyed to see Isabella and Robert. Their own son, Frank, had left to work in Bradford when he turned 17, and only the two younger girls were now still at home. They thought it grand to have a lad about the place again, and Isabella's sisters used to argue with each other, when Robert was little, over who should take charge of him. They were happy times. Mrs Outhwaite always had a meat and potato pie and mushy peas ready in the oven when they arrived, and there was always cake, eggs, butter and cream to take back home.

28

1851

It was late September, and Isabella and her son set off for their weekly walk to Newsholme, the six-year-old Robert stuck tight to his mother's hand as they walked quickly against a warm head-wind. They made good time, and were glad of the customary welcoming meal and the roaring fire at the farmhouse.

'Better not stay too long today, dear,' said Mrs Outhwaite as she poured custard over a steaming sponge pudding. 'The weather doesn't look too good, and we would not like you to be caught in a thunderstorm, would we?'

She might as well have saved her breath, for before they had finished the meal an almighty crack of thunder rattled the window pane and heavy drops of rain began to fall. Mr Outhwaite had been out tending the cattle, and he came in now, shaking water off an already very wet coat.

'Better bide awhile and let this storm blow over. It's fairly coming down just now.'

They waited an hour or so, and when the storm had given no sign of abating Mrs Outhwaite suggested that Isabella and Robert stay the night at Newsholme.

'John won't expect you home on a day like this. You can have Frank's room and go home tomorrow.'

'I think John will worry,' said Isabella. 'He won't know whether or not we have set off. I think we should go home.'

A little while later the rain eased. The thunder and lightning seemed to be spent, and Isabella was determined to leave. Mrs Outhwaite sounded worried as she bid them farewell.

'Take care, love, see you next week if the weather's better.'

There were ominous black clouds higher up the hill, so Isabella decided to take the short cut across the fields in the hope of getting home before the rain came on again. The field was muddy but passable, and they were soon down at the foot-bridge over the river in the valley bottom. Higher up the hills there had been a cloudburst, and the river was in full spate. Isabella had never seen it like this before. Normally it was little more than a stream, and if they came this way in the summer-time Robert often paddled across. Now the water was rushing by at a terrifying speed, roaring past the stone pier supporting the bridge in the centre of the river and splashing over the two wooden planks which formed the bridge. Isabella was reluctant to cross and wondered if they should re-trace their steps and follow the road – but she knew the bridge had withstood many storms, and it was only a short span, they would be across before they knew it! With Robert in front of her, she stepped onto the bridge and began to cross. The water came over their shoes, and Robert looked back for re-assurance.

'It's all right, Robert, we'll soon be over.'

She had hardly uttered the words when with a terrible 'whooshing' noise the stone pillar collapsed and the wooden planks gave way beneath them. Robert and Isabella were thrown headlong into the raging torrent. There was no time for Isabella to reach out for her son. She tried to see where he went under the water, but he was gone and in another instant she was being swept downstream at a terrifying pace. Vainly she tried to catch overhanging branches as she was swept along, and more than once was dragged under and her lungs filled with water before she thrashed her way to the surface again. One of the planks, which had caught momentarily on a trailing branch, broke free, and hurtling down the river it hit Isabella on the head and everything went black as she lost consciousness.

Robert had fallen into a faster current. Briefly taken under the water, he was soon forced to the surface, gasping for air. He heard his mother call his name as he was carried swiftly away from her. About 100 yards further along, where the river made a sharp bend, he was thrust against the bank and held there by a boulder jutting out into the river. The terrified boy screamed until he felt as if his lungs would burst and then, real-izing that no one would ever hear him above the noise of the torrent, he tried to pull himself from the water. Twice he slipped back into the churning river, but fear lends strength to those who need it, and he finally managed to haul himself onto the bank, where he lay fighting for his breath. There was no sign of his mother, and Robert knew what he had to do. He ran as fast as his legs would carry him back up the fields to the farm. Banging on the door he shouted for Grandfather to go and help his mother, before collapsing into his Grandma's arms. Little as he was, he would have gone back down the river if Grandma hadn't restrained him and taken him in to dry him by the fire and give him a warming cup of tea.

It was almost two hours after the collapse of the bridge that Grandfather and a neighbouring farmer and his son found Isabella. She was lying face-down on a large flat rock in the middle of the water about a mile down river, and it took the strength of all three men to get her back to the bank. She was unconscious and deathly pale and her father, afraid that they had arrived too late, sank onto his knees beside her in the wet grass.

'There's a pulse,' said Bill Mawden suddenly. 'Quick, get her over onto her front.'

As they rolled Isabella over, water spurted from her mouth and involuntarily she gasped for air. Bill pressed up and down on her back a few times to help her lungs to fill with air, and after a while, although she didn't regain consciousness, it was clear that she was breathing a little more easily, and they thought it would be safe to move her.

'Better bring her back to my place,' said Bill. 'It's a good bit nearer than your house, and the sooner we get her where it's warm the better.'

When they arrived at Spring House Farm Bill's wife, Nellie, immediately took charge. Her son was sent to fetch the doctor; Bill was told to put the kettle on to boil and then light a fire in the grate in the spare bedroom. Turning to Mr Outhwaite she said,

'You'd best be fetching 'er 'usband. She's not looking too good and he'll want to be 'ere.'

She stripped Isabella of her sodden clothes, dried her and then put her into one of her own warm flannel nightdresses. The bedroom fire was by this time already blazing in the hearth, and with her husband's help Nellie carried Isabella to the bed and piled thick wool blankets over her. She was

228

worried by Isabella's paleness and the bluish colour of her lips, and never left her side, all the while rubbing her hands and arms to try to get her circulation going. After what seemed a very long time indeed her colour slowly began to return and her lips lost their deathly blue tinge. Moaning softly, Isabella opened her eyes.

'Thanks be to God,' muttered Nellie. 'There, there, you're all right, just you rest awhile.'

Isabella closed her eyes again, and the farmer's wife wondered if she had any idea what had happened to her or where she was now.

Doctor King ordered complete bed rest for at least three days. He said Isabella was lucky to be alive and was in deep shock. Throughout her stay at Springhouse Farm John refused to leave his wife's bedside. He had been horrified when news of the accident reached him, and he blamed himself for not foreseeing the bad weather and sending the trap to pick up his wife and son. He wanted to be there when Isabella woke to reassure her and to tell her that he loved her and so that, together, they could give thanks to God that both she and Robert had survived the accident.

After the first 24 hours Isabella seemed to recover quickly. She sat up in bed, ate everything that Mrs Marsden brought for her, and laughed and talked with John, but they took heed of the doctor and she stayed with the Marsdens for another two days before John collected Robert from his grandparent's house and took them both home.

It was almost a week later that Isabella took a turn for the worse. She developed severe chest pains and a harsh cough and had difficulty getting her breath. By the time the doctor arrived Isabella was running a high fever and was delirious. It didn't need Dr King to tell John that the situation was very grave.

'She has double pneumonia, and there is little we can do. Keep her warm and free from draughts, and try to get her to drink frequently. She needs to be kept quiet and will need all her strength when the crisis comes.'

Again John never left Isabella's side. When she was awake he supported her and tried to get her to sip water, but she needed a lot of encouragement and was obviously getting weaker. He tried to keep her mouth moistened, as she was becoming dehydrated and her lips were cracking. Isabella was fighting for her life. For more than a week she drifted in and out of consciousness, and there was little that John could do but pray. He was unkempt and unshaven and deadly tired when Dr King finally pronounced that the crisis was past and Isabella would recover. Taking his wife's hand, John felt hot tears of gratitude coursing down his cheeks.

All Christmas invitations were cancelled. There would be no parties or other festivities this year. John knew that his wife needed peace and time to regain her strength, and that it would be better if the three of them spent Christmas quietly together.

Isabella asked that her bed be brought down to the conservatory, where she would be surrounded by the plants she loved. They had two caged canaries in the conservatory, and by day the birds sang their hearts out, bringing added joy to the invalid. She was content there, and with servants to look after her John was able to get back to the quarries and make sure everything had been running smoothly in his absence.

By Christmas Eve Isabella was much better. Though still in bed she was able to help wrap sweets and make paper flowers, which she gave to Robert to hang on the pine tree which John brought into the conservatory. This new idea had spread rapidly since Prince Albert introduced a Christmas tree at Windsor ten years earlier, and now nearly every home had a gaily decorated tree. After tea, when it was dark, John lit small candles he had attached to the branches and told Robert that it was to remind children everywhere of the starlit sky on the night of Christ's birth. Robert climbed onto the bed beside his mother, and she told him the now-familiar story of Mary and Joseph and of the baby Jesus in the manger. He loved to hear how the shepherds and wise men came to the stable bringing gifts for the baby and how all the angels in heaven sang for joy, although by this time he was excited by the prospect of Father Christmas bringing him presents that very night.

Downstairs his parents were content to spend the evening talking quietly together. John sat on the floor with his back to the side of the bed, and Isabella ran her fingers through his dark curly hair. The canaries were still singing, though the only light came from the flickering candles, and John and Isabella

230

felt relaxed and happy, and again thanked the Lord for at last bringing them safely through what could have been a terrible tragedy.

'I don't know what I would have done if you had been taken from me, Isabella,' whispered John. 'I love you so very much and am only waiting for the day that you are truly well again.'

'I love you too, John. Thank you for being here. I know that your love brought me through. I could feel it. Even in my confused state I knew that you were here for me.'

John kissed her gently, telling her to sleep, and went to bed.

Robert was up bright and early on Christmas morning and eager to open the large parcel he found beneath the tree. He was overjoyed to find two sets of model soldiers. The first was the Duke of Wellington's regiment, smart in red uniforms, and the second was a set of French soldiers, dressed in blue, which his father told him was the army of Napoleon Bonaparte.

With John's help Robert set out the soldiers on the floor of the conservatory, and after a little history from his father he soon had Napoleon's army in retreat. Whilst his son played, John gave Isabella a small package tied with red ribbon. Inside was a small box with 'Fattorini, Bradford' written on the lid. Opening it, Isabella gasped with delight, for inside was a beautiful gold heart-shaped locket studded with a small diamond. Taking the locket from its box, she turned it over in her hand and saw on the back an inscription which read 'To my Darling Wife' and underneath the initials 'J&I'. Tears filled her eyes as she tried to express her thanks, but John just kissed her tenderly, and taking the locket from her he fastened the chain around her neck.

'I'm afraid your present was too big to wrap,' smiled Isabella, 'and you must wait a while, but all will be revealed in one hour's time.'

At exactly 10 a.m. a horse-drawn cart came up the driveway and stopped beside the lawn directly opposite the conservatory. Bob Wood, the carpenter, was driving and George, the gardener, was with him. Together they unloaded a beautiful dovecote which they quickly erected on the grass. A handful of grain was placed around the base, and then from a wicker basket George produced six fan-tailed pigeons which were soon busily pecking at the bird food and looking for all the world as if they had always lived there in John and Isabella's garden. John's face was a picture.

'I could not have had a nicer Christmas present. You know I've always had a fancy for keeping pigeons. Thank you very much, darling.'

He kissed her lightly on the cheek. 'And you all did well keeping the secret!'

Bob and George were invited in for a seasonal drink of port wine and were given huge pieces of Christmas cake and cheese. They all raised their glasses for John's toast.

'A very happy Christmas, everyone!'

Christmas dinner was almost finished. The roast goose and chestnut stuffing had been followed by a rich, dark plum pudding with brandy sauce, and John and Isabella were enjoying another glass of port wine when a group of boys appeared in the driveway. They were wearing mufflers and gloves, but the cold weather hadn't affected their voices for when they began to sing the strains filled the garden and soared over the treetops. Robert left his soldiers to sit at the window to watch and listen, and when John saw tears in Isabella's eyes he reached out and took her hand. They found out, after the singing, that the boys were from the Parish Church choir and were doing a round of carol singing, especially for old or sick people.

'Well, I feel very much better for your efforts,' said Isabella as the boys drank ginger beer and munched warm mince pies, which the cook brought out. As they left, John thrust two gold sovereigns into the leading boy's hand.

'Well done, lads, and a Merry Christmas to you all.'

He watched them jostle down the drive, warmed by the mince pies and excited to have 'struck gold'.

Isabella was tired by all the visitors, and John took Robert to the billiard room so that she could rest for a while.

'Bring your soldiers, Robert, we'll have the Battle of Waterloo today!'

'I will be Wellington,' said Robert, gathering the horses and men and putting them into their wooden box, 'and you must be Napoleon and command the French soldiers. We'll win, of course!'

John laughed at his son's excitement.

'I'm sure you will, but it will be a hard battle. The two

232

armies fought all day, and it was only when the Prussians arrived in the evening that Napoleon was finally defeated.'

Robert tipped the soldiers onto the billiard table.

'Who are the Prussians, Daddy?'

'Prussia was a German state. The people were great fighters, and they joined forces with us and Russia against Bonaparte.'

'Why did everyone want to fight Napoleon?'

'Because he wanted to rule everyone. He wanted to be Emperor, and we have our own Queen – King then, George IV – and we don't want anyone else to tell us what to do!'

The green baize was soon transformed into the battle scene, and they had great fun lining up the soldiers in square formations. A whole British regiment, ten of Robert's men, were slaughtered, and Robert was unsure if he would win after all, but he kept taking the figure of Wellington on his horse, Copenhagen, to the front shouting, 'Shoot,' and 'Kill them,' until finally John gave an anguished cry. 'Mon Dieu, the Prussians have come. We are finished,' and knocked over all the French soldiers.

Robert laughed, 'I knew we'd win. Wellington always wins!'

John left his son re-setting the battlefield and went back to the conservatory to his wife, and as he neared he heard her coughing. Isabella was not asleep. She motioned to John to sit beside her, and he was concerned to see that she was paler than she had been in the morning.

'It's nothing, darling. I've just tired myself a little with all the excitement. I'll be fine tomorrow.'

She took a pair of small scissors, and without a word reached out and snipped one of John's tight black curls and proceeded to put it into her locket.

'Thank you again for my gift, John. It really is beautiful and I will treasure it always.'

John felt a lump in his throat. He loved his beautiful wife and wanted her to know how very much.

'It is heart-shaped because I give it to you with all the love of my heart, and the diamond represents our first-born child.' He took her hands in his. 'How many more diamonds will be added before our family is complete?'

Isabella didn't need to think about it, she answered straight away.

'I would like three children; two boys and a girl...' she paused then and looked away '...oh, if only I were well.'

'You just concentrate on getting better,' said John. 'There's plenty of time for children once you're well.'

Three days later the weather turned bitterly cold. Dr King arrived to check Isabella's progress, and before he left he stressed to John that Isabella must be kept warm at all times.

'Her lungs are not free of infection. She must remain in bed, but I'm not sure the conservatory is the best place for your wife right now.'

'Oh, it's fine, Doctor. The heating system for the conservatory was one of our priorities when building the house. We've plenty of fuel, and the gardener does a good job of keeping the boiler well stoked.'

Robert persuaded the doctor to have a look at his armies whilst he was enjoying a glass of sherry, and the doctor explained some cavalry tactics.

'By flanking the infantry, right and left, you cut off their escape route, and sometimes it is good to make it appear that all your forces are to the front and then spring a surprise attack from the rear.'

He declined Robert's invitation to re-enact the Battle of Waterloo, saying gravely, 'Wars are terrible, young man. Let us hope that you never have to fight for your country.'

With that he took his leave, eager to get home as snow had begun to fall. It fell heavily all afternoon and evening, and outside the garden was blanketed in white. The branches of the trees were hanging low with the weight of the snow, and the new dovecote, now peaked in white, looked like some mysterious Eastern temple.

Still the skies were heavy and the snow continued to fall. From the warmth of the conservatory Isabella watched with John as the garden was transformed into a winter wonderland. There is something very calming about snow when it is not being whirled and driven by fierce winds. Today there was hardly any breeze and the flakes fell thickly but gently, shutting out the rest of the world until all else was forgotten. There was no noise to spoil the magic of that evening, only a deep silence of which the two young people felt very much a part. They didn't need to speak. No words could have more adequately expressed the love they felt for one another than the simple sharing of this silence. At last John took Isabella in his arms and kissed her long and tenderly.

'Sleep well, my darling,' he whispered. 'I'll see you in the morning.'

As he left Isabella was snuggling down into her warm bed. She looked happy and contented. Please God, he thought, make her well soon and let us lead a normal life again.

It was bitterly cold now outside; winter had really taken its grip and, mindful of the doctor's warning, John decided to go into the basement before retiring and to check the boiler for himself. All was in order. There was plenty of wood stacked against the far wall and coal in the adjacent cellar. The fire was good, but John put on even more fuel and then lowered the damper to reduce consumption and ensure that the fire would stay in throughout the night.

Isabella didn't know what time it was when she awoke, but it was still dark and the house was quiet. The cold had awakened her. She was shivering, for there was no warmth now in the conservatory. Knowing that the boiler must have gone out, she rang the little hand bell on the table beside the bed. She rang it gently at first but, when no one heard, more urgently until her arm ached. Still no one came. When all the doors were shut the conservatory was too cut off for anyone to hear. The house was silent. Isabella didn't know what to do. The snow-filled garden frightened her now. It no longer looked pretty and had lost its magic. The steely whiteness was menacing and she felt so cold – so cold! I must get help, she thought, I must go and waken John.

She slipped her feet from under the cover and onto the thick rug beside the bed, but when she tried to stand her knees buckled and she fell back onto the mattress. She was frantic now. Again she rang the bell and called out as loudly as she could, but no one heard. Pulling the covers tightly around herself Isabella drew her knees up to her chest, wrapped her arms around them and prayed that morning would come quickly.

John found her there and thought at first that she was dead. She was so desperately cold, and white as the bed sheet, and he could not rouse her. Lifting her into his arms he raced through the house and upstairs to their bedroom, screaming for the servants to light the fire, bring hot-water bottles and more blankets and send for the doctor. John lay with her in the bed, holding her and willing her to take the heat from his own body. He rubbed her hands and arms and breathed hot breath against her neck. Please Isabella, do not die. Please God do not take her from me; not like this! The servants scurried round, and in no time stone hot-water bottles were in the bed and a huge fire was roaring up the chimney. Only then did John leave Isabella to others' care whilst he went down to the basement to investigate what had gone amiss with the heating. George was already there and re-lighting the boiler.

'Fire bricks collapsed, John, whole grate'd given way. I've fixed it and I'll have it going in a jiffy.'

'I should have seen it,' cried John. 'I was here last night to check the fire, and I never saw it.'

'Now how could you? No one could've seen what were going on under that furnace. You mustn't blame yourself.'

'My wife might have died because I didn't listen to the doctor's warning. I'll never forgive myself!'

Dr King was quite frank. Isabella's life hung in the balance. The shock from the cold, so soon after the previous shock of the near-drowning, was almost too much for her weakened system. Her pulse was indistinct, her blood pressure had dropped and the poor blood flow could well have affected her internal organs, particularly the lungs, which were already badly damaged. He recommended that a nurse be hired and promised to call back in six hours time.

As the house grew warm Isabella's temperature very slowly returned to normal. The deathly pallor left her face and a faint tinge of colour reached her cheeks. When the doctor called again he found her very slightly better.

'She's not out of the woods yet, but with good nursing she should continue to improve.'

Isabella was determined to get well, and day by day, little by

236

little she did seem to be on the mend. By mid-January she was spending time each day out of bed in an easy chair, but John was still worried. The cough which she'd had ever since the accident wasn't getting any better. In fact, if anything, it seemed worse now, and sometimes she was coughing up nasty-coloured phlegm. Her breathing was shallow, and on a bad day any slight exertion would leave her gasping for breath.

At John's request Dr King brought a chest specialist from Leeds. They had studied medicine together, and Dr King knew him to be the best in his field. Silently the physician examined Isabella, listening to her chest both back and front, taking her pulse and watching her as she moved to allow him to proceed, coughing at each turn. Leaving the bedside to look out of the window, he spoke at last but made no mention of the illness.

'What a beautiful garden, Mrs Pickles. I see the snowdrops are here at last. Brave little things aren't they, poking out their heads when it's still so cold? Soon the daffodils will be here, and then before we know it all the other flowers will follow on.'

He stayed on a while, chatting about the garden and about the lovely leafy plant which Isabella had had brought up to the bedroom. Downstairs he gave the nurse some medicine to help relieve the congestion and also told her how to make Isabella more comfortable and help with her breathing. Neither Dr King nor the specialist had given any indication of the diagnosis, and John could not let them go without talking it through.

'Please be frank, sir. What is your opinion of my wife's condition?'

The physician looked at John's troubled face. He knew that the truth had to be faced eventually and, hard as that may be, the time had come for this young man to know the worst. Looking him straight in the eye he said, 'Your wife's lungs were badly affected by the river water, and unfortunately they have deteriorated since. There is nothing more that we can do for her.' He paused before saying, 'I'm afraid your wife will only live a few more weeks. I'm sorry.'

John thanked him for being open with him and thanked both men for coming. As he closed the door the physician's words pounded round his head. He closed his eyes and leaned heavily on the oak door. His heart was beating too fast and a strange tightness gripped his chest. She was dying. Isabella was dying. He had known, of course, deep down, but until the doctor had said the words he could pretend it wasn't happening. Now he could pretend no longer. Isabella was going to die, and he didn't know what to do. Should he tell her? Should he continue to pretend for her sake? Please God, help me. Tell me what to do!

When he had composed himself he went back upstairs and into the bedroom smiling brightly. He knelt by the bed and embraced his wife, kissing her several times and trying not to show that he wanted to hold her forever. Still holding her, so that he didn't need to look at her, he said, 'That specialist knows his stuff. He's left some medicine that's going to work wonders. It'll get rid of the phlegm, and you'll be right in no time.'

Isabella pushed John away and looked him full in the face.

'Tell me the truth, John, what did the specialist say? I know I'm going to die, and I want to know how long I have left.'

John hugged Isabella to him. Angry tears fell down his face as he cried, 'No, Isabella, no! You're not going to die, I won't let you die!'

Isabella waited until the outburst subsided. She felt calm and in a strange way happy that the truth which she had so feared was out in the open at last. She pulled away from John.

'If we only have a short time together, Johnny, we have to use that time well. Let us not part with things unsaid, and let us not waste one second on tears.' She laughed then and with an air of frivolity said, 'Why don't we have a party for our relatives and closest friends?'

Once the idea was born there was no stopping Isabella. Organizing the party gave her something to think about, and she seemed to find extra strength to make endless lists for John. A list of guests: 1. My parents and sisters, 2. Paul, Molly and the children, 3. Harold, Alice and family, etc. A list of foods, a list of drinks, a list of removals: 1. Me to conservatory! 2. Piano to conservatory, 3. Daffodils to conservatory – lots!

It was easier for John to put on a brave face when Isabella was so positive, but when she fell into one of her frequent restless sleeps he often sat in a chair close to her bed just watching her, and it was then that the tears flowed. No one else saw;

238

he could not bear the thought of losing her, for she had been a tower of strength to him. Right from the start she had had a good grasp of the business and often knew the answers to his problems. His thoughts flew back to their meeting in Bradford. How proud he had been of her then; so beautiful in the russet dress he bought her. It seemed as if fate, or God, had brought them together, but if it was God why did He now want to end this perfect marriage and take Isabella from him?

He knew how much she was looking forward to the party, and decided whilst she slept that he would do everything in his power to make it very special for her.

'And I shall buy you a new green gown for the ball, Princess,' he whispered.

He asked the village dressmaker to make her the softest, thickest, richest, green dressing-gown ever seen.

The party was in full swing. Isabella, having slept most of the morning, seemed to have found new energy to meet the occasion. She had been thrilled when she awoke and found the velvety dressing-gown over the foot of the bed, and despite her paleness, when the nurse helped her to put it on and brushed her still thick hair, she felt very special. Now with good food, balloons and streamers the party was going well. The two Ryan boys were of a similar age to Robert and they played well together. The adults were determined to be cheerful, and they all did their best to make the party a success.

Isabella surprised everyone when she asked John to lift her onto the piano stool so that she could play for them. Everyone gathered round to sing the familiar songs, but both Mr and Mrs Outhwaite had a hard time fighting back the tears when Isabella played their favourite tune. Each person there wondered if this would be the last time that Isabella would sit at her piano. Trying to keep the party going, Paul and John set the children marching up and down the conservatory whilst Isabella played a rousing tune. They were turning to come back up the floor for a second time when, with a crash, Isabella slumped over the keys exhausted. Robert ran to her crying, 'Mummy, Mummy! What's the matter?'

John lifted Isabella back into the bed.

239

'Mummy's tired, Robert. She needs to rest. Take Samuel and Jack to the billiard room and play with the soldiers, there's a good boy.'

Soon afterwards the guests departed. All said how much they had enjoyed the party, but in their faces John saw everything which was left unsaid. He was grateful to them for coming and grateful for the smiles they had found for Isabella.

Somehow Isabella found the strength to write. Propped up in bed, she slowly and painstakingly filled the small piece of paper. Her breathing was laboured and her fingers ached, but no amount of entreaty from John would persuade her to rest until she had finished. Then, without a word and without showing John what she had written, she folded the paper tightly until it was small enough to fit into the locket which hung around her neck. Only then did she sleep awhile, but on waking she asked for more paper and began again. This time she handed the completed sheet to John.

It was difficult to read the list through his unshed tears, but somehow John got through it. Isabella's handwriting was not so clear as it once was, but her brain was as sharp as ever and she had thought of everything.

'1. Robert must learn to swim; teach him,' he read.

'2. When the time is right I would like Robert to attend Sedbergh Boarding School for Boys.'

Isabella interrupted. 'It's a good school with a reputation for being strong on learning and character development, and it has an excellent sports record too.'

She knew this last point would squash any doubts John had about sending his son away to school, and she was right, but John was thinking of how proud Isabella would have been if she could have seen her son start out for that first day at school. He went back to the list.

'3. Money in my own private account is to be used to build almshouses in the Worth Valley to be rent-free to deserving elderly people.'

John smiled, 'I expect you want Mr Day as architect and a local builder to do the work, eh?'

Isabella squeezed his hand and smiled back. They didn't need a lot of instructions, for they knew each other's minds and Isabella could trust John to do what she would have wanted.

Her next part of the list referred to the funeral, and John felt a lump rising in his throat and could not read the words out loud.

'4. I would like Bob Wood to make me a coffin of English oak with brass handles. I want to be buried in my beautiful new dressing-gown in Slack Lane Cemetery so that I am overlooking my father's fields.'

John could hold back the tears no longer. He sat very still, staring at the paper but seeing nothing. Isabella reached out and touched his arm, saying softly, 'Please don't cry, Johnny, I am no longer frightened of death, it is not the end it is the beginning, and wherever I am going I will wait for you, my darling. Thank you for giving me the most wonderful eight years of my life and for being the best husband and father in the world.'

John wanted to say that *he* should thank *her*, that she had made his life complete and given him a wonderful son, that she was beautiful and bright and brave and the light of his life, but no words would come. He held his wife in his arms and sobbed bitterly.

Two days later Isabella was dead. John never left her side, and she died in his arms with the words 'I love you' on her lips.

29

Though not quite eight years old, Robert was sent to the boarding school in Sedbergh soon after his mother's death. John told the grandparents that it was what Isabella had wanted, but if he had been truthful to himself he would have admitted that the boy was far too young and it was because he, John, could not bear to be reminded of the happy times when they were a family, that he had sent his son away. He didn't want to be in the house at Oakworth either, it held too many memories. So John divided his time between the two quarries and the timber yard, burying himself in his business and spending long hours both at the books and at the quarry face.

The hands-on work suited him. He could vent his anger on the stone and work through the sad moments by wearing himself out physically so that at last he could drift into uneasy sleep. He drove himself hard taking huge orders and trying to meet them all by himself. It still seemed that where business was concerned he had a magician's touch. The profits continued to rise, but instead of easing off John drove himself harder and diverged into transporting building materials by barge on the Leeds–Liverpool Canal. Three more boats were bought, and when these made money John invested in the Lancashire and Yorkshire Railways. He opened yet another quarry, at Fly Flats near Halifax, to meet the demand for stone for rail tunnels and bridges.

Paul and Molly and Mr and Mrs Outhwaite were all concerned about John. He was driving himself too hard, and they worried that he would crack under the strain. George tried to involve John in his garden, but he only stopped long enough to growl 'Do what Isabella would have wanted', and showed no further interest.

When the Sedbergh school closed for the summer everyone thought John would come home each day now that Robert was there, but the little lad was left with the servants and spent most of his days helping George planting and pruning in the garden. After trying in vain to persuade John to spend time with his son, Mrs Outhwaite suggested that perhaps Robert would be better on the farm with them for the summer. John was only too pleased to accept her offer, and Mrs Outhwaite had the task of trying to explain to a tearful seven-year-old how much his father was grieving over his mother and that he really did still love him very much.

To his business associates John was the perfect gentleman. He never allowed them to see the anger and hurt inside him, and he was viewed with respect. He was so highly regarded that he was asked to stand for the parliamentary elections for the Halifax constituency – but though he had such wide, commercial interests he had no burning desire to step into the political arena, and when arguments in favour of the idea gathered strength he remembered the advice Mr Fielden had given him some years earlier: 'Don't get involved with politics – stay neutral.' John thought it good advice and turned down his would-be nominators.

The teachers at Sedbergh were concerned when a very much quieter Robert returned to the school in the autumn. His father's rejections had hit him hard, and he was much less confident than before and spent a lot of time on his own instead of enjoying the company of other boys. Misunderstanding the cause of the change in his pupil, the headmaster wrote to John telling him that Robert was still grieving for his mother, and suggested that it would perhaps be better if the boy was to postpone his schooling for a while and return home.

John wrote a curt note back.

Robert is a strong boy and will come to terms with things in time. I prefer him to stay at the school to receive the education his mother wished for him.

Yours faithfully, John Pickles.

243

Things continued much the same for John until December. Work, work and more work. Anything to stop him having to think; to stop the memories of Isabella flooding into his mind. Things came to a head at Christmas. John was feeling the strain, and once again it was Harold who saved him.

When Robert came home from school for the holiday John took him straight to the farm at Newholme. Mrs Outhwaite didn't want to take him. She thought the boy should be at home with his father for Christmas, but something in John's manner stopped her saying so and instead she said, 'Come on in, Robert, Grandfather needs a hand with the cows, and there'll be holly and laurels to bring in for the Christmas decorations. We surely need you here!'

John rode off with barely a backward glance for his son and spent the next two days pick-axing gravel from a new dig at the quarry. He didn't even go home to sleep. When it was too dark to work he curled up in the foreman's hut with a bottle of whisky for company, and didn't care whether he was warm or cold.

The quarries and timber yards all closed down completely for three days over Christmas, and John had to go back to Oakworth Grange. How different this from last year; no tree, no holly, no parcels. Nothing. Cook tried to tempt John with a festive duckling, but he pushed it away and went into the conservatory taking a bottle of whisky with him, and finally gave way to the grief that he had been fighting for the past ten months. It was there that Harold found him on Boxing Day.

'Well, I hope yer proud of yerself, lad,' Harold knew how John had suffered, and he felt for him, but he showed no sympathy now. 'Are you drunk at Christmas? And yon little laddie with his grandparents when he's missing his ma so. You ought to be ashamed of yerself!'

John eyed him stonily. He was not drunk. Though he had supped a good deal of the whisky, it had somehow left him cold sober, and he didn't want Harold interfering and telling him what to do.

'And what's it to do with you?' he asked icily.

'It's everything to do with me. We went through a lot together, and I'm not going to let you sit there and rot when you've a whole life before you!'

244

John turned on him angrily.

'I've no life now. Without Isabella my life is worthless. I'm making money – big money – but for what? What's the point? Isabella is dead!'

'I know she is, but your son is alive, John, and 'e needs you.' Harold suddenly became angry too. 'You of all people must know 'ow much a boy needs 'is parents. You were left alone in the world, but Robert still 'as a parent. Imagine 'ow 'e feels, knowing that 'is father 'ates 'im.'

John was aghast.

'But I don't hate him, you must know that?'

'I know, but does he? All 'e knows is that you can't bear to look at 'im and 'es too young to understand that it is the loss of Isabella that you can't bear and that 'aving 'im near reminds you of 'er. 'E thinks you blame 'im.' Harold shrugged and made to leave. 'What's the use in my talking? You're too wrapped up in your own self-pity to see 'ow much a seven-year-old boy needs you.'

When John strode into the Outhwaite's warm kitchen no one spoke. Robert was at the table with his grandparents, enjoying cold turkey left over from the Christmas dinner. Mrs Outhwaite was anxious to know why John had come and nervously began twisting her apron in her fingers. At last John spoke.

'Are you coming home, son? The soldiers are all ready to do battle, but they're waiting for the Duke of Wellington!'

Robert rushed across the kitchen into his father's outstretched arms and Mr and Mrs Outhwaite smiled at one another; everything was going to be all right at last!

Gradually things returned to normal and the house at Oakworth again became a happy place to be. John took an interest in his home and rejoined the cricket team. He still kept a tight rein on his business, but he no longer felt the need to spend every working hour at the quarry or the timber yard. Paul was welcomed now when he called round to while away an evening at the billiard table and talk over old times as they used to do. In the holidays John taught Robert to swim where the beck was dammed, and many times Jack and Sam would join them too.

At the end of the summer term John took the three boys to Whitby on the east coast, where they enjoyed sea fishing and watched an exciting local cricket match. Robert was a different boy, strong and confident with a maturity beyond his eight years born from the grief of the past 12 months. As John watched him cast his line from the jetty, his heart swelled with pride. Never again would he allow such a gulf between himself and his son.

30

Three years had passed since Isabella's death. It was June, and John decided it was high time he called a truce with God. When Isabella died John's faith had died too. He blamed God for taking his beloved wife, and he would have nothing more to do with the church. However, over the past 12 months he had begun to feel differently about it all. Isabella's fall into the river had been an accident. God hadn't decreed it. These things just happen. John had gradually begun to see the beauty of the world again and feel the joy of living and had learnt to appreciate every day. He and Robert had grown very close since that awful Christmas of 1852. They often talked of Isabella, and both felt that her spirit was ever present in the house guiding and protecting them.

Before the accident they used to attend the Scar Top Wesleyan Sunday School Charity. John had been to the annual event ever since first coming to Sladen Bridge at ten years old, and it had been one of the highlights of the year, but since Isabella's death he hadn't been able to face it and had stayed away. If the weather was fine the Charity – or Anniversary – was held outdoors on a piece of raised ground below the chapel facing Stanbury. It was a widely known event, and up to 2000 people would gather in the fields around to hear the preacher and join the hearty hymn singing. People came from as far afield as Wycoller and Colne, Hawksbridge and Oxenhope, and even Pecket Well, for no one wanted to miss hearing the preacher and listening to the fiddles, flutes, clarinets and trombones. All manner of people turned up with instruments. Some mill owners supported small brass bands, and their members would all turn out for the Anniversary. Those folks who could not play a musical instrument all sang their hearts out. People arrived early in the day, bringing picnics, so that they could listen to the players and choirs practising before the afternoon and evening services got underway. Not least of the benefits of these preachings to the multitudes was the fact that huge collections were made for the chapel and for local charities.

This year they would go! Robert, home for half-term, was excited, anticipating the picnic and all the thrill of the crowds and music, but when the second Sunday in June dawned the skies were black and heavy rain was falling. It continued to rain throughout the morning, and John knew that most people would not be making the trek to the little chapel on the hill. Certainly none of those from the distant towns and villages would come. Only the local people would be able to squeeze inside the tiny building, and it would be a poor collection this year. Nevertheless, having decided to make that leap back to the church, John was determined he would attend. Robert was disappointed that his day out had been spoilt, and when he said that he would rather stay at home and play with his soldiers John didn't press him to go.

'Another time, son,' he said ruffling the boy's hair. 'I know you have plenty of religious education and services at the school, so I'll not insist you come.'

John set out in the trap with plenty of time to cover the three-mile journey before the service began, but the wheel hub cap became loose and John had trouble securing the wheel from dropping off. A nearby farmer came with a spanner and fixed it for him, and by the time he pushed open the church door the congregation were already singing the first hymn. There was very little room inside the chapel. Every pew appeared to be full, and John thought he would have to remain standing, until the steward handed him a service sheet and indicated an empty seat at the far end of the back row.

As quietly as he could John slipped into the pew and tried to find his place in the hymn. The woman next to him pointed to the third verse, and as she did so a faint whiff of a familiar perfume teased John's nostrils. His heart missed a beat and he felt as if his stomach muscles were held in a vice. He could not take his eyes from the hymn sheet, dared not look at the person next to him, but he knew, without a shadow of a doubt,

248

that the woman here, in the pew, was Leonora. The singing was finished and everyone sat down, but still John did not turn. His mind was racing over the past years, trying to decide what Leonora would think of him now. He remembered how he had loved and needed her, and how rejected he had felt when she married Oscar Beale. Did she still love that man? Did Leonora ever think of him, John? Did she know that he too had married? What should he say to her? He didn't hear the preacher as he rambled on and on through his long-winded sermon, but sat rigid in the pew staring straight ahead, unable to control his thoughts. 'Oh, Leonora, my first love!'

As they stood to sing the final hymn her fragrance wafted over him again, and he was surprised to find that his knees went weak. At last he turned to look at Leonora. She was watching him, waiting, just as apprehensive as he, but as their eyes met all doubts dispersed and the years seemed to melt away. She smiled and then instinctively, almost as if at a given signal, their hands joined. They didn't sing the hymn for neither of them could find a voice, and the words on the paper were just a blur as all kinds of mixed emotions surged through the pair.

After the service it was frustrating for John to have to greet all the people who were so pleased to see him there, whilst all the time trying to keep his eye on Leonora and make sure she didn't disappear into thin air.

'Thank you, Reverend. An inspiring sermon.' 'Mrs Brown, hello, how are you? ... And Mr Brown is well, I hope?' 'Yes, yes, and nice to see you too, Mr Sugden.' 'Good-day, Frank.'

At last he was free, as he stepped out of the chapel entrance door and the sun was shining with a blue sky above.

'Leonora, shall we walk?'

They took the path down to the river and followed its winding course towards the Donkey Bridge. They chattered all the time. John talked about the weather, the Anniversary service and the state of the country. Leonora asked after mutual acquaintances she had spotted in the chapel, and talked about paintings and the wildlife and plants they happened upon in the fields. At the bridge they stood looking into the clear, rippling water, watching fishes in the shallow pools as they had so often done all those years ago. John could stand it no longer.

'And what about you, Leonora, have you been happy?'

Leonora turned tearful eyes towards him.

'Oh, John, I have always wished that things could have been different. If only you knew...'

'Tell me, Leonora. I want to know. Tell me everything.'

They sat for a long time on the stone parapet of the bridge and Leonora told John all about her fateful marriage to Oscar Beale. How her father had been convinced that John had taken the missing mill money and had been influenced by Oscar's smooth-talking charm and his position at the bank.

'He encouraged Oscar's attentions towards me and would not let me visit you at Armley. Your name was forbidden in our house. Oscar told me wicked lies about you which, stupidly, I believed. It all seemed so possible then. Oh, John, was it very terrible in the prison?'

John smiled. 'Not too bad. I'll tell you all about it some day, but just now I want to hear about you.'

'As you know, I married Oscar Beale. Looking back now, I don't know why I did except that, with you gone, my life felt worthless and I just didn't care what happened to me. It pleased Papa and it seemed the right thing to do. Poor Papa. He died last year. I came to see him when he was ill, and he told me he was sorry to have pushed me into that marriage and he asked for my forgiveness. There was nothing to forgive. I didn't blame my father because he only ever did what he thought was best for me.'

Leonora went on to tell John a little of what her marriage had been like.

'How different Oscar was once the knot was tied. He had no time for me when we were alone together and he humiliated me in public. In many ways it was a relief when he was jailed and I was able to seek a divorce. The last time I saw him, I was so angry when the truth was known, I took off my wedding ring and threw it into his face.

'The only good thing to come from my marriage is my daughter Sarah.'

Leonora brightened visibly when she spoke of her child.

'She's twelve years old now, and perhaps I shouldn't say this, but she's growing into a lovely girl. She's at the Moravian Boarding School at Fulneck, Pudsey, and by all accounts is a bright scholar.'

'I'm sure she is,' said John, 'but is she as beautiful as her mother?'

Ignoring John's question, Leonora smiled and continued, 'I've moved to a nice house in Pudsey, quite near to the school, so that Sarah can spend most weekends with me. I hate for us to be apart.' She paused, looking up the hillside to where the roof of Laverock Hall was just visible. 'We sold Laverock. When Papa died Mamma decided to go back to her family in Italy. She always hated the cold Yorkshire winters and knew that Lake Como would suit her better. Sarah and I spent a few weeks out there last summer. It really is a beautiful place.'

It was John's turn then to tell Leonora all about Isabella and Robert and about the quarries and the timber yard and the canal barges. He told her about the accident and how his wife and son nearly drowned, and of Isabella's ensuing illness. Leonora laid her hand gently on his arm.

'I heard when your wife died, John. I'm very sorry. I saw her once, a long time ago, she was very beautiful, and she sounds to have been a very special person.'

'She was, and I will never forget her. Isabella was a tower of strength when we were building up the business. She was a good mother and a wonderful wife, and when she died I didn't know how I could carry on. But time is a great healer, and Robert and I manage very well now. He's away at school too, at Sedbergh. I think you'd like him. He has a lot of his mother in him, but he has my black hair!' John paused as if uncertain about what he was going to say. 'He's home at the moment. If you're not dashing straight back to Pudsey, perhaps you'd like to meet him?'

'I'd like that very much,' said Leonora.

Rather stiff from sitting on the stone wall, they decided to wander up the fields a little way, and almost without thinking they took the path to the little hollow which had once been their favourite resting place. The afternoon took on a dream-like quality as hand in hand they walked over the grass, vividly remembering the happy hours they had spent there. Now, as then, blackbirds were whistling amongst the late May blossom on the little trees above the hollow. A colourful carpet of buttercups, milkmaids and clover was spread beneath their feet, and a startled rabbit, who thought he had the place to himself, scampered off to find refuge in his burrow, his white tail flashing as he pounded away. Unseen a sheep bleated as if in warning 'Baa!' They both laughed and John drew Leonora into his arms and kissed her. Time stood still. Leonora was back in 1841 with a young John, carefree and happy. How well she remembered his embrace, how alive had been her memories of his kiss. All the magic was still there; the attraction just as strong. Please God, don't take him away from me again!

At length they drew apart.

'I still have your rose, Leonora. I pressed it between pieces of leather, and for a while it gave me hope and courage to face some of the hardest times in jail.'

'Keep it, John. My heart came with that rose, and it has never been reclaimed for anyone else. I have always loved you.'

Leonora had taken a room at the Black Bull for the night, so John retrieved the pony and trap from near the chapel and drove her into Haworth. They dined together and enjoyed a bottle of wine, and there was so much of their lives to catch up on that they never stopped talking. The evening flew by and it was dark before John reluctantly took his leave, promising to return for her early the following morning.

The next evening found them once again dining at the Black Bull Hotel, and if the landlord was surprised at John's presence he never said. He was happy to supply the second bottle of wine that his customers had ordered that evening. They were deep in conversation.

'Robert is a credit to you, John. He has a lot of common sense for one so young. You must be very proud of him.'

Leonora was thinking too how handsome the boy was. Very like his father after all, with his shock of dark hair and those wise, dark eyes. If he was like his mother, it must be in character, because his looks were all John's.

'I am proud of him. He's been through a lot and really missed his mother, but somehow it has made him a stronger person. I wonder sometimes where his life will take him. I'd like him to run the quarries after me, but nothing is for certain in this life and he must make up his own mind when the time comes.'

252

When Robert had left for school after lunch, John had shown Leonora round his house and garden before bringing her back to Haworth for the evening meal. The day had been a great success as hour by hour they realised how very much they still enjoyed each other's company. The hotel was quiet and they moved to the lounge to finish their wine. For the first time they were suddenly quiet, content just being together and not wanting to make any sound lest it break the spell which was weaving itself around them.

John sat looking at Leonora who was watching him. She was sparkly eyed and a slight smile played at the corner of her mouth. She is so beautiful, thought John. She must be 36 years old now, but her skin still has the bloom of a young girl's and her hair is just as I remember it, so thick and shiny. He was reminded of the first occasion that he saw her at the Butterworth's wedding; it had been her hair and eyes that had attracted him then. Nothing has changed, he thought, after all this time, being close to her still excites me. The power of their first love had not died, it had only been submerged, and as the evening wore on, and the wine did its work, the desire to be together was overpowering. When the last of the wine was finished John finally spoke. Never taking his eyes from Leonora's he said very softly, 'Is the bed you have here big enough for two?'

A slow smile spread over Leonora's face.

'I was hoping you would ask me that. As it happens it is a large four-poster, but had it been only a single bed my answer would still have been yes!'

Much later as Leonora lay relaxed and warm in his arms, John looked up at the four oak posts of the bed and the lavish canopy overhead and laughed.

'Well, this is the grandest bed I've ever had the good fortune to lie in!' He turned and kissed Leonora. 'But without you here with me it would be no more than a sack of hay. You are wonderful, Leonora, and the memory of only one other night comes near to this one, and that was a long, long time ago in a bed with a beautiful embroidered Italian counterpane!'

They kissed again. Long and loving, lingering caresses. The natural expression of a deep love that had already soared the

253

heights of sensuality and stirred them into a frenzy of desire which had spent itself in joyous, uninhibited union so that now they lay together, entwined almost as one, deeply grateful to have been given a second chance of the happiness which had once been so cruelly snatched away from them. Leonora, so happy, was surprised to suddenly find warm tears washing her face.

'Hey! What's this?' asked John, wiping her cheeks. 'Why the tears?'

'I love you, John. I have always loved you, and I have missed fifteen years of the life we could have had together.'

'Then let's not miss another day. Marry me Leonora! Will you marry me?'

The tears fell even faster. 'Yes, John. Oh yes!'

A little over a month later John and Leonora were married at Haworth Parish Church. They would have preferred the service to have been in the tiny chapel at Scar Top, and had been disappointed to find that it was not solemnized for marriages, but they had been appeased by the chapel organist saying that he would come along and play for the wedding. At Leonora's request it was a very quiet affair. Only Paul and Molly with their two children, Robert and Sarah, Harold and Alice, and Mr and Mrs Heaton of Ponden were invited. After the ceremony the happy party went by waggonette to the Silent Inn at Stanbury for the wedding reception.

As the meal ended Paul rose to toast the newlyweds.

'Before we drink to the health and happiness of John and Leonora, I should like to say a few words. Firstly, I want to thank John for his friendship. As you all know, John and I were together in the Blue Coats Orphanage at Liverpool, and on my first day there John befriended me and we have been pals ever since. No, we have been more than just pals; we have been like brothers. Our bond has stood the test of time. John has supported me through rough times and smooth, and I hope he knows that I have always been there for him. He is the most loyal and true friend anyone could wish for.' Paul paused, turning to look at the bride. 'And Leonora! Our acquaintance goes back many years and all that time ago, when you so staunchly cheered on our cricket team, turning up on cold, cold days when few others would brave the wind, I thought you were the perfect partner for John. Now that you are together at last, I wish you good health and a long and happy married life. Please everyone raise your glasses, to John and Leonora!'

They all had to raise their glasses a second time when Harold praised John for rescuing his family from poverty. He thanked him.

'On behalf of all t'other families in t'valley who've 'ad full bellies since t'quarry opened.' He held his glass high as he finished, "Ere's to you, Johnny Big Block, and to that lovely wife o' yours. We all 'ope you'll be very 'appy!'

Finally it was John's turn to thank everyone for coming and helping to make their wedding day such a joyous occasion. He proposed a toast to their continued friendships in the years to come.

A honeymoon at the Grand Hotel in Scarborough had been Leonora's idea, and Robert and Sarah were thrilled to find that they were to be included. Thoughts of the promised cliff walks, beach excursions and deep-sea fishing trip filled their every waking moment, and they were almost bursting with excitement by the time the train puffed into Scarborough station. The Grand Hotel certainly lived up to its name – it was very grand indeed, having been described as the 'largest and most handsome hotel in Europe'. It even had the latest ducted warm air to the bedrooms and cold and hot water to the bathrooms. It attracted an exclusive and select clientele – landed gentry, aristocracy, wool barons of the West Riding, coal-mine owners from south Yorkshire and shipbuilders from Tyneside all flocked to the Grand.

Sarah gasped in amazement when they entered the hotel lobby. It was illuminated by huge crystal chandeliers and had the largest staircase she had ever seen sweeping to the floor above. Leonora followed her daughter's gaze.

'Apparently the staircase is in the style of the one in the Berlin Opera House, designed so that two fully crinolined ladies, with their escorts, might pass in comfort.'

She could see that Sarah was amazed by the splendour and said, 'I've heard that it took eleven and a half miles of carpet-

255

ing to cover the floors of this hotel, and they even have fresh sea water on tap for those who wish to bathe in it!'

They hadn't even managed to book in at reception before John was hailed by a group of men he knew to be mill-owners from the Bradford area. It transpired that they were here on a fishing trip and had just had a very successful day.

'We've had some good catches, and if the weather holds we're going out tomorrow to try out luck with the blue-fin tunny.'

John was surprised.

'I didn't know we had tunny fish in the North Sea!'

'Only at this time of year. When the waters warm up they come north to feed off the herring, mackerel and whiting. They dive through the shoals in a frenzy of feeding, and if you're lucky you can see them leaping clear of the sea. Splendid sight! They grow to quite a size – up to ten feet long, they weigh over a thousand pounds. They are very exciting to catch. We go a long way out, probably about twelve miles, so we'll be off early morning, but come down to the harbour tomorrow afternoon about three and you'll be able to see for yourself what we've caught.'

The travel-weary family were all so tired by the time they were finally escorted to their suite of rooms that John asked for supper to be brought up and then they all had an early night, eagerly anticipating the day to come.

The first week passed in a flurry of activities. Robert and Sarah found that there was so much to do in Scarborough that the days raced by. A morning spent watching the fishing boats; an afternoon on the beach, swimming from their beach hut, building castles in the sand or catching crabs; an evening walk along the cliff tops as far as Cayton Bay or climbing Oliver's Mount for spectacular views along the shore. Whatever they were doing they all enjoyed themselves, and John knew that this was the beginning of a very happy family life.

One afternoon they listened to the brass band of the North York Rifles, often called the Green Howards Regiment, playing on the promenade. It was a recruitment drive, and soldiers in smart uniforms were doing rifle drill and marching back and forth in time to the music. Robert was enthralled by the 'real-live soldiers', and nothing would have enticed him away from the parade. John winked at Leonora.

'I think the company just won its youngest recruit!'

Robert turned to him, eyes bright and shining,

'Oh yes, Father! When I grow up I want to be a soldier, just like these men!'

Over the middle weekend of their stay another party of men arrived at the hotel. They were members of the Bradford District cricket team who had arranged a friendly match against an East Yorkshire gentleman farmers' team to be held Sunday. The men were in high spirits, enjoying a 'boys' own' weekend without their wives and fiancées. They had been at the harbour on Saturday afternoon, sampling shell fish sold from striped booths on the quayside, and they had followed that by the four-course meal at the Grand before rounding off the evening with rather more drinks than was wise.

On Sunday morning two of the party were worse for wear – they swore it was from the shell fish they had eaten and not the effects of alcohol, but whatever the cause it meant that the team was one man short, having only brought one substitute. They had heard of John's former prowess with the bat, and when they learned that he too was staying at the Grand they asked him if he would join them. John hesitated. He had played very little cricket for some time now, and thought he probably would not have an eye for the fast balls and he knew he could not run like he used to. However, the Bradford lads would not hear of a refusal. They brought him some sports clothes and John good-naturedly agreed to be in the team, providing he could play late in the batting order. Leonora said it would be interesting, and that in any case the exercise would do him good!

The afternoon was perfect for the match – sunny and warm for the spectators, dry on the field and just enough breeze to keep the players cool enough to run. Leonora, Robert and Sarah were lucky to find seats in the pavilion, as it filled up quickly after their arrival and late-comers had to sit on rugs on the grass at the edge of the pitch. Supporters had come from far afield to watch the match, and there was the usual banter and rivalry and expectations of a good game when play commenced.

The gentleman farmers' team won the toss and selected to bat first. They played hard and well and made 356 runs before the tenth man lost his wicket. John had already proved his worth, catching two balls which were hit sky-high and intended for a boundary four. As the crowd cheered Leonora flushed with pride. She was reminded of the old days with the Haworth Church team and of how proud she had been of John then, and she realized that her love and admiration for him were now even greater than before.

The Bradford team had already scored 231 runs when John went in to bat at number eight. As he walked from the pavilion across the pitch, bat in hand, Leonora's heart was pounding. She knew how much it would mean to John to play well today. At first she was disappointed. The flamboyance of his early years was gone. There were none of the wide swings, sending balls roaring over the boundary for six, which had characterized his youthful cricket successes. John played the ball cautiously but steadily and notched up only 35 runs in the first hour. As a young man he had been known to make a century in not much more than 60 minutes, but his policy today was to take no risks and thereby protect the batsman at the other end. For two hours he held his wicket, and when he hit the four which brought his score to 101 the crowd was ecstatic. It didn't matter that with the very next ball he was caught out. Once the tailender had slogged the three runs required, John was voted 'player of the match' for all his efforts in securing Bradford's victory over the East Yorkshire side.

Next morning the local paper's sporting headline ran,

'CRICKETER'S COMEBACK CRACKS COUNTY'

It was followed by a glowing report of John's play, and naturally it was the talk of the day, especially amongst the fishing party who had decided to take a break from the deep seas and had joined everyone else at breakfast.

'Well done, John!' 'That's the way, show them what the West Riding can produce.' 'Best in the county, we are. Good for you, John!'

Eventually conversation turned to other things and plans for the day were discussed. One of the mill-owners, with whom John had previously done business, told them that they were planning to go and catch crabs out to the flat rocks at Crook Ness.

'We'll spend some time there, have a picnic and such, and then walk back along the cliffs. We've a couple of spare places if the young people would like to come along.'

Robert and Sarah were thrilled and Leonora thought it an excellent plan, so it was arranged that they would meet the party in the foyer at 10 a.m.

John and Leonora felt a little guilty as they waved them off. Each was secretly pleased to have the day to themselves, and they wondered what they should do to make the most of it. Leonora had the first idea.

'You'll probably think I'm rather foolish, but I'd like to have my fortune told. Remember the woman in the town who always tries to draw us in? I'd like to go there.'

'Oh yes, Gipsy Rose Lee! "Cross my palm with silver and I'll tell you what you want to hear",' teased John. He laughed at Leonora's whim, but they made their way down Newborough Road past the little shops, side stalls and cafés, until at last they saw her standing on her doorstep tugging the sleeve of an unsuspecting passer-by.

'Let me read your hand, luv, it mirrors your future. Advice given in health, business and matrimony.'

As the accosted lady made her escape John approached the fortune-teller.

'How much does it cost to find out what's in store?' he asked.

Gipsy Rose quickly took in John and Leonora's elegant attire. 'A guinea for the gentleman and his lady for half an hour.'

John laughed. 'Robbery!' he declared, pressing the money into her hand. 'But we'll come in just the same.'

As they crossed the threshold the aroma of home cooking filled their nostrils.

'That smells good,' John remarked. 'Liver and onions.'

'Yes, and dumplings too,' said Rose Lee. 'How did you know?'

'It's one of my favourite meals,' said John, and Leonora smiled.

'I'll remember that when we get back home!'

The fortune-teller took them through a curtained doorway into a small, dimly lit cubicle with heavy chenille drapes of a dark plum colour covering the walls. A small red lamp in the corner cast a rosy glow on a crystal ball at the centre of a circular table at which there was just room for the two chairs set

259

ready for the visitors. Gipsy Rose sat down on a stool opposite them and closed her eyes. Something in her manner made John and Leonora indisposed to speak, and they all sat in silence for what seemed quite a long time until at last the gipsy opened her eyes, and spreading her hands around the base of the crystal ball she gazed into it.

'Ah! I see a wedding. You two dear people are newly wed? And to be sure it is a match made in heaven! There have been stormy seas but they are past, and now there is much happiness. I see wonderful gardens, full of flowers and I see coins, golden coins; you will not be short of money, for I see it everywhere.'

She paused then and looked a little puzzled.

'There are children ... but no babies ... ah, I see it now. A girl and a boy, and they are here already, perhaps?'

Leonora nodded but had no time to speak as the fortune-teller continued.

'The girl, one day she will be very beautiful and become a successful business woman, VERY successful. I see a fine young man in uniform. He is very brave... A leader.'

Gipsy Rose turned the crystal ball in her hands and was silent for a minute or two before she went on.

'Now what is this? I can see stones, huge stones, the likes of which I've never seen ... oh they are being pulled from the ground by a giant crane with chains... Take care with these chains, mister ... yes, take good care.'

Slowly she turned the crystal ball again, and as she did so her manner suddenly changed. For a fleeting moment Leonora thought she saw a look of horror on the gipsy's face, but if she did it was gone in an instant for Gipsy Rose masked it with a forced smile and, rising from the stool, she said abruptly, 'That's it, folks. The reading's over. Thank you for coming.'

John was a bit indignant.

'We haven't had our half hour yet. Come on, fair's fair!'

But the gipsy was adamant and seemed keen for them to leave.

'I'm sorry, that's all I can see. There's no more and now, if you don't mind, I have to make my husband's dinner.'

John would have insisted, but Leonora laid her hand on his arm.

'Let's go, John. We've heard that we're to have a happy marriage and great wealth, what more can there be?'

260

She smiled brightly as they left and said nothing at all about the look of horror she had seen on the face of the fortune-teller.

They strolled along to the harbour but the tide was out and there was little activity, so they continued up Castlegate and eventually found themselves at the old church of St Mary's.

'I believe this is where Ann Brontë is buried,' said John, opening the gate and waiting for Leonora to lead the way into the churchyard. They found the grave and sat for a while in the long grass, thinking of the times they had met Ann and her sisters at the musical evenings at Ponden Hall.

'Now they are all gone,' said Leonora, voicing both their thoughts. 'How sad for Mr Brontë to have lost all his children. He must be so very lonely.'

Leonora remembered Gipsy Rose Lee, and though it was warm and sunny she suddenly felt cold. Turning to John she said earnestly, 'We must make the most of every single day, John. We have been given such happiness, and we mustn't waste it.'

Taking her in his arms, John was surprised to find that his wife was trembling.

Ever since seeing the eight large fish caught by the businessmen on their second trip to sea, Robert and Sarah had eagerly awaited their own fishing expedition. The highlight of the holiday had been saved for the middle of the second week, and on the morning of the excursion they had to be up at the crack of dawn to catch the early tide. They breakfasted and donned the thick warm clothing that they had been advised to wear, before hurrying down to the harbour to find the fisherman they had hired to take them out already waiting to cast off. Rods and tackle had been stowed away and the tide had turned, so no time was lost in getting aboard so that the crew could slip the moorings.

John and Leonora were equally as excited as the children as the fishing boat cleared the harbour. The four watched as the north bay came into view. They could see the castle standing guard on the cliff top, and soon Robert pointed out the rocks at Crook Ness which he and Sarah had visited a few days earlier.

It was a fair morning, but despite the warm clothing the wind felt cold once they left the shelter of the land. The little boat was tossed into deep troughs as the swell increased, and the passengers began to feel unwell. Only Robert kept his colour. John, Leonora and Sarah turned varying shades of green and began to wish they hadn't eaten such quantities of bacon, eggs and fried bread. All three breakfasts ended up in the sea, and the two were relieved to find they felt much better from then on.

About eight miles from the shore the surface of the sea suddenly began to boil. Dense shoals of herring glinted green and silver and, as promised, large tunny were leaping and diving at terrific speeds.

'Look, look there!' shouted Robert, pointing to one side and then the other as yet another giant soared above the waves, its dark back glistening in the early sunlight. The fisherman produced a rod and line for each of them and gave instructions for getting a bite. Within minutes Robert felt a terrific pull on his line and was so unprepared he nearly dropped the rod. The fish raced away at tremendous speed, and whatever was on the other end of his line was too powerful for young Robert. John had a leather harness attached to his body, and taking his son's line he followed the fisherman's instructions and eventually landed a massive tunny fish almost eight feet long. Robert's eyes were bulging in disbelief, and even the fisherman begrudgingly admitted it was 'a fair size'. Not many minutes passed before Sarah too had a bite. Once again it was John who landed the fish and, though not quite so big as the first, it was still a whopper and caused great excitement.

In the next three hours they caught several more fish, mostly considerably smaller specimens and only one that gave them the same thrill as the first two. It was Leonora who landed the big one. Or to be more precise, Leonora took the bite, but it needed John and the fisherman to help her to get the monster into the boat. It was a beauty and all of nine feet long.

They had to wait for the tide before returning to land, so they sailed south to view the 85-feet-high lighthouse which tipped the white cliffs of Flamborough. Robert wanted to go in close under the cliffs, 'like pirates might have done,' but the fisherman explained that it was dangerous owing to treacherous

262

currents around the promontory, and instead he headed back to Scarborough and the safety of the harbour.

John kept the largest fish, and on the advice of the fisherman he visited Cox's chemist and arranged to have it stuffed and set in a glass cabinet.

'I shall display it in the billiard room at my home,' he told the taxidermist, 'and I shall be proud to say that my wife caught it!'

As a special treat, for the last night of the holiday, John and Leonora allowed Robert and Sarah to stay up late and watch the dancing from the balcony in the ballroom. Throughout their stay they had heard the strains of dance music drifting through the lobby and up the main staircase, and had seen the ladies in their evening dresses coming downstairs to dance. Sarah was entranced. Never had she seen such exquisite gowns. It made her long for the time when she would be old enough to wear such fine clothes and attend a ball such as this one.

'Don't you want to dance, Mother?' she asked.

However, Leonora and John were content to stay with their children and watch the swirling throng below. They smiled at each other, remembering another time, another ball. Leonora took John's hand.

'Thank you for a wonderful holiday. Scarborough will always be a special place for us, and I think it will hold happy memories for our children too.'

31

Haworth

'He's going to close the quarry, be sure of it! I've known John Pickles a long time, and if he says he'll do a thing then that's what he'll do. If your men don't turn up for work on Monday the quarry will be shut down – and where will that leave us all?'

Alice Wainwright had been right. The women were worried enough that their menfolk had not been to work this past week, and were wondering what they would do about paying the rent if it went on much longer. The last thing they wanted to hear of was the closure of the quarry. Alice had their attention now, and she wanted them to listen!

'Mr Pickles gets good orders and keeps the men in regular work. He pays living wages and provides work-clothes and boots, not to mention keeping the bairns from going hungry with food parcels when the winter frosts and snows hit us. What more do you all want?'

Alice stepped down then, and the vicar took his turn, climbing onto the upturned beer barrel after her.

'My good ladies, Mrs Wainwright is correct. A tragedy it will be if we allow the quarry to be closed down. The families with children will face great hardships, worst in the winter months. There will be no food on the table and no fire in the grate. I implore you, go home to your husbands and make them see the stupidity of this strike. May the good Lord go with you and help you to make them see sense.'

John had known something was amiss before they reached home after the holiday in Scarborough, for the valley was strangely silent. There was no sound from the cranes and stone-saws of the quarry, and no familiar cloud of steam rising over

264

Dimples Hill. The quarry was deserted, except for Harold who came out of the blacksmith's shop when he heard John's horse approaching.

'Am I glad to see you back,' he said. 'We're in real trouble. Yon Obadiah Fothergill 'as stirred up trouble among t'men. 'E's been shouting 'is mouth off in t' Black Bull and King's Arms about decent wages and such, and like a flock of sheep t'others 'ave followed 'im and gone out on strike! There's not a one dares set foot in t'place whilst Obadiah's on t'war path. 'E's a right wrong 'un. I warned thee when tha set 'im on that 'e'd be nowt but trouble!'

John was unable to contain his anger. He knew that they would now be way behind with the order for the Leeds Post Office building and would be heavily penalized if they didn't deliver on time. He banged his fist against the door with great force.

'I'll give them until Tuesday morning. If they're not back at work then I'll close the quarry down.'

Harold looked startled.

'Nay, lad, don't do that. There'll be a lot o' folk out o' work wi' out t'quarry.'

'They should have thought of that when they took up with Obadiah Fothergill. Eight o'clock, I'll dismantle the cranes and take all the tackle over to Hebden Bridge!'

He strode angrily away, leaving Harold scratching his head and wondering what on earth he should do.

Later, when Harold told his wife of John's intentions Alice was furious.

'He can't go closing the quarry. There'll be a lot of hungry children in this valley if he does, and all because of that muck-stirrer, Obadiah Fothergill, opening his big mouth. I could swing for him and for all those other stupid fellows who can't see a good thing when they fall over it! They have regular wages and a good boss who treats 'em fair. John isn't like them millionaire mill bosses who think their workers are slaves and pay 'em a pittance and sack 'em if they so much as straighten their backs. Leave this to me Harold. We'll see what the women-folk have to say about it all!'

Alice had put a notice on the church gate calling all the women to a meeting at 2 p.m. on Monday afternoon, and had spread the word that the quarry was to close. As she had expected the wives turned up en masse, with babes in arms and young children and toddlers in tow. Not one would have missed this meeting, for they were all alarmed at the prospect of the quarry closure and angry at their husbands and sons for having brought this situation about. When Alice stood on the beer barrel to speak they cheered her, and they listened to what the vicar had to say too, but when an aged woman standing on the church steps began to speak she was booed and jeered for everyone knew she was old Mrs Fothergill, mother of the troublemaker Obadiah. Some instinct prompted Alice to quieten the crowd and ask them to let Mrs Fothergill have her say. It proved to be the right thing to do, as the old woman had advice that neither Alice nor the vicar would have thought of giving.

'As ye all know, I'm the mother of Obadiah Fothergill – but I ain't proud of it. Though 'e's my own flesh and blood 'e's always been an awkward bugger. 'E were a right Johnny-opposite when 'e were nowt but a little lad. Stubborn as they come, and wi' a chip on 'is shoulder t'size o' one o' t'quarry blocks! 'E can talk t'hind leg off a donkey, but that's all 'e's good at. If 'e could work 'is 'ands as good as 'is tongue 'e'd be some use to mankind! Aye, my Obadiah's a bitter man and, tho' I says it who shouldn't, 'im being my son, 'e's nowt but trouble. Now, get ye all 'ome and tell them 'usbands o' yours what I've said, and if they still won't go back to work stay out o' their beds and sleep wi' yer children. That'll learn 'em!'

There were loud cheers from the women, who were glad to have an ace up their sleeves. They walked in procession down the main street, stopping at all the public houses, calling for their menfolk to return to work.

When the quarry gates were opened at 7.00 a.m. on Tuesday morning a stream of shamefaced men filed back to work. Obadiah Fothergill was not amongst them. His mother had finally thrown him out, telling him never to darken her door again, and some time on Monday night he had left the Worth Valley for good.

Later that morning a notice was posted in the quarry, asking for volunteers to work longer hours to complete the stone order for the Leeds Post Office. It stated that there would be a five-guinea Christmas bonus for each man if the deadline was met.

32

The Mayor & Corporation of Halifax

Request the honour of
Mr & Mrs John Pickles

Company at the Opening of the Town Hall by
*His Royal Highness **The Prince of Wales***
*Accompanied by Her Royal Highness **The Princess of Wales***
On Tuesday 4th August 1863

J.S. Walsh
Chairman of the
Town Hall Committee

Town Hall 15th July 1863

An immediate answer is requested. Should this Invitation be honoured.

Leonora gazed in amazement at the invitation in her hand. She could not believe that she and John would actually be meeting royalty.

'I'm a bit surprised too,' said John. 'I was only involved with the building at the last minute, and then only because the plans were changed yet again and it was decided to replace the flat roof with a mansard roof. I didn't expect to be invited to the opening, but I would not miss it for the world.'

'Nor I, but I'll need a new dress, John. Nothing that I have is suitable for such a grand occasion as this.'

'You shall have the best that Bradford has to offer; whatever you want! It's not every day a prince comes to these parts. In fact, I shouldn't be surprised if this isn't the first time any member of the royal family has been to Halifax.'

The eight years of John and Leonora's marriage had proved

good for all the family. The house at Oakworth had been a happy, bustling home during Robert and Sarah's holiday visits, and when they returned to school Leonora had enjoyed the quiet times, delighting in Isabella's garden and immersing herself in her favourite pastime of painting. Sarah had stayed at school until she was 18 and had then spent a year in Italy with her mother's family, improving her Italian and absorbing all the sights and sounds of that wonderful country. She was young and fresh, and Italy amazed her. Art, opera, architecture, she loved it all and gained much from the experience. It was a much more cultured woman who came back to England to take up her place at a teacher training college in Oxford in the autumn.

Now 18, Robert had just finished his final term at Sedbergh and had his sights on a military career. However, John was still half-hoping that he could change his son's mind and persuade him to join him at the quarry.

As Gipsy Rose Lee had predicted, John was now a very wealthy man. The quarries still continued to produce vast quantities of stone for the burgeoning towns of the industrial West Riding. Anglican churches and Methodist chapels were springing up like mushrooms across the countryside, and libraries, hospitals, schools and meeting halls were being built in the prosperous towns. John had sold most of his canal barges and invested heavily in the fast-growing network of railways, which he now used for most of his transportation. However, it was through his timber-merchants' business in Halifax that he had become involved in the Town Hall and had been invited to attend the royal audience.

A new town hall had been proposed for Halifax as far back as 1847, and since 1856 various schemes had been put forward and rejected, and it wasn't until the spring of 1860 that work finally began on the present building, designed by Charles Barry.

John had been disappointed at that time to lose the contract for the stonework to another firm, but he had been interested to watch the magnificent building taking shape. There had been delays when the stonemasons went on strike and when changes were made to the original drawings, but this latter had been to John's advantage when huge timbers were needed quickly to continue the newly designed roof and to raise the tower a

268

further 20 feet. John had built a reputation on holding large stocks in his yard and was known for selling long lengths of good, straight-grained, clean timber imported from the Baltic or Canadian parts. When summoned by the Borough Engineer and the building committee, John was able to assure them that he had half their requirements in stock and that a boat due into Liverpool the following week had ample lengths on board for him to supply the remainder within 14 days. There had been much discord and argument about the alteration to the plans, and it was a great relief to all concerned that building could now continue. It was John's part in easing the strain of the situation which had secured him the invitation to the opening celebrations.

The royal visit was a two-day event, and 60,000 visitors arrived in Halifax by train to join the many thousands of local people who had turned out to watch the spectacle. The Prince arrived on the 3 p.m. train and was greeted by the Mayor, Aldermen, Councillors and a guard of honour formed by the West Yorkshire Rifle Volunteers. The Council, the Railway Company, the Military and the Police had all been involved in planning the spectacular decorations and ceremonials. The streets were garlanded with flowers and bunting, and crowds of cheering people lined the roads waving flags and banners.

Like many other women, Leonora was disappointed to learn that the Princess of Wales was unable to come owing to illness, but she eagerly awaited seeing the Prince of Wales at the Piece Hall, where 16,000 Sunday School scholars and teachers had gathered to welcome him. Accompanied by 300 musicians a huge choir sang the 'Hallelujah Chorus' from Handel's *Messiah* and followed it with 'God Bless the Prince of Wales' and the National Anthem. A great feeling of national pride swelled the hearts of everyone in Halifax that day.

Several factory visits had been arranged for the Prince after the welcoming, and during the evening he was guest of honour at a banquet at Manor Heath whilst the Town Hall was illuminated by 16,000 gas burners, 4,000 of them forming the Prince of Wales plumes on the clock tower. However, it was to the next day's events that John and Leonora were looking forward.

It was raining that Tuesday when the Prince of Wales, with local dignitaries resplendent in their new ceremonial robes,

269

proceeded through the triumphal arch, which had been erected in Princess Street, and mounted a raised platform to duly declare the new Town Hall officially open. Inside, waiting in line to be presented to His Royal Highness, John glanced at Leonora standing beside him. She looked radiant. The new royal-blue gown suited her well and the sparkling diamond necklace and matching tiara, which they had found in Fattorini's jewellery store, were breathtaking against her still dark hair. Watching her now, John could hardly believe that 23 years had passed since he first caught sight of her at Ruth Turner's wedding. His heart had skipped a beat then, and she still had the same effect on him after all this time! John was so lost in his thoughts that the Prince was almost upon them before he realized it, and he was just in time to take the proffered hand and execute his practised bow. Leonora made a deep curtsey, and the three of them conversed for a moment or two before His Royal Highness moved on down the line. Their special meeting had passed in a blur, and afterwards neither of them could be exactly sure what they had said to the Prince of Wales.

33

Robert had at last made his father see that he had no intention of working with him either at the quarry or the timber yard. Ever since the holiday in Scarborough, when he had watched the soldiers drilling, he knew that that was the life for him. He had enlisted as soon as possible, and after three months basic training with the Green Howards Regiment in Richmond had been accepted by the Royal Military College at Sandhurst as an officer cadet. The training was as he had imagined, intense and disciplined, but Robert had thrived on the challenge and had enjoyed all aspects of the curriculum. Whilst at Sedbergh he had proved to be a good sportsman, becoming captain of the school's rugby team, and at the college he had taken up other sports in which he also excelled, soon winning the rifle-shooting competition. He was thoroughly enjoying his time in Berkshire. The military life suited him, and in his first few weeks he had taken up with a young girl from the area called Kitty Marchant. Robert felt that life was good and he could want for nothing more.

He had met Kitty on one of his free afternoons. Setting out to explore the route of the Roman road a couple of miles north of the college, he had caught up with Kitty, who had been visiting an aunt in Crowthorne and was walking back to her home, a farm on Surrey Hill. As they happened to be going in the same direction Robert suggested that they walk together, and each had been easy in the other's company and had enjoyed the time together. When Robert hesitantly invited Kitty to a cadets' dance she readily accepted, and their friendship very quickly deepened into something much more special. He had been invited out to the long red-brick farmhouse, where he

271

had taken afternoon tea with Kitty's mother, father and two younger sisters. Her parents had thought Robert very agreeable, and Kitty's sisters had giggled and said later that he was 'dashingly handsome'. Kitty had laughingly agreed.

'He is, isn't he? Apparently he's a replica of his father; their build, colouring and lovely thick, curly hair are all exactly alike. I'm looking forward to meeting Robert's parents.'

She would not have to wait long, for in four weeks time Robert would graduate, and he had sent a letter to Oakworth telling John and Leonora all his news and inviting them down to the graduation ceremony, when he would be presented with the silver trophy for rifle-shooting and, more excitingly, would receive his commission. He had also managed to obtain graduation day tickets for Mr and Mrs Marchant and Kitty. He already felt quite serious about Kitty, and he thought it would be an ideal opportunity for the two families to meet.

John and Leonora travelled down by train, happy to have an excuse to take time off from the businesses and see something of the countryside outside Yorkshire. Neither of them had been to the south of England before, and they were keen to see as much as possible from the train windows. They watched as the mills and factories of the West Riding were left behind and the moorlands of Derbyshire came into view, to be followed by flatter, more open land. Acre after acre of green, rolling countryside unfurled before them. Farms, hedgerows, villages with steeples, rivers and woodland came into view and disappeared like the scenes in a dream when the sleeper can never quite decide exactly where he is. The train swept on at great speed, all the time bringing them nearer to Sandhurst and the eagerly anticipated passing-out parade.

The weather was fine and sunny on the appointed day. Seats had been provided around the arena, and a military band was playing lively music as John and Leonora arrived in the college grounds. A major welcomed all the guests, and they were treated to a spectacular drill parade by the cadets. Various cups and awards were given out, and John and Leonora felt very proud when the Lieutenant-Colonel presented Robert with his trophy. At 19 years of age Robert was on the brink of manhood and had the world at his feet.

When the graduating cadets had received their pips and all the ceremonies were concluded, Robert introduced his parents to the Marchant family. Leonora smiled at Kitty and took her hand.

'How lovely to meet you. Robert has told us a lot about you in his letters.'

She was surprised to find that Kitty had long, blonde hair and bright blue eyes. For no sensible reason, Leonora had imagined Kitty would be dark like all of them. However, she found the girl's fresh face and open smile appealing and warmed to her immediately. The Marchants were invited to dine with them at the hotel in Sandhurst so that they could all get to know one another better. Mrs Marchant, a tall smart woman, was sensible and forthright, and John and Leonora liked her. They didn't take to Kitty's father quite so readily. Though pleasant enough, he was rather bumptious and tended to dominate the conversation at the dining table. However, from the reactions of the landlord and other locals, it seemed that he was well respected in the district. He told them that his family had farmed at Surrey Hill for generations and could be traced back to before the Civil War. The Marchants, originally 'Marchand', had been wealthy French traders who, it seemed, had come to Britain late in the sixteenth century to escape the Protestant persecution in their homeland.

Unlike the hill farms of West Yorkshire, the land here was rich and fertile, and the farmers of southern England were much more affluent than their northern counterparts. Henry Marchant was comfortably well-off and had more of the air of a country squire than of the farmers that John and Leonora knew in the Worth Valley. As the remains of the meal were cleared away he turned to Robert.

'Now then, young Robert, what's your commission? Where are you to be?'

'I've been assigned to the First Battalion of the Green Howards Regiment. Just what I wanted! I think eventually we are going to India, but I've no details yet.'

Kitty looked crestfallen. 'I'd hoped you would be staying in

273

England for a little while before shooting off halfway round the world.'

Seeing the smile disappear from Kitty's face made Robert see, perhaps clearly for the first time, that there was a down-side to this military career he so cherished.

As if on cue an officer from the regiment, a Captain Forbes, stopped beside their table and shook hands all round.

'A fine day for the ceremony. I hope you all enjoyed the parade.'

John assured him that they had had a wonderful day and asked the Captain if he would care to join them. They learned from him that the 1st Battalion would be leaving for India very soon.

'We need a continuing British presence in the Northern Territories to prevent Russia getting ideas of invading India and to keep Pathan rebels under control. There was a campaign last year to quell the Yusufzai tribesmen, and the British Army had difficulty holding out in the Ambelo Pass until reinforcements arrived. We never know when there'll be another skirmish with these fanatics, so we need to get the men over there where we can train them in mountain warfare. Robert will be sailing from Southampton in ten days time.' Leonora looked concerned. They had been so happy and proud this morning to see Robert in his smart uniform, but marching on a parade ground is one thing and fighting hostile tribes, in some foreign mountain range, is quite another.

'Don't worry, Mother!' laughed Robert. 'I'm ready to go. After all, that's what I joined the army for.'

Leonora and Kitty were both subdued at the news but the menfolk seemed to take it in their stride and were soon deep in conversation, discussing the merits of the East India Company, and overseas trade in general, and the job of the British Army to safeguard the nation's interests abroad.

Noticing how quiet Leonora had become, John turned to her.

'How would you like to stay down here for a while? We would perhaps have chance of seeing a little of Robert and Kitty, and we could make our way to Southampton in time to watch the ship leave.'

Leonora smiled and squeezed his hand.

'You have a way of knowing exactly what I need, John. Thank you. I'd like that very much.'

It had been an emotional farewell. Robert had looked so young in his officer's uniform, the bright scarlet tunic set off by a white shoulder strap and black shako, plumed and blazoned with the badge of the regiment. Too young to be in command of the men marching onto the dock and filing up the gangway, he nevertheless had an air of confidence and waved jauntily to John, Leonora and Kitty: a young man off on his first big adventure. They had smiled and waved back, but both women wept and John had a lump in his throat and didn't trust himself to speak. They stayed on the quayside watching until the ship slid out of sight into the Solent. It was then that John told Leonora his plan to spend a few extra days in Hampshire, and after seeing Kitty to her train they started out for a hostelry in the New Forest.

The thatched roof gave the white Buck Inn an olde-worlde charm. Set in a leafy lane just outside Cadnam it was small, quiet and comfortable, and the backdrop of the forest gave it an air of timelessness and medieval mystery. John had chosen this area because he thought he might be able to do some business here, as Hampshire is noted for its good trees, ash, beech and oak, all of which were in great demand in the timber trade back home. Leonora had laughingly complained that she thought this was to be a holiday not a business trip, and he had assured her that he intended to spend most days fishing for trout in the River Test or walking in the famous woodland.

They had an idyllic few days. The good food and wine at the Buck Inn relaxed them, and the dry, warm weather was perfect for John's fishing. Leonora was happy to sit in the shade of a tree and read, occasionally breaking off to watch as John cast his line or netted a fish. Once or twice they wandered arm in arm through the forest before making their way back to the inn, where the landlady had been happy to oblige them by poaching the trout John had caught earlier.

After four days John reluctantly decided that they must return home. He was beginning to feel anxious about the quarries, for he had been away for almost three weeks and he had not forgotten what happened, many years earlier, when he had left others in charge whilst on honeymoon in Scarborough.

After their meal they spent the last evening wandering through the village, marvelling at the profusion of flowers in the gardens and lanes. Honeysuckle climbed over the tops of cottage doors whilst beneath, delphiniums, hollyhocks, peonies, poppies and red-hot pokers vied for pride of place. Everywhere the lanes were sweet with the scent of briar roses, bursting out between the hawthorn bushes and the trailing brambles. The warm day had left a soft haze over the woodland, and the late-evening sun was like melted butter through the misty veil. John and Leonora felt mellow and contented when they returned to the Buck Inn and climbed the stairs for bed. They lay quietly together, Leonora nestled, as always, in John's arms, each lingering over thoughts of the day and feeling blessed at sharing their wonderful, mutual love. Their kisses were warm and soft, lingering and loving, until eventually, melting into the feather bed, they fell asleep.

Cries of alarm awoke Leonora from her dreams. It was the middle of the night, and at first she didn't know what had disturbed her. Then she heard the cry again, 'Fire! Fire!' and in the same moment she smelt the acrid smell of smoke and heard the crackle of burning wood somewhere beyond the bedroom door. Horrified, she awoke John with a jerk in the ribs, and in an instant he was out of bed and across the room. Just in time he realized that thick, black smoke was curling under the door, and he heard the ominous popping, smacking, cracking noises of the fire beyond. There would be no escape for them that way.

Grabbing the counterpane, he stuffed it into the gap at the bottom of the door then shouted to Leonora to open the window for some air. Ripping the sheets from the bed, John pushed the feather mattress through the narrow window and let it fall, before knotting the sheets together and fastening one end firmly to the foot of the iron bedstead. With her back to the window Leonora had watched all this as if in a trance. She vaguely heard voices below: 'Jump!', 'Get out whilst you can!', but everything was drowned by the awful sounds of the fire. Spitting, hissing, crackling, banging. Noises of hell! Orchestrations of the devil!

Leonora put her hands over her ears to blot it out and turned towards the window, but then she saw the bright glow of flames reflected in the open pane. Time was running out, the flames had reached the thatch, and with a fierce 'whoosh' the roof was ablaze. John shook Leonora and pointed to the sheets. He had to shout above the noise of the fire, 'You go first,' and he half lifted her onto the window sill. Suddenly she snapped out of her shocked state and, hesitating only a moment, began the descent.

All went well until her nightdress snagged on an iron spike supporting a thin, garden trellis. Frantically trying to free the material, Leonora became more and more ensnared on the climbing rose tree snaking up the front of the building. She could move neither up nor down. The landlord and his wife, and one or two other people drawn by the blaze, were shouting below but they, and John watching from the bedroom above, were helpless to assist her.

As the fire raged across the roof and began licking at the trellis work under the very next window, Leonora panicked and wrenched at her nightgown, ripping the material and trying to free it from the thorns. Now, with only one hand on the sheet, she lost her grip and with her added weight the nightgown finally tore right through and Leonora fell backwards with a scream. She landed half on the mattress but banged her head against a stone balustrade and lay motionless as a dark red patch began to spread over the path.

John hardly touched the sheet as he threw himself off the window ledge and half-climbed, half-jumped to the ground. He was beside Leonora almost as quickly as the bystanders, but there was nothing to be done. Leonora was dead.

John didn't remember being taken to a nearby house. He remembered nothing of the blankets and the brandy and the anxious faces of the villagers. He didn't know, at that time, that the landlord had brought Leonora into the house and that his wife had laid her on the bed upstairs and washed away the soot and blood before covering her with a clean white sheet. He was swallowed up in blackness. A blackness darker than the despair of Armley, blacker than the desperate days following Isabella's death. This was black as coal, or tar, or jet. The darkness of the deepest mine where no light has ever shone. This blackness engulfed his very soul.

For a long time John remained in a state of shock, unmov-

277

ing, unhearing. Then for the third time, it seemed Harold was to come to his aid. John saw his friend in front of him; or, to be more exact, he saw his face, gently smiling and still with the unlit pipe between his teeth. He was saying softly, 'Remember St Michael. Pray to St Michael of All Angels, he understands and he will help you.'

John prayed as he had never prayed before; he prayed for help, he prayed for strength, he prayed for Leonora and for Sarah. He mouthed the words but no sound came, and the worried villagers thought he might be going mad and they sent for both the doctor and the vicar. Still John prayed until, at last, light filtered into his darkness and he could begin to face the enormity of his loss.

With consciousness came pain, physical pain which John hadn't even noticed until now. His leap from the window had resulted in a broken leg, and he had to grit his teeth whilst the doctor re-set the bones and applied splints to keep the leg rigid. The vicar of Cadnam was a great help to John, understanding his hurt and loss. He comforted him with quiet words and prayers before dealing with the practicalities as well. It was he who called for the undertaker to supply a coffin and who made arrangements for the railway company to take Leonora's body back to Yorkshire.

How different from the last time, thought John. Then the fields were dull and wet, the skies were overcast, and a cold March wind had whipped between the gravestones. Today the sun was shining from a blue, blue sky, and a bright carpet of yellow buttercups lay over the adjacent fields. John knew that he must find an inner strength today, for there was another in need of consolation.

Standing beside him in the cemetery, Sarah was distraught. She looked so vulnerable and, in her grief, so much younger than her 21 years. She had held back the tears throughout the service and had walked bravely behind the hearse bearing her mother on her final journey, but when she saw the newly opened grave a low moan had escaped her lips and tears had washed unchecked down her pale cheeks. As the coffin was lowered on its leather straps, and the vicar intoned the final committal, heavy sobs wracked Sarah's body and John drew her to him and held her tightly, wishing that in so doing he could draw away her pain and bear it all himself.

At last it was over. Leonora lay with Isabella, at peace on the sunny hillside, and John and Sarah rode home together to a life without a wife and mother; a life that could never be the same again.

Sarah returned to her studies at Oxford and John sought solace in his work, but unlike before he didn't cut himself off from his friends but rather turned to them for companionship, often inviting Paul or Harold to his home for a game of billiards and a drink. He spent most of his free time maintaining the garden which first Isabella and then Leonora had tended with such loving care. He drew comfort from the fragrant blooms, and he never ceased to marvel at the wonderful variety of plants which thrived in this one small plot of God's garden, Earth.

He set himself another task that summer; to carve a headstone for his wives' grave and find some apt inscription for its face. Of course the stone must come from Dimples Quarry, and John selected it with care, for it needed to be large enough and workable, but must also weather well if it were to stand the ravages of countless Yorkshire winters. At last he was satisfied and began chiselling the huge block.

In Loving Memory of
Isabella Pickles
d. March 1852 aged 27 years
And also of
Leonora Pickles
d. June 1864 aged 44 years
Devoted wives of
John Pickles

He left a gap then so that later the date of his own death could be added, and then he began again.

Shortly after Isabella's death John had opened the locket he had given her that last Christmas. Inside he had found a lock of his own hair and a small, folded piece of paper. John had

279

wept when he read what Isabella had written, and taking no comfort from it then, he had put the paper and the hair back behind the glass and thrust the locket beneath his shirts in the drawer of the dresser. Now he remembered the poem and knew that it was just what he wanted. Retrieving the locket, he read her words again. Isabella spoke of the future, but John knew that now it was a very present truth, so changing only the tense he began his inscription:

Though I am gone from you, do not weep at my grave.
I am with you all the while and in timeless peace.
Nature has been my mentor.
I am in my father's fields,
Where the wind whispers through the rushes by the stream,
And where the primroses grow.
My spirit soars like a bird in circling flight;
Up with the skylarks, through the clouds.
To light and joy and truth. Stillness and Peace
Where all is pure and clear and loving.

34

India, 1864

Nothing could have prepared Robert and the other men for India. It was both a climatic and cultural shock for all of them. They had been at sea for almost four months and, although conditions aboard HMS *Crocodile* were not bad, they were bored and restless and looking forward to disembarkation at Calcutta. The heat hit them as soon as they left the open sea behind and the ship sailed into the estuary and up the Hughli River to the docks. Before Robert had made his way down the gangway his hair was already matted to his head and his new, white-drill summer kit was soaked with perspiration. On the quay a cloud of flies descended to buzz incessantly around his head, and the humid, sticky air felt oppressive, draining him of energy. He knew that, after months at sea, none of the men were very fit, and he wondered how they would ever get back to peak condition in these temperatures.

However, he soon forgot his discomfort as the sights, sounds and, most of all, smells of Calcutta bombarded his senses. Splendid marbled buildings with domes and minarets pointing skyward were a grand contrast to the narrow streets and crowded bazaars. Here, richly patterned brocades and silks were displayed alongside softer cottons, copper jugs and bright, jangling jewellery. Fish, gutted and spiced, hung from roughly lashed poles to dry in the sun. Varying-sized mounds of tea, millet, rice and curious smelling spices were piled on jute sacks on the ground, ready for sale alongside exotic fresh fruits and vegetables. Bullock carts, loaded with grain, carpets or pots and pans, trundled between the stalls, and everywhere a jostling crowd bartered and haggled, bought and sold, or gossiped as they watched the snake charmers draw weird sounds from their curious instruments to tempt their captive reptiles from the woven-bamboo baskets.

It was all strange, new and exciting to the young Englishmen, and Robert felt that a month would have been too short a time to absorb all that Calcutta could offer, but very soon they were leaving it all behind as they headed north by railway on the first stage of their long journey through India. Even on the train, there was no respite from the relentless heat. The air was too warm to create the breeze which travellers in England can expect, and a lot of the men settled down to sleep for a good part of the journey. Robert wanted to see as much as he could of this new country, and for a while he watched as rice paddies, jute fields, waving palms and big-leafed plantains slipped past his window, then he too dozed, then slept. When he awoke the train was rattling through a forest, and he sat up quickly hoping to catch sight of the tigers, but these elusive animals were either keeping well-hidden or lived in another part of India, for Robert never saw any.

At Benares, where they were delayed for a number of hours, Robert found himself gravitating, with many others, towards the Ganges. The river was busy with rice-boats, boats filled with pilgrims travelling to visit one of the many shrines of the Ganges, and a countless number of other tiny vessels with canopies strung amidships to give some shelter from the fierce sun. The northern side of the river is steeply banked, and here many wonderful temples and palaces had been built, each with wide steps leading directly onto the river. From these worshippers were scattering offerings of rice, milk and flowers on the Ganges before bathing in its holy waters. The men stripped to their loincloths, but the women waded into the water in their brightly patterned saris and submerged themselves fully clothed.

A little way down the river a thin wisp of smoke rose from a funeral pyre, burning on one of the ghats, or platforms, built beside the steps. Robert shuddered. This was so alien to him and yet it seemed that the whole family, from young to old, was here to watch the burning!

As Robert left to retrace his steps, he was confronted by the spectacle of a colourful procession heading towards him. A strange carved figure was being borne along the street accompanied by an excited throng of people. Some were riding in tasselled howdahs, high on the backs of elephants whose hides had been gaily painted for the occasion. Some were astride snorting camels, and others walked or rode on decorated carts. Everyone was brightly clad in clothes of red, gold and blue fabrics and wore garlands of fresh flowers. They moved to the sound of hand-beaten drums, and over all the shrill, wailing notes of the peculiar, wooden pipes filled the air. Robert pressed himself against the wall and, fascinated, watched as the parade passed and made its way down to the river. He would have liked to have followed, but time was short and he had to content himself with finding out later that the idol was Kali, black goddess of darkness, who, once a year, is immersed in the River Ganges at sunset on this festival day.

As the train took them yet further north, darkness fell and with it came a slight relief from the relentless heat of the day and chance to sleep and build up reserves of energy for the route march to come in a few days' time.

Looking back on those first few days in India, it seemed to Robert like a dream. He had written to his father, telling him of what he had seen then: of domed, marbled mosques and lavish temples, of camels, elephants and monkeys; of boys squatting over looms, weaving wonderful patterned carpets; of jakins, or holy men, sitting cross-legged hour after hour, and of the emaciated cows who wander everywhere unimpeded because they are considered sacred.

He didn't tell him of the heat and flies, the squalor and the poverty, and he didn't want to alarm him with details of how men had died of disease only days after the regiment began to march north. It had taken 73 days to reach Nowshera, walking about 13 miles each day, and in that time they had lost 14 men. It had been especially difficult to keep up the men's spirits when one of their number succumbed to the dreaded cholera. Time and again Robert impressed upon his company the need for careful hygiene but, on the march, in this land of heat and flies, it was easier said than done.

The time spent at Nowshera was somewhat of an anti-climax. After an initial rest period the men were keen to go forward into the hills, where unruly Pathans were attacking villages

283

which had been promised British protection, but it was some months before the order came to proceed. The men were not left idle. Excursions into the local hills were organized in order to accustom the soldiers to the terrain and teach them the tactics of hill-fighting. Robert ensured that every man was meticulous about cleaning his kit, especially his rifle.

'Remember the maxim,' he said, 'look after your kit and your kit will look after you!'

There was another outbreak of cholera, and men who were fit enough to take part in drill one day, were dead and buried the next. Robert was concerned for his men, and made great efforts to enforce the strictest hygiene. By always taking a positive attitude he helped reduce the level of fear engendered when yet another soldier died a sickening death.

At last, the order to march had come and they had moved to Peshawar, from where they had regularly patrolled the hills and periodically skirmished with the Pathan tribes. The hills of this area are barren and rocky and offer very little herbage for the animals of the herdsmen, who have no other resources and who have, for centuries, lived on what they could get by way of trade and plunder. They resented the British intervention which threatened their livelihood, and they were fiercely independent. Their fanatical coverage, during the raids, made them fearful opponents, and they were skilled marksmen, some said, able to hit a man in the eye at a thousand paces with a ball shot from their long-barrelled jezails.

The fighting against the tribesmen was never easy. The British had superior weapons, but it was difficult to anticipate the raids as the Pathans had the ability to materialize as if from thin air and then melt back into the rocks again as silently as they had come. There were a number of tribes scattered through the hills, and they fought independently of one another, summoning their men by the sound of their drums and gathering beneath huge flags hung on 20-foot-high poles. Usually their method of attack was ambush but sometimes fanatics would rush the troops, bandishing their curved swords, talwais, with their blood-curdling cries filling the air. It took a stouthearted soldier to stand his ground until they were in range, hoping that, as usually was the case, a few well-aimed shots would curb the attack.

By no means all of Robert's time in India was spent on hill patrol. The companies did turns on garrison duties at Rawalpindi and road-building south of Abbotabad. The six guns of the Royal Horse Auxiliary were pulled by elephants in the North-West Frontier Campaign, and good roads were needed for all this heavy weight.

When not engaged in the campaigns the men easily became disgruntled and bored. Aware of this, Robert arranged sporting competitions with other companies and organized fishing expeditions and other activities to keep up morale. During these times he thought much more often of England and the people who meant most to him. He wrote to Kitty and his father, and felt sad to think it would take all of six months for his letters to reach them. That brought home the reality of the distance between them. He enjoyed army life but he missed Kitty very much, and he had wondered, at first, about asking her to join him. Some of the officers' wives were with them and it would have been possible, but the heat and prevalence of disease put that idea from his mind.

It was almost ten months after Leonora's death before Robert received his father's letter, telling him about the fire and its tragic consequences. Robert could hardly take it in. After only this short time, England, and all that he had left there, seemed so remote. Leonora dead! Poor Father. He would be quite alone now, for Sarah, he knew, would still be at Oxford. When he first read the letter, Robert wished that he had never come to India and that instead he had joined the quarry as his father had wished. He knew that John would need him now. However, in time, he accepted that he could not have foreseen Leonora's death, and that if he hadn't joined the army he would have regretted it all his life and would probably have grown resentful towards the quarry and his father. John's next letter, some months later, set his mind at rest. It was a normal family letter, full of news of Sarah, Paul, Harold and the Heatons, and updates on the quarries and timber yards. His father didn't sound despairing.

It was after the Black Mountain Campaign in October 1868, that Robert finally decided to ask Kitty to marry him. The fighting had been particularly fierce. Extra troops had been withdrawn from road buildings and from the garrison towns for an expedition into the Hazare region, where 4000 Yusufzai tribesmen were scattered amongst the hills waiting to face them. It was a fearsome prospect, for these warriors, tall and lithe, could swarm through the mountains at terrifying speed. They were gaunt-featured, with hooked noses and cheeks calloused from the stocks of their rifles in frequent recoils, and they were brave fighting men. Their dusky brown robes were perfect camouflage against the dusty landscape, and it was Robert and one or two other officers, who came up with the idea of dyeing their own white cotton drills to try to even their chances in the hills.

The soldiers of the Green Howards, the Royal Warwickshires and the South Staffordshires, who joined forces in this campaign, were all highly trained. There was strict discipline and tight, organized command and control of the troops. The newly issued, breech-loading, Snider-Enfield rifles, capable of firing ten rounds per minute and accurate to ranges of 1000 yards, gave the British much greater fire power so that, in the end, it took only nine days to subdue the rebels, and there were few British casualties.

Back at the operations base Robert thought over the last three weeks. They had travelled light, taking no tents and with only a greatcoat for warmth against the freezing cold of nights at this altitude. They had to be ever-alert and wary, for the Yusufzai fighters could creep within firing range without being seen or heard, and they were keen marksmen. The campaign was short, but there were some nights when no one slept or left their positions, and three weeks with little sleep and no shelter had meant that the men were living on their nerves. Even on the march back to barracks they had had to remain constantly vigilant.

Now there was time for reflection. The recent fighting had driven home to Robert the preciousness of each day and the fragility of life. He no longer wanted to be here, putting his life at risk. He wanted to be with Kitty, safe in England, and he knew that the only way was to resign his commission and leave the army.

He wrote to Kitty immediately, asking her to marry him

when he returned. Robert hadn't heard from Kitty for some months, but on receipt of her last letter he had felt sure of her love. Now he was filled with apprehension. Suppose she had met someone else or ceased to love him – after all it was more than four years since he left England! It was no use being anxious or impatient; Robert knew it would be many months before he could expect a reply, and in the meantime he had men in his command.

The troops could not fully withdraw from the mountains as it was an uneasy peace. Young Pathans refused to accept defeat and, as before, often broke out in the hills. Robert's company had completed another term at the garrison at Rawalpindi and were leaving for their final spell of duty on hill patrol when Kitty's letter arrived. She had accepted his proposal and would be his wife! Not only that – he had a son! Kitty had given birth to his child eight months after he had left England, and she had never told him. A son! He must be four years old now! Robert was swamped with a flood of emotions, joy, guilt, excitement, anger, pride. He didn't understand why Kitty hadn't told him. She said it was because she knew how important his career was to him, but could not she see that she was important too? It only took five minutes for all the negative emotions to fade and then joy and pride remained. Robert wanted to set off home immediately. However, he spoke with the Colonel, who made him see the sense of sticking out these last two months. After all, his company was being recalled then and they could all return to England together.

After the march to Peshawar, a minor skirmish took Robert's mind off home, and it was a month later that he wrote to his father to tell him of his plans. He sent the letter, knowing full well what joy it would bring the recipient.

All was quiet for a week or two until news came that a small village a little way north had been attacked during the night and two villagers had been killed. Robert was ordered to do a reconnaissance, and taking 12 of his men, he set out up country. It was not hot at this time of year in the hills, and they made good progress over the stony lower foothills before climbing to the craggier hills. They crossed a wide, shallow river and beyond, amongst the rocks and stunted scrub, they flushed out three of the enemy tribesmen, who fired wildly at them before

287

fleeing with Robert and his men in hot pursuit. The Pathans
sped over the rocky terrain like mountain goats, heading for a
ravine where the river wound between high rocky banks.
Robert's group had been in India for four years now. They too
were very fit and, gradually, they gained ground on the rebels,
closing fast as they neared the gully.

Suddenly the Pathans stopped and turned, firing at close
range. One bullet whizzed past and there was a yelp as it
grazed the skin from the cheek of one of the men behind.
Robert killed one of the rebels with a shot from his pistol, and
the other two men dived for cover behind rocks in the water-
course. Only then did Robert realize that this was a set-up.
Pathans are past masters at ambush, and he had fallen for one
of the oldest tricks. Along both banks of the river tribesmen
squatted behind crags and boulders. They were outnumbered
and in real danger. There was no way out, except back the way
they had come.

Robert ran, simultaneously shouting to the men to retreat
and take cover. He realized in a few seconds that his sergeant
was no longer with him, and glancing back he saw that he was
lying injured about 50 yards back, right in the enemy firing
line. Without hesitation, Robert ordered the rest of his men to
hold their retreat and give him covering fire. Bending low he
raced back to the sergeant, zigzagging to avoid flying bullets,
and despite the injured man's pleas to leave him and save his
own skin, he hoisted him onto his shoulders and carried him
back to where the men were waiting. He almost made it without mishap, but five yards from safety, he felt a searing pain in
the small of his back and he half-stumbled, half-fell the few
remaining steps. Seven of the detail kept the rebels at bay with
their fine marksmanship whilst the other four helped the
injured men to high ground, where they had the cover of some
large rocks and could maintain their position until the sun went
down. Under cover of darkness they very slowly made their way
back to the main force.

The army doctor was called, and he dealt first with the
injured sergeant, who was in a poor way, having lost a lot of
blood, and was drifting in and out of consciousness.

Robert had felt little pain after the bullet's initial impact, but
it must have been his own instinct for self-preservation which

blotted it out because once back at base he collapsed and had to grit his teeth to bear the agonizing waves of pain that hit him. He filled his mind with thoughts of England, imagining his homecoming and Kitty waiting on the quay. The boy would be waiting too! Robert was trying to imagine what his son would look like when he heard the doctor come in.

'Now then, sir, let's take a look at you. Where have they got you? Ah! We'll have you patched up in no time at all!'

35

Oakworth

Robert was coming home! John could not have wished for better news than this. His son was coming home and would join him now and take over some of the running of the business! With great excitement John re-read Robert's letter. This was his first communication for many months, and there was so much to take in. It was a long time since those early epistles, full of the sights and sounds of a strange country. The first three pages of this letter were full of the many skirmishes with the Pathan rebels; and how the men of these tribes, strong and fearless, and with many dead, continued to fight. The soldiers were unable to protect the many isolated villages, which were attacked and left deserted. Troops on the move were ambushed by huge bands of tribesmen, who seemed to materialize out of nowhere, and counter-attacks failed when the Pathans melted back into the hills, their dirty robes giving them camouflage against the dusty landscape.

Robert told of endless nights of marching, when the scorching heat of the day made any move impossible and the nights were only marginally cooler, and of the difficulty in keeping up morale when cholera and typhoid swept through the camps. But he also wrote of courage and friendship and the camaraderie born when men are thrust together in adverse conditions. John was stirred to think of Robert caught up in all of this, but it was the last page which gave him the greatest thrill and shock. The regiment was to leave India in three weeks' time, and on return Robert would resign his commission. John read on.

I don't take this step lightly as I find army life suits me

well, as I knew it would, but I have good reasons to come home. Firstly, Father, Kitty and I are to be married as soon as I get back to England! I wrote and asked her several months ago, and upon receiving her reply I went straight away to the Colonel to ask about my release. He wasn't too happy at first and tried to dissuade me, but when he saw that I was set on it he wished me well. And now for my other news. I have a son! Kitty only told me after I proposed and said that I intended leaving the army, as she knew how much I had wanted this career. Now all I want is to be home with Kitty. Imagine it! I have a boy, four years of age. I can't wait to see him and to bring him to Yorkshire, as soon as possible, to meet his grandfather.

So if you still want me I will be able to join you at the quarry after all!

Looking forward to seeing you very soon.

I remain,

Your loving son, Robert

If I still want him; of course I do! John poured himself a stiff drink and tried to work out when Robert would be home. Letters travel no faster than men, so with luck Robert should be in England within a couple of months.

The time flew by. John busied himself at the quarry, where trade was booming. He had secured a contract to supply stones for building a railway viaduct, but was having difficulty hauling the huge blocks to the quarry top from the bottom of the rock-bearing face some 100 feet below. None of the cranes was strong enough to lift blocks weighing 20 tons or more, and John was stumped. It was the crane driver, Harry Little, who had worked for John for some years, who hit on the idea of using two cranes in unison.

'I'm sure it could be done,' said Harry, 'but it'll be a dangerous job. T'cranes would have to work together at exactly t'same speed, and if a cable broke, or there were engine failure, t'whole bloomin' lot 'ud end up in t'quarry bottom, cranes 'nd all!'

John didn't need telling that this would mean certain death

for the crane driver, who would not only be crushed and trapped in his cab but would be horrifically burnt by red-hot coals and steam. John shut the picture from his mind. He was determined to find a way to make this work. Despite his own warning, Harry said that he was willing to give it a go if the blacksmith would first cut out a door at the back of the cab so that he could jump clear if an emergency arose.

It was less easy for John to find a capable person who was prepared to drive the second crane. He asked Harry Little's son, Felix, but with a wife and six children to think of the younger man didn't want to take the risk. Never one to be beaten, John decided to drive the crane himself. He instructed Harry to get the two largest cranes in top working order, check all moving parts and grease them well. He asked Harold Wainwright to put on new steel cables and chains and cut escape hatches at the back of both cabs. He didn't want the work hurried; everything must be double-checked and in good shape before they reported to him that the cranes were ready.

John had just reached the entrance of his drive leading up to his home when he saw an army officer alighting and standing by the front door of the house. Robert? Eagerly he urged the horse on, but as the trap reached nearer he saw that it was not his son standing there but a higher-ranking officer of the same regiment. The gentleman did not smile as he shook John's hand, and a cold dread filled John's heart. He knew without a shadow of a doubt what the officer had come to tell him.

'Colonel Isherwood, sir. Green Howards. May I come in?'

Once in the drawing room John poured out two glasses of brandy and handed one to the Colonel. He knew he had to listen, but he didn't want to hear what this man had to say.

'I'm sorry to be the bearer of bad news, Mr Pickles, and I'm afraid there's no easy way of saying this. Your son, Robert, was killed in action six weeks before we were due to leave India.'

John drained his glass and sat down heavily as the Colonel went on.

'He was a very gallant officer, and I wanted to come personally to tell you of his bravery.'

He related the details of a reconnaissance party, led by

Robert, which was ambushed by Pathan tribesmen and of how Robert had gone back into the firing line to rescue his injured sergeant, with no thought for his own safety, and had been shot in the back. He paused and without looking up John asked, 'Did he die immediately?'

'No, the men brought him back and we fought for his life. The army doctor did his best, but the kidneys were damaged by the bullet and it was impossible to save him. Robert was courageous and knew that he would die. He sent a message to tell you that he is sorry to let you down over the quarry.'

John groaned and sank his head into his hands.

'How could he think that he ever let me down?'

Colonel Isherwood was finding this difficult and would be glad when it was done. He went on swiftly, 'I was with him towards the end, and he asked me to also give you a message for Kitty – he was to have been married, I think?'

John nodded.

'The message was "I love you and please, take the boy to see my father".'

John topped up their brandy glasses and indicated that the Colonel should sit. They sipped their drinks in silence for a few minutes before the Colonel spoke again.

'He was given a full military funeral with his own squad as firing party at the burial. The injured sergeant insisted on leaving his sick bed and being carried to the graveside. I am so very sorry. Robert's death is a great loss to the battalion. He served us well, with unremitting attention to detail and with concern for the comfort and efficiency of the men under his command. Although he was so young, he was highly regarded by all who served with him and he died as he lived – a chivalrous gentleman and officer. I intend to put his name forward for a special commendation.'

Colonel Isherwood rose to his feet.

'If you will be all right alone, Mr Pickles, I'll take my leave as I have to make my way back to North Yorkshire today.'

He had deposited a leather bag in the hallway on his way in and indicated it as he left, telling John that it contained his son's personal effects. They shook hands again, the Colonel apologizing once more for being the bearer of bad news. John thanked him for taking the trouble to come and for all his kind words, and then with a heavy heart he closed the door and, taking the leather bag, went back to the drawing room.

Paul and Harold marvelled at how well John coped with his son's death. He appeared to have accepted it calmly and quietly. There was no frenzied pursuit of work nor angry outbursts as there had been when Isabella died, nor did the black void, which engulfed him with the shock of Leonora's death, descend again, but if his friends could have seen into his heart they would have known that something else had died along with his son. John's zest for life was gone. With Isabella, Leonora and Robert all in their graves and Sarah away, he was very lonely, and although he continued his businesses and was polite and friendly to those around him, he had no real desire to do anything or see anyone. The exception was his interest in the conservatory and garden. He was obsessed with growing ever more exotic plants, starting an orangery and growing peaches under the glass, and even trying his luck with banana trees. Two parakeets shared the conservatory, and eventually he trained them to answer his 'Hello' with 'Hello, Johnny' 'Hello, Robert'.

There were some things, however, that had to be faced, and one of these was to let Sarah know what had happened. When she completed her training at Oxford in the summer of 1866 Sarah had taken up a teaching post in a school near Reading, in Berkshire. It was to this address that John wrote, as soon as he felt able, telling her of Robert's death and as much as he knew of the circumstances surrounding it. He then told her about Kitty Marchant and her child, and how she and Robert had planned to marry on his return. He asked Sarah to seek out Kitty at the farm near Sandhurst and pass on the tragic news. John enclosed a letter for Kitty, in which he thanked her for making his son so happy and inviting her and the boy to come to Yorkshire for a visit. He felt it was what Robert would have wanted, and he was curious to see his grandson.

On the first Saturday after receipt of her father's letters, Sarah set out for Surrey Hill. She was not looking forward to telling Kitty the news of Robert's death, and was almost sorry the journey was not longer than the eight or nine miles from the school. In the event, she didn't see Kitty that Saturday and found herself most unwelcome at the farm. Sarah thought it was probably one of Kitty's younger sisters who opened the door to her and discovered who she was speaking to.

'Oh goodness, why have you come here? You shouldn't have come. She doesn't live here any longer; not since the...'

'Who is it, Emma? Show them in!'

A large red-faced man, whom Sarah took to be Mr Marchant, came into view behind his daughter. He smiled.

'Good morning, miss. Don't think I've had the pleasure?'

'Father, this is Sarah Pickles. She came to see Kitty...'

Mr Marchant's attitude changed completely at the mention of Kitty's name.

'She's not here. No one of that name here. Go inside Emma, now!'

He glared at Sarah and would have followed his daughter, without another word, if Sarah had let him.

'Please,' she pleaded, 'I need to see Kitty. I'm Robert's sister and I have some sad news for her.'

For a moment she thought Mr Marchant might relent when she spoke of 'sad news', but then his features hardened and, drawing himself up to his full height and fixing his gaze somewhere above the top of Sarah's head, he said purposefully,

'As I said, there's no one of that name here. I no longer have a daughter called Kitty.'

Without giving Sarah chance to speak, he went inside and shut the door behind him.

Quite nonplussed, Sarah was unsure what to do next, and for a few minutes she stood on the doorstep staring at the closed door. She contemplated knocking again and pleading with Mr Marchant to tell her where Kitty was, but thought that would probably do no good, so she returned to the cab at the gate, thankful that she'd asked the driver to wait. Sarah had intended to spend the weekend in the locality, thinking that Kitty might need someone close by who had known Robert, and, in truth, she had hoped it would provide mutual comfort, as she was finding it hard to come to terms with the news herself. She had noticed an inn when they had passed through the village of Crowthorne, a couple of miles back, and, for want of a better idea, she asked the driver to take her there now, although there seemed little point in staying now that she knew Kitty wasn't here.

By the time she reached Crowthorne, Sarah had made up her mind. Since this appeared to be a fruitless mission, she would find somewhere to eat and then head back for the school. Later she would write to Mr Marchant, explaining why she had come and enclosing the letter for Kitty. She would appeal to his better nature and hope he would have the decency to forward it. Sarah felt better once she had decided on a course of action, and she enjoyed the cold chicken and salad that was the only thing on offer at the inn at that time of day. She had just finished and was about to pay the bill when a tall, well-dressed woman approached her.

'Miss Pickles? I hoped I'd find you here. I came as soon as I could get away, on the off-chance that you might make a stop here. I'm Mrs Marchant – Kitty's mother – and I apologize now for my husband's unforgivable rudeness!'

'Mrs Marchant! I'm so pleased you've come. I did so hope to be able to get in touch with Kitty.'

Sarah paid for her food and the two women found a quiet corner where they could talk. Sarah came straight to the point.

'I'm afraid I have bad news for your daughter, Mrs Marchant. Robert told us in a letter that he and Kitty were planning to be married, and Father was so thrilled ... and then, only last week, we heard that Robert was killed in action in India.' She filled up then and found it impossible to go on.

Mrs Marchant laid a hand on her arm.

'I'm so very, very sorry, my dear. He was a lovely young man, and I'm afraid Kitty will be heartbroken – she was so looking forward to his return and to being married. Oh! Poor Kitty! And you too; I'm sure you will miss your brother dreadfully.' She waited awhile until Sarah seemed more composed, and then went on to tell her all that had happened at the farm. 'When my husband found out about the baby he was furious. He held such a lot of store by his reputation, you see, and he felt Kitty had shamed him. It was such a terrible time, he told Kitty to leave, and no amount of tears or pleading would change his mind. I tried everything I could to make him see reason, but he would not listen. No one had to mention Kitty and he still refuses to acknowledge that he has another daughter! I keep in touch with Kitty and I think Henry has guessed but he never asks after her nor enquires where I am going when I go to Southampton each month.

'That's where Kitty is now – Southampton. After her father threw her out I helped her to find a position with a sea-captain and his wife. She cooks and cleans for them in return for a room and board for her and her son. It's not what I wanted for her, but it's all worked out quite well as the captain is away at sea for months at a time and Kitty is company for his wife whilst he is gone. Thankfully they were quite accepting of the baby; in fact I rather think they enjoy having the little boy there. They are childless, you see, and I have the feeling that it has been a great sadness for them. Of course Kitty was devastated when she had to leave home, and she misses her sisters, but she settled in happily enough in Southampton, once her son was born, especially after Robert asked her to marry him and she had so much to look forward to. Oh dear, I don't know how she will be when she hears this news!'

It happened to be the very week of Mrs Marchant's monthly visit to Southampton, and so it was decided that she would tell Kitty of Robert's death, take her John's letter and ask her to contact Sarah with a view to making arrangements to visit Yorkshire during the summer. Mrs Marchant had to leave then to get back to the farm before she was missed, and taking leave of her, Sarah headed back to Reading, wondering how Kitty would cope with the news her mother brought her.

At the end of term Sarah came home with Kitty and the child. John was outside to meet the coach which brought them, and the first person to dismount was a stocky little boy of about four years old who had a head of thick curly hair, not black like his father's but shiny-gold in the sun. He was followed by his mother, Kitty, who looked pale and sad, and older than John remembered, and lastly by Sarah. Kitty bent down and said something to the boy, and without more prompting he ran straight to John, who picked him up and hugged him.

'And who might you be, young man?'

'I'm Robert,' the little lad replied before wriggling to free himself so that he could run back to his mother.

John embraced both the young women and enquired about the journey. He was so very pleased to see them all, but felt sorry for Kitty, whose grief was palpable. It was probable that seeing him reminded her of Robert, for he knew his son had been very much like him. However, he wanted this to be a happy visit and he wasted no time at all before taking them all to see the parakeets.

'Hello, Johnny,' 'Hello, Robert,' they piped as the party entered, and young Robert laughed in delight.

'I'm Robert, how did he know?' he asked, chuckling again as the birds repeatedly squawked his name.

Cook had prepared a meal in readiness for their arrival, and as they ate the house suddenly felt to be 'lived in' again. After dinner John took Robert round the house and gardens. He showed him the large fish in the glass case in the billiard room and told him that his daddy once caught one just like it.

'It's a very big fish,' said Robert gravely, but he preferred the live goldfish in the pond and tried to grab them until John laughingly explained that they were happier in the water.

The following day dawned fine and bright, and John suggested they ask Cook to pack some food and then take the horse and trap up onto Haworth Moor to visit the waterfalls where the Brontë sisters took inspiration for their sketching and writing.

The ride was enjoyed by all. The country lanes leading to the moors were bordered by dry-stone walls, and there was much to delight the eyes and ears of the little party. A wren hopped in and out of the hollows of a moss-draped wall before flitting to the topmost stone to deliver its shrill warble in short repeated bursts. Though enchanting, the little bird was no competition for the song thrush which they heard soon after, singing its wonderful melodies from the tree-top perch high above. Butterflies fluttered amongst the white campion, feverfew and tall thistles which grew amongst a profusion of grasses beneath the thicket and bramble, which was adorned with a mass of delicate, pastel pink flowers.

As they left the lanes and climbed the last rough track, the landscape opened up in front of them in a wonderful display of heather in full bloom, purple and pink as far as the eye could see, way up to the distant moor tops. As the trap jolted up the rough stony track there was a flash of white tails as

298

startled wheatears took flight, only to settle again a little way ahead to repeat the performance when the horse drew near. Above, the curlew cried its lonely 'coorli-coorli', prompting them to watch its graceful, swooping flight.

At last they reached the narrow valley where the falling water tumbled over rocks and boulders and under the little slabbed-stone bridge that enabled travellers to arrive dry-shod at the outlying farms higher up the moor.

They picnicked beside the stream as the clear, sparkling cascade bubbled over the glistening stones. Little Robert tossed pebbles into the pools, laughing at the plopping sound they made, and later he sat on a smooth flat rock and splashed his feet in the cool water whilst his mother and Sarah chatted as they watched over him. John was relieved to see Kitty smiling; the change was doing her good.

His thoughts went reeling back then to his youthful courtship of Leonora. They had spent many happy times on these moors, and if he closed his eyes he could see her as she was then, beautiful and lively and so full of fun. His heart ached and as the sadness washed over him he sighed, causing Sarah to ask what he was thinking.

'I was remembering your mother, Sarah,' said John. 'This is where we used to walk thirty years ago. We were so full of hopes and dreams ... so young...' His voice trailed off but Sarah saw the emotion in his face, and going to him she put her arms around him tenderly and kissed his cheek.

'You're very lonely, aren't you?'

When John didn't reply she went on. 'I'm not going back to Reading. I've decided to stay here, at Oakworth, and look after you. I'll help you with the business too.'

John thought perhaps he should insist that she return to the school, but he didn't have the will. Instead he turned and smiled at Sarah, grateful for her offer. How like her mother she had grown, not only in looks but in mannerisms and the way her smile lit up her eyes. A lump came to his throat, and squeezing her hand he simply said,

'Thank you, I should like that.'

By the time the trap was back at Oakworth Grange young Robert had fallen fast asleep. John carried him upstairs and watched as his mother carefully undressed him and laid the bedcovers over him. He felt humbled by the sight of that flushed face against the pillow, and knowing that he had thought that life was not worth living. He was glad to once again have people around him who loved him, and whom he could love in return.

Ever since Sarah had told him of Kitty's plight, John had been wondering how he could help her. He knew now that he wanted them all to stay here, with him, at Oakworth. Sarah had already decided to stay, and John felt sure that Kitty would take very little persuading, for it seemed that her own father would never relent and welcome her back into the family fold. It might even be possible, in the future, to arrange for Kitty's mother and sisters to visit her at the 'Grange'.

John went across to the bed and gazed down at the sleeping child. His heart ached; for the little boy who would never know his father, and for his own son, who would never know the joy of watching his child grow to be a man.

'Well, young Robert. Let's hope your mother agrees. If she does we'll have lots of time together!'

He kissed the boy's forehead and left, quietly closing the bedroom door.

Cook had sent an extra place for dinner for Mr David Winstanley. John had invited his old friend and family solicitor to the house, and had persuaded Sarah and Kitty to take a walk so that he and Mr Winstanly could have a long chat. When his guest arrived the house was quiet. Robert was taking his afternoon nap, and the two men enjoyed a game of billiards before settling in the conservatory with a glass of sherry each.

Mr Winstanley knew there would be business to attend to, and he liked to get on with things.

'Now John, you didn't ask me here simply to play billiards. What's on your mind?'

'I want to make a new will. The bulk of my estate was left to Robert, but now that he's dead...'

'Yes, I thought it might be that. I was very sorry to hear of your loss. Dreadful shame! It is a good idea to get these things sorted, and you've only Sarah now, haven't you? It should be quite straightforward.'

300

'Not so straightforward as you might think,' said John and he proceeded to tell Mr Winstanley how Kitty and Robert fitted into the picture. He told how Kitty's father had disowned her before Robert was born, casting her out without a penny to her name, and how Kitty had now agreed to come and live at Oakworth Grange. The solicitor raised his hand to stop John.

'You do know that you're not legally responsible for either of them, don't you? Under the law you have no duty to make provision for them.'

'I know that, but I have a moral duty to the boy, for Robert's sake, and it is my wish to name him in the will along with his mother and Sarah.'

Mr Winstanley nodded. 'I would expect nothing else from you, John.'

They talked at great length until finally the details of the will were decided upon. After a few small legacies, such as the ones to Paul and Harold, the remainder of John's estate was left in equal third parts to Sarah, Kitty and Robert, this last share to be held in trust, with the boy's education being paid from it. Robert would inherit a great deal of money when he reached the age of 23 years. John was glad to have everything sorted out.

'That's settled, then. If you will draw up the document tomorrow morning I will call at your office at three p.m. and sign the will. We'll tell Sarah and Kitty what has been decided over dinner.'

Sarah had been showing an interest in the quarry, and as she had already told John that she would help him with the business side of things he thought it would be useful if they went up to Dimples Hill to give her some insight into the process she would be involved in. Kitty expressed a wish to go too, so a few days later they left Robert in Cook's care and headed for Haworth. The two women were fascinated watching the men hoisting blocks of stone from the quarry bottom. Neither of them had any idea that stone was dug out from such a depth, and they were rather awed by the huge cranes and stone saws. They watched as the stones were cut to the required size and shape, and realized that the men handling the saws and chisels were skilled craftsmen. John left them in charge of one of the hands, telling him to show them whatever they asked to see, whilst he went to the steam cranes in search of Harry Little.

'I see the blocks are ready for lifting, Harry. Are the cranes prepared?'

'We're waiting for you, Mr Pickles. I'm ready when you're ready. There's fella's up in t'ale 'ouses 'aving a bet on this. Some sez t'blocks *will* come up, others sez they *won't*, but they all think we should 'ave a third man to give instructions to the two drivers. Them cranes operates on different speeds, and it'll be a job keeping an even pull on t'blocks.'

'Fire the boilers early tomorrow, Harry. I'll be here at nine to get started.'

For a first time in months John felt a buzz of excitement at the prospect of the challenge. 'And ask Felix to be third man, will you? He knows those cranes as good as any.'

When John arrived at Dimples Hill the following morning there were already quite a number of bystanders waiting to see how the operation would go, and he was surprised to see Paul amongst them.

'I've heard of nothing else for days now,' Paul explained, and the betting's been heavy, so I thought I'd come along and see for myself.' He looked a bit embarrassed as he added, 'I'm not sure it's a good idea, John. Those blocks are mighty heavy. Are you sure you know what you're doing?'

In the cab, John was checking the steam pressure and all the levers.

'Don't worry. We've overhauled the cranes, fitted new chains and cables, and so on, and we've talked it all through. It'll be just fine.'

Paul moved away for a better view as John gave Felix the thumbs-up to tell him that all was now ready on his side. In the other cab Harry was still checking, and 100 feet below men were manoeuvring the claws and chains around the first of the giant blocks – ready to hook them to the massive cables swinging from the cranes. The crowd at the quarry top had swelled visibly as all the quarry men not involved in the operation had downed tools to watch. Harold had left the forge and was

302

standing with Paul in a perfect viewing spot, directly opposite where the stones would be landed.

At last all the preparations were made, Felix waited until the men at the bottom of the quarry were well clear and then raised his hand to show that all was ready. Everyone fell silent, and Felix gave the signal that John and Harry had been waiting for. Together they depressed the steam levers and set the cables in motion. The chains tightened with a jolt and the 20-ton block of stone began to move. Slowly and steadily it rose from the quarry floor, and dozens of pairs of eyes were riveted to the progress of the block. Only Paul glanced away and saw that beads of perspiration had appeared on John's brow. About halfway up the stone suddenly tilted. A gasp arose from the onlookers, but Felix was ready for it and his flattened hand told Harry to ease the pressure, and the stone levelled again. There were no more problems, and after swinging over the quarry edge the block was landed safely. A great cheer rose from the spectators, and workmen threw their caps in the air and shook each other's hands, thrilled to see the job accomplished but, no doubt, also thinking of the winnings they would collect from their bets.

There were 11 more blocks of this size to lift and three larger ones, each weighing 25 tons. By 1.30 p.m. they had 12 of the stones out of the quarry, and John called a halt. The three men had worked well together, and most of the stones had come up without a hitch since that awful moment when the first one tipped so alarmingly, but the concentration levels were high and John's muscles ached with the unaccustomed tension.

'We'll have a break and begin again in an hour's time. There's only the three big ones left and, with any luck, we'll be finished by four.'

Despite the success of the morning Harry Little was apprehensive about the 'monsters', as he called the three remaining stones. He re-checked everything in his cab and before he started again he swung open the escape door behind him. The crowd had dwindled somewhat as the morning progressed without excitement, but there were still several dozen men lining the quarry top when they recommenced.

The first 'monster' came up like a dream. They had no

303

trouble with the cranes hoisting the weight, and it was landed safely beside the smaller stones. The second one was the same. Slowly and steadily it was eased from the quarry and over to its designated place. The last stone was hitched ready, and John smiled at Harry and put his thumbs up as if to say 'we've done it'. It didn't look like a monster way down there, 100 feet below them at the bottom of the quarry. With a jerk they began to lift the block in the now familiar way and, like the previous ones, it rose slowly and smoothly.

It was almost up when an ear-splitting crack rang round the quarry. Metal casing fell from the pulley wheel bearings on the jib of Harry's crane, and the steel cable lost all tension. Someone screamed as the huge stone swung across the quarry, smashing its full weight into the base of the other crane, crushing it like cardboard and sending the whole thing crashing into the quarry bottom, with John inside. As the stone fell the other cable used up the remaining slack, and Harry's crane too was pulled into the yawning hole. It was all over in a matter of seconds, but just as the second crane went down Harry flung himself through the escape hatch and landed half over the rock face. Someone pulled him to safety and he lay stunned, knowing he was lucky to have made it.

There was no escape for John. He was still alive when Paul and Harold reached him, but he was trapped by the twisted metal across his chest, and red-hot steam was belching over his legs. Harold took off his coat and wrapped it around the broken steam pipe. He closed the firebox door to prevent the burning coals from spilling out over John, but there was little else that they could do until someone brought down the tackle to cut John free. He was drifting in and out of consciousness, and realizing that his friends were near, he tried to speak. When Paul supported his head and shoulders and told him to lie still, John smiled at him and said quite clearly,

'St Michael won't be coming. He will miss me out this time.'

And before Paul could ask what he meant, his eyes closed and his head fell sideways against his friend's chest. John had taken his last breath and was gone.

It is a sad fact that we can never know our worth, in terms of value to others, during our lifetime, but if John had been able to see his own funeral he would have had a good idea of how loved and well respected he had been. Hundreds of people flocked to Oakworth's Slack Lane Chapel to pay their last respects to the orphan boy from Liverpool who had had such an impact on so many lives. They came from Keighley and from Bradford, from Halifax, from Todmorden and from Hebden Bridge, and Mr Turner, now a very old man, had travelled all the way from Buckden in the Yorkshire Dales. Workers from the quarries and the timber yard sat beside the Heatons and the Butterworths, whilst the doctor, the solicitor and the vicar of Haworth Church sat with the gardener, the cook and all the household staff.

Everyone felt a great loss, and all bowed their heads as the chief mourners followed the coffin out of the chapel to the grave. Sarah, Kitty, Paul and Harold and their families wept openly as John was laid to rest with his beloved wives, Isabella and Leonora.

When the mourners had left it was Paul and Harold who quietly filled in their friend's grave and replaced the gravestone, which John himself had so lovingly carved.

EPILOGUE

1989

All through the winter months I was busy writing this story of the life of John Pickles – 'Johnny Big Block'. I had enjoyed it but was glad to be finished, thinking this would finally put an end to it all. Not a bit of it. The night I finally laid down my pen it all began again. My usual nightly trip to put the cat out was interrupted when Tom stopped in his tracks, tail erect and fur on end, just as he had done all those months before. He did a U-turn back to the kitchen, and I felt my spine tingle as I noticed that the bunch of keys in the lock was swinging like a pendulum. Taking a deep breath, I hurried to the door and peered through the glass pane. I saw what I expected to see, Johnny Big Block, in his top hat and riding coat, smiling at me from the yard, and I had the distinct feeling that he wanted more; there was something else he wanted me to do. I felt I'd done enough, but never one to leave a job unfinished I decided to revisit the Spiritualist Church in Keighley and see if I could get my answer there.

Quite accustomed now to the format of these services, I took a seat in the front pew and joined in wholeheartedly with the first hymn. The visiting medium, a man from Bradford, said he hoped we had all heard God's promise of a life hereafter and knew about the spirit world and how happy our dear, departed loved ones are who have 'passed over' into that realm. Then straight away he came to me, saying he had a big, powerful man beside him who appeared to be dressed for riding.

'It's old-fashioned clothing, breeches and a top hat and such,' he said. 'He says you are to burn the papers. Does that make sense?'

When I nodded he continued.

'Burn the papers and keep the rest for your efforts. He's smiling and saying "Thank you".'

After the service I had the opportunity of speaking with the medium whilst we all shared coffee and biscuits. I told him a little about my 'ghost', and he said that John must be an earth-bound spirit, and tried to explain.

'Often when someone suffers a violent or sudden death they do not realize that they have died. They still have an attachment to someone, or something, on this earth – in this case it seems to be the stables – and they find it difficult to move forward into the spirit world where they belong. These spirits require sympathy and understanding, and often need our help to free themselves from the conditions in which they are trapped.'

Well, at least I knew what I should do next, and the following week I organized the local Boy Scout troop to help me to manhandle the wooden boxes down from the hayloft to my back garden. (They were as excited as I had been by the secret door and the hidden room.) Once the papers were down, the boys had a whale of a time burning them all on a bonfire, and when I gave them £5 for their funds and agreed that they could keep the boxes for their camping gear, they went away very happy.

That dealt with, I turned my attention to the problem of the jewellery. It was very nice – well, superb! – but it wasn't quite the sort of thing that I was ever going to be able to wear, so I decided to take it to a jeweller in Bradford and have it valued.

When I put the casket on the glass counter and opened the lid the young assistant gasped in amazement at the sight of the tiara, earrings and necklace glinting inside. Her polished nails flew to her gaping mouth, and muttering, 'Gosh, they're fantastic,' she hurried off to fetch the manager. By the look on his face I doubt whether he had ever had such valuable pieces brought into the shop before, but he tried to appear as if he dealt with such gems every day.

'Ah yes, beautiful pieces, quite exquisite! The matching set must be very valuable indeed. I would not like to put a price on it; several thousand I should say. You keep them in a bank, I presume? No! Well, I would strongly recommend that you don't take them back home with you. They are really wonderful pieces, and I would not be surprised if they are over a hundred years old. It's a job for one of the London auction houses really, and if you would like me to, I could arrange for them to be sent down for valuation or sale. The firm I have in mind charge two per cent commission on any sale, and we charge a small handling fee on top.'

When I agreed that this would be a good idea, the jeweller gave me a receipt and took details of my name and address and telephone number, and I felt as if a weight had been lifted from my mind to have all that sorted.

I was about to leave when I remembered the gold locket, but it was a bit of an anti-climax after the excitement caused by the other items. Funnily enough, after everything that I had learned, this was the piece I liked best of all, but I was told that although very pretty it probably had more sentimental than intrinsic value, and I made the happy decision to keep the locket for myself.

Six weeks later I received a letter from the Bradford jeweller, enclosing a cheque in my name for the staggering sum of £280,000! I could not believe my eyes and rang him immediately to see if there had been a mistake. He assured me that the figure was correct. A wealthy American had bought the treasures as a set, and after commission and handling charge as detailed in the letter, I was left with this phenomenal amount. I thanked the jeweller for what he had done, poured myself a large brandy and sat down to think things through. It's not every day that one inherits such a large sum, and I'm not sure if it was the money or the brandy that went to my head, but I really shouldn't have been driving the car when I took the cheque to Barclays Bank later that morning!

I thought a lot about everything that had happened to me since I came to Oakworth; about the papers, jewellery and other things I had found in the stable block, about Johnny Big Block's diaries and all that I had learned of him, but most of all I thought about the money – £280,000!

That night I dreamed of Seth. At least I dreamed of *my* Seth, for the face was all from my own imagination, but I knew it was him because he was wearing the blue naval officer's uniform. He was on board ship in the wildest sea, with white sails billowing in the wind and huge waves tossing the ship as all hands struggled to keep her ploughing a steady course. He was laughing and enjoying every minute of it, for Seth loved the sea.

Unusually, next morning I remembered the dream and suddenly it was clear what I should do. I rang the Trust House Forte Hotel in Liverpool, booked a room for three nights, and after stowing everything I needed for the trip, I climbed into my little Ford Fiesta and headed for Merseyside.

The weather was perfect, and I really enjoyed Liverpool. I spent the first couple of days absorbing the sights of that wonderful city. I visited the Maritime Museum on Albert Dock and saw models of the sailing ships such as Captain Blanchard must have sailed, and of the later, faster clippers and steam ships that did much to increase Liverpool's trade.

I learnt that in just 100 years, between 1830 and 1930, more than 9,000,000 people from all over Europe had sailed from Liverpool, hoping to find a more prosperous future, for themselves and their descendants, in new far-off lands. Raw cotton was imported here for manufacture in the Lancashire mills, and then the ships were filled with emigrants bound for America, South Africa or Australia.

I learnt too about the earlier slave runs, all tied in with the lucrative West Indies sugar trade. The museum's tableaux of this period were fascinating, but dark and sinister, and so realistic that I was glad to step outside and back into the twenty-first century.

I must have walked miles around the city, marvelling at the magnificent buildings which reflected the wealth and prosperity of the last 200 years. The merchant banks and insurance houses, the town hall, library and groups of fine Georgian houses, such as the one where W.E. Gladstone, PM to Queen Victoria, was born, all added to the splendour of the city. I even found the old Blue Coats Orphanage in School Lane, now the Blue Coat Chambers; it is a lovely old, brick building set round three sides of a courtyard behind imposing iron gates. It houses many small businesses – shops, galleries and the like – but standing in the flagged square, looking up at the tiny, circular, third-floor windows, it was easy to imagine the inquisitive faces of small boys peering back at me. I was standing where John and Paul and Albert must have stood over 150 years ago, before being taken, at the tender age of ten years, to work long hours in the mill at Sladen. I felt privileged to have had a glimpse into their lives.

On my last morning in Liverpool I set about fulfilling the tasks I had set myself. I had brought with me a cardboard box, and into it I now put Seth's wooden leg and his naval uniform – still bright-buttoned and complete with tricorn hat. I put a brick on top of them for added weight and I felt sad when I closed the box and tied it up with string, but I knew I was doing the right thing. Before I could change my mind, I walked down to the Pier Head Ferry Terminal, with the parcel under my arm, and booked a ticket to cross the Mersey.

It was 11 a.m. and relatively quiet on board, the commuters who packed the ferry earlier being now ensconced behind polished desks in modern air-conditioned offices. As the boat slipped from its mooring it was hard for me to imagine the hustle and bustle of the docks in the middle of the nineteenth century. I could see brightly clad tourists drifting along the re-paved quays following painted signs pointing them in the direction of the Maritime Museum, cafés and bars, or to another museum dedicated to the Beatles, or the tall ship on display in dry dock. Seats were dotted along the waterfront, where holidaymakers were resting, licking cool ice-creams purchased from a gaily canopied booth. Young teenagers, on their summer break from school, jostled one another in fun, or sat with their legs dangling over the dock, listening to the radio and watching older boys swimming in the deep water.

It was all a far cry from the Liverpool of 1829 when Seth arrived, on the brink of death, after losing his leg at sea. Then boys, younger than those that I had watched on the docks, would spend long days filling sacks with dusty grain or shovelling coal, or worse, in order to take home a pittance to help to feed hungry brothers and sisters. I sighed and closed my eyes for a short time whilst the sights and sounds of the modern age drifted away behind me. Then I made my way to the stern of the boat and was thankful to find I had this part of the deck to myself. I didn't want an audience.

About halfway across the river I quietly held my parcel over the rail and let it drop into the water. It fell into the bubbling wake of the boat, so I didn't hear it splash, but I watched for a few seconds before it sank. As it disappeared beneath the waves I said a little prayer for the souls of Mary Ann and Seth, in whose lives Liverpool had played such an important part.

I had a welcome cup of tea outside the restaurant on the Birkenhead side of the river. Sitting in the sunshine, I looked across the Mersey to the three splendid buildings which dominate the Liverpool waterfront: the copper-domed offices of the Dock Board on the right, the Cunard Building in the centre and the Royal Liver Building on the left with the two liver birds perched on its twin towers, 300 feet above the city which they symbolize. I was content. I felt that I had done all that Johnny Big Block wanted of me at last, but there was something else which I had decided upon that would make me even happier.

I was light-hearted on the return trip, and when I disembarked I walked around the Albert Dock until I found what I was looking for – a mail box that I had seen on the day of my arrival. It was an early-style pillar box recently repainted bright red and with the royal crest proudly displayed on top. Into it I dropped an envelope addressed to a well-known orphanage organisation and containing a cheque for £280,000. I had enclosed a short note asking them to acknowledge receipt and stating, quite firmly, that I wanted no publicity or thanks, as this money had come to me by chance, having once belonged to an orphan boy from Liverpool who, long ago, made good.

Back home I spent hours in my garden. After long days cooped up writing in the winter months I was glad to be out of doors, and gradually my hard work, digging, planting and fertilizing, coupled with plenty of sun and rain to help, paid off and the garden was a blaze of colour. I was rewarded with a marvellous show of dahlias, chrysanthemums, michaelmas daisies and cornflowers. These beautiful flowers filled me with wonder and with a spiritual awareness that made me feel at one with Mother Earth and in touch with all that has past and all that is to come.

I wanted to share my feelings and thought that sharing my flowers would be the way to do it. I'm not certain why I had the idea of visiting the grave at Slack Lane, but once I'd thought of it I could not start soon enough. I cut a large bunch of chrysanthemums, and taking a vase and a bottle of water, I set off through the park and along the old track to the graveyard.

Having no idea whereabouts the grave was situated, I started working systematically along the rows starting at the gate. The morning was fresh and sunny with a clear sky above, and I found it interesting reading all the family names on the gravestones. I eventually found the one I had come to see, right at the bottom of the sloping cemetery, overlooking a field where cows and sheep were grazing. It was such a tranquil place. The only sound was of running water in the little valley below, and I knew it was the same stream into which Isabella had fallen. It didn't worry me now, for nothing could disturb my peaceful state of mind.

I set the vase of flowers on the grave, and then for the first time I read the words which John Pickles had carved on the headstone. The two names at the top and the long poem beneath were expertly carved, but the middle section of the stone was a little clumsier and the letters not so well proportioned. It began:

In Loving Memory of
Isabella Pickles
d. March 1852 aged 27 years
And also of
Leonora Pickles
d. June 1864 aged 44 years
Devoted wives of
John Pickles

And then in a rougher hand it continued:

Died tragically at Dimples Hill, Haworth
August 1870, aged 51 years
Well respected and sorely missed.
'Johnny Big Block'

I didn't need to read the poem for I knew it by heart by then, so I closed my eyes and said it softly.

> Though I am gone from you, do not weep at my grave.
> I am with you all the while and in timeless peace.
> Nature has been my mentor.
> I am in my Father's fields.
> Where the wind whispers through the rushes by the stream,
> And where the primroses grow.
> My spirit soars like a bird in circling flight,
> Up with the skylarks; through the clouds.
> To light and joy and truth. Stillness and Peace
> Where all is pure and clear and loving.

As I opened my eyes I heard the song of a skylark, and looking upwards I saw not one bird but three, hovering directly over the grave. As I watched they spiralled upwards, all now singing, and their liquid notes fell over me like welcome rain on parched earth. Higher and higher they soared, and still their melodies sprinkled down. I watched for a full five minutes and, even when they were no more than specks in the blue heaven, their songs never ceased. Shelley's 'Blithe Spirit' came to mind, and I too found it hard to put an earthly mantle on these birds. I like to think that in the graveyard that afternoon I saw the liberated spirits of John Pickles and his two wives.